AUTHOR'S NIGHTMARE

BOOK THREE

AUTHOR'S NIGHTMARE

BOOK THREE

Ian B. Urns & A. C. Erinle

Podium

Podium

AUTHOR'S NIGHTMARE

BOOK THREE

CHAPTER ONE

Solitaire's POV: Day 104
Current Wealth: 722 gold, 0 silver, 37 copper

We'd needed food. It was a ludicrous thing to run out of, given the amounts of everything else we'd been burning through, but life was funny like that sometimes. Usually right before it tried to kill you. Still, what could you do?

Well, not die. Ideally.

One small problem with that plan; we had to leave the nice, comfy mansion I'd spent weeks turning into the most immoral fortress I possibly could. Could be worse, of course; we did have superpowers now. Small ones, at least. The main question confronting us was who exactly to send out.

Shango was a no-go. He was busy doing Shango things with our money. Beam too was a bit preoccupied trying not to congeal on the sofa we had him strewn across. That complicated things because we needed to keep a guard of certain strength in the mansion, always.

That was the only way to keep the incredibly juicy target that was my laboratory from being raided by the locals.

In the end, there was only one decision we could've made. And it satisfied exactly no one.

Phelia had to go—her buying power as an established noble was just too much to ignore—and I had to accompany her. I had things cooking, and nothing to do. I was among our best fighters. I was the paranoia freak, which made me ideal for spotting ambushes.

Alora accompanied us, and Magnus alongside her. Otherwise it was just us and a carriage. We set off with about as much enthusiasm as you might have expected.

Our vehicle was not the standard for Redacle, I'd seen to that myself. Though it had started as nothing more than a heavy-duty transport, my work had transformed it into something a great deal more *secure*. I'd bolted sheets of thin tool steel along its sides, each one less than a millimeter thick but easily enough to stop a bodkin-pointed arrow if it came down to it. The simplicity of them had let Ardin produce a lot, and we'd mostly been using them for testing. That we now hid behind them as protection had been the plan from the start, of course. I tried not to make things with only one use when time was a commodity.

At the front was Phelia, and at her side was me. This was so that I could keep an eye out for any rat bastards trying to kill us, and she could deter them with her nobby face respectively. In the back were Alora and Magnus, squatting and ready to come flying out and mutilate whoever we told them to.

All in all, not a bad arrangement if I did say so myself. The only downside was that it left me sitting right beside a frothing bitch queen from hell.

We rattled along the road, horses hauling the few hundred kilos of extra weight without much issue, ground protesting with each turning of the wheels. It got me thinking. We'd kept the armor thickness low to allow the vehicle to keep moving; that was just the natural limiting factor on any piece of armor. That and mobility. But horses weren't the be-all and end-all of locomotive power, and I reckoned I knew enough about physics and math to either reinvent or just invent a steam engine more efficient even than the ones actual humanity had abandoned their own horses for.

My rediscovery of the tank was interrupted, however, as I suddenly caught a whiff of emotion from Phelia, distractingly strong and sharp.

It was fear I smelled. And that was fair enough. Subverting my friend group, manipulating Shango, twisting everything to her advantage, and putting all of us in danger—Phelia had done a lot to necessitate *fear* around me.

But I didn't like smelling it. I didn't like *feeling* it. I didn't like my head being fucking noisy, even when I had a mere three people around me. And certainly not when I'd be stuck with the feeling for hours.

So I spoke.

"What's wrong?"

I hadn't meant to growl it. That was just sort of how it came out. Phelia seemed to recoil, as if I'd just started licking her. Come to think of it, that would've been pretty funny, but I figured it wouldn't exactly forward my current goal of calming the bitch down, so I abstained.

"What's wrong?" she echoed, seeming *surprised*. And cautious. Well, no shock on the latter point. If I were a woman, living among several billion giant baboons who might beat me to death in a moment of berserk rage if I misread their emotions, caution would be my default setting. In fact, it bloody *was* my default setting, and I was one of those baboons.

"I'm asking you what's wrong," I repeated. "Something's clearly gnawing at you. It's me, and it's pissing me off. So tell me what's the matter so I can fix it."

She stared at me that way people did when they thought I might kill them.

"You choked me half to death," Phelia replied, voice so tight it was almost like my hand was still around her neck.

"You tried to kill my family," I countered.

"I didn't *try* to kill anyone!" she spit. "I just—"

"Withheld information that might have gotten us killed."

That deflated her, but . . . interestingly. The way she paused, the way she halted, it was like she was actually *considering* what I'd said. I wasn't aware upper-class people could do that, and studied her for any signs of imminent combustion.

". . . I'm sorry," she said at last, squirming. Fearful. I still felt that much, fearful. She didn't think apologizing made any difference at all, didn't think I could be deterred in the slightest. She was watching me for any sign of an attack like . . .

I swallowed. She was watching me like a very stupid boy had once watched a very violent woman.

"I'm sorry," I said at last, not looking at her.

She smelled of betrayal, that was what I'd been missing. But not mine. I'd seen the way she and Shango had been looking at each other, the revolting, putrid affection growing between them. *Love.* It made me ever so slightly sick. Definitely the worst of all the fucking emotions our dumb ape ancestors had thought were a good idea to evolve.

But there was no denying that that's what was blooming. Probably she'd made Shango promise not to leave her at my mercy. Probably she saw this as some sort of failing on his part.

Well, she was right. Stupid bastard never did let us mere mortals move his convictions when he'd dug them in.

"You're sorry?" Phelia didn't sound convinced obviously, but she did sound surprised. She got over it fast. Quick, that one. Dangerous. "Right, forgive me. I—Of course. I forgive you."

Well, that just tasted sour. I was being handled like a wild animal. Not much to do there in any case. Anything I said would, at best, just be a continuation in what she saw as a lull before the next outburst. I fell silent and tried to tolerate the feeling of her jagged emotions scraping my brain.

She was being sincere for the most part. And she'd been acting out of self-preservation before. I couldn't blame her for that, not really. Not when I'd done what I'd done for that very same reason.

Guilt started gnawing at me, but at least this was my own instead of someone else's. I let it sizzle away in my mind while the cart continued on its path.

The city was warmer today than it'd been in a good long while, and getting warmer. Winter was almost over. The sky was lightening. I let myself focus on that, let myself focus on everything. Split my attention that special way I'd never met another person capable of managing.

And it was a good thing I did too. Because if I hadn't—if I'd still been busy moping around and self-pitying over my own damned choice to strangle a woman—then there was every chance I'd have missed that faint, slight whistling in the air as something moved through it.

Without that moment of forewarning, my diving tackle probably would've come too late to keep Phelia from being decapitated.

CHAPTER TWO

Beam's POV: Day 104
Current Wealth: 722 gold, 0 silver, 37 copper

While Solitaire was busy fighting for his life, I had a challenge of my own to contend with. Putting on my pants.

As far as struggles for an Olympic athlete went, there were certainly *less* ignominious ones to be having. Still, it beat bleeding to death in the middle of some arena.

"You're not going to ask for help?" Helena asked, sticking to me like a shadow since I'd been hurt. She was doing better recently, much better. Almost back to fighting strength. I doubted she'd last long if someone of actual power attacked us, but I'd still put my money on her against nonsuperhumans.

"Would you give it?" I frowned, surprised by her question.

"No."

I sighed and continued the task of getting my fucking pants on.

"Do you think Solitaire will be alright?" Helena asked as I kept at it. It wasn't that I couldn't move much, or even that I couldn't move fast; it was that I couldn't move *consistently.* Something that was fine one moment would be pure agony the next.

"Why wouldn't he be?" I grunted distractedly.

"I don't know," she replied, quickly enough that Shango or Solitaire would've read something in it. My pants though were a far more pressing concern. Little bastards were trying to run away from me.

"He'll be fine." I sighed. "Solitaire always is. Do you know anything about his mother?"

Helena hesitated.

"Bits and pieces," she replied. "Some mad magus, right?"

I felt a smile at that. Yeah, it was about right.

"More or less. Well, she was about the best person anyone could ask for in terms of teaching about *survival.* I've seen Solitaire disappear for weeks on end while police—uh, guards—searched for him, and they didn't find so much as a trace of his existence. And you've seen how . . . careful he is."

She relaxed somewhat, and I finally clothed myself. I got to my feet, wincing, sighing. Everything hurt.

Everything hurt, and I still didn't remember why. It wasn't like I'd been concussed—God knew I'd felt a few of those, and they were different from this. It was like I just . . . hadn't done anything. But everyone else remembered what I didn't, and my body certainly agreed with them.

You there?

Of course, the voice said nothing. My little helper had been awfully quiet since the fight, quiet enough that I'd been left to simmer with the question of what was going on. She—it felt like a she sometimes—seemed to be diminishing in what she knew of me. Time was my thoughts were being answered with her words before even I'd noticed them. Not anymore. She questioned me on occasion, didn't always know what I was doing. I didn't know whether that was good, but it was definitely relieving.

"You're not allowed to train, you know," Helena noted, and I froze. I eyed her, considered exactly how much she'd been sticking to me and what her current condition was.

Not enough to win a fight reliably against anyone who might be sent to assassinate me, but more than enough to bully me in my current position. I reminded myself just how sneaky Shango could be when he felt like it.

"Well, fine," I said, doing my best to hide just how fine it wasn't. "I wasn't going to anyway."

"Yes you were."

Helena, if anything, had gotten harder, not softer, after being brutalized in the arena. I wasn't sure why. Obviously, I was happy to see her keeping her chin up and spine steely after such an ordeal. At the same time though, it made it rather unpleasant to find yourself at odds with her.

"Well, whatever I may or may—"

"Oh my God?!"

That didn't sound good. I didn't hurry to the source of the noise—well, actually I did, but my body only allowed for so much hurry before the risk of an impromptu disassembly became too much to ignore—but I reached it soon enough all the same.

Elizabeth was the source of the scream, and Shango was standing right next to her as both of them stared aghast through an open door. The door to Solitaire's lab.

"What's—"

"Don't," Shango snapped, turning to me before I could even finish the sentence. "Just . . . Holy shit, just don't." He closed the door, swallowing, sighing. "We need to get him some better locks."

Well, we sort of already had. Or rather Solitaire had. The actual mansion was about as impenetrable as something you'd compare a mansion that had recently been renovated by a schizoaffective terrorist to.

"He'll be back soon?" Elizabeth asked, suddenly seeming worried. "I don't want . . . that left unattended."

"He'll be back soon," Shango promised her. "Beam, how are you holding up?"

"I'm not," I growled, feeling a twinge in my everything just from him saying it. God, I might have gotten the worst ass kicking in my entire life before. Well, worst so far.

Including the bear.

"That's a shame. We might need you to be fighting ready sooner rather than later." Shango said it with the same easy smile he said most things with, but he seemed tense at the same time. It was the face he had on during deals. Not relaxed, just forcibly controlled.

"Tournament's over," Elizabeth added. "Means attacking us won't be fucking with money anymore."

"As I was thinking," Shango agreed. Helena shifted behind me.

"I won't be ready for combat for a while," she noted. "And Beam will be longer."

"So we play for time." Shango smiled. It didn't even come halfway to his eyes. "Shouldn't be too hard. Solitaire's already made enough toys to overthrow a small nation."

An exaggeration, at least by Earth standards, but I could believe it might have actually been true here. Our limit now—and for a while really—had just been on manpower. The sooner we could see to that, the better.

"We'll need men," Helena noted, as if she'd read my mind. Smart, our new friends, all of them.

"We can't get them." Shango sighed. "Not without risking infiltrators."

"And why not risk them?" Elizabeth cut in. "Our reputation's spread now, so it'll be easier to find recruits, and we'll be that much scarier for people willing to spy."

Shango pulled the exact face most men did when we found ourselves pinched between two women with good points, and hesitated.

"We'd need to have them all watched," he noted.

"Would we?" Elizabeth countered. "Solitaire told me not to step into his laboratory without permission or I'd be instantly killed. Was he lying?"

Shango paused again.

"Probably not," he admitted.

"So what's the problem then?" Helena added. "We don't need to recruit a whole gang—we can pick them partly at random, just a few dozen. Train them up, arm them. Hell, we can even see about changing the loyalties of any spies when they realize what sort of equipment they're getting."

That hardened his eyes rather than softening them.

"And in doing that, we'll be giving them all samples of Solitaire's technology to run off with and show around to be studied and replicated."

It was my turn to reply then.

"Uh, Shango, I don't think you realize how hard that would be. We're talking about guns, right? How many people in this world do you think can copy them?"

"I've heard of some who have weapons like yours," Helena noted. "We fought them on occasion. Eastern raiders weren't that uncommon in Vittonia, but they looked and worked differently from yours."

Probably she was describing one of the magitech factions with arcane gravity- or wind-based force guns. And she was right in those being different from our weapons, though not by as big an amount as I'd have liked.

"The powder is already being sold off, right?" Elizabeth asked. "And that's what makes them work."

That, it seemed, was what had Shango decided. His posture shifted, crumpling as his mind changed and threatened to crush the rest of him beneath its titanic weight.

"Fine." He sighed. "Fine, fuck it, you've won me over. If you can convince Solitaire, then we'll do it."

We all blanched at that. Elizabeth, me, even Helena in spite of her soldier's stoicism and newfound fondness for him. Solitaire was not the most predictable guy. Ask him not to rig a grenade under your bed and he got pissy. Ask him to invite strangers into his home . . .

My odds of being reflexively shot in the face this week were upsettingly high, I decided.

CHAPTER THREE

Solitaire's POV: Day 104
Current Wealth: 722 gold, 0 silver, 37 copper

I almost forgot to make sure I took most of the fall, which was dangerous for Phelia given that she didn't have superhuman durability. Fortunately, I was quick-witted enough to avoid turning my sister-in-law into a particularly sticky piece of modern art.

Ridiculously, Phelia screamed and hit *me*. Her fist bounced harmlessly off my face—forget the strength of a woman, most men couldn't have even made me flinch anymore—but it did a fine job of distracting me while I tried to locate the source of our enemies.

"Stay down, you stupid cunt," I snapped. "Someone's trying to kill us."

No sooner had the words left my mouth than they tried again.

First rule of getting jumped: Don't. Second rule: Be clever. I knew their target was Phelia; I thought back to the attack they'd tried. Solid, notable travel time, massive and large enough to leave a sound in the air as it whipped by. Probably, it could be blocked. I rolled off my sister-in-law and froze the air above her by banishing away all the heat. Steam erupted in a great torrent over the slab of ice just as it came to rest atop her.

Phelia was completely flattened under it, screaming and weakly flailing below the freezing mass. She'd *probably* live for a while underneath it, and that was a damn sight better than if she was exposed.

Besides, it served her right for acting like I was some sort of psycho.

I didn't need vindication for that, but if I had it would've come a moment later when something—the same attack that had almost killed her—smashed downward on the ice. An instant slower, a quarter second more hesitant, and I'd have watched Phelia die. As things were, the bar of iron hit the barrier, left a meter-wide crack across it, and rebounded with about as much control as a tased drunkard.

The iron rod bounced away, toward me. Pure luck, and I capitalized on it fast. I grabbed the thing, concentrated, felt all the rust spreading as oxidation stripped the metal's strength far in advance of its age. Then I quickly let go as a telekinetic force tore it from my grip, dragged it a meter away, and sent it spinning back.

A few weeks ago, I'd have been in trouble. I still was, being fair. Beam's growth was far beyond anything I'd gotten. But I had an edge over my old self, and I recognized the prick attacking me now. Knowledge was power and all that. Well, power actually was power.

I twisted aside, then heard something else. String twitching, bolts moving. The crossbows caught me dead-on—a dozen projectiles slamming into me from the side. Skull, neck, kidneys. The wind was punched out of me, and I fell, head ringing, life over.

Well, that was a hell of a way to die.

And apparently not mine because I was still alive. The dirt tasted bitter. I spit it out, frowned. Got up. My ears were still ringing, and the battle had changed in those brief moments of confusion—Magnus and Alora were throwing themselves into it now. And I still wasn't bleeding to death. I looked around.

The bolts were right beside me, and they had blunt heads. I thought about it for all of a second before stumbling onto the obvious.

Apparently our attackers, the Dead Edge based on the return of the Iron Bar Fucker, knew who was responsible for our technology and wanted to take me alive. Well, I wasn't complaining. I was *alive* after all.

I turned, scanned the fight.

Twenty men, on the dot. Most moved like normals—people without the strength-augmenting powers native to Redacle. One I recognized. The Iron Bar Fucker, keeping his distance this time and standing behind a big man with a big hammer. Alora sent her chained blade spinning out, its recently finished tool steel edge opening a man's throat up down to the bone and braining another as she dragged it back. Magnus fell in before her, making himself the vanguard and raising his shield high to block a volley of crossbow bolts.

These ones were pointed, I saw. Six shooters, fast at reloading and nicely accurate, hanging back. Fortunately, all our enemies seemed to have bunched in at the same side. Amateurs—we'd be dead to rights if they'd surrounded us with this number.

Well, their mistake was my fortune. I got moving.

I dragged the heat from a section of air in front of me, chilling it to ice. Then I tried something new. The ice had been made with a hollow airtight section sealed at the top, which I synthesized nitroglycerin into. Then I changed a section of the back to steam, leaving a rim protruding up around it. The effect was just as I'd have hoped. Explosive.

Steam was less dense than ice, by a factor of . . . oh, around fifteen hundred times or so. Turn the latter into the former while something solid was pinching it, and it wanted *out.* The steam shot away like the jet stream of a rocket and threw my makeshift projectile as fast as any arrow could have gone. Faster. It was inaccurate, missing its intended target by a good few meters, but that didn't matter much. I'd left around a hundred grams of nitro in there, and when it went off, it sent splinters of ice shooting out to lance through its poor victims.

Aiming is a bit redundant when you're throwing frags at people.

I watched the closest man keel over. Another just seemed to fall. The rest only stumbled. Mixed success, I'd say, but not bad for an experiment. I was almost disappointed to be on them before getting the chance to shoot off another.

The first one I punched, using every bit of my now considerable strength. It was like hitting . . . well, something less durable than a skull, that was for sure. I felt it crack, the bone shifting under my knuckles with a tangible displacement. He dropped like a sack of shit, and I stepped over him to reach the next.

He was ready for me, abandoning his crossbow for a knife. I have a rule about people who try to stab me. I put the metal deep into his guts once, twice, three times. He dropped, hands tight around his ruined belly as I whirled and dragged the stolen edge across another man's face. It was a good swing, timed well. Split the bastard up right before he could stick me. More were coming. Coming slow, but coming in numbers. If I backed off, they'd swamp me, so I charged instead.

The paranoia saved me, as good at preserving my life as it was at ruining it. If I wanted to smash someone fast enough to dodge my weapons, how would I do it? Wait for him to get focused attacking someone else, then hit him in the back. And I'd kept ducking under, so the bar would come low. I was already ready to move when the wind first pricked my ears, and I did with a jump.

With the use of both hands, nitro congealed in the air before me. I let it form, focused again on ice, had a platform right below me just as the mass of liquid exploded. I'd leaped as high as I could, and the concussive force gave me an extra few feet even as it snapped my makeshift platform in half. I cleared the heads of the idiots in front of me, watching the bar sweep their legs out from under them with a few sickening cracks. Then I landed.

A glance showed me that Magnus and Alora's situation had deteriorated. Good fighters—great fighters—but four-to-one odds were four-to-one odds. I resisted the apish urge to help them and made myself act a bit more constructively, heading for the Iron Bar Fucker.

Well, he was expecting me. The weapon came up just in time to avoid my hastily cast shield of ice. It hit my ribs, *hard*. I moved with the impact, leaning back, twisting. Angling and shallowing it as much on instinct as anything else.

Had I been as tough as I was when I'd first arrived, it probably would've broken several ribs like kindling. Lucky me then that it only bruised or cracked one. I wheezed, breaths suddenly coming hard, eyes suddenly watering, pace slowing. I thought things through.

Alora and Magnus were losing, but they were . . . fast. Faster than their enemies, that was sure. We could run, thanks to that. The one complication to a sudden flight would be the Iron Bar Fucker. I saw his weapon readying itself for another strafing run and knew I could stop it. But not physically.

If I exposed Phelia—their first target—and bolted in the other direction, what would they do? With a dozen men already dead or dying, their little ambush had already lost its teeth. Keep fighting us, maybe they'd win. Maybe they'd lose; maybe they'd all join their friends. Humans were stupid for the most part, but I thought even the average idiot would be capable of that basic arithmetic.

And I knew that Phelia would be a tempting target, even without it. She was our in with the nobility, the source of our connections. Shango could work around her sudden loss, I knew, and in fact her death might even benefit us in the long term by letting us keep the title and free him up to use marriage as a political offer once more, this time from the seat of nobility. But they probably didn't know that—else they wouldn't have attacked her first.

I would condemn a woman I didn't like, I would buy my allies and myself the chance to flee, and I would preserve the most valuable asset we had, all while strengthening our position long term and bloodying our enemies' noses with a petty victory. It was the smartest choice.

Shango loved her. It hit me like a stiletto to the scrotum, as the truth tended to. He'd been more than just morally disgusted with me, and he'd not just lashed out because I'd egged him on. The rift between us—the ruination our friendship had become—was caused because there was an emotional element to this marriage. It hadn't taken long; no doubt the relationship would go up in flames as so many fast loves did. But it was there. It was strong enough to hurt him if Phelia died.

The Iron Bar Fucker struck, weapon flying like a thrown javelin, heading for Alora. Everything slowed, my brain quickened, my mouth moved, and my words shot out with a volume to match their mountainous power.

"I surrender!" I called out, almost buckling under the strain of even saying that much. The world froze.

CHAPTER FOUR

Shango's POV: Day 104
Current Wealth: 722 gold, 0 silver, 37 copper

Alora was drenched in sweat, and Magnus looked barely better. Both of them were littered by bruises, pale skin already darkening and bleeding to blue where impacts had landed too hard and too frequently. Neither one was meeting my eye. It only made my nerves more jagged.

"What happened?" I asked, keeping my voice under control only through a great deal of effort.

It was Alora who told me, while Magnus kept his eyes on the ground. Shame, I noted. He considered this his own failure. I tucked the knowledge away for later use while I listened.

She spoke quickly enough, hitting all the important facts and making me stop her for elaboration on a point only once or twice. By the time she was done, the full gravity of the situation had hit me.

"Were you able to figure out where Solitaire and Phelia were taken?"

"Byror's mansion," Alora told me, looking away as she said it. "We would've gone in after them, but . . ."

She didn't need to finish. Doubtless the place had been prepared ahead of time to hold them, and if they could send out dozens on a capture run, there were likely scores sticking around the prison itself. We wouldn't be getting in there. Not by force.

"I need to think," I told her, and turned. Someone called after me as I headed off to my room, but nobody stopped me from locking the door behind me. I took a seat at my desk, hands resting down beside me, and thought. The quiet helped, but the isolation helped more.

There was a sense of shock needling me, obviously, but it didn't sink deep. I was almost surprised, but it made sense. Solitaire four gone; so was Phelia. Beam was being told even as I sat there, but he was still in recovery and too weak to even win a fight against Argar for certain. This was all on me. The pressure hardened my thoughts instead of softening them, and I emerged again after only a few minutes. With a plan.

Everyone was waiting for me, of course. Beam included. They seemed . . . put out. It must have been how calm I was. People tended to be unnerved by that, and any other time I'd have considered hiding it for their sake. But now wasn't the moment to be focusing on other people's comfort.

"Our first priority is food."

The stares were like sledgehammers against me, and I watched as the seconds ticked by while everyone tried to make sense of what I'd said. Alora was the first to protest.

"That's what Solitaire and your wife were grabbed getting," she snapped. "Why the hell would that be your first thought?"

"Because we still need food," I told her. "And, more to the point, from what you told me, Solitaire already bloodied their noses in being captured, which means they'll be hesitant for another engagement. If we let them recover, our odds of getting attacked on a food run, that we have no choice but to make eventually, are much higher than they are now."

She hesitated, and Beam spoke up.

"I can go on the next run," he said, and now it was his turn to be stared at.

"No, we need you resting and healing as fast as you can. Corvan, however tired you are, power through and speed up his recovery. How fast can you have him fighting?"

Corvan paused, considering it.

"Fighting? A few days. He won't be in peak condition for over a week though."

It wasn't ideal, not at all, but if we played for time . . . It might be enough.

"Then, Arthur, we're going to need you to be ready for anything. If things escalate, you're our main line of defense for a while."

By the look on his face, I could tell Sir Nightne was planning on packing up and fucking off that very night. I'd need to find a way to keep that from happening.

"Understood," he replied, blandly courageous and unflappable as ever. On the outside. It seemed to instill a bit of confidence in everyone else at least.

"I say we charge in and smash the bastards' heads open," Argar growled, and I only sighed.

"We can do that in the future, if we live through this. We're getting stronger, and they know it—that's why they attacked when they did. But for now, we can't afford that sort of recklessness."

Argar was not happy. He'd never been one to take defeat easily, but you could've cooked bacon on his face with how hot the blood seemed to be pooling under its skin. I made sure to keep a gentle tone while contradicting him. It barely worked.

"What do we do then?" he croaked. This was killing him, and I felt for the big guy. But barely. My emotions were distant right now, as they needed to be. It was just me. No Solitaire. Whatever plan we went with would come out of my own mind. So I hardened it.

"We've already had some of us captured, but we have nothing to worry about now. An offer will come soon, and I have a plan for it." I turned to Elizabeth. "Everyone, mind giving us a word alone?"

She seemed more disturbed than surprised, though that was hardly an atypical reaction from her. The room soon cleared, and the two of us were speaking together.

Elizabeth didn't like what I had to say, but I'd figured as much. The important thing—the only important thing—was that she agreed to it. After seeing to that, I made my way out too. I wasn't at all surprised to find Beam waiting for me beyond the door.

"We're getting him back," he said. It wasn't a question, which was fair enough.

"Both of them," I replied, feeling a strange tugging in my gut at the thought of Phelia. I buried it.

"Good." Beam nodded. "It's just that you seem quite calm about all of this."

I could see the frustration in his eyes. He hated how little he could contribute to this. No doubt if he wasn't hurt, he'd already be trying to barge his way into wherever Solitaire was and spearhead an assault right for him. No doubt, after his performance against the King, he'd have a fair chance of managing it.

But there was no point in dwelling on hypotheticals.

"What do you want me to do?" I asked him. "I'm focused on getting our friend back. Sorry if I can't be a bleeding heart while I do that. I'll make sure to cry a river when Solitaire's home safe."

Beam eyed me for a moment, then nodded. We got to work.

It may come as a surprise to you, given the success rate of our operations at the time, but we actually *managed* to get the food. I know, our competence truly does know no bounds. The hitch did come of course, but not until we'd already started on our way back to the mansion.

We'd gotten to keep the carriage after the first ambush, which meant we were in it for the next one. The enemy was polite enough not to open up with an attempted assassination this time though and settled for merely encircling us. We were forced to stop as the row of men halted ahead, spears outstretched, formation tight. Like a giant hedgehog with bristling steel quills.

The carriage stopped, and we all got ready. Argar was compressed into the back, axe quivering in his hand and two-hundred-kilo body coiled up like a spring. Alora and Magnus were squeezed in beside him. Corvan was hidden, tucked behind a thin wooden compartment we'd had hastily made to give whoever attacked us a nasty surprise when the magus came out hurling fireballs. We had Arthur sitting in front of it, to draw the eyes of anyone facing them disastrously away right before surprise jumped out.

In the front, shielded by plates of thin iron, was just me. My gun was beside me, and that was company enough.

Ahead, the men parted slightly to let a newcomer stride out from among them. I recognized him instantly of course, his face as smug and infuriating as ever. Lord Byror cut a rage-inducing figure, standing there in the setting sun. I did not shoot him on sight. Sometimes one must play the grown-up, after all.

"Lord Velaharo," he called out, speaking as if he could read my mind and knew for a fact he wasn't going to die. Maybe he just hadn't heard much about how my gun worked. "Might I have an audience? Seeing as how I have you so splendidly surrounded."

Elizabeth wasn't here, and in her absence, Alora was the best set of eyes we had. She leaned up from the back, keeping herself obscured from the men ahead as she whispered to me through the paneling.

"They have us at the back too, almost as many men as at the front. Archers on roofs, and Corvan says he senses someone using magic. Maybe forty men in total."

Forty was . . . too many. Particularly when I saw Aja the Pit Hound step out among them. Without him and the magus, we might've managed it, depending on their skill and level of superhuman abilities. As things stood, I wasn't going to risk it. Not with all the chain mail I saw covering them.

"Stand ready but don't escalate," I whispered back. "I'm going to head off with him. It's a plan."

"A stupid on—" I got up and got down just as Alora started speaking, leaving my gun where it was. Wouldn't do me much good anyway, so I'd rather avoid it catching their eye. I headed over to Byror and waited for the fear to bubble up inside me.

It didn't. I felt just as hollow as before, just as clear.

"It's been a while," he said as I came in, resisting the urge to hover just out of spear range and stepping in deliberately close. If they wanted me dead, there wasn't much to do about it, so I might as well look unfucked about it.

"Not really," I told him. "Can we get this over with? You obviously have some reason for being here personally."

His eye twitched. Not one to take being disrespected well? No, he'd been fine enough with that when Solitaire mouthed off in our first meeting. He didn't like being underestimated. Didn't like the idea that someone didn't fear him. I tucked that information away for later.

"I'm here to ensure that you don't give us any trouble as my men escort you elsewhere," he explained at last. I considered that.

Lying, I knew it. But he seemed . . . defensive, even annoyed by the question. Why? I'd have to find out later.

"And you'll kill my associates and brother if I do," I guessed, earning a smile from him.

"How astute you are, my lord."

"Just get it over with."

CHAPTER FIVE

Shango's POV: Day 104
Current Wealth: 722 gold, 0 silver, 37 copper

Say one thing for Byror, he didn't waste time. Not much at least. I was marched off road and onto a carriage within the minute, and far from the point of my abduction in only three more. His vehicle was a lot more comfortable than ours. Or, as Solitaire would say, insecure. The walls were pretty wood, not clumsily bolted steel. The whole thing seemed to glide over the ground, rather than shiver each time its extra ton of weight was rocked an inch too far, and the air within lacked that dirty, metallic reek I'd come to grow accustomed to.

The company, of course, was a downgrade. Byror didn't share it with me, which was definitely the smart choice on his end. Instead, I got to enjoy the presence of four men who each individually looked like he'd sworn an oath to do one push-up every time he breathed through his mouth.

Fortunately, I wasn't riding with them for long. We soon arrived at Byror's mansion.

Not as big as mine. Somehow, that took the edge off the moment. Phelia's house was broader, and just as tall. The grounds were the real difference though, and probably a good acre removed from the new Belahont headquarters. It didn't do anything to diminish Byror as a threat, mind, but it felt good enough. I soaked in more while being ushered in through the building itself, though didn't get much noted down before we finally came to his office.

It was a nice room, well decorated and warm against the winter. But it felt icier than the taverns my brothers and I had spent our first days shivering away in. I took the seat gestured to me—opposite Byror's desk—and readied myself for whatever was coming.

I wasn't waiting long.

Byror dropped himself down facing me and smiled.

"We both know where this is going, I think," he noted with the tone of a man who thought he knew more than he did. "I need your secrets. All of them. The secrets to your technology, your tactics, your brother's impossible growth. Give them to me and I will have no further incentive to harm you."

I thought about convincing him torture didn't actually work very well, but decided against it. If the CIA had made anything abundantly clear, it was that violent morons didn't easily listen when told how pointless their methods were.

"And if I refuse?"

It was so obviously what he wanted me to ask that it would've been rude not to. Besides, if I kept on *not* giving him what he wanted, his ego might've gotten pricked. Stupid people with pricked egos and power over others were a disaster in the making.

With a gesture, Byror had a door opened and passed. Through it came a large group. Three among it were tall men whose bodies clinked with thick steel plates, each of whom had physical stats in excess of a dozen. Between them was a terribly familiar face.

Tall, as ever, wiry as ever, and vibrating, as ever, with the concentrated urge to kill every single person on the planet. Solitaire was bound in thick enough chains to hold the giga-troll as they hauled him in. He looked around the room with the sort of expression I'd expect to find in the eyes of a rabid dog. It barely softened as he recognized me.

I didn't soften at all, in turn. There was some part of me that rejoiced at the sight of him, but it was deep and buried, and through no great effort on my part. I'd figured out what Solitaire had turned himself in for—figured out he'd thrown himself away to save Phelia—and I loved him for that.

But now wasn't the time for love, not even for a brother's. The icy tendrils tightened their grip on my thoughts, keeping me calm and clever. I turned my gaze to Byror as if Solitaire was no more than a poker chip.

Byror, it seemed, was dumb enough to buy the act.

"As you can see," he said, sounding about one-third as confident as before, and only slightly angrier, "we have your brother."

"I knew that already." I sighed, as if he were being incredibly tedious. "But you should know he's not the best way to hurt me."

The noble stared at me, almost offended.

"Do you take me for a fool?" he snapped. "I—"

"Solitaire pinned my wife against her desk," I cut in, crushing his words under mine. "And threatened to break her fingers. He held her like this—terrified—for minutes, all over nothing more than a suspicion. You've heard the stories. He's a mad dog, and if he weren't so useful to me, I'd have had him put down long ago."

"Bastard!" Solitaire snarled, thrashing against his chains and almost making me flinch. There were few things in the world more terrifying than watching him lunge for you when you'd seen him fight. If it was an act, it was good enough to fool me. At least in my moment of panic.

Certainly, it fooled Byror.

"You . . . This is the man you're partnered with," he whispered.

For one single stunning moment, I understood Byror, and he understood me. We looked at each other not as enemies, but as two men who were both in the presence of *Solitaire.* Basking in the snarling, screaming, jagged bundle of nuclear misanthropy that was my friend and leaning on each other for mental support. Hugging in the eye of the storm.

Then the moment passed, and we were all business again.

"We all make concessions." I shrugged.

Byror was quick to adapt at least, if only by moving on to the *second* most obvious chip.

"And yet we still have your wife too."

I tensed at that, all deliberate and controlled. Nodding after a moment.

"You do," I replied, speaking through carefully tightened teeth and vocal cords. If I do say so myself, I did quite a good job of making the words sound reluctant. I did care about Phelia of course, but . . . Well, that care was as distant now as everything else. If emotion gets in the way of thought, better to throw it away and pick it back up when it's useful. Of this, I am the master. More than Solitaire, more than anyone. My mind does nothing I don't want it to.

And in that moment, I wanted it to do nothing but think.

"I can offer you . . . some schematics," I said at last, taking my time as if it was a difficult choice.

"The fuck you can!" Solitaire roared, then gasped as someone hit him. I resisted the urge to look over instantly, turning my head slowly, instead, to make sure he was uninjured with a colder and more lethargic eye. Our gazes met for a moment, and I flashed him the quickest, shortest expression I could. Anyone else would have missed it—because eye blinks were faster. Solitaire flashed me one back to let me know he'd seen.

I turned back to find Byror was smiling, which was an entirely expected response. Everyone smiled when they thought they were winning. It was a good sign.

"Excellent." The noble beamed. "I might have expected as much, of course. Word has already begun to spread of you and yours you know, my lord. It is rather well-known, even now, that you are the reasonable brother."

The reasonable brother. What a curious thing to be known for. I just shrugged.

"I suppose I am." And I supposed truthfully. Without another word, without asking for permission, I got up. Byror beamed wider.

"By all means, make your way out. We're not holding you prisoner, after all! Indeed, you'll find a carriage awaiting you outside."

I'd known all of that of course. With Solitaire already a prisoner, they'd want to ensure whoever else they strong-armed for information had a path back to the laboratory where we were developing all our technologies. It had been a few more layers of guesses and hopes than I was typically comfortable with, mind, but then I'd been doing a lot more of both than I'd ever have wanted to since coming to Redacle. It had paid off this time, at least.

Solitaire swore after me for each and every step I took to the door, and I just ignored him too. Better that than look back. Now, above all other times, I had to keep up my feigned indifference.

The plan relied on Solitaire, after all. And if the enemy got even a whiff of what it was, I doubted he'd survive the night. The temptation to volunteer just how much of our technology was stored specifically in his head was almost irresistible.

But I did resist, because indulging the urge to protect him in the short term would doom him in the long. I was cold, clever, and calm. And for the time being, I was free.

CHAPTER SIX

Solitaire's POV: Day 104
Current Wealth: 722 gold, 0 silver, 37 copper

Shango had flashed me a look there, for just a second. Too fast for anyone but us to know, but just long enough to convey its meaning. As limited as communication done with facial twitches alone was, I was fairly sure I'd gotten the meaning too. It was a secret "go on an insane psychotic rampage and kill as many people as you can" look.

I couldn't know that for sure, of course, so I decided to play things safe and assume that it was. After all, in the worst-case scenario, I was still too useful to kill. Good thing about being imprisoned for vital information is you're the most important person present.

My three escorts—who I had nicknamed Grongle, Dumbo, and Chungus on account of their subbrick intelligence—were relaxed slightly after my lack of violent insanity at Shango's presence. That had been deliberate, of course, as had been the rest of my performance over the day. Slackening up slightly when they hit me, flinching, letting them think I could be deterred with a pinch of pain.

Ridiculous. My mum hit harder than these dumb cunts, and more regularly too. Say one thing for mother dearest, say she was good at preparing you for the worst.

We turned a corner and started heading down, walls losing their paper and wood, yielding to hard stone. A few more steps and we were in the dungeons, the most secure part of the building.

That was, of course, the perfect time to strike. Because I didn't think I could physically get out no matter what, which meant the benefit of extra-tough walls around me was no benefit at all to my enemies. And if they relaxed thinking it was, then it was actually my weapon. I did give these things a bit of thought, you know. If you thought I just improvised it all then I can only apologize for spoiling the magic.

My shackles were thick, heavy things. But they were bigger than they were solid. I focused on building ice around the locking mechanism, shielding it from sight so my enemies wouldn't notice.

Oh, I wasn't freezing the metal. That would've been pointless. Iron this thick? I'd need to be able to bench a hundred of myself to even have a chance of snapping it, and even bringing steel into the negative hundreds Celsius left it with an appreciable fraction of its strength. No, the ice was protection. Because once its shell had thickened to about an inch, I got to work on the nitro.

Every step taken as I flooded the hollow interior of my shackles with the stuff felt like it'd detonate the liquid prematurely. Even with ice now covering the shackles and as much of my hands and arms as I could manage without giving up the game, it wasn't wholly pleasant. But it took me only a few seconds to completely fill it. Then I turned around and swung the shackles up for Dumbo's face.

Boom. Nothing like the sound of a nice explosion to wake you up in the morning, better than caffeine! Not for Dumbo though. It did the opposite to him. I'd made most of my icy wards on the *wearer's* side, so much of the blast got deflected directly into poor Dumbo's face. He dropped like a sack of shit, and I whirled to see Grongle and Chungus were reeling.

Honestly, some people. Set off a tiny, piddly nitro bomb next to them and they go completely witless.

Well, witless was what happened to Grongle next. I snatched a particularly big bit of mangled iron out of the air and jabbed it into his neck as hard as I could. It wasn't that sharp, or big, and I don't think I hit any arteries, but the moron was clutching at himself to stem the bleeding anyway. A fair precaution, but unfortunately one that occupied both of his hands. I grabbed his temples and started head-butting, once, twice, five times. By the time I stopped, my forehead had finished testing his jawbone and found it wanting. He fell with a chin that was rather lumpier than before. Two down.

Of course Chungus had a baton, and he was almost as big as me. But he also wanted me alive. Doubtless Byror—who seemed desperate to control everything—had made a stupidly vicious threat to anyone about what would happen if they killed me. Chungus was probably thinking of that now, which meant my neck and head were safe from bludgeoning. The baton was affixed at his left hip, and he was to my right, so it'd be whipping to me roughly from behind as I was facing to Grongle's left.

I darted back, turning and catching the bludgeon in my shoulder. It was a few inches lower than I'd have guessed, but I was right enough to blunt its impact. I'd caught the weapon halfway through its acceleration, and for my next trick I caught Chungus and started leaning in.

He'd seen me bite someone, so he panicked instantly, and I used that moment to break contact, twist the baton from his wrist, and start swinging. Heavy thing, maybe a kilogram in total and running about the length of my forearm. It came down hard on the back of his neck, shoulders, and skull. Chungus went down shortly. Three for three.

But I wasn't out of the fire yet because when you start your escape attempt with an IED, it tends to gather attention. I knew for a fact there were seven guards lower in the dungeons, where I'd been held, and if the ones I'd seen on my way up were still where they'd been, there were four more who were closer. I turned down the hall and started sprinting up out of the dungeon and into the mansion proper.

Lo and behold, the four guards were ahead of me soon enough, gathered up, armed and shaking as they awaited my approach. I did hate being right sometimes. As a paranoid, it rarely brought good news. My baton was better than fists, but each of them was armed with a spear now. And they wore chain mail. Better equipped than some street toughs, these were Byror's personal guards.

Well no pain, no gain.

I came on as fast as I could, then leaped right before we crashed into one another. Their spears were outstretched, which would've made me the loser of that. I darted to one side, kicked off the wall, and turned as much of my sprinting speed into flying speed as I could. And it worked pretty well, if I say so myself, sending me far over their heads to land behind. I was swinging before any moved, cracking the baton into someone's chest and feeling bones *give* beneath it. A spear flashed for me, and I twisted aside into the path of another that barely glanced off my own weapon. The third chased me back.

All their motions were slow, like watching men moving through water. Which was the only reason I hadn't been stabbed to death already. They advanced as I retreated, then the sounds of footsteps reached me from behind. More enemies, a good number, and fewer than twenty paces away. I threw myself at the spears again.

With another baton swing, I snapped one's head off, but the other two were too steady and too long to close. I hissed as this time one of them opened a cut on my cheek. A splash of nitro eviscerated one of the wielders, then the newcomers closed. They went to restrain me, not kill me. Which meant fists and grappling. I dropped the baton as arms closed on my body, knowing it'd be useless at this range, and got fighting.

All told, I did a bit of damage. One man lost an eye to a headbutt; another's head hit the wall so hard I heard either brick or bone break apart. But there were a lot of them. Fists came down like rain, and though I was a great deal sturdier than back on Earth, damage like that adds up impossibly fast. Soon enough, I was buried under several burly men, limbs held in vise grips and body pinned fast. I struggled anyway, and actually shifted them a few inches.

Then the fist came down on my temple, and I decided that being taken easily was the better part of valor.

Well, I'd had a good run, and I'd hospitalized a few of the enemy at least. Now it was out of my hands. Whatever Shango had needed me rampaging for would either work or it wouldn't.

I considered, as they hauled me off, the idea of trying another nitro blast. No. Knowing my luck lately, I'd end up killing myself.

And the world had been doing a fine enough job of that already without my help thrown in.

I t was cold out, but the snow had stopped. That left Elizabeth miserable, exposed, and without the reduced visibility she'd have enjoyed from having the air clotted with debris. About the perfect conditions to not be infiltrating Byror's mansion in, but beggars couldn't be choosers. She should know. She'd begged a lot.

As far as mansions went, Byror's was on the larger side. Ordinarily that meant it was easier to get into, all things being equal, but all else was not equal today. It was practically *sweating* guards. Elizabeth gave her best go at counting them but gave up somewhere around the fiftieth.

She circled it, hugging her clothes—thick and warm, thankfully—tight to herself as she searched the place for any possible flaw. There seemed to be none. Clearly Lord Byror was one used to staving off malfeasance from his enemies, for he'd taken no chances in the defenses of his home. Elizabeth was just starting to consider heading back to report a failure when she caught sight of the guards outside starting to turn back to the mansion.

Odd, that. She closed in more, studied them harder, and saw more and more of them fall back into the building as if they were . . .

As if they were hurrying to respond to some disaster. Elizabeth smiled to herself. Looked like Solitaire had gotten the hint.

She moved fast—not as fast as Beam could now, damn it—and scaled the outer fence. It was one of those expensive ones, wrought from iron with jagged barbs covering it. Her new clothing took care of that though. An inch of quilted wool staved off the tearing hooks of metal and saw her safely over it. Then she was running.

Elizabeth had always been a sprinter, and always the best she knew. It was over a hundred yards from fence to mansion, but she crossed the distance within five heartbeats and slipped inside as quiet as a cat.

Nice place. Well decorated, expensive. Elizabeth felt irritated, for a moment, that she was on business too important to justify taking a break to loot the mansion of its valuables. She settled for wiping her shoes on the most expensive looking rug she could find, then took off again.

Shango hadn't been able to find actual plans of the mansion, and with Solitaire captured, they'd not even been able to test his bizarre numerical magic on scrying her destination from the outside, but Elizabeth had been in enough mansions of similar design that she wasn't entirely lost. Mostly, it was just trial and error. Which meant her success would depend on how long the distraction lasted. And no small amount of luck.

There were more guards around still than she'd have liked, but Elizabeth slipped them by without much trouble. If nothing else, the escapade was a good lesson on why exactly her bosses had insisted on everyone living and working in such a small section of the Velaharo mansion. The idea of securing the entire thing was made more impossible with each step she took. Eventually, Elizabeth came to the living areas and wasted no time in barging past one door and another in search of the prize.

By luck alone, she reached him with only her fourth attempt. Elizabeth stepped in to find a large room, floor littered with toys that each looked more expensive than everything she had on her. A little boy was lying in a large bed, fast asleep.

He looked so peaceful. Innocent, as all children were, and utterly oblivious to what was happening around him. Elizabeth felt a lump in her throat, suddenly struck by the urge to turn and abandon her job.

But she couldn't. Not now. Steeling her nerves, she headed in and gently raised the boy into her arms. He was so very young and small that even she could manage his weight without much effort, but she still hurried on her way out. As she was now, Elizabeth wasn't nearly as confident about outrunning any pursuit as she'd have preferred to be. Better to not need to.

Elizabeth was like a gust of wind sweeping through the corridors, and she'd almost gotten out of the mansion when the mass of guards caught her eye. She froze, huddled behind a wall, glanced at the child to make sure he was still asleep, then studied them. Among the men, snarling and occasionally thrashing, remained Solitaire.

He was hurt badly, face littered with bruises and crusting blood, hands skinned raw where they'd been mashed into other men's skulls. By the looks of things, he'd done more than just cause a distraction. No wonder so many of the guards had left their posts.

Disaster, a guard started turning for her. Then another. Elizabeth's mind blanked as panic struck away her thoughts, freezing her in place, leaving her to do nothing but await discovery. The only way for her to run was back—which would only trap her in the other end of the mansion. If she was to cross the grounds with a child in her arms, she'd need to take the shortest route, and the only path to the exit leading there was ahead. It was over.

Then Solitaire punched one of them. The man's feet actually left the ground for a moment, then the rest tackled her boss all over. Elizabeth stared for a single second before hurrying to the window and leaving through it. She realized what had happened only when cool winds hit her.

Solitaire's little attack had been timed too perfectly for a coincidence. Somehow he'd known she was there and done the exact right thing at the exact right instant to let her leave. He hadn't even glanced her way. Sometimes that man was bloody frightening.

The boy stirred in Elizabeth's arms, cold threatening to wake him where motion hadn't, and she sped up. By the time she was at the fence, he was stirring. Elizabeth reached down for its base and set up her little mechanism. First the thick furs over the metal, to protect her cargo, then the ropes strewn over and knotted at the base. She bound the boy in a makeshift hammock and climbed over, pulling him back after her by levering his weight over the fence itself. He woke midway into the fall, but she caught him and sprinted off before anything could come of it.

Elizabeth was faster than a carriage, even with the boy slung over her shoulder. Carrying him all the way tired her. By the time she reached Velaharo Manor and found Helena and Arthur ready to escort her in, she was sweating so profusely that her skin shuddered like a creaking oak at every gust it caught.

Both of them saw the kid, and Helena in particular seemed almost disbelieving. Neither said anything though, just took her to Shango.

By then the boy seemed confused and growing increasingly close to upset, which only worsened as Elizabeth left him in the small room they'd agreed would be his temporary quarters. Shango was with her soon enough.

"You managed to get him," he noted. His voice was blank, face blanker still, eyes blankest of all. Like a corpse, as if everything around him were nothing more than some idle fact to be cataloged and considered for later use. It made Elizabeth shiver, but she suppressed it. Showing weakness went against her every instinct even more than keeping calm while Shango stared at her like a blunted tool he was deciding whether to repair or discard.

"I did," Elizabeth replied, surprised by the venom in her voice. "And I don't want you to ever ask me to do something like this again."

She'd thought she could do it. She'd thought, oh, it was just some rich boy, some spoiled little brat. How hard could it be? Then she'd felt the panic take him as he realized he was surrounded by strange faces and no parents. Felt his tiny body wrestling for freedom as she handed it off. She wasn't going to feel that more than once.

"You won't have to," Shango replied at last. "We only needed this as leverage, and only because the enemy has hostages too."

The enemy. It made her skin crawl to hear the phrase used so casually. Were they at war now? Elizabeth barely stopped herself from bolting then and there. Barely stopped herself for Solitaire.

Elizabeth headed for the door, as much to give herself an excuse not to look at Shango as to leave.

"Is this going to save Solitaire?" she asked.

Her boss paused a moment.

"I can't know for sure."

CHAPTER SEVEN

Shango's POV: Day 105
Current Wealth: 721 gold, 18 silver, 30 copper

I woke up to knocking on my door. A heavy knocking, the sort that came from hammers rather than fists. Given that I did not live with any pathological vandals—at least since Solitaire's capture—that narrowed it down to Argar.

"They're here," he growled, finally losing patience and barging in just as I got out of bed. He wasn't bothered by my near nudity, and neither was I.

"Let him wait," I said. "I'll be down quickly—but don't tell him that."

It was one of Solitaire's old tricks. Leave someone to stew; let their emotions multiply. He was so much better at playing them than me, but that didn't mean I couldn't pick up a thing or two. And I'd need all I could get now.

I got dressed and thought while I did. Then I made my way downstairs at a brisk enough pace to be quick, but not so brisk that I'd seem disheveled or out of breath when I arrived. I found Lord Byror at the head of what was *almost* an army when I finally reached the blockade my men had set up just within our own walls.

They were encircling most of the mansion and watching the rest. Outside the outer fence, for now, but pressing in dangerously close. If Solitaire were here, he might've given me a head count with one glance. Instead I had to turn to Alora.

"Have you estimated how many there are?"

"Close to five hundred," she replied, face tight. Five hundred. That seemed small, somehow, for the amount I thought I was seeing.

"He didn't have anywhere near this many guards," Elizabeth added. "He can't have. Byror, I mean."

"So other members of the coalition are here," I concluded. Good, if anything that would make this work better.

I didn't need to ask where Byror was becuase he made himself very easy to pick out as he stormed through the gate and hurried toward me.

Lucky he didn't try scaling the fence, I noted, right before he was in my face spitting and snarling. No guards came after him, I noticed, and none of my own moved to cut him down. Everyone was worried about escalation?

Perhaps.

"You fucking fuck!" Byror screamed, practically frothing at the mouth as his own guards hurried to catch up with him. He wasn't in control at all. Good. *"My son,"* he roared. *"Give me back my son."*

I kept my face as neutral as I ever had in my life and found the task remarkably trivial.

"I have no idea what you're talking about, my lord," I told him. "Your son is missing?"

"Bastard!" Byror was halfway through his first step when I realized he was going to hit me. That wouldn't be good. If we attacked back, it might escalate things with his men. If not, we looked weak. I spoke fast, and quietly. Waiting until he was within arm's reach and moving in before the blow could come.

"Touch me and Byror blood will coat my grounds."

I might have encased him in concrete and not frozen him as thoroughly as that sentence did. His face paled, like the blood was running out of an opened artery, and I waited for his response to come. Sluggish as all the others. I really did miss Solitaire.

"You . . . You . . ." He was stunned, disbelieving, desperate and with his thoughts scattered by all the cognitive ripples I was going without. So I chose then to speak again.

"I really have no idea what you're talking about," I pressed. "Why, just ask anyone. I'm the calm and reasonable brother. You captured the mad one already."

He wasn't lost for words this time. If anything he had them in excess, stumbling over his own tongue before speaking.

"I demand to see my son," he whispered, grabbing me and earning a cautious hand toward every weapon present except my own. With a slight gesture, I had my men standing back and waiting.

"I'll drop him off under the bridge at the outskirts of town," I murmured back, keeping my voice low and letting body language imply I wasn't speaking at all. "Come alone to pick him up or I'll kill him in front of you. We got into your mansion. We'll know if you try a double cross. If you want to bet your son's life on us missing it then feel free."

He held his courage, but not for long. There was no courage when you got a threat like that.

"Threats do not work on me, boy. You will give me my son back in two hours, or I will storm this mansion and level it in the searching. If you kill him, I'll have your whore wife raped by every man in my garrison and dump her head outside your gates," he hissed pitiably. Quietly. There was menace in his eyes but mostly . . . This was just an attempt to hurt the one who'd hurt him.

There was no courage when you got a threat like that, but for me there was no fear either. I just stared at him as he turned around and shuffled back to his men.

Beam watched him leave for a moment before closing in at my side, face almost folding in over its frown.

"What was that about?"

He hadn't heard, and that had been intentional. I needed everyone to not hear this. Everyone except Arthur, whom I'd pressed into complicity before he got the chance to flee so that he'd have no choice but to help beat the man whose son he'd kidnapped. Elizabeth had been brought in by unfortunate necessity, and Helena . . . Well, she seemed strangely, fiercely loyal to Solitaire. And she had a certain iron to her that I'd—rightly—figured would make her okay with it.

But not Beam. Never Beam, no matter what.

"No idea." I frowned, as if I were anyone other than the culprit of a kidnapping. "Bad luck, I'd guess. Poor bastard's son went missing and . . . Well, given the timing I guess I'd probably assume we had something to do with it too. I can hardly blame him."

Beam nodded thoughtfully, looking concerned but not even flashing a moment of worry about the events. It was nauseating, sometimes, the faith he had in me. I should have taken it as a sign of his friendship—and I did, sometimes—but right now it was just a reminder that everything truly was on my shoulders.

Though even that was distant compared to the simple pragmatics of everything.

We all took cover, and we all waited. Tempers frayed, but everyone was too busy being miserable to vent them. Corvan sat with us—which surprised me. I'd expected him to bolt whatever I did. Apparently he'd decided to bet on the long odds for better returns later. Didn't look like he'd get to see his money back with how things had gone though.

My only hope now was that two hours was enough time for Byror's doubt to fester.

Slowly though the change came. Men shuffled about their ranks in the surrounding army, and we all tensed and prepared for boots to hit the ground and explosive violence to come.

Instead, their formation parted, and some figures came striding out. Two figures, one short and trembling, the other tall and . . . also trembling, but for very different reasons. Solitaire and Phelia hurried as they headed over to us.

"Solitaire!" Beam grinned, his face almost splitting as he stared at our brother. I turned to Phelia, surprising myself by hugging her, and being surprised as she hugged me back. I looked up just in time to see Solitaire squirming.

Dangerous move on Helena's part, hugging *him* like that, but she won the game of Solitaire roulette and didn't get bitten. This time. He still looked properly miserable as she stepped back.

Solitaire turned to me then. He was friendly, of course, pleased to see me. Thing was, Solitaire's friendliness looked very much the same as a bulldog's. His smile showed a row of the world's most dangerous teeth, and his face had a sort of naturally angular shape that made his eyes just a little bit too wide whatever he did with it.

No wonder we got along so well. I was no more perturbed by that than I'd been by anything else over the last day.

"You got me out," he said at last, having taken an uncharacteristic pause. I shrugged.

"You gave yourself up."

I understood why, and he understood, in that instant, the exact nature of my understanding. I wouldn't embarrass him by letting everyone else know he'd done the right thing. However irrational, he wouldn't want them to be told. But I needed him to be aware that his goodness had been noticed.

Needed him, but not with any emotional pull. It was all purely cognitive. Morality, not decency. Correctness, not rightness.

CHAPTER EIGHT

Byror's forces—not really an army, but not really not an army either—didn't take too long to leave after the negotiations were finished. They'd fucked off within half an hour, leaving a nice surplus of breathing room around the mansion. Solitaire, I noted, seemed a bit disappointed to not have seen any of his defenses used.

Somehow, I got the feeling he would.

Well, that was a concern for later. The celebration was a concern for now. I looked around at the jubilation on display and felt . . . none of it. That was to be expected. I was still in a thinking mood. Still in a *doing* mood. That didn't mean I couldn't appreciate my friends' joy as I saw it happen around me.

Argar was the loudest, and seemed to be undergoing a new form of training where he did his best to find the absolute limits of how much alcohol a single liver could process without melting. Helena was careful to stop him from getting too rowdy, and mostly failed. Elizabeth seemed to find it all amusing. Ardin was more relieved than happy, wrung out and drained the way I usually got after a close call. Magnus was almost matching Argar for enthusiasm, Corvan calm as ever, and Arthur . . .

Well, Arthur was eyeing me with a silent hatred. He was a smart man. He'd realized what I'd done by having him be the one to handle Byror's son. The kid wouldn't give much of a useful testament—I was certain of that. It had all been too quick and too jarring for the boy, Elizabeth's work done perfectly in keeping him asleep for so long. But as far as Arthur knew, he was pinned to us by the threat of other people's revenge. Not the best bond to have in a subordinate, I knew, but a smart one could be trusted not to try any stupid betrayals. It was better than having him leave and take half our fighting power with him.

Phelia sat down beside me. It was abrupt and untelegraphed, but I wasn't surprised. When I got like this, I tended to keep my focus unaimed and scattered, watching everything at once. She hesitated as I turned to her, voice a small and uncertain thing. She began with something she hadn't come over to say.

"You got me back," Phelia noted, going exactly nowhere with the remark and, I suspected, only giving it voice to give her mouth something to do while she continued thinking about how to broach the apparently uncomfortable topic she'd actually come over to bring up. I could hardly blame her and played along.

"I had to," I replied, which I knew made it sound more formal and dutiful than it was but didn't bother correcting. Phelia seemed to take it well, though a distance grew between us. That distance made it easier for her to say what came next.

"I would like to speak about our child."

I eyed her.

"Are you . . .?"

"No," Phelia hurriedly replied. "No, not . . . not yet. No, I'm talking about . . . you know, our efforts to try for one."

"Right." I gestured for her to keep going, and she did.

"I'd like to put them on hold," Phelia said at last. "For now, at least. Given the . . . danger around us, I wouldn't feel comfortable bringing a child into the situation until we know it's improved."

She stared at me as she said it, suddenly intense and searching the way a woman being threatened might look. That, I'll admit, did confuse me.

"That's your choice," I said slowly. "If you don't feel ready, we'll wait."

Her face sort of . . . melted, going from stiff and hard to all . . . runny around the edges. I was confused, for the briefest instant, then recognized the relief on display. Relief and . . . gratitude?

Right. She was a woman living in the fucking Middle Ages.

"Thank you." Phelia sighed.

Thank you? Yes, of course, thank me by all means. It is after all my due, to be thanked for deciding not to fucking rape you. How kind of me, how decent, how superlative in moral character and integrity. I surely deserve a prize.

I didn't let any of the thoughts show on my face of course, just nodded again as Phelia took her leave back across the room. She passed Solitaire on the way, flinching back as usual. He didn't so much as glance at her, fortunately, and came to stop just before me. He spoke with none of her hesitance. When Solitaire had something to say, it got said. Especially if it was sexist.

"How'd you do it?"

Well, he obviously had bigger things on his mind than a bit of misogyny now. I hadn't really expected any different.

"Charm and cleverness." I smiled. "I knew Byror couldn't kill you, because then he'd have no leverage, so I didn't give anything up to incentivize him holding on. Let him think he might get what he wanted another way."

Solitaire smiled too, just as hollowly as me. He could've made it more convincing but didn't. Deliberate then. Meeting me falsity for falsity.

"You're lying," he noted.

I let my own mask slip to make him feel more at ease. Empaths did so hate being lied to.

"I am."

He eyed me, not angry but certainly far from pleased.

"And you can't be convinced to tell the truth?"

No. Never. Not with this.

"I can't," I replied. "Regardless, I've given you the story that's going to float around."

"The one that suits you best to be floating around," he observed. I shrugged, no point denying the obvious. Solitaire sighed as I started to take my leave, waiting just a moment before he spoke next.

"I'm sorry, Shango. For everything."

I didn't pause. But I didn't ignore him.

"I know" was all I said, then I left.

The entire sky had been eaten by night by the time I reached the alley, which was just as I'd planned. The place was conveniently close and conveniently far—I could sprint back to base if I had to, and wasn't at much risk of being stumbled onto while I concluded our business. As expected, Byror was waiting for me there.

He hadn't slept. He hadn't slept when we'd last spoken, a few hours ago, and he hadn't slept since then either. The fatigue had grown, not lessened, and whatever vitality had been remaining in the man before was fully wrung out of him now. He looked just fragile enough to . . .

Well, to meet me in a dark alley alone.

"My son," Byror snapped. "Where is he? I demand to see him."

He wasn't shouting anymore, but there was still that odd weight to his voice. The pressure of words formed by a man who expected obedience. Even now. It was inappropriate, to say the least. Byror's power lay in wealth and influence, not physicality. Within this alley, within the reach of my hands, he was no more potent than any peasant in the city. Less even.

I wasn't a fighter, but I'd collected levels in just the same way my brothers had. I wouldn't lose to a normal human. Wouldn't even struggle.

"He's not here," I replied, watching the terrified spasm across Byror's face for a moment. "He's already back at your mansion, dropped off, safe and unhurt."

Byror exhaled as if someone were squeezing his lungs empty and didn't appear able to speak for a good long moment. When he did, it was with anger.

"So this is some sick joke?" he snapped. "You dragged me over here just to get your jollies?"

I was calm, still, when I replied. Never calmer.

"I don't find anything that's about to happen funny."

Byror's feet left the ground when I hit him, his head snapping back and mouth exploding in a spray of blood and teeth. He landed hard, and confounded.

I'd brought a knife to do what needed doing next, but somehow that didn't make it any easier for me. Nothing would've made it easier, because it wasn't hard to begin with. It just needed to be done.

The blade came down and up while Byror was still gasping in confusion, slicing off one finger and another before he'd even realized what was happening. His shock hit like . . . a breeze, sliding off me as I focused on the task. An entire hand was mutilated before his screams started.

I silenced them with another fist, gentle to make sure he lived.

"You've made me sick," I told him. Not sure why I was speaking, not caring to stop. "Sick of my family not being safe, my friends not being safe. Sick of needing to do things like this just to survive. You didn't leave us alone, insisted on coming at us. So now you're going to become our deterrent."

Slice. Slice. Slice.

Difficult to do damage a magus can't fix, with enough time. Dismemberment was a start, but if you really want to make it hard, you'll add a bit of magic to the wound. Like the kind that comes from superhuman strength. Burns? Those were one thing. But a missing appendage with magic at the cut? I wasn't sure how many people in all the world could heal that.

So I started pinching the stumps, crushing the flesh as best I could and twisting what was left. There wasn't much left by the time I finished.

"My family magus," Byror gasped. "I . . . My family magus." I'd tuned out so much of his begging that I almost missed the critical tip there.

A magus. Worse, the personal magus of a powerful noble family. If he was only as strong as Corvan, I'd be screwed. If he was stronger, I'd have been screwed even with help. So I was now working on a time limit.

"Well, I'll be done before he's here," I whispered. "And you'll be a living reminder of what happens to our enemies. Just as intended."

I brought the knife down, now, to Byror's groin. I saw the fear flare up in his eyes just an instant before the cutting began.

"If my brother were doing this—Solitaire, the mad dog—he'd enjoy it, you know. He was practically vibrating when you did what you did to Helena. I'm almost surprised he didn't kill you then and there. I'm not Solitaire."

Soon enough, Lord Byror had relinquished his family jewels to a bloody, clotted mess on the floor. He was still alive, twitching and moaning, and, to my surprise, even speaking.

"You . . . How . . . How can you do this . . .?" he gasped, whimpering, crying. Voice trembling with the shiver of a man who didn't believe what was happening to him. "Do you not feel anything?"

Oh, I saw it now. He was confused. He kept expecting guilt to stop me. It'd never done that before.

Morals stopped me. The simple, intellectual rationality of what was right and what was wrong. I never did understand people who deviated from that on some emotional whimsy. I still didn't.

But right now, the best I could do was keep maiming him. Solitaire would've loved that, I knew. He was about as utilitarian as a trolley, but always to serve the ends of venting out what was in his gut. Not me.

I didn't feel anything at all as I worked, save the resistance of flesh against steel.

Father had been ruined in a way Varder had not, until first seeing him, even known men could be. His body was not just damaged, or even destroyed. It was a ghost. Limbs near useless where tendons had been cut, hands mangled and sliced into jagged stumps, vitality burned away in the fires of his agony and . . . at least from what the healers had told him, manhood missing altogether. He might have taken notes at seeing so potent a message, were it not for the revulsion of knowing that it was his own father who had become it.

His own father.

The disgust Varder felt looking at him, let alone laying his hands upon the wheeled chair to push him, was almost too much to bear. He bit it back only with great effort, forcing himself steady and calm as they moved through the corridors.

"We'll make this right, Father," he whispered. "All of it. We'll make it right, and we'll make them pay."

His father didn't answer. Just a week ago, Lord Byror would have been burning like forged iron for vengeance, but now he seemed unable to even muster the will for that. He just shrank deeper into his chair. Varder kept pushing, and soon they were at their destination.

The chamber was as large as could be managed without compromising its necessary subtlety and convenience, just barely fitting the twenty-something nobles cramped within and eyeing Varder as he entered. Their expressions were a mix of many things, pity and disgust chief among them. It enraged him to see.

But Varder buried that rage. The pity was useful, and so was the disgust in its own way. He'd gathered everyone here by name, deliberately and after a careful selection. All were members of the Elswick Coalition of course, and each of them was among the ones most directly loyal to the Byrors. That was vital for what he intended to do next. What he needed to do.

"Greetings, everyone," Varder managed, leaving his father and stepping slightly to one side, and slightly more ahead of him. They needed to see him at the forefront before they heard it, needed to understand the role he would be enjoying in this meeting. They had come on his word, and it was his words they now waited to receive. "I thank you for coming. As you can all see . . . I had good cause to call you."

Eyes flickered, inevitably, to his father, and Lord Byror shrunk back from them all. It was so revoltingly uncharacteristic of him that Varder felt the sting of seeing it even more sharply than he had the sight of his father's crippling.

"I am sure you all have questions, and while I can answer them myself, I believe it will be quicker and more efficient for my father to." Varder gestured to him as he said it, and quietly stifled the sudden fear that his father would go back on their pre-agreed-upon tactic and lock up.

He had found speech so very difficult already, and this was the first group of such size he'd faced since the incident, let alone of former subordinates and friends.

Fortunately, his father was still his father. Even ruined and crippled, there was a large enough sliver of his own strength to do what needed doing. If Varder was to use this—to exploit their thin silver lining—and rise to one of the coalition's heads, he would need to speak. He spoke.

"It was the oldest brother, Shango. The one with foreign skin. He . . . I met him in an alley. He'd promised to deliver Jeshuai, but it was just us. He told me . . . told me he was tired of being in danger, that it was my fault, and then he started . . . Then he drew out his knife and started cutting."

Hearing him reach the end, let alone for a second time, was the hardest thing Varder had ever done, and he barely kept himself from placing a hand upon his father in solidarity. Such a display of weakness was unthinkable now.

Before Varder could speak again, and capitalize on his father's testimony, another voice rang out. Lord Caltan. He had been among the Byrors' closest allies, or so Varder thought, and yet now his face was colored by doubt and hesitation, his voice a blossom of skeptical contradiction.

"You say it was Shango who did this," he began, tentatively and cautiously. Like a man speaking to some wounded animal. "It's just that, well, not to doubt you, but this seems far more like the work of the Solitaire."

A spasm of worry ran through the room, and Varder allowed himself a moment of appreciation for the man's reputation, if not his nature. The stories were spreading far about that one even after only a few months of prominence, and each one seemed harder to believe than the last. A black wizard, able to eviscerate entire hordes of undead with a single great fireball. A demonic cannibal who feasted on other men's flesh to empower himself. A madman, who found impossible knowledge whispered to him among the delusions and thus knew things about people they themselves may even have gone without realizing.

If anyone were expected to have done such a thing, it was certainly the Solitaire. But Varder's father had said what he had.

"Do you call my father a liar?" Varder asked. "Or merely too broken to even recall his own attacker? It was Shango Belahont. All that Solitaire's absence proves is that any one of the Belahonts can be just as monstrous as their worst. We were right to suspect them, and now we must crush them."

It was perhaps as well as he could have played it, and might even have been enough. On another day. But luck was against him.

The door swung open with a jerky grind, old hinges and older frame protesting as Lord Viras stepped in. Varder turned to him with a barely suppressed wince and felt the hope run out of him like blood from an opened vein. He'd almost had them there. Almost.

But there was no having anything in Lord Viras' eye, unless one was Lord Viras himself. The man entered like a lizard on ice, tall and sinewy, creeping into middle age and yet potent regardless. He moved as if each step had been planned months in advance and spoke with a greater control even than that.

"A secret meeting. How quaint," he murmured, like it was all terribly amusing. As if it were some mere fancy he'd stumbled onto by accident, rather than the most hidden event Varder could manage. He didn't smile as he said it. Viras never felt the need to smile, even when he was playing gentle and charming.

Varder just bit his tongue.

"I see that Lord Byror has finished his treatments," Viras observed, barely even flicking his eyes toward Varder's father as he noted his presence. "You have my sympathies, my lord. A true tragedy, what befell you. I can only hope we find whoever was responsible and bring them to justice."

"We know who did this," Varder spit, swallowing the bait whole and feeling its not-so-hidden hook stab clean into his maw. "It was Shango Belahont, and we were just discussing how best to go about—"

"Shango Behalont?" Viras cut in, trampling Varder's voice without so much as raising his own. "That is curious, because I have it on good authority that all the brothers—Shango Belahont included—were seen at their mansion on the night of your father's . . . suffering."

Varder tried to control his temper, but something about Viras' cadence—his apparent disinterest in the entire affair—needled him like few things ever had.

"My father himself identified Shango Belahont," he managed, and felt his despair mount ever higher as Viras only shook his head pitiably.

"And I am afraid Lord Byror has been through a lot, particularly in those moments."

Varder eyed his father and found that he was remaining silent. Unwilling to contradict Viras now of all times, of course. Viras used the chance to speak more.

"Other parts of the story, I am afraid, do not line up. Your brother was not delivered to the alley, despite his meeting there. We had the Belahonts' men all followed during the night of the incident and found only the woman Elizabeth left at all. She was alone when she did."

"They could have used her as a distraction to send our spies away before Belahont exited," Varder noted, and Viras only hummed.

"And yet your brother was, in fact, returned. Do you suppose they would have missed the child if he had accompanied her? Regardless, the Belahonts are powerful now. They have numerous strong fighters, and the strongest of them—Beam Belahont—has hastened his recovery. Capturing one for interrogation was a fine idea, but there will be no chance to repeat the effort now that it has failed. It is over."

The finality was what crushed Varder most. The total, inarguable, mountainous end to the topic that Viras so effortlessly turned his response into. How did he do that? Speak as if he were explaining the world to everyone around him, stare with those empty eyes and that motionless voice while he tore apart whatever argument was hurled his way?

Apparently realizing that Varder didn't have it in him to push back any longer, Viras moved on to his conclusion. He didn't even pretend not to have planned it already.

"I would say that Lord Byror was happened upon by a group of common thugs, perhaps even some other of our enemies taking the opportunity to let the Belahonts be blamed for their own transgression. Speaking for the greater part of our coalition, now that I remain exclusive in my seniority and leadership, I shall inform you all that any who pursue the Belahonts will do so alone. And if they are, in fact, responsible for this atrocity . . . Well, I can hardly imagine them being *more* merciful than they were already."

The silence was heavier than steel.

CHAPTER NINE

Beam's POV: Day 112
Current Wealth: 733 gold, 47 silver, 16 copper

A week of healing wasn't really that much in the grand scheme of things. Even in combat sports with gloves and health-preserving rules, I'd frequently needed several times that between matches. But Corvan made it go a lot further. By the seventh day since Solitaire's return, I felt like most of my strength was back.

Of course feelings could be deceptive—if they weren't, then Solitaire's feelings would add up to a literal apocalypse every week—so I put that to the test too. Fortunately, I had as big an abundance of sparring partners as ever.

Argar's improvement had started to slow somewhat, but the big guy was still formidable. It just didn't help him much. He was slower than me obviously—he'd always been, and though he'd gotten a lot more technically sound, reading space better and telegraphing less than even a week before, there was no comparing us. None of that was a surprise. What was surprising was that I was stronger than him now. Much stronger.

His swings didn't even register to me as testing, and I smacked axes aside like they were feathers. Argar was soon panting, sweating, swearing, but I was just barely warming up when he finally called it quits. It was a good moment, satisfying after a week of infirmity.

Then Arthur kicked the crap out of me. Well, some things didn't change so easily.

Fortunately, my embarrassment didn't last for long. I'd gotten closer to Arthur's sheer physicality than I expected to, but even with that the gap between us was insurmountable. Whatever I'd done to fight the King—and I still didn't even remember that—it apparently wouldn't be done again. And my little helper had been silent about it ever since, to boot.

Well, that much was typical. I'd learned a long time ago not to rely on the voice for . . . much of anything, really. They apparently had the ability to deny me access to my powers, but they sure as shit didn't care much about speeding up their growth. In fact . . . I was beginning to wonder if they even could.

I wasn't given long to continue testing myself, of course. That would've been too pleasant. It was Solitaire who called me up, and I hurried as best as I could, finding Helena already there with him when I arrived. She was looking much better, healthier and more mobile of course, but mentally too. There had been a weight to her that wasn't there anymore, a weakness that had been displaced by something of her previous strength.

The *actual* strength I could see demonstrated by how easily she was moving around the solid tool steel spear went a long way to conveying it all, I had to admit. I almost didn't see the new faces behind her and Solitaire.

"Took you long enough," my brother grunted, gesturing to them. "Beam, these are the new recruits. New recruits, this is Beam. He's going to be teaching you how to fight alongside Helena."

Neither Helena nor I looked particularly happy about this. I reckoned my reasons were a good deal stronger than hers.

"Solitaire, a word?" I asked. He smiled.

"No. I've got to go and do something. Have fun, kids." Before I could so much as protest, he was gone. Asshole. I turned to Helena, questioningly, silently pleading for her to take the lead. Thankfully, she'd always had a knack for other people's discomfort and realized how lost I was before the recruits did.

"Line up!" she barked. All of them froze rigid and didn't so much as twitch, let alone form up. I realized about when Helena did that, evidently, she was used to training people at a different stage of the process than completely raw new joins. I spoke before anything else could wrong.

"Form ranks in a straight line, one next to the other, shoulder to shoulder and facing us."

Thankfully, that seemed to be enough clarification that they'd done as told within a few moments more. It gave me a good chance to count them too.

Fourteen men. All of them were short and wiry, as people tended to be in Redacle, and half looked like they'd been homeless the day before. As far as starts went for a new personal army . . . we'd had better.

Then again, we'd had worse too. Fourteen men was still fourteen men. Particularly when we outfitted them in the way Solitaire's laboratory made possible. Even without that, I reminded myself, this gang could've beaten me and my brothers down with ease the day we arrived. Oh how far we'd come.

"You're all lucky enough to be joining the Belahont Company," Helena said, speaking with the confidence of someone who was near certain she'd not be interrupted and the aggression of one who almost hoped she was. "Here, you will be changed from the pitiable, mewling wretches I now look over and turned into hardened killers. This will not be easy, and it will not be quick, but I will see to it personally, and anyone who drags this journey of yours down will have to *answer* to me personally."

They looked awed and terrified. More terrified than awed, it had to be said, but both could bring about obedience, and Helena was the expert. I remained silent.

"Now to start with, we're going to go over some spear fighting," she continued. "I'm a spear fighter, as you've all probably noticed, and there's no better weapon for combat in formation. In the corner, you'll find a row of practice spears with blunted heads, as well as some actual shields. All of you will take one of each, then assemble back into your ranks and await further instruction."

And so they did, and so she gave it, and so the training began. It was a dull affair, at least at first, but as it progressed, I started to appreciate the differences between training one person and training an entire class. More, I appreciated the gap between simply teaching a group to fight and teaching that group how to fight as a group. It made me realize how flimsy my own tutelage in Rinchester had been.

For a while, I just watched as they ran laps, practiced thrusts, obeyed everything Helena said as if they were sheep and her the shepherd. I actually started to wonder about what purpose I was even meant to be serving there, but that was put to an end when the first break came about. A short one, just a few minutes as men panted, cooled down, and desperately guzzled the free drinking water we'd lured them into training by providing. Helena seized the chance to take me aside and speak.

"What do you think?" she asked, throwing me for a loop.

"Your training is very impressive," I replied, flashing a smile that withered, died, and decomposed into rotten sludge with a single raised eyebrow from Helena.

"About the recruits," she clarified. "What are your thoughts?"

It was an embarrassing question to be asked, as would any other question be coming from an expert and aimed at a layman.

"I don't know." I shrugged. "I'm not a trainer. The only reason I even had a go at it in Rinchester was because—"

"You have a way of moving and watching movement," Helena cut in. "I've seen it. I don't know how you do it, but it's like watching a snake coiling, and sometimes you'll be avoiding an attack before it's even come. So don't tell me you have no insight about what you've been watching."

It was a slap to the face, but it got me thinking, at least. She had a point. I couldn't know which direction their training needed to be heading, but I could certainly identify where they were going wrong. What would I take advantage of if I were fighting them?

"That tall, thin one," I began. "He needs to try gripping his spear a hand lower down than the others. His body is weirdly shaped, and doing it the standard way is screwing up his control. The one on the far right has something off with one of his ankles that makes his footwork clumsier. Teaching him to move more from his knees and focus on faster, shorter steps will do a world of good. And—"

I continued, prattling away about every minor and major problem that came to my mind until Helena stopped me.

"Don't tell me," she cut in, sounding suddenly rather impressed. "Break's about to end. Tell them."

And so I did, learning names and faces, discussing styles, and tweaking techniques. I was surprised to receive an incredibly warm—even enthusiastic—welcome when I injected my input into things, and Helena picked up on that near instantly. Soon enough, I was more involved, repeating orders I had whispered to me from the Vit and watching as men scrambled to obey.

Half the day went by before we were finally finished with the training, and I almost felt fatigued for just having watched it. As the men began filing out, heading to their new sleeping quarters in the mansion to enjoy the luxuries of insulated shelter and actual bedding, my new instruction partner turned to me. She looked pleased.

"You did well."

I wasn't sure how to reply, so just shrugged. Helena grinned.

"God, you really are different from your brothers. Shango and Solitaire eat up compliments like they're starving for them." I cracked a smile at that.

"They're not as different from each other as either of them thinks."

She looked thoughtful at that, and it made room for a question of my own.

"Why me?" I asked. Helena caught my meaning fast. She seemed surprised to even be asked.

"Isn't it obvious? "

I looked at her in a way I hoped conveyed that it was, in fact, not obvious, and Helena continued.

"Beam, you fought the King of Blades and wounded him. You've killed enemies by the dozen within individual fights. The whole world watched you go from near the middle to second in the entire tourney over a few weeks. You're famous. Why wouldn't they be thrilled to learn fighting from the city's best fighter?"

I felt like I'd just been gutted.

CHAPTER TEN

Shango's POV: Day 112
Current Wealth: 733 gold, 47 silver, 16 copper

I'd needed the week off since finalizing my plan to take care of Byror, and I'd spent it all well. As far as rest and relaxation went, it was certainly a lot easier to make progress when one lived in an increasingly well-heated mansion than when one was sleeping in the streets, drinking from puddles, and periodically waking up to avoid police officers. The company of one of the most attractive women I'd ever seen was, likewise, a fairly big upgrade over my brothers'. It's not that I didn't love Beam and Solitaire, of course. It's just that a man who pathologically trains himself in martial arts and a violently deranged drug fiend are about the least relaxing company one can keep in *any* circumstances.

Getting married in my early twenties had never really been the plan, but then neither had getting forcibly inserted into the edgiest dark-fantasy world I knew. Somehow, I was coming to like the former.

Phelia was brilliant, and now that things had calmed down, and she'd been brought back, I'd started spending even more time with her. Just talking for the most part, because there was a damned lot to talk about. Politics, mathematics, history. As far as sheer knowledge went, there were a few areas she lacked in, as someone from a world centuries less advanced than mine, but her raw intellect and wit made the discussions fascinating anyway.

That she had sex with me pretty much daily was, I assure you, entirely unrelated to our growing fondness. I'm a perfectly classy guy you know, more interested in brains than what's below the neck. Honest.

Well, that morning we were in bed together and in one of those moods where getting out to face the cold air seemed nightmarishly difficult.

Something tickled my nose, and I grunted, turning to see Phelia's hair had somehow billowed out to splay itself up over my neck, jaw, and face. It did that a lot,

I'd learned. Seeming animated by some external force to end up in all the places most irritating to me whenever we shared a bed. The one time I'd complained, of course, she'd gotten pissy, but even disregarding that, I didn't feel like complaining now.

"You're awake," she noted, turning to look up at me. Must have heard my breathing change. Clever as ever.

"So are you," I observed. "Ugh, mind lying in for a bit?"

"It's cold," Phelia replied by way of agreement.

"Always cold here," I grumbled. I'd grown up in Nigeria and the warmer parts of the US, which meant weather that was a great deal warmer than the vaguely European climate we'd based Redacle on.

"I don't know why your family lived here for so long." I sighed. "You've told me about the heights of your glory days. I'd have used that fortune to move somewhere sunnier."

"Would you now." Phelia hummed. "Well, you're free to move out of my giant mansion whenever you want, dear."

I smiled.

"Perish the thought," I replied with false severity. "The lord of a household can't leave it unmanned now, can he?"

Phelia snorted.

"The lord of the household?"

"Yes." I nodded with a feigned fervor. Then added, a shade more warmly, "Forever."

She leaned in, lips inches from mine, when the door soared open as if someone had kicked it.

In fact, someone had. A tall, wiry someone with eyes that bulged to an almost insectoid size and hands fidgeting with all the nervous energy of a crackhead three days into confinement. I shot up, and Phelia screamed as the figure grinned.

"Relax!" He laughed, face splitting to show large, pointed teeth. "It's me! Solitaire!"

I did relax, slightly. Phelia screamed even louder upon hearing him identified and didn't stop for a good few more seconds.

"What do you want?!" I snapped, finding my head suddenly throbbing and relaxation suddenly dissolved at the intrusion.

"We have a visitor." He grinned, sweeping his eyes across the room and, to my genuine surprise, not ogling Phelia's half-covered body like a slab of meat. "Thought you'd want to see them personally, but if you're busy then it's no problem. I can handle it on my own."

Solitaire had once lit someone's hemline on fire for calling him a Liberal, so I actually didn't think he *could* handle a social situation on his own. Not unless it devolved into a conveniently violent ambush, at least.

"I'll come." I sighed, climbing out of bed and wincing at the frosty greeting of morning air. "Go on ahead of me but wait a minute or two. I'll be there."

Solitaire nodded and was gone with his usual spasmodic hurry. Phelia exhaled as he left.

"He saved me you know," she whispered, staring at the door where my brother—for everything that entailed—had just been standing. I froze and waited, knowing she'd be going somewhere important with the thought.

"He did." I nodded, having figured out on my own what he'd done on the day of the capture. "How . . . do you feel about that?"

Phelia swallowed.

"I don't know," she admitted. "But . . . there's more to him than I thought."

That, I knew, I could agree with.

"There is." I nodded, back to dressing myself now. "There always has been. Beneath it all, there's more than just cleverness, even more than just that sense for other people he always has. There's decency. Goodness, even. Kindness."

It was just a shame he insisted on keeping it hidden away, where it was at no risk of stopping him from hurting people. I finished pulling my pants on and straightened up, planting a kiss on Phelia's cheek and realizing how reflexive the motion had been only when it was completed.

I was out into the hall moments later, and true to my word no more than a minute or two behind Solitaire. Even so, the conversation was already ongoing when I came out into the gardens of our mansion to find both my brothers facing off with a newcomer.

The man was tall for Redacle, though by the expensive make of his clothes, I guessed he was probably just an average-height noble. He was definitely not young, black haired and with a horse-ish, lined face that was rather too long and too thin. His whole body was thin, actually, in the same way Solitaire's was before Beam's training regime, though something told me he didn't share the Scouser's freakish hidden strength. When he spoke, his voice was more or less the exact sort I'd have expected from him, almost uncannily appropriate.

"Finally." He exhaled, apparently relieved. "Lord Shango Belahont, I presume?"

He had the good manners to feign uncertainty as to whether there was some *other* tall black man wandering around the otherwise homogeneously white region, and so I had the good manners to just reply as normally.

"I am." I nodded. "And you are?"

"Lord Appleberry," he replied, missing Solitaire's not-so-subtle dry heaving at the ridiculous posh Britishness of his name. "And I come to you on behalf of Swanhen."

I sifted through my memory quickly at the mention and found it bearing fruit with satisfying speed. Swanhen was a local settlement maybe twenty miles east, just important enough to have been among the notable names I recalled, just unimportant enough to take me a hot minute to recall it.

"What about it?" Beam prompted.

Appleberry swallowed before he continued.

"My town has been assailed by orcs, foul gray-skinned savages from the north. They are near uncountable and attacking with insane vigor. I have come to you because I heard tell of your exploits in saving the town of Rinchester from undead and hoped your righteousness would send you to our aid as well."

"Bullshit," Solitaire cut in, stifling a yawn. Appleberry stared at him, but I started at Appleberry.

"Excuse me?!" the man gasped, suddenly flustered. That was what settled it for me.

"He's saying you're lying or leaving something unsaid," I explained. "Which is it?"

For one moment, he was defiant. Then it all melted out of him, and he deflated into truth.

"I've spoken to every noble I could reach in this entire city, and yours is the last family on that list. I'm desperate and without hope. If you turn me down, then I don't know whom I can turn to who might still be able to save Swanhen." His voice was wavering like a hypothermic man's by the time the speech ended, and I was actually convinced he was telling the truth. Amazingly, so was Solitaire.

"Proceed." He shrugged as I looked at him. "I don't have any contributions to make when they're not lying or planning to kill us."

Appleberry did not look particularly pleased, but at the very least, the conversation was moving again.

I gave the idea some thought.

"You're asking us to take a big risk," I noted. "But . . ." Swanhen was a mining town, and a fairly big one population wise, at least. If we gained control . . . "Provided you promise us ownership over half of the town's mines, and first rights to all their product, we'll agree to help."

Appleberry looked aghast.

"I will do no such thing. My family's birthright is not on offer! I will not sell my legacy!"

"Even if it could save lives?" Solitaire asked. Appleberry's eyes hardened.

"Honor is worth more than life."

Beam actually had to stop Solitaire from pouncing on him like Gollum, and I hurried to bring an end to the conversation.

"We'll think about it," I promised.

It was the most unpromising promise I could have made, and not by accident.

CHAPTER ELEVEN

Solitaire's POV: Day 112
Current Wealth: 733 gold, 47 silver, 16 copper

S hango had hurried us all away for a group discussion in private. As I might have expected, he was actually considering *helping* the fucking moron. As you are probably expecting, I was opposed.

His argument was the precise one I would have made, one wearing the disguise of pragmatism.

"Swanhen was a big deal once. Okay, not compared to cities, but as far as towns go? It was profitable as hell, and if we come out of this with pull there, then that'll make *us* profitable too."

I bit back my annoyance.

"Except we won't, will we?" I asked. "Because Lord Fuckwad has promised not to give us anything for our trouble and apparently doesn't much see the value of human life."

I saw Shango consider pointing out how little I valued it too, but he decided not to as he replied.

"You know that isn't right. Showing up as the big damn heroes will win us popularity. It *might* get us more recruits, it *will* get us more noble support, and the more our reputation spreads, the more unpopular anyone who plans on attacking us will become. We're not strong enough yet that we can afford to ignore a set of armor like that."

Well, that was Shango for you. He knew me well enough to guess which points I'd find heaviest, and he had the brains to hit every single one with a single verbal barrage. Still, Mama Solitaire didn't raise her no quitter. I'd started this argument, and if I had to keep shitting myself until I won it, then so be it.

I'll spare you the slow, painful crawl toward the inevitable. I did not win. Shango did his best not to look too smug after I finally conceded—as if I couldn't *smell* it on him anyway—and Beam looked rather relieved. He always gave away his standing on a topic by the reaction he had at its end.

Still, our concurrence here just meant we were ready for another topic. The more important one too, I would say.

"And how sure are we that Appleberry will become our bezzie mate after this?" I challenged.

That had Shango pausing.

"I don't know," he said at last. "But if nothing else, there's a lot more to gain than just that."

"And we can trust him," Beam cut in, sounding uncharacteristically certain. "I'm used to his type. We can rely on him to respond in kind if we help him out."

"Right," I grunted. "I forgot, that's what the upper class is famous for. Rewarding people fairly for their labor."

Beam smiled, but he remained intense.

"Trust me," he answered. It took all my concentration not to spit at the very concept, but I considered things and realized that we already looked to be doing this anyway.

"I trust you," I lied and felt a stab of guilt at how Beam's face lit up. Well, what are friends for if not comforting one another with happy untruths and kind deceptions?

"The land is in a pretty good position too," Shango added. "A fair distance from Elswick, but close enough to reach easily. It can make a decent retreat for us if we need it to."

"You've convinced me already," I grunted and felt another spasm of irritation. I'd be saving lives, okay, sure. But did Appleberry's really need to be among them? Putting aside the fact that he cared about feeling cool more than saving people, his name was fucking *Apple berry*. And he ruled *Swan hen*. Ugh. Looked like Redacle's habit of filling in the gaps with our world-building was making no distinction between naming schemes we used as teenagers and ones we used now. I was almost embarrassed.

"It's a big town," I noted at last. "Good few thousand people live there. If the orcs are threatening it in spite of that, we're gonna need a lot more than just us."

Both of them looked soured at that, but the truth tended to have such effects.

"We have fourteen new recruits," Shango reminded me, turning to Beam. "How are they going?"

He thought for a moment.

"Helena is a good teacher, and they seem to be . . . inspired to move along quicker . . ."

That'd be my idea to have him present and helping. I'd hoped that his reputation would add a certain weight to their training, and apparently I'd turned out to be right.

"But it'll take a while before they're proper fighters even with that."

"How long is a while?" Shango pressed.

". . . Weeks, at least." Beam sighed. "It takes time to teach people how to fight."

"Especially real fights," I added. "Most people just freak out and either get in the way of those or contribute nothing."

Shango didn't look happy, but he took it all in quickly enough. He'd always been good at accepting inconvenient truths.

"What do we do then?" He frowned.

"Well, obviously we need to take the time to actually finish up our miniature army," I noted. "And while we do that, I'll see what other weapons I can prepare. If we give it about six weeks, then that should be a half-decent job, right?" My question was addressed to Beam, who gave it a fair amount of thought.

"With a lot of training every day, yes. At least they'll be good enough to meaningfully help on a consistent basis."

"Then that just leaves us to outfit them. We've started that already, so it shouldn't take much longer."

"What are you giving them?" Shango asked. "Plate armor?"

"Fuck no," Beam and I said at once. I let him explain.

"Remember how long we took to move in that? We had superhuman strength that made it feel almost weightless, and even now, weeks later, we still get caught on doorframes and shit. No, that's a nonstarter. Especially with how long Ardin takes to make it."

Shango was looking half annoyed and half thoughtful, like he always did in those rare conversations that happened past his expertise.

"Then what will we give them?"

"Brigandines," I explained. He eyed me blankly, so I elaborated. "Basically secondhand steel plates bolted together and pinched between layers of leather. Think Sean Bean in *Game of Thrones*. Not as good as plate, not as consistent, but a lot quicker and easier, lighter, and, fortunately for us, something we already have a head start on from all the damage and replacements our full plate armor took during the tourney."

Hearing that they would, in fact, be wearing a *kind* of plate armor seemed to do wonders for Shango's optimism at least, and he relaxed.

"Alright then. So we'll prepare in . . . the ways we have been, I guess. I'll see about balancing the funds while we pay for our new recruits, perhaps getting more before we arrive. You two just keep doing what you've been doing."

I resisted the urge to giggle at that, having gotten over the annoying part of my new project and graduated to putting on its finishing touches. It was nice and *mobile* too. A horrible little surprise for whatever was waiting for us at Swanhen. Shango and Beam seemed to notice my enthusiasm, taking short steps away from me as it became more evident.

Honestly, some people were so puritanical.

CHAPTER TWELVE

Solitaire's POV: Day 112
Current Wealth: 733 gold, 47 silver, 16 copper

Ever since the invention of the gun, the technology has been plagued by a single crippling flaw. No, it's not the noise. It's not the recoil, or anything lame like the inherent nature of potent violence to inspire the worst in men and drive us into an ever deeper downward spiral of barbarity, othering, and hatred. It's the rate of fire. The fact that there's such ludicrously long pauses between each shot is a vital factor holding us back from meeting our full killing potential. I'd not managed to fix this, but for my part, I like to think I made steps in reducing it somewhat.

The Gatling gun was a very significant leap forward, historically, in the delicate art of killing people very quickly. I'd replicated it. It had been *hard*, mind. Fucking infuriating, in fact. But I'd done it. The trick had been a new kind of explosive, mercury fulminate. Shock activated and powerful enough to ignite black powder in even tiny amounts while not going off if you looked at it too angrily like a certain explosive liquid I could name. Pack a bit at the back of a cartridge, which we were making out of linen, then a single oscillating hammer mechanism could strike it, detonate it, and trigger a proper firing. Slot this into a rotating barrel mechanism, figure out a way for new cartridges to be rotated in and empty ones out, and soon enough you have a gun capable of firing . . . fucking, I don't know, like, ten shots a second or something. Pretty fast anyway.

Of course there were drawbacks. There always are.

Mercury was fairly expensive, even for "alchemical materials," which meant that creating literal tons of ammunition had been out of the question. One-quarter of a ton, more or less, was the best I could manage within a few weeks. Fortunately, I didn't need as much mercury fulminate as I did black powder—finding that about a four-to-one ratio of them was enough for the cartridges to fire. The hard part came with actually assembling the cartridges themselves. I found out the hard way how slow a process that would be after two hours netted me about forty rounds. Enough for eight seconds of shooting.

Yeah, fuck that.

I brought in Elizabeth, since she wasn't doing anything, and Alora too. Then upon being accused of asking specifically the women to do handicrafts, I realized that they actually had a point and called Magnus on board so they could all suffer more egalitarianly.

We got to work, and within a few more hours, we'd made around three hundred more. Enough for *seventy* seconds of shooting, including the forty I'd made alone.

God, this was going to be so annoying.

Soon enough, the limiting factor became raw materials again, so much of my time was spent on whipping up new batches. We wasted some in making the rounds of course, and we really did need quite a lot, but with all of us doing our parts, we started making steady progress toward a useful pile of munitions. As a British man, I have a great deal of knowledge as to just how effective musket balls are against technologically preindustrial natives. In fact, you might even say it's genetic memory. We could devastate infantry formations with just a few seconds using this weapon.

But that didn't mean we could *win* by firing it that long. I wanted minutes of shots, not moments, so we all continued our work. Those fleeting moments between, I spent on other projects.

What? I hear you think. *Other projects? Why, Solitaire, does your unbelievable handsomeness and genius know no bounds?* It's funny you should ask that, because no it doesn't!

A big problem we'd been having in all our fights was that, after we'd finished erasing the hordes of weaker enemies, something stronger and faster would show up to beat us all up. Now Beam had gotten nice and powerful. In fact, I was certain now he was in the top ten thousand deadliest people on the entire planet and throwing him out like a Pokemon had been working decently . . . *so far*. The problem was, there were still ten thousand on his level. Or, failing their appearances, numerous magical creatures which were simply *far more powerful* than humans by nature. That vampire we'd fought had been a small fry, almost a fledgling, and vampires weren't the deadliest undead out there either. If something like a demon made an appearance . . .

Well, if a demon showed up, I was fairly sure we were fucked even if I spent the next few weeks making a howitzer and it was polite enough to stand still while I fired it. So best to focus on the things we could account for.

Something big and powerful, more so than Shango's gun. But also small enough to be aimed at an individual target. For that matter, we could use more guns too. That was more Ardin's area though unless the design changed. And I was getting off topic.

Something man portable and easy to aim that could take down big, tough enemies immune to gunfire. It didn't take me long to land on the obvious solution, and so I started working on my rocket launcher.

Now, the history of rockets in warfare is actually a great deal longer than most people know. Even in Europe. They were used to some extent during the Napoleonic Wars and beyond, though never very accurately. I'd never looked into the precise designs of those primitive ones, but I did know that projectiles prone to doing somersaults were not what I was looking for.

So I got to thinking. It's amazing how much you can figure out just with a bit of abstract consideration, especially when you're me. I figured I'd need some way of keeping the rocket on target and that its long shape and low mass, compared to a cannon ball at least, would combine with its inevitably lower velocity to make drag force and sidelong wind pressures a huge problem.

Spin it then. That was the universal fix for stabilizing things over distance. The only issue was how to go about it. I called on Beam, during his downtime between training sessions, and we got to work.

The first obstacle was finding somewhere to actually test them. Phelia refused to let us do so inside, for some reason, and Shango backed her fully, which ended up forcing us out into the gardens. The second obstacle was that it turns out rocket science is actually really hard. Who knew?

Rifling the barrels turned out to not work so well, and half our early days were spent just figuring out the best way to maximize velocity. Eventually we managed to get them moving at, what I estimated, was about two hundred miles per hour. Not bad, but still incredibly inaccurate. At fifty paces, we'd be lucky to hit within five meters of our target. Not ideal for what was meant to be an anti-individual weapon.

It took me an embarrassing amount of time to stumble onto the obvious, and when I did, Beam wasn't able to make it for me. Gun barrels were one thing, but tightly measured holes at sharply cut angles were something that demanded Ardin's touch. He wasn't too happy to be given the job, but he got to it.

The next day, we were able to try his work out. It failed. We tried again the next, and again. Studying the effects of each minor change, predicting which others might follow, seeing what happened instead. On the second day, we'd finally managed to perfect the design, but it wasn't until the fourth that we showed it to Shango.

He wasn't exactly in a good mood when we did, despite being assured that I'd made something really, *really* cool. In fact, if anything, being told just how cool it was seemed to make him less happy, and more nervous and worried. Well, he'd always been a strange one. I suppose some people just need a visual demonstration to grasp things.

"That," I told him, gesturing across the field as he stood beside me, "is our target, scientifically chosen for the purposes of this test."

The scientific process in question, of course, had been finding the heaviest boulder Beam and I could carry together. It weighed a ton. Or, to be more precise, it weighed 1.4 tons. A roughly hemispherical block of granite measuring four feet at the base, a nice stand-in for about the toughest castle walls we'd be likely to run into for a while.

"Big target," Shango noted.

"*Tough* target," I replied. "And I'll aim for the center. If it hits more than half a foot from the median line, then we'll consider it a miss." Anticipating his complaint, I'd illustrated just that line from top to bottom with a nice length of pasted-on mud. "Ready?"

"Fire away," Shango invited, now seeming rather more . . . excited.

I fired.

One of the first things we'd done, in the early fixes, was make the muzzle velocity lower. This is because a six-pound projectile hitting three hundred miles per hour really *isn't* producing the kinds of momentum we're designed to handle. My super-human physical prowess seemed to give me some innate ability to resist being moved, but there was a limit to even that. So when the rocket exited its barrel, I was treated to a good few moments of it accelerating as it tore away.

Barely half a second later, impact followed.

The boulder seemed to shudder and might even have been budged slightly. Chips of stone flew outward in all directions as the rocket bounced off, then shot spinning and spitting for a good few hundred more paces before smashing down into the dirt just shy of the railing. Lucky that, it'd almost hit one of the—

"Holy shit!" Shango gasped, and I saw he was gawping at the point of impact.

Well, I couldn't blame him there. Where the rocket had hit, a chunk of stone about as big as André the Giant's fist was now missing. The spot still smoldered, jagged and rough. But it was a good foot off target.

"Give me five more shots," I told Shango, and he agreed. These ones were far better aimed.

In the end, the solution I'd coined for the drag problem had been little angled vents on the outsides of the rockets. Black powder was carefully packed to burn slowly and imperfectly, providing a constant thrust alongside the main charge at the back. So each one spun, and screamed, and whirled like a firework before impact. The first hit, burying itself a good five inches in the stone. The second hit outside the median line; the next one hit slightly worse than the first.

Then the fourth came and buried itself a good seven inches, thanks to the tool steel point we'd had put on as an experiment. Shango was very impressed with that right up until the final rocket hit dead center and split the entire boulder in half with a sound so loud it was as if God himself were drunkenly back-handing it.

When the debris finally cleared, we had a lot to talk about.

"Mercury fulminate filling," I told him. "About a kilogram of the stuff, not as powerful as TNT but . . . well, not that far either as you saw."

"How fast can you make it?" he asked.

"Not fast enough that these aren't more difficult to produce than the other rock-ets, but they'd serve as good frag rounds too. We made the metal casing out of cast iron. Hard, brittle. It shatters under the explosion. You didn't see it here with all the flying rock, but anyone within single-digit meters of that blast would get shredded by shrapnel."

Shango gave me one of those "my best friend is a psycho" looks that I know and love, then licked his lips.

"Make it fifty-fifty then," he said at last, frowning. "Fuck, Solitaire, you've leveled up."

CHAPTER THIRTEEN

Shango's POV: Day 117
Current Wealth: 742 gold, 16 silver, 21 copper

[Appraisal]
Class: Revolutionary
Level: 19
Condition: Fine
Modifiers: +5 Speed, +7 Toughness, +4 Alertness, +6 Strength
Statistics: Strength 13, Speed 12, Dexterity 8, Stamina 6, Toughness 12, Alertness 12, Charisma 3, Intelligence 10
Inventory: Local wear, shortsword, knives (x3), plate armor, shortspear
Class Abilities: Detect Element II
Current Experience Points: 118/580
Unspent Skillpoints: 6

"Oh, fuck, I have," Solitaire gasped, eyes bulging even wider than usual and threatening to consume the rest of his face in the process. I was almost too distracted to ask my next question, but I did.

"How did you not notice?"

This must have come from the Gatling gun and rockets. It was stupid enough of me not to check, but Solitaire should have felt *something* change. He'd leveled enough times by now for that.

"Looks like inventing new things earns you XP," I observed as Solitaire spent it. "But only when you don't know how to make it already. You did need to essentially come up with the designs for the Gatling gun and rocket launcher yourself, right?"

"Right," he replied, sounding rather sour over the fact. I supposed Solitaire had never liked struggling with things. He'd always somehow seen the right answer as his due. The idea that he'd be forced to keep doing this as a means of progression was . . .

Kind of funny actually.

[Appraisal]
Class: Revolutionary
Level: 19
Condition: Fine
Modifiers: +7 Speed, +8 Toughness, +6 Alertness, +7 Strength
Statistics: Strength 14, Speed 14, Dexterity 8, Stamina 6, Toughness 13, Alertness 14, Charisma 3, Intelligence 10
Inventory: Local wear, shortsword, knives (x3), plate armor, shortspear
Class Abilities: Detect Element II
Current Experience Points: 118/580
Unspent Skillpoints: 0

Well, Solitaire hadn't wasted time spending his points. And he'd done it the way we were all learning was the best way—a roughly even spread to ensure our super-humanity grew into that of jacks-of-all-trades.

"How much can you bench?" I asked, entirely jokingly. Solitaire either missed the humor or decided *not* to miss his chance to show off.

"Six hundred kilos, thereabouts." His nose wrinkled. "Still only half as strong as Beam."

It was a very Solitaire response to improving one's superpowers so much within the span of a mere few seconds, but I could see that his mood had lifted. Somewhat, at least.

"Well fortunately, we don't need to rely on it. If you can keep us stocked with rockets and ammo, we may not even need to swing a single sword."

Somehow, I doubted things would be that easy. Even if I hadn't, convincing Solitaire would be hard. So I saved my energy and headed off.

Of course he wasn't the only one who'd been powering up over the last few days. It was actually that that made me feel so . . . *embarrassed*. Not even checking his stats had been a ridiculous oversight on my part. I'd pulled them up now, not as much because I expected a change as because the change I had seen was still new enough that I was continuing to draw no small sliver of satisfaction from it. Reassurance, it was. A reminder that despite everything, we were growing stronger. Frighteningly so, almost. Two months ago, Beam had been lifting grown men like they were children and punching hard enough to require he hold back or risk killing everyone he fought. Now he was hauling boulders mostly by himself, and the other day I'd seen him actually send Argar a meter back and a good few centimeters off the ground with an uppercut.

I wondered when I'd be able to do that.

[Appraisal]
Class: Emperor
Level: 19
Condition: Fine
Modifiers: +8 Toughness, +6 Strength, +6 Speed, +4 Alertness
Statistics: Strength 13, Speed 12, Dexterity 6, Stamina 5, Toughness 13, Alertness 12, Charisma 9, Intelligence 8
Inventory: Local wear, plate armor, repeater, shortspear
Class Abilities: Appraisal II
Current Experience Points: 143/580
Unspent Skillpoints: 0

Even with Solitaire's new leap in power, I actually wasn't that far behind him anymore. Maybe less than our builds would've indicated. If his estimates were right, and they usually were, twelve strength would make me somewhere around half a dozen times the strength of an average man. That was a lot less than I'd have *preferred* of course, but ideally I wouldn't be fighting up close anyway. God had made me for many things, but being a front liner was certainly not one of them. That's why the world had its Solitaires and Beams.

I made my way through the mansion, quickly reaching my office and taking a seat inside. It had, technically, been a storeroom, but at Solitaire's not-so-unreasonable insistence of solidarity, we'd had it emptied out and furnished with all the necessities of a workspace. A desk sat in it, and upon that desk was a carpet of papers each holding the word of one noble or another. I took my seat and got to looking through them.

Honestly? It wasn't that bad. Say one thing for human society since the medieval era—and you really can say more than one thing—but it's gotten more *complex*. Compared to the infinite dynamism of a billion-dollar corporation, a single family's affairs, limited as our holdings and funds were, were pretty trivial.

It helped of course that I was, for once, taking over from a competent person. My father was many things, you see. Stupid? Yes. Arrogant? Also yes. Evil? Of course. Impulsive? Yup. Moronic, delusional, idiotic, prone to inspiring repeated synonyms of "unintelligent" when described? Yes to all the above. Phelia was his exact opposite.

Well, okay, I was being unfair to the old man. He was smart. For a normal person. Certainly smarter than most of our economic peers. It wasn't that Solitaire was *right*, it was that he had a point. Sometimes I felt the gorilla comparisons when speaking to most of my species too, and that was never so strongly as when I saw them trying to manage their own success.

Because it really isn't hard to keep track of your funds and deals. You just need to look at all the angles.

The best thing about the Velaharo family, easily, is the combination of their age and their history of actually not-shit rulers. The result of this has been an extraordinarily large library that, up until just a few years ago, was decently well maintained, and to this day still includes records on . . . well, everything really. People, of the past of course. Families. Lands and areas, buildings, resources. The filing system was a bit archaic. Sorting everything by matter of relevance rather than alphabetic or chronological order—separating stories about Sir Etron the Savior from historic tax returns took some doing—but I'd always had a knack for blood-hounding my way through filing systems, and within a few days, I'd mastered the art of digging up whatever info I needed.

Which meant I could look at all the offers around me with a very informed eye. Intelligence is good, of course. But never, ever underestimate knowledge. You are what you know, and I knew something about everything.

I couldn't have done half as well without Phelia, who'd not only memorized a scary fraction of the information in question—and thus saved me precious search-ing time very regularly—but had been sure to gather what knowledge she could on more modern sources too. Even if she hadn't the time or funds to put it all down on paper.

Together, we assessed our options.

Offer for land in Belvort, a village just ten miles off. No, unthinkable because Belvort's current governor had been recorded three times bucking under other nobles' leadership, had ties to Lord Byror, and, most crucially, was stupid enough to do something he shouldn't.

Offer for more iron, more cheaply than Wilskasai was offering and in impossibly great volumes. Nope. Actually worse than unthinkable because the iron in question was famously of shit quality . . . one hundred years ago. It'd faded into obscurity since the little fiasco of its current owners' ancestor trying to do just this and finding his reputation badly damaged only after some poor sod had forked over a great sum on dog-shit ore.

No offer, and yet an opportunity, where the village of Ghortan was sending people out in search of work after their lord's efforts to have its too-large popu-lace strategically die in the winter fell through. That interested us, and with just a few strokes of my quill, we had eight more recruits, bringing our total up to twenty-two.

And so it went.

Each day there was some small advantage to find, or some disaster to avert, and as the weeks passed on, I found our resources growing rather than shrinking. There wasn't much to it, just cutting costs and growing profits. I got us potassium nitrate for cheaper by cutting a deal with some local alchemists, which let Solitaire make as much black powder for less. I was brought the prospect of outfitting our higher-ranked recruits—Alora, Magnus, and such—with firearms like mine and figured out a work rate that would leave Ardin room to do that by dripping some of his labor off to assistants.

As time passed, business started to boom. It wasn't hard to see why. The coalition had left us completely unmolested since Byror's crippling, which meant that, bit by bit, the braver families of Elswick were starting to come out of the woodwork to try their luck working with us. Not all had good deals, mind, and most had agendas, but that just meant more time to spend sifting the good from the bad. There wasn't a lot that couldn't be managed if you were willing to take your time and do it right, from top to bottom. I could've managed alone, and so could Phelia. With both of us combining our skills, we practically sprinted by the offers. By the standards of painstakingly diligent proofreads at least.

Which was, itself, a sign of something off. We should've been getting a lot more with the looming threat of Byror and pals fading. I took the question to Phelia one day, who, completely unsurprisingly, gave me an answer.

"It's because of your strange standing." She shrugged. "You're nobility in legal terms, that much was seen to by our marriage. As the last Velaharo head, my name is preserved and passed on to my husband. But that doesn't mean you're seen as Velaharo, or nobility. There's a culture there, a history, that you have so far simply refused to engage with. You're still leaving yourself an outsider."

I chewed on that and didn't take long to realize she was right. Looking at it from the nobility's perspective, we were a new, growing power of unknown motive, intents, and nature who barely saw fit to interact with them. Of course they were suspicious of us and, more to the point, suspicious of people who'd try to partner with us in spite of that. We were probably getting so many shit deals because of a selection bias to only receive deals from either desperate people or idiots.

So I decided to change things. We were in a good spot now, and I'd come to trust Phelia enough that I didn't mind leaving her in charge of the mansion while I looked into more social affairs. Even if we both went, there was enough stability in our position to leave things for a day.

I began looking into social gatherings among the nobility.

CHAPTER FOURTEEN

Beam's POV: Day 123
Current Wealth: 755 gold, 42 silver, 33 copper

I'd seen a lot since coming to Redacle. The inside of a bear's throat, from several feet away. Zombies. A vampire who could turn your own fears against you, a man strong enough to launch people in plate armor ten meters back per swing. And methods of death so revoltingly excessive that their victims couldn't even be identified with dental records back on Earth. Terrible things, scarring things. Things that, even if I made it home the next day, would stick with me for the rest of my life, right up until the moment my heart stopped. Out of them all though.

Shango and Phelia's flirting took the cake.

We were all crammed into a carriage, some old heirloom of the Velaharo that Shango had paid to have repaired purely to make an entrance, despite Solitaire threatening to go into convulsions at the idea. They were seated opposite me, touching and hugging, caressing and kissing. I was doing my best not to projectile vomit over them both.

Look, I can understand the appeal of women. I've spent my share of time enjoying them, after all. But at a certain point, a person just needs some sense of dignity. Is there anything in the world as revolting as a man in love? I was thinking no.

"You didn't need to come," Shango growled, clearly picking up on my discomfort and looking somehow affronted at it. I rolled my eyes.

"I'm not leaving you both alone. If someone tries to kill you, then I want to be there to stop it."

The only one better in a fight than me was Arthur, and at a social gathering where things like full plate armor were considered improper attire, my ability to conjure my own equipment on the fly might have actually given me the advantage over him. Shango clearly understood as much too, but he didn't look any happier than I was. Good. Misery loves company.

Besides, this was a closed affair. Family of nobles only. The only alternative was Solitaire, which . . . No.

We arrived after a tediously long ride, the carriage having been built for luxury and showing off rather than speed, but the journey was soon forgotten as I laid eyes upon our destination. It was a mansion almost the equal of Phelia's, in size. But its decoration—its staff—were a different thing altogether. Filling out the grounds in a way that felt somehow surreal. I'd gotten used to big things with little human habitation in them. This was something else. And we were heading right for its maw.

"Relax," I heard someone say, turning and finding myself surprised to see Phelia addressing me. "This isn't a fight, and while there will be rivals there . . . they should be fearful of us. We gave no warning about our coming beside the barest polite word ahead. And we're an unknown factor. The advantages are ours."

Right. They didn't know what we could do, how we'd move, where our skills lay. Thinking about it like some match let me frame it in terms that made sense of that and made our situation seem that much less precarious. I frowned, looking back to Phelia and seeing a knowing smile on her face. She'd done that on purpose?

She really was a good fit for Shango.

Our carriage parked as close as it could, but the sheer size of the place meant we were soon foot slogging our way into the building. I took point of course, doing my best to compensate for the lack of Solitaire's natural insanity by keeping an eye out for anything that looked potentially trap shaped. Soon enough, even that instinct faded as we entered the building proper, and then, after another minute or two of strolling through elongated halls displaying various trophies and artworks, the three of us came to a sprawling epicenter.

The hall was at most half full, but there had to be well over a hundred people there. It was only one-third the volume of its equivalent in Velaharo Manor, but that was no small thing.

Everyone present was wrapped in so much finery I half expected them to topple under its weight, and a lot glanced toward us as we stepped in. I felt nothing. A lifetime before crowds had prepared me for such attentions, and by the looks of things, Phelia and Shango were similarly inured. Still, I did get an awful sense for how screwed we *would* be if this was a trap.

Ugh, I was starting to actually think like Solitaire. If talking to yourself was the first sign of insanity, that would probably be the six hundredth.

"I say we split up and mingle," Shango suggested. "Let them see us as individually social. Not to mention the places a woman can go that a man can't, and vice versa."

"Agreed." Phelia nodded, watching as he peeled off from us and disappeared into the social canopy of the hall. Phelia on her part headed the other way, and I waited a few moments to tail her. If push came to shove, she was a lot less capable of defending herself for those initial precious moments of combat than Shango.

She headed on, slipping through groups of chatting nobles, and I clumsily waddled after her. Within about thirty seconds, I almost bumped into someone. Freezing instantly and apologizing quickly, I was surprised to find it was a woman, staring up at me with a smile on her face.

"Beam Belahont?" she asked, with the tone of a woman who already knew. "My, you really are tall. I've heard about you, you know. Is it true you single-handedly bested a vampire at Rinchester?"

"Uh, not really." I replied, trying to peer ahead to catch sight of Phelia again. "Excuse me—"

I tried to step past her, but somehow she moved, just an inch, and I was right in front of her again.

"You know, I've been fascinated by some of the stories about you. What would you say to *accompanying* me to my manor and regaling me about the details? I'd love to hear it all straight from the source."

I had no idea why she'd stressed the word accompanying, and I was too distracted to care. I sidestepped again, using the full length of my stride this time to plant myself firmly from her path as I hurried off.

"That sounds lovely, but I'm afraid I'm only here as a bodyguard, not to socialize. Sorry." She was left frowning in my wake, and I made it no more than another ten paces before some other woman ambushed me with a conversation, this time leaning in much closer. Close enough that I could actually feel her breath on my face as she spoke.

"Hello there," she breathed. "I don't think I've seen you before. What would your name be again?" It took even longer to disentangle myself from this one, and by the time I did, more seemed to be slowly closing in, waiting for their chance to approach. I reached Phelia only after wading my way through a solid dozen other women, each one more uncomfortably forward and presumptuous than the last. It was a relief to finally be in the company of my sister-in-law.

So much of a relief, in fact, that I momentarily forgot I was meant to shadow her in the relative luxury of having her there to stave off other people's attentions.

"Enjoying yourself?" she asked, taking the sort of amusement I'd expect from Solitaire in my plight.

"They're all over me," I snapped. "Like, like rats, practically crawling over one another to get at me."

Phelia grinned, eyes dancing with good-natured mockery.

"Oh, but can you blame them? You're Beam the Breaker, legendary hero. Savior of Rinchester, vanquisher of vampire elders, rival to the King of Blades himself—"

"Enough." I cut in, finding myself suddenly harsher and more severe than I'd intended. Phelia paused, taking a moment to eye me, then nodded.

"Sorry, brother," she said at last, inspiring a spasm of guilt to replace my annoyance.

"What have you done now?" a new voice came. I turned to find Shango approaching with one of his least false-looking grins plastered across his features.

"Saw the two of you were huddling again, so I thought I'd complete the set. Anything important going on?"

"Your brother has been experiencing the horrors of heroism," Phelia told him, and Shango cracked a smile at the fading irritation on my face.

"Well at least we've all been getting our names out across the room." He shrugged. "I've been finding some very productive talks myself. Elswick really was holding its best business back from us." He seemed mildly peeved at that, but I could tell the emotion was blunted by finding so many new opportunities unrolling before him.

I was starting to hate these periods. Long, mundane stretches of peace and calm. They always made me feel so . . . useless.

"I've made other connections," Phelia noted. "Less overtly useful perhaps, but the women of this city's nobility are rather eager to win my friendship all of a sudden." She glanced at me, knowingly, and then back to Shango. "Give me a few weeks and I may have quite the source of information and rumor."

Shango was smiling wide at that, and a shudder ran down my spine. He was absolutely smitten, I realized. Tragic. Before either of us could say anything, though, a new figure approached. He was tall, thin, but powerfully built and looked like he stood on the wrong side of fifty. He spoke without introducing himself or mincing words, and I found myself suddenly wary of him. It might have been ridiculous in another world, but old men could be dangerously powerful in this one. Even without their influence and wealth.

"The Belahonts." He smiled, eyes flitting over each of us. "Lord Viras, a pleasure. I've been meaning to meet you for quite some time, but . . . Hmm, the third brother, Solitaire, he is not here?"

"Busy," Shango replied, matching the man's smile. Each of them seemed as false as the other. Like watching a pair of cats stare each other down.

"A pity." The newcomer sighed. "I'd been hoping to meet that one too. Well, no matter. Tell me, Shango Belahont, would you mind if we had a word? Just the two of us. I have certain things I'd rather like to discuss with you."

"Of course," Shango replied, still matching the man beat for beat. It was like watching him speak to an aged reflection. Well, aged and whitened. "Lead the way."

"I'm coming," I cut in, finding myself suddenly on edge about . . . everything. Viras, whatever he wanted Shango alone for, and, once again, the fact that we were deep in enemy territory with nothing but one another as company.

"No," Shango shot back, not even looking at me. "Stay by Phelia, please."

I paused, and by the time I'd even thought of a suitable response, they were already gone.

Phelia and I stood side by side for a good few long, painful seconds before she finally broke the silence by speaking.

"You're staring at them both like a hawk."

"Am I?" I replied without thinking. Yes, I realized, I was. They were only a few dozen paces away, close enough that, these days, I could probably sprint over in under two seconds. Still, I was on edge.

"You really care about them, don't you?"

It took me a moment to realize she meant my brothers, not Shango and Viras specifically. I risked a glance back at her, uncertain suddenly.

"They're . . ." My friends? Cowriters? "My brothers," I said, realizing it really was the best word for it. Phelia smiled.

"And yet you're different from them, aren't you? Shango is the spider at the center of a web, Solitaire a snake waiting to strike. But you. You're like a hero come to life, as if you walked out of some old folk tale and into reality."

I didn't know what to say to that, but fortunately she wasn't finished.

"I love you for protecting us, Beam. And I would ask that you keep doing it. However I ended up here, you are my family now. The Belahonts. And I would see you preserved."

Even Solitaire? I wondered, skeptical at the thought. Phelia smiled again.

"Yes, even Solitaire."

Great, another mind reader in my company. Just what I fucking needed.

CHAPTER FIFTEEN

Shango's POV: Day 123
Current Wealth: 755 gold, 42 silver, 33 copper

There was something different about Lord Viras. I didn't feel it. I rarely got gut feelings in general. It was more that I . . . saw it. Calculated it. All his responses, the little flashes of emotion that naturally lived in a person's face, were too long in happening and lasting. His words stuck together with more symmetry and logic than was natural. It seemed like everything about him was an artifice.

And it was a damned good one. Better than I could do, when I let myself untether and focus purely on strategy. Much better. This here was a master in the same field I'd been making a study of. I was tempted to try to learn a thing or two.

"You know, I've sacrificed quite a bit of myself to get what I want, how I want, where I want." Viras spoke differently now that we were alone, more flatly. It was like someone had taken the voice of a man and stripped it of everything other than the simple, bare facts of what it was conveying. Like some binary expression of human thought, cold and inorganic where ordinary speech was hot and . . .

Animalistic? I was going to think animalistic.

That had been a strange reaction on my part, but I wasn't given the chance to dwell on it. Viras was speaking still.

"You share that, don't you?" he asked. "That calmness in the face of what must be done. How else could you have inflicted what you did on Byror and remain so unflappable now?"

I wasn't taken aback by the accusation. Throwing something like that at someone and studying their immediate reaction was one of the basic plays in my own book. And without that crucial surprise, its effect was blunted.

"I am aware of the rumors, but I truly have no idea what you're talking about," I told him. Viras smiled the way statues that had been carved into the expression did.

"It was cleverly executed," he continued as if I'd not even spoken. "But you are young. Unmentored, I imagine? Everyone needs a mentor. My own was Azelis."

The statement was like a fist in the gut. Azelis was a figure in our books, a long-dead magus of incredible power and genius. Essentially Redacle's Merlin—or one of them at least—responsible for codifying so much of magic into its modern structures.

It was not a good thing to meet someone personally mentored by him. Not at fucking all. For one thing, it meant Viras was older than he looked. Because Azelis had died a lot more than fifty years ago. Magi with supernaturally long lives often achieved such through bargains, more often than not Faustian ones. Which meant many of them were desperate as well as powerful.

"Thank you for your offer," I said quietly. "But I must refuse."

Azelis had taken only thirty disciples, fewer than half of which we'd actually named in the books. It was entirely possible Viras was telling the truth, and if he was he *would* be one of the more powerful magi—most powerful humans—in the world. Top one thousand, perhaps even stronger. Strong enough to kill Corvan even if a dozen more Corvans attacked at once.

But I couldn't risk associating with him or giving him the chance to access our materials.

My answer seemed to surprise the man—the magus—enough that it actually showed a crack across his chisel-made face.

"That is an interesting response," he noted. "There are not many who would turn down alliance with one such as myself. Or do you disbelieve me?"

"I don't know what to believe," I told him flatly, realizing the mistake just a moment after it was out of my mouth.

"So then, it does not matter to you even if I am who I say I am." He frowned now, thinking. "Interesting. Very interesting. What sort of magics has your family created since you last engaged in battle that you are more fearful of my learning their secrets than you are eager to learn the teachings of Azelis himself?"

Fuck. Fuck fuck fuck, he was good. Dangerously good. Of course he was. His amount of experience, with magic slowing the ravages of time on his brain, meant his potential as a thinker was, theoretically, superhuman. I'd misstepped once already. I couldn't afford to do it again.

"You're too dangerous to ally with," I lied. "Students of Azelis are noticed. Students of students of Azelis are noticed. Even if you aren't advertising it at will, there'll be powerful people who know. If they see you teaching another, I become a target. I can't take that risk."

It was perhaps the best lie I could have come up with, as told as well as any might have been in this situation. And were it almost anyone else, I'd have been confident about seeing it swallowed. But Viras didn't look convinced.

"So quick-witted," he breathed. "Truly, I must have you as my student and see this mind turned to true magic. You're simply too dangerous not to. I ask again: Will you accept tutorship under me?"

It was honestly tempting. If I was learning as fast as I was with some roughly average hedge magus as my teacher, I shuddered to think what I might do under Viras. Would I make the same progress in half the time? A third? Even less? What secrets did Azelis pass on to him that I couldn't get anywhere else?

But all the best traps had tempting lures, and I wasn't stupid enough to let that distract me.

"I'm sorry," I said, actually earnest now, to my own surprise. "But I can't accept this offer."

Viras looked at me with a touch of what, I thought at least, was genuine sadness. He shook his head slowly.

"Then I am afraid I must destroy you," he whispered.

I met his eye.

"Yeah. I have to destroy you too," I replied, just as regretful.

Odd that, that sense of regret. I barely knew Viras, and what I did know of him painted a picture of sociopathic apathy and murderous ambition. But I felt reluctant to kill him. I realized why only as he was walking away. Viras was like my father. Not my actual father. He was like a father I would have had if I'd been given the luxury of a parent who was to me what others' were to them. The master to my student.

And he would have to die. I knew that without question. Because he was just too dangerous to leave alive. I stared down at my hands. My lessons in magic had continued of course, and continued fast. Most magi took twenty years to become average. I was almost average after a few months.

But Corvan was still stronger by far. How long would it take for me to equal him? Months more? A year?

How much longer then to equal Viras? Several years at least. Maybe a decade. Maybe more depending on his age. Magic was a slow thing to learn, and he'd had over half a century's head start, as well as enough talent to attract the eye of Azelis himself. And I'd gotten us into a conflict with him. What had I been fucking thinking?

Beam came over, looking somewhat uncertain, and stopped just beside me.

"So," he started. "How did it go?"

I thought about it.

"Badly," I croaked. "Very, very badly."

CHAPTER SIXTEEN

Solitaire's POV: Day 123
Current Wealth: 755 gold, 42 silver, 33 copper

I was in the middle of testing how many times a single human being could fold strips of linen in a row before killing himself when Shango called on me, interrupting my work, fortunately, and bringing me bad news to compensate for the upward tilt of fortune.

"I won't be coming to help you in the battle. I need to stay in Elswick."

As far as revelations went, it registered somewhere between "I'm pregnant" and "I'm a fed, and you're under arrest" in terms of the sense of molten dread it sent bubbling down my body.

"Explain," I replied, quite reasonably I thought. Shango stiffened, as if he was preparing for a fight of some sort. Which was ridiculous because if I'd wanted a fight, I'd have let him know by smashing a hammer across his face without the slightest telegraphing, warning, or threat.

But then Shango spoke, and he told me where he'd been, what he'd done, what had happened. He talked of Lord Viras, the man's weird similarity to him, his claim of tutorship from one of the world's foremost magi. And his promise to destroy us. By the end, I was still uncertain, but I had a lot more to think about than just my former friend.

"You realize he might be trying to split us up."

"I'd considered that." Shango nodded. "I wasn't sure why he'd tell me he planned to destroy us if he didn't gain something from it."

I thought about that.

"Well," I began, "I wasn't there, but if he reciprocated this sense of connection you felt, I can see that being why. People are weird about feelings of belonging and kinship." I knew that better than most, having already felt the experience of meeting a singular man of roughly comparable intelligence after years of wading through morons. "But, still, it could be a trap regardless."

"Does that make any difference?" he asked.

"No," I hissed, finding myself particularly irritated by the fact. Even if it was a trap, we didn't have any real choice here. Either we let ourselves split up, or we let our workstation remain completely unguarded with an active enemy who had his arm elbow deep in the local law enforcement's asshole. Not a real choice at all. We could try dismantling it, but even that would set us back . . . an unthinkable distance. And as of now, we needed all the time we could manage to perfect our weaponry and defenses.

"So," I said at last. "You're staying behind."

"I'm staying behind," Shango echoed, seeming about as happy with the fact as I felt. "And I'll need a few of the men too."

I nodded, thinking about the best picks almost subinstinctually.

"Arthur should stay with you," I suggested. "The point of this little trip is to spread our reputation and earn favors. Not having an already established hero there will make it easier to have people coming away with the idea that we're the ones doing everything. It just won't hit home the same if one of our subordinates kills as many as all of us combined."

Shango hesitated.

"You sure about entering the fight without him?"

"Yes," I told him. "And I'd rather have him here where all my stuff is even if I wasn't."

"Alright then." Shango thought a moment more. "Alora. I'll have Alora here too. A trained gunman, or training rather, would go a long way if I have her fire out through the windows."

I smiled. "We'll make a terrorist of you yet," I complimented him, finding myself rather perturbed to see Shango seeming reluctant to accept the praise, and even put out by it. Some people.

"What have you been working on here?" he asked abruptly. "Any new weapons or . . .?"

"Okay, so you know how I have a new shock-activated explosive that goes off when it's impacted?" I prompted.

"I do now." Shango nodded. I sighed. Sometimes it hurt how little people appreciated my work.

"Well, I'm . . . Fuck it. Grenades. I'm making grenades. They're grenades. You ruin everything."

Far from being concerned with the savage emotional attack he'd just inflicted upon me, Shango seemed suddenly captivated by the project.

"What do you mean grenades?" he pressed. "Like, you throw them and there's an explosion?"

"Yes, I do mean things with the literal definitional function of grenades." I nodded. "Watch this."

I gestured him out across the room, to where I'd prepared a series of stone slabs for testing new devices without targeting any load-bearing beams, again. Rifling around produced two of the new spherical objects, and I hurled one through the air to impact the target nice and fast.

Even standing where we were, a good ten paces back, I felt the shock wave like a harsh gust against my face. Shango yelped and covered his eyes, I giggled at the sight, and once our ears had stopped ringing, he glared at me.

"Flashy," he noted, glancing over at the stone slabs. "Powerful too," he added with a considering glance to the large cracks running a meter across them. "But I don't see how this isn't just a worse-ranged version of my rifle."

It really was nice having intellectually comparable company.

"Because it's not done yet," I told him. "I'm working with Ardin to make casts for lead balls, and we're gonna add an outer section around the explosives filled with them."

"You're going to fill them with bullets?" he asked, getting it now. "And they'll be launched outward when it goes off. Fuck, how fast?"

"Subsonic." I sighed. "Though not by a lot. Maybe two hundred meters per second. It's hard to estimate properly without decent equipment. About half or less the speed of your rifle's rounds. They're reasonably big, but plate armor will have a fair chance of stopping them. The main purpose of these is to blow up larger formations of lightly armored enemies. Which brings us to our next innovation."

I reached into another pile, drawing out the schematic I'd been working on.

"Grenade, meet grenade launcher."

It was, roughly, as primitive a grenade launcher as you could possibly imagine, really more categorically akin to a scaled-down nineteenth-century mortar than its contemporary kin. Shango looked nice and impressed though. Well, good, I should bloody hope he did.

Shango took in the design, its weirdly short frame; squat, wide barrel; bell-shaped mouth; and robust construction. One upside to using this thing would be that, if its wielder were ambushed in melee, they'd already be holding a perfectly serviceable club.

"How's Ardin getting along with the other guns?" he asked finally.

"Almost done apparently." I grinned. "With the first one, that is. He's had a lot of other stuff to work on. The plan is he'll have two done by the attack, one of which for Alora."

Shango nodded. "Well, three gunmen is better than one."

"Unless you're the enemy." I smiled. It was a nervous, fidgety smile. The conversation wasn't actively unpleasant, but it was a distraction from my work. And my work, in turn, was a distraction from the imminent danger I had no choice but to sprint at.

Preparing the most dangerous and destructive weapons I could had always been soothing in times like that, and most certainly was not "probable cause," regardless of what the cops said. I bit back my growing anxiety, steadying my mind.

"I think we have decent odds of coming out of this alive," I told Shango, realizing he'd been asking for just the same reasons as me. "You've seen a pair of big reasons for why, but there's also our personal growth. Remember how the vampire ended up after we survived a night? If the enemy doesn't eradicate us all at once, we've got very favorable chances to stave them off nearly forever."

"Right." Shango nodded, inhaling, exhaling. His fists were tight when he finished. He was furious. No, wait. Shango didn't show emotion. He just wasn't built for it. By his standards, this was a stroke of murderous rage, borderline manic hatred. It was almost as intense as a passing irritation was to me.

"I thought we were done with this," he spit. "I thought . . . I thought I'd gotten us done with this."

"Some people just need killing." I shrugged. "You took care of one problem, Byror. But there's others. We'll be done when everything with ill will toward us is either very far away or decomposing into more black powder."

He stared at me.

"Simple as that?"

I stared back.

"People hurt one another. If you have something they want, they hurt you even harder. This isn't going to stop. It's not going to end. There's no peaceful solution here. We're at war. If we don't kill we die, if we die we lose, and if we lose more people die. Yeah, it's as simple as that. Some people need killing, and when something needs doing, it's better to do it than sit around agonizing over a world where it doesn't need to be done."

"And if they surrender?" he challenged me. I felt myself sneering.

"They're welcome to surrender before they try to kill me. After that, they're an example for the next cunt who thinks about it."

Shango said nothing for a few seconds, then nodded.

"Right. Good talk, Solitaire," he replied, distance popping up between us again.

He left.

CHAPTER SEVENTEEN

Beam's POV: Day 137
Current Wealth: 776 gold, 41 silver, 48 copper

The two weeks still left went by like blurs, and I barely even kept days separate in my memory. When I wasn't training new recruits—who'd shot up in number to twenty-two early on—I was sparring with Arthur. When I wasn't doing that, I was helping Solitaire with heavy lifting or Ardin with metalworking. I wasn't in a unique place to complain though. Everyone was busy with something, and most of us were with several things.

And behind it all there was that sudden worry of Shango, Arthur, and Alora being left to hold down the fort by themselves.

Still, that preparation wasn't for nothing. By the time we were ready to leave, our new recruits had gone from homeless people to decently trained, violent homeless people, and they'd been equipped with the best gear we'd been able to manage on short notice. Each one had a spear tipped with tool steel, sharp enough to skewer a man clean through lighter armor and tough enough to hold that edge for a good long while. Their armor was brigandines made from our own scrap metal, and I'd seen for myself the demonstration where even thousand-pound crossbows had failed to penetrate them without hitting soft spots.

I wasn't sure how they'd measure up against the professional soldiers of this world. Their training had been a step above the norm, with Helena having one hell of a knack for it and things being made smoother by my presence. But it had also been just a mere few weeks. Not very long at all, really, to pick up more than the basics, even with a full five or six hours dedicated to it daily. But they were well equipped at least, and bolstered by some of the heavy weapons Solitaire had coined I was convinced they'd make a very strong defensive force.

We just couldn't use them to swarm any positions. Morale was the main issue at this point.

Setting off was an unexpected inconvenience, with us now traveling with around five times as many people as we were used to. In the end, we had to use carriages, simply for the speed, transport of heavy weaponry, and shelter, but hiring them cost us a pretty penny. It bothered Solitaire, I knew, to not be seated exclusively in preprepared armored vehicles. Poor guy was twitching like a fresh corpse the whole trip, even after we'd already been at it for a few days. As we got closer, he became more erratic, snappy, angry. It was a familiar pattern that all the regulars were used to, but it terrified the poor recruits who, for the most part, genuinely thought he was some dark explosion-wizard.

Powerful evil magic and violent instability. Not a reassuring combination.

On the second day of our journey, I was surprised to be approached by none other than Lord Appleberry himself. He'd accompanied out convoy from the start, but still the man seemed hesitant, almost awkward, as he came over, a reaction I'd certainly not come to expect from Redaclans who stood higher on the social totem pole than whomever they spoke to.

"Beam Belahont," he greeted me, using my full name but without any sort of formality to his voice. A weird combination.

"Hello," I replied awkwardly. I wasn't sure what he wanted, but I mentally prepared myself to explain that whatever Solitaire had threatened to do wouldn't actually happen unless he touched him.

"I've been meaning to speak with you," he continued, seeming to grow more friendly with each word. "Terribly sorry for taking so long, but you'd seemed preoccupied with your men until now."

Well, I'd spent a lot of the journey trying to keep their spirits up, or at least keep them from actively fleeing before we arrived. I couldn't blame him.

"It's fine. What did you want to discuss?"

He chuckled nervously.

"Oh, no, nothing in particular. Just . . . Well, I've heard the stories, you know? I wanted to speak to you in person, just the two of us. Not often one meets a hero in the flesh, eh?"

"Hero?" I replied before I could stop myself. Appleberry beamed wider.

"My, and modest too. Yes, of course, have you not heard what they're saying? I know of your deeds. Rinchester, battling that vampire, going toe-to-toe with the King of Blades. Even allowing for the usual exaggeration, I dare say there are few men who'd be your equal."

It didn't happen like that, I wanted to say, but we were marching to fight ten, twenty, or even a hundred times our number in orcs. Somehow the idea of correcting him, of denying him this small reassurance, felt cruel. Maybe he needed to believe he was fighting next to another Arthur.

Appleberry continued praising me, bringing up one feat or another—none of which were ever quite how I remembered them actually occurring. It was a relief when I was finally called on to sprint off ahead and scout the area out beyond us.

The thing with being me, or rather the thing with being me in excess of level twenty and with a speed stat of seventeen, was that it meant I was actually the better option for such things even compared to a man on horseback. I cleared a mile every other minute, and by the time I'd swept the area for geographic features and potential hostiles to return, less than half an hour had passed. It made me realize how easy it might be to be seen coming by our enemies too. After all, I was far from the most physically powerful man in the world. Hell, even this region alone boasted Arthur, the King of Blades, and a few others above me. My performance in the tourney's final round had been . . . weird. A fluke that I barely recalled. There was every chance we were having our movements reported back by some scout able to sprint faster than I could.

It was fortunately only one more day before we finally came to Swanhen, or at least until we were close enough for me to run into it while scouting. The town was, as we'd heard, bigger than Rinchester, though clearly a few steps removed from true city status. Its buildings were squat and somewhat packed together, and running along its outer edge was a tall wooden wall reaching maybe fifteen feet off the ground and looking thick enough to stop a car.

The first bit of good news was there was no siege camp outside. Orcs in Redacle had a tendency to be smarter than humans expected, and Solitaire in particular had always gotten a sick glee from writing stories about upper-class gentlemen finding their armies torn apart by so-called animals with a great deal more ingenuity than they'd expected to face. There were orcs out there who'd have had trebuchets to bring to this attack, let alone other siege engines. But those did not seem to be the ones we'd be facing.

In fact, there didn't seem to be any orcs at all.

I circled the city, slowly and carefully, ready to sprint all the while as I studied its surrounding environment to see what features it boasted. The ground around it was vaguely flat and level, which was definitely good for farming but not ideal when one was being attacked. It meant the enemy had plenty of space to work with in doing whatever they wanted to beyond the walls. The walls in question were periodically dotted with siege engines. Catapults for the most part, but the occasional ballista too.

It didn't look like a great defense, I had to admit. Velaharo Manor probably would've stood up to an assault better after Solitaire's renovations, but at the very least, the town had plenty of spots we could deploy some of our new weapons from.

That was, assuming we were allowed in past the walls. As I looked closer, I could see those walls had taken more than a few batterings, and their gates looked like they were replacements of replacements of replacements. From what I saw of the buildings poking over the top, the place had taken some battle damage too. Evidently the orcs had gotten inside before, and maybe not just once.

With everything I could hope to glean already taken in and processed, I gave it all one last study to see if I'd missed anything. I had, as it happened, something big.

The orcs were already fucking inside the town. Suddenly hollowed out by the realization, I turned and started the journey back, raising my pace a shade beyond the usual comfortable effort I went out scouting with to compensate for the extra time I'd spent studying our destination.

Before nightfall, we'd be at Swanhen and ready to help. But I wasn't sure now how much we could do. It all felt so real all of a sudden.

CHAPTER EIGHTEEN

Solitaire's POV: Day 140
Current Wealth: 781 gold, 34 silver, 47 copper

Bugger," I replied calmly. "Bollocks. Oh bosh, heck, even, and, dare I say it, ploppies." As far as displays of my anger went, I actually thought I was doing a pretty good job. I wasn't even swearing, really. Beam apparently disagreed.

"Can you stop punching that dead deer, please?" he requested. I looked down to my hands, covered in blood and fur, then up to the now rather less deer-shaped deer. With a sigh, I acquiesced.

"This isn't good," I grumbled, kicking the ground and sending a big tuft of cold-solid dirt ripping free. It would've been a satisfying display of my strength, had that strength been enough to kill several thousand gray-skinned bodybuilders.

In a protracted fight, Beam might've been worth a hundred of them. I was probably more like fifty, including my ability to hilariously prank them with nitroglycerin, while most of our elites would've been perhaps ten or fewer. The basic soldiers we had would've been one each, maybe less. In total, our force was equal to perhaps two hundred orcs. Not bad, considering we numbered less than thirty. With Corvan to help, we might've even tipped that up to three hundred.

But that still wasn't enough, even without the disadvantage of the enemy having a manned defensive position. The siege engines, in particular, were a concern. So we got thinking.

We could see a few details about Swanhen from the outside, and Beam had spent a good while studying it, but otherwise there wasn't much to go off. Around the town, woodland grew thickly enough to hide us from sight. This meant we had the chance to take our time in planning, but that still didn't give us more info to work with. Intelligence, in the end, was our crucial shortcoming.

That in and of itself made the plan fairly obvious though, and shortly after coming to the realization I'd formulated it. The men weren't exactly happy about the fact, but then people rarely were happy to have a giant deadly fort pointed out to them and then hear the phrase "get 'em." I decided I could make do with their poor moods.

We cooked and ate the deer, which was if anything even more delicious following its several-minute tenderization, and though there wasn't much when split so many ways, it certainly had an effect on morale. Then we all ran screaming like lunatics at the orcs.

The good thing about being so heavily outnumbered, charging a fortified position, and with few to no actual siege weapons to help us break it was that the enemy was entirely surprised. That was, unfortunately, the literal only benefit we gained from the situation. Unless one counted the way maddened adrenaline kept us running.

Well, it wasn't such a small thing. We were mostly to the walls before any actual siege weapons could even be fired.

That went a long way because by then we were close enough that none *could* be fired with any real accuracy. The volleys of arrows were of greater concern. Big, heavy, fast things driven by massive composite bows with too heavy a draw for most humans to manage. The orcs did just fine though, spitting their projectiles our way with velocities eerily close to my own rocket launcher.

Corvan came in clutch there, of course. The air ahead of us coiled with force as grass and the increasingly thin snow were torn away. Arrows, even these ones, were slower than bullets, and they were far, far less dense with a much bigger surface area. Corvan didn't even need a barrier to stop them, just blasted them off course with a few meters of gale-force wind. By the time the second volley had missed its mark, our men were dropping down and readying their retaliation.

Of course, they used the hand mortars.

There was a certain satisfaction to seeing weapons I'd worked so hard on finally used in anger, and I had to suppress a giggle as the sight of orcish flesh flying in all directions hit me. My old therapists might have called these "disturbingly sadistic tendencies," but considering they ended up stuck in a career where they asked children about their feelings for money, I didn't really think they were in a position to judge. Certainly, their advice didn't compare to the dopamine hit from weapons well-made.

Not all of them were accurate. Some grenades went over the walls, detonating out of sight within the town. Others were short and hit the wall itself, blasts shaped away from their intended targets by the sloped designs.

Enough hit home though. We'd not put as much time into drilling on the grenade launchers as we might have, but even a fraction of the shots hitting did wonders to freak the fuck out of the orcs. They probably thought they were getting blasted by an entire host of magi. Idiots.

Well, Corvan added a bit of weight to that misconception with his own, actually magical attacks.

Fire ran along the wall like a sheet of rain, scorching everything in its path. Siege engines were charred into ruined husks, ropes snapped and whipped around like burning ribbons, and the poor sods actually manning the stuff either perished instantly if they were lucky, or slowly if they weren't.

It only took us a minute, maybe less, to de-man an entire section of the outer wall, a hundred or more bodies crushed, eviscerated, or immolated into death. I'd been an idiot to overlook our heavy weapons. They doubled or tripled our effectiveness easily. But the enemy was mounting their defense soon enough. Other siege engines farther from our section were turning, other bows were readying, and the gate was starting to rise as enemies prepared to charge down and swarm us in melee. I initiated the next step of my cunning and masterful plan.

"*Retreat!*" I screamed, making a solid example of the order by turning to leg it myself.

If there is one order you can count on being obeyed by scared, half-trained men, it is an order to run the fuck away. These ones were very *eager* to do so. Corvan whipped up more winds around us to cover the flight, though with so many arrows from so many directions, we found them getting a bit closer than would've been ideal. I saw one bounce off a man's brigandine and almost trip another before it came to stop, but we were soon out of bow range entirely and back safe at the tree line.

Of course, the siege engines started firing back at us. None hit. Even discounting the range and limited visibility, I'd parked us behind a nice, big slope, and most of the best positioned had been taken down in the attack.

"Everyone still alive?" I asked, while the recruits panted and heaved and our elites looked around doing a head count.

"Yep," Argar grunted, his mood pretty foul what with all the fighting he hadn't gotten to do. "Nobody's even hurt."

That actually did surprise me. I'd expected at least an arrow wound or two, armor or not. Looked like we'd gotten lucky with this one, even with the sudden devastation and quick retreat. My good mood didn't last long though because a certain whiny prick's voice soon took to the air and got to work on ruining it.

"That's it?" Appleberry snapped. "That's what you call an attack?"

Of course, Appleberry had entered that attack in full plate armor. Even orcish arrows hadn't had decent odds of hurting him at the range we were catching them from, and it probably hadn't even occurred to him that we'd gotten lucky to have escaped with no wounds at all. In his eyes, casualties were just an expected price. In his eyes, the real waste was losing the chance to capitalize on all the dead poor people and take back his shit.

I didn't hit him. Partly because I'd run a fair risk of killing him, in my own plate armor, and partly because I had to reluctantly admit there were more productive ways of handling our little disagreement. Even if none were as fun as watching him go flying back and bounce off a tree.

"That's what I call a diversion," I explained to him calmly. Appleberry paused through what looked like it had been about to be a secondary rant and looked thoughtful all of a sudden.

"A diversion," he echoed. "Explain."

Hearing it phrased like a command with so much confidence that I'd oblige him actually made me incredibly tempted to not answer out of spite, but that wasn't a serious option. If Appleberry was left in the dark, he would do something stupid, inevitably. And that could only end badly even if it had the bonus of getting him killed.

"You haven't noticed yet because you're stupid, but Beam isn't here," I pointed out. Appleberry realized what I was saying a moment later, eyes widening. I continued anyway. "That's because he's inside Swanhen. Our biggest issue was we didn't have much information to go off for an actual plan of attack, but now we have a man on the inside."

CHAPTER NINETEEN

Beam's POV: Day 142
Current Wealth: 781 gold, 34 silver, 47 copper

I honestly don't know how Solitaire talked me into heading inside the walls. He's persuasive, that much I've always known, but I didn't know he was *that* persuasive. Fucking Shango wasn't even that persuasive. I must have lost my mind. Unless he'd drugged me?

Well, I was inside now, and I didn't exactly have the luxury of backing out. My friends were counting on me, the people of Swanhen were counting on me, and besides all that I wasn't too confident about keeping myself free of arrows as I sprinted away from the walls.

A hero. People were calling me a hero. I wasn't—that much I was painfully aware of—but somehow I felt like I had to act the part at least. The idea of giving them that hope and just falling short was too awful to consider. I got to work.

Swanhen was actually pretty similar in layout to Rinchester, and moving through it brought back memories. Not pleasant memories, mind, and each one left me significantly more pissed off than the one before it. With the snow receding and the orcs still busy at the walls, I actually got quite far before even encountering another person.

I managed a good look at the place.

Swanhen was locked down tight, probably to keep people like me from getting in and doing exactly what I was doing. I wasn't as sneaky as Solitaire—nobody I'd ever met was even half as sneaky as Solitaire—but I was faster and stronger, which meant that in the time an orc patrol took to turn their backs, I could already be several paces to one side and on top of a building. It made avoiding their eyes pretty trivial.

Heading around, I noted that there were still quite a few humans in the place. In fact, though I couldn't exactly judge them based on a glance like Solitaire, it seemed to me that it was roughly as populous as Rinchester had been, just with our kind's numbers more . . . compressed.

Well, no surprise there. It tended to happen when your home was invaded and you suddenly found yourself a prisoner. I continued my travels, learning what I could, seeing what I could. I found the gear for more siege engines of course, which was particularly important as Solitaire had been hoping we might ambush the orcs as they headed outside to cut down trees for more of them. I found their ammo stores, which were plentiful, and what I thought were some barracks. The orcs in Swanhen had been oddly well equipped. It was hard to see from the walls, but now that I could study them at my leisure, I saw they all came plated in metal.

Iron, I thought, rather than steel, at least if my lessons with Ardin were leading me right. But it was thick still, formed into cuirasses and greaves, bracers and helms. Maybe a quarter of an inch in all. That wasn't good. A quarter inch of iron might well stop Shango's rifle, and I didn't know how well our Gatling gun would defeat it.

Nerves fraying, I kept up my examination. Now that I'd gotten the basics down, I started running interference too. There were a few thousand orcs in Swanhen? Alright then, I'd see what I could do about that. Fighting them all was out of the question, but with those numbers I could kill twenty and reduce their strength by 1 percent.

It wasn't much, in the grand scheme of things. But if I killed twenty more, and another twenty on top, it'd add up. We needed all the advantages we could get, so I worked to start getting them. If nothing else, the big, cumbersome iron armor made it a shade easier to sneak up on them.

This was how I passed much of my first day in Swanhen, and I had to say it was almost fun. I was faster now than even I'd realized, watching orcs turn in slow motion, twisting around, and cutting throats before my presence had even been fully noticed. Sometimes I'd be shot at, of course. And the arrows were *slow*. Faster than I could run, naturally, but not by as much as I'd have thought, even fired from those stupidly big recurve bows. On more than one occasion, I actually dodged one after it was fired, and I had no trouble keeping ahead of the sluggish marksmen wielding them.

Of course, one could only kill so many people before those people's allies decided you were a high-priority target. By the time orc number twenty-nine had met his maker—which, now that I thought about it, was actually me—I caught word of some alert running through the city as they scrambled to respond.

Thing was though, they were responding quite . . . quickly. Sharply, as if on some prearranged schedule, and when I kept an ear to the ground I heard mention of resistance fighters. None had made the connection that their recent enemy's attack had deposited someone inside the walls.

Which told me that they already had problems bubbling up within.

* * *

I looked into it, naturally. And was rather proud to find I was right. From what I could gather—mostly by grabbing orcs' heads and angrily yelling questions at them before I chopped them in half—this resistance had cropped up a while ago, and it was led by quite a charismatic figure.

Obviously, the orcs did not know who that figure was. Or else they'd be a dead charismatic figure. At the very least, they were competent enough to evade detection though, and doing that without my literal superpowers was probably no mean feat. So I looked into finding this leader myself.

It was actually not that hard, if only because I was a very big, scary man who'd already become famous for killing—by now—thirty-two orcs. I shook down a few human locals, most of whom knew nothing, some of whom knew something, and none of whom were cooperative. At first. Fortunately, fear and orc blood did a great job at lubricating my investigation, and soon enough I'd managed to narrow down my suspects through a combination of one part Holmesian deduction, and 999 parts intimidation and persistence.

It was quite a Solitaire thing to do, and I won't pretend otherwise. But it needed doing. I wouldn't fail my family.

To my surprise, I didn't find any guards at the leader's location. When I entered, cautiously and with full readiness to hurl myself from a window if it turned into an ambush, I found none inside. Only a single woman.

Tall, even by Earth standards, and well-dressed. Very well-dressed actually, clothes made of silk and other cloths that were prohibitively expensive in Redacle, with their tailoring fine and careful enough not to be visible even at a more thorough inspection. She was black too. Not as dark-skinned as Shango, but close. Her hair was braided into dreadlocks, and her face was sharp and aristocratic.

She looked like she'd been expecting me, and at the risk of sounding like Solitaire again, I almost dived through the fucking wall to escape when I realized that.

"Greetings," she said, looking at me like I'd come to expect people would in this world. As if I was some tool of unknown use, to be assessed and planned around. "I have been expecting you."

"I can tell" was all I thought to respond with. She gestured to a chair opposite her.

"Sit?" she offered.

"No thanks," I replied, wanting to remain as mobile as possible in case this was a trap of some sort.

The woman hummed, not looking annoyed, nor pleased, at my response, and she was speaking more before I could even wonder what to read from that.

"My name is Adannaya," she said at last. "Lady Adannaya. And I have been waiting to meet you, Beam Belahont, for quite some time."

CHAPTER TWENTY

Shango's POV: Day 142
Current Wealth: 781 gold, 34 silver, 47 copper

I'd been working hard on making sure our place in Elswick was secure. Unfortunately, it wasn't. It wasn't that we were relatively poor, still, by noble standards, or that we lacked manpower, or that most of our forces were off elsewhere being heroes. It wasn't that we were seen as illegitimate by a lot of Elswick's powers. Well, actually, it was all those things to some extent. Mostly though, it was that if Lord Viras decided to make his move and come for us, nobody would stand in his way. Not merchants, certainly not nobles. Nobody.

The man was powerful, established, and scary. Meanwhile, we were only two of those things, at best, and plenty didn't even have the intellect to realize that much. Our fundamental issue was a lack of deterrent, especially with our forces split. So that was what I got to work on.

I couldn't win over the nobility. They cared about time and legacy too much. I might not even get them on our side in a generation. The mercers and middle classes might be easier, but that would mean diverting precious funds, and only to get a meager few whom Viras could probably buy away from us anyway.

No, we needed actual loyalty, and we needed it from a source the rest of this city wouldn't have poisoned already. So I turned my focus to the peasants.

The good thing about poor people—especially poor people in the past—is that they're so used to being shit on by wider society that it's ridiculously easy to get them on your side. Hell, you don't even need to stop the shitting. I saw people calling my father a genius back on Earth while he was having people piss into bottles for his sweatshops to meet quota. Like some bizarre, large-scale Stockholm syndrome affecting half the population.

And it meant that you could turn that zeal into much, much stronger zeal by actually engaging in a bit of philanthropy.

It was kind of ridiculous. No, not kind of. It was just ridiculous. Altruism was so alien to this shitty planet that I was practically inventing it here. How much of that was our edgy teenage writing, and how much based in reality?

I didn't care. The important thing was that it benefited our plans a lot. I started looking into holding a ball for specifically the peasantry of Elswick. Such things were not generally done, and suggesting the idea to my men got me mixed responses. Still, I got to work preparing the funds and ended up settling on a seventy-gold budget.

It hurt to use up such a big slice of our savings, but it'd hurt more to have our home stormed by Viras' men and watch all our shit get stolen. Besides, I was already saving money by using Velaharo Manor as our venue.

Which, of course, caused its own problem too. This time of a domestic kind. Phelia called on me shortly after I started making my preparations, and she looked incredibly unhappy.

"Something the matter?" I asked her, my husband senses nascent and undeveloped compared to some, but still vibrating with terror at the sight of her worsening mood.

"Yes," she replied, voice dripping with false sweetness. A lie, I knew. The scent of sugar luring unwitting flies into the mouth of a Venus flytrap. I watched her cautiously. "Dear," Phelia began, "I just heard that you are, apparently, intending on hosting a ball of the peasantry . . . in our home."

I kept my face level, knowing that if I showed even a minuscule crack, Phelia would pounce on the weakness without even the slightest hesitation.

"That's correct," I told her. "We need allies, and since the nobility and mercers are beyond reach, I thought it'd be best to go for the city's peasant class."

Phelia's jaw tightened, subtly and slightly. It was the sort of expression she'd mastered, conveying absolutely nothing to me except an urge to take back whatever I'd just said. But I didn't.

"And you decided to do so by hosting a party for them," Phelia began, as if she were merely observing some idle fact. As if it were mere coincidence, not intended by her, that her words were coming in a tone that promised an ever-greater length of time without sex for every syllable she conveyed.

"I did," I told her, deciding to let her obvious anger sizzle and cool against the ice of my calm. It did the exact opposite, as if Phelia took my lack of reciprocated irritation as some personal challenge, inspiring her to yet taller heights.

"And do you care to explain why you chose to host this party, of which the main guests are unwashed, uncultured peasants, within my family's thousand-year-old home?"

Ah, there it was. The crux of the issue. I probably should've guessed from the start.

"Do you have a more specific problem with that?" I asked, deciding to let her try, at least, to communicate what was fundamentally no more than an icky feeling in her gut. If nothing else, it would be interesting to watch how stupid such a clever woman could sound when venting pure bigotry from her mouth.

"A specific problem?" Phelia glared. "Other than opening my home to thievery and plunder?"

I sighed. "This will earn us the favor of the most populous group in Elswick, and we need all the favor we can get. After this, I'm going to make connections with dissenters among them, spread charity, do things to make the Belahonts a very beneficial force for the peasantry. Make it so that they stand to tangibly lose if something happens to us."

That's the trick with causing a rebellion. It's not what you do to the people, not really. Humans are robust, complacent, long-suffering creatures and will shrug off any number of vicious cruelties or prolonged societal tortures. It's what you give them and then threaten to take away. All the biggest revolts of history followed a period of better living standards giving way to worse.

But Phelia didn't have my modern historic context to draw on, and even if she had, her mind was clouded by tribalism and prejudice. It was like trying to explain color to someone who insisted on viewing the world through lenses of red.

"You really expect gratitude from these people?" she scoffed. "When have they ever given that?"

"When have they ever been given a reason to?" I shot back before I could stop myself. That lit the fuse on a rant grenade that I absorbed the blast of at point-blank range. It was all I could do not to fall off my fucking chair as Phelia just. Kept. Going. If it wasn't their being allowed to live on noble lands, it was their lack of work being tolerated. If not that, their free defense from all the hostile monsters of the world. I'd never realized just how much she had on her chest about poor people before.

Well, now I knew.

"Phelia, I understand what you're saying," I soothed. "But we still need to do this. You just don't understand the lower classes as much as me."

"Why?" she snapped. "Because of your madman brother?"

She paused then, eyes widening, as if she'd somehow crossed a line.

"Yes," I told her. "Because of my madman brother, and more specifically because of our friends, and a thousand other experiences I've had. You can trust Solitaire to invent weapons from the future. Can you not trust me to do this?"

It was, perhaps, the most ridiculously unfair and cruel thing I could possibly have done. But it was necessary. Phelia though only glared.

"Say no," she growled, "and I'm placing you below your violent savage of a brother mere moments after forcing you to admit his madness. Very slick, Shango. Very clever." She turned and stormed out without another word. I didn't go after her.

Seeing her not only recognize, but dissect my attempted manipulation so instantly, I reckoned the very least I owed her was a bit of time to herself.

Besides, I'd gotten suddenly tired of speaking with intellectual equals. It really did take a lot out of a man.

CHAPTER TWENTY-ONE

Solitaire's POV: Day 143
Current Wealth: 712 gold, 26 silver, 14 copper

With Beam inside the town, and the rest of us still waiting beyond it, I didn't really have much direct action to take. That didn't mean I didn't get myself busy of course, because there were always precautionary measures to take. And that wasn't even me being a paranoid either! The orcs could've gone out looking for us, and if they'd sent even a fraction of their forces, we'd have been outnumbered dozens to one. So I gathered up the men and started working on a decently defensive perimeter to make sure that they had as miserable a time trying that as possible if it happened.

There was a secondary purpose to this too, of course. The men were feeling a bit crushed. They'd just gotten into a fight with orcs—surprisingly advanced orcs—and though none had been seriously wounded, in their eyes, we'd all failed to breach their defenses. They considered themselves to have been repelled, and the fact that it was all according to plan didn't seem to mitigate that. Being given a bloody nose by what they saw as semisapient primates was hardly something to uplift morale, and it was always smart to keep a large mob of violent men busy if you didn't want them to get angry and suddenly hang you.

So, we got busy.

While preparations got underway, I considered our enemies. Siege engines of the kinds they'd shown hadn't been expected even on my part—though that was because my friends tended to nerf my genius by insisting I not exercise the full might of it on imagining how everyone might try to murder us—and they indicated . . . something. There was a cause for everything, and even if you weren't a smart person, you'd be amazed how much you could figure out just by slowing down and taking the time to really dissect some of the things you saw. Nothing just happens. It all comes from somewhere. Taking that for granted is like going through life with your eyes closed.

I actually *was* intelligent though, so it actually took me less than two seconds to figure out what was going on with the orcs. It was almost funny. You can wait to find that out later. It's funner that way.

We had our camp's basis up after a while, a small thing that was nonetheless densely packed with defenses. At home, I'd tried to make a swivel turret for the Gatling gun. It hadn't really worked, but I got busy here again. The issue had been making the thing light enough to be practically mobile, and I circumvented that issue here by just cannibalizing one of our carriages and assembling one on-site. By the end we had, more or less, 360-degree coverage.

That, and the large barricades encircling us, the fact that we still had all our rocket ammo and most of our grenades, and the handful of low-level superhumans among us, told me that we wouldn't be at much risk of attack from the orcs. Especially because most directions, they'd be forced to charge us uphill, and thus give the Gatling gun extra time to punch holes in them.

But with that done, we soon ran out of jobs, which meant it was back to thinking time.

Helena fixed that with the men, of course. The sight of soldiers with free time seemed to offend her on some deep, almost ontological level, and she quickly got to barking them into running laps, practicing thrusts, and sparring with the blunted weapons she'd insisted on bringing. Elizabeth watched, giggling and shouting out unhelpful orders, then started swearing when Argar hauled her off her feet and started making her sprint right next to the rest.

But I just sat down and thought.

Beam was in the town. My friend, my brother. He'd gone in because I'd told him to, and I'd yet to hear anything about him since. I hadn't fully expected to yet, mind. Sending regular letters would make his movements predictable enough that the risk of being caught would raise exponentially, but still . . . It needled me. And not just in the paranoid way. He was my friend, and he was there because of me.

All I had to do was ask, and Beam did it. No hesitation, he just did it. Like he was some soldier, some champion rather than a friend. Did that say something about me, or him?

Him, I decided, because he'd have done the same with Shango, if not quicker. Who would he follow if Shango and I had a real falling out and our differences proved too much for us to even cooperate anymore?

Yeah, that question didn't take long for me to answer. He'd follow Shango, obviously. I could be honest with myself, at least. Very few people would be friends with me if given a real choice in the matter, and I wasn't delusional enough to think Beam considered me the equal of his noninsane one.

And since I was being honest with myself, I thought I might as well take a look at this plan of mine. Oh, it was very clever as usual. But it all hinged on my friend being seated right in the heat of the biggest danger in the region. Would it work? It might well. In fact, there might even be better than fifty-fifty odds of that. Would Beam survive?

Probably, if he succeeded. Maybe not if he didn't. Beam could always bug out if things went wrong. At this point, he could sprint faster than a racehorse, and his ethereal armor would stop orcish arrows without a problem. But they might corner him, or get a lucky shot to one of the gaps. I didn't think twenty times a normal person's durability would stop the projectiles we were seeing yesterday, not if they hit the neck and clipped an artery.

I'd not even thought about it. Just decided on the best course of action, the effective course of action, and sent Beam to do it. My friend might be on his way to die, and it might be my fault.

"Something on your mind?"

It was Argar, dropping down into a seated position beside me. The redhead was, as usual, so big there was a moment of brief stunned staring to see him so close so suddenly, then I was talking.

"Just worrying about victory."

Argar eyed me, frowning.

"Beam?" he asked.

I considered lying but decided I couldn't be bothered.

"Mostly Beam." I nodded. He sighed.

"And you already know he's the best fighter either of us has ever seen, capable of killing orcs by the dozen if he has to, and probably dancing around their patrols by jumping from roof to roof."

"Yep."

"So me telling you that doesn't actually achieve much," he continued.

"That's about right." I nodded.

Argar grunted again.

"Well, you've been told anyway. Beam will be fine, and it's not on you if he isn't. This needed doing. Sending anyone else to something he might have failed at would just be sending them to their death. Besides, he was the only one who could scale the wall fast enough."

When he put it like that, it was so very tempting to actually stop being pissed with myself. Instead I just got to my feet with a grunt.

"I'm in the mood for something to take my mind off of it," I growled. "Let's go a few rounds."

Argar grinned.

Fighting Argar is an exercise in arrogance, at least when one happens to have the superhuman strength of ten adult men in a single body. He was still stronger than me, by a fair amount, but that difference wasn't exponential anymore, and I was a lot faster. I danced around him, clipping him with jabs and smacks while he hissed. The pain wasn't really anything significant for him. We were sparring with thick wooden swords that, if I had swung hard enough to actually hurt Argar, would have snapped in half. But it annoyed him. It annoyed him very much.

Every now and then, Argar would catch me with his own swing, and Helena had to order him to switch to big logs after the second consecutive practice sword he snapped against my body. I was fine of course, though bruised. And the sparring continued for a good hour.

By the time we were both done, muscles burning and bodies so exerted that I actually felt hot despite the cold around us, the sky was darkening. We took our seats around one of several fires set up in the camp.

It wasn't more than a few minutes after the night came until I was thinking about Beam again. It was all well and good to distract myself, but the simple fact remained that my friend might die at any moment. And I'd be the reason if he did. I didn't sleep well that night.

CHAPTER TWENTY-TWO

Beam's POV: Day 143
Current Wealth: 712 gold, 26 silver, 14 copper

Lady Adannaya had a disquieting way of talking as if she were giving orders that, for reasons unknown to all but her, she already knew for a fact would be obeyed. I figured she was an Akanite, one of Shango's contributions to the lore. West African inspired from some distant lands, and they had their shit together a bit more than the regions we were currently stuck in. Lucky me.

"You will tell me your intentions and plans for Swanhen," she said, sharpness in her voice just a hair beyond schoolteacher and a whisper shy of angry general.

Faced with that, I couldn't really think of anything better to do than just obey.

"I'm here to help," I told her. "Swanhen, its people. Whoever I can. I'm here to liberate the town from the orcs, and help people regain some semblance of peace in their lives." It sounded pretty good, said aloud. The sort of thing an actual hero might say, but Adannaya did not seem impressed.

"And did you consider the effects of your interference?" she pressed. "That you might inspire further cruelty from the orcs, which, in your absence, will be taken out on the people you claim to be here for?"

I had, actually. Solitaire had mentioned it, and I'd come to picture it myself. Something about living in Redacle taught you how bad people think. Maybe it was the constant exposure to bad people.

"Yes," I replied, meeting her eye, not blinking. "But I'm not going to be held accountable for other people's cruelty. If the only way I can help is by causing more harm in the short term, I'll do it. It'll be worth it if people end up freed after the fact."

Adannaya looked at me long and hard, then nodded.

"Good," she said at last. "I am glad to see you are not a fool who failed to consider such things, or a coward who would be daunted into inaction by them. I believe we can work together."

It was a bit jarring to see her leap from conversational threads like that, and more jarring still to find out I had, apparently, been sitting through a test this whole time. I tried to keep up anyway.

"What do you know of the orcs?" I asked. She was answering almost before I'd finished speaking.

"They are organized, uncommonly so, and their technology is of almost human grade. They number perhaps six thousand, or as low as four, and seem to be taking efforts to obfuscate their true count. I would imagine they are closer to the lower end based off of this. Their leader is Guraganar the Machinator. Have you heard of him?"

I had not and saw no point in hiding my ignorance.

"He is one of the deadlier among their kind," she explained. "Perhaps in the top three or five among them in martial skill. And at least is believed to be the reason for their unusual technological potence. Here in Swanhen, he leads the orcs. Do you know how orcs select their leaders?"

I considered it. "Strength." I shrugged. "Charisma also."

"Charisma," she echoed. "That is what it comes down to in the end. They are emotional creatures, and unlike us have little control over their instincts. Orcs will invariably follow whichever among them seems most impressive, with little thought to their particular suitability for the role of leader. Which means that their impression of which orcs would be best to follow after as a leader are inherently subjective and variable."

I nodded along, seeing the logic now.

"You want to assassinate Guraganar," I noted. "And hope that his death will cause their cohesion here to collapse."

"I do," Adannaya confirmed. "And thus far, I have been met with a single major obstacle. He is seven feet tall, as strong as twenty men, and blocked the last assassin's sword with a forearm before proceeding to remove their head with strength alone. The wound left in his flesh was shallow enough to heal in a week. He was not wearing his armor."

Ah. Yeah, now I saw how it was. Sneaking one assassin into one room was easy enough, but Adannaya's issue was that unless she found a particularly tough one, she'd need to sneak in a dozen, or a score.

And I, as it happened, was that particularly tough one.

"So you want *me* to assassinate Guraganar." I smiled to hide my nerves. "That's an awful lot of risk being taken on my part."

She held my gaze, as if it were perfectly natural to ask a man to risk his life.

"You said you wanted to help." She shrugged. "Here is your opportunity to do so. Unless you have a better way to damage the orcs on a grander scale? They really are numerous, and so far you've killed . . . a hundredth of them? Less? I don't suppose you plan on remaining undetected and prolifically violent for months to whittle away their numbers and hoping all the while that they do not become more active in hunting you down?"

It was like talking to Shango, worse than Solitaire in some ways. Everything I said was just ammunition she used; everything *she* said gave me something new to be uncertain about. Always twisting my own mind up in knots until I wasn't even sure what I was doing. It was eerie. We really were meeting a lot of bizarrely clever people in this world, and not all of them, I realized, would be allies. Our luck wouldn't hold against people who saw all the angles like my brothers did. It wouldn't hold at all.

"You're really sure that killing Guraganar will cause that much damage to the orcs' organization?" I asked, not actually that skeptical, but wanting to see how she'd go about defending the idea.

"Much of what galvanizes these orcs," she began, impatiently—almost irritably—"is the image Guraganar has cultivated around himself. He presents as some genius revolutionary, a being of impossible, even miraculous insight. He seems to deliberately leave it ambiguous, where possible, how much of his work is produced by knowledge of physical matter and how much from some arcane or even demonic power. That sort of weight of reputation is not something that will be easily replaced once removed from the forces."

Put like that, it made a fair amount of sense. There was really only one small issue.

"How exactly do you expect me to close in and kill this orc when, presumably, he's surrounded by a lot of others, all of which are better equipped than most of their kind and stronger than almost all of ours?"

It wasn't that I wasn't *willing*, it's just that I didn't want to die horribly for no reason and achieving nothing. Fortunately, Adannaya seemed to have a solution for this just as she had all others. It was delivered, of course, without the slightest smile.

"There's a woman he sees," she told me. "A human woman. A traveler, I believe, unfortunate enough to get caught up in this affair, then more unfortunate still in catching the orc's eye. Guraganar is rather regular about visiting her, and you will find him doing so tonight."

Not the most pleasant scene to be waiting at, but then assassination wasn't the most pleasant job to be waiting for either. I'd done worse, anyway, since coming to this world. And helped a whole lot worse still. You didn't come through Redacle with clean hands. At least not if they were still attached to you.

"Alright," I said at last, steeling myself like I always did. This wasn't about me; it was about my brothers. What they had planned—what we were going to do. The people we could help if we'd just stop groveling around powerless and scared. The world we'd built to be so shitty and now had the chance to save. "I'll do it."

It really wasn't that hard to get into the building, even without being seen. You'd be amazed how infrequently people look up. People who aren't Solitaire, that is, who was ever vigilant about keeping himself safe from ambush by the Fogmen. I don't know what that means, but I do know climbing. I got myself up onto the building's roof and in through its top windows in moments.

The longest pause had been in preparation. I'd asked for a bow and arrow first and stashed that away on myself before hiding. I wasn't going to use either for combat. Their function was far more important. The woman whose rooms I was in didn't even know I was there, and shortly after, we were no longer alone. Guraganar entered with footsteps so heavy I heard the floorboards creak even from my hiding spot, and he was loud about getting down to business. I waited though.

He was alone, but he was still powerful. I wanted him as distracted as possible before I made my move. One second, another. Then I came out. As long as I was willing to wait, with what was about to happen to that woman, and as little as I could afford to risk. But my error became clear as I exited.

Guraganar was not, in fact, alone. And he wasn't busy. He was staring at me straight ahead, with four others right next to him. Each one was taller than me, all of them were almost a meter wide at the shoulder, and all of them were covered in metal. They didn't look happy to see me.

CHAPTER TWENTY-THREE

Beam's POV: Day 143
Current Wealth: 712 gold, 26 silver, 14 copper

It was times like this that I really felt the difference between my style of combat expertise and Solitaire's, because my reactions were terribly, critically slow. Long moments of staring incomprehension and inactivity as the orcs moved for me.

Fortunately, I'd gotten so fast that what felt like a full second for me was barely the blink of an eye for them. I'd already whipped into motion before any of them had more than halved the few meters between us.

I turned and ran like fuck. *Obviously.* Because no matter what people called me, I actually wasn't a hero, and I wasn't going to die like one. Heroes died in much the same way as dumbasses and were differentiated in memory mainly through other people's fondness. The window smashed in front of me—wood, not glass, and reduced to a blizzard of splinters as I crashed into it. Ahead was a thirty-foot drop down onto hard cobbled road.

But thirty feet was an age to fall, for me, and I'd twisted in the air to land on my feet long before impact. I barely even felt the shock of it run up through my ankles, then I was running. I was probably a good twenty, maybe thirty meters from the window when I heard the bowstring from back where I'd leaped. My thoughts were quickened by fear, and my armor formed around me just in time. I felt what *seemed* like a punch to the back of the head and only realized otherwise when the snapped pieces of projectile went spinning ahead of me as they bounced off.

Lucky, that. But I'd need a lot more luck, because now I saw the teeth of the trap. More orcs, closing in and cutting me off as they stepped out into alleys and . . . Well. Everywhere else I might run, including the tops of roofs. There had to be a hundred of them.

Certainly felt like there were a hundred arrows. They came at me from all sides. Big, sweeping, jagged, and . . . slow. I dodged, watching one whip by where my face had just been, then another. It actually made me giddy. I was dodging *arrows*.

Well, not for long. Soon enough, I was taking more hits than not, and most I didn't even see coming. There were just too many orcs, firing from too many sides, and they were closing the distance with each barrage. My armor was holding—though shivering with the strain—but I couldn't count on that for long. I picked out the weakest-looking section of enemies . . .

Then went for the second weakest. I really wasn't in the mood to be ambushed again.

A dozen orcs up ahead, half had bows. I was ten meters from them when the volley came and I swept out with my ethereal sword. One arrow just came apart into a cloud of wooden slivers as I clipped it; another glanced from the base. One more I dodged. The remaining three hit my breastplate and went flying away, leaving little cracks to remember them by. Somehow I knew that if I'd only been in chain mail, any one of those would have killed me.

The orcs seemed just as surprised as I was, and a lot more scared. Those who hadn't been armed with bows stepped forward, swinging axes and clubs that were slower even than their arrows. I smacked them aside, twisted out of the way. Battered each and every swing from reaching me like I was watching limbs dragging through water, then I countered. Big as they were, armored as they were, it didn't even take all my strength to kill each of the orcs with a single swing. Iron fell in fractured chunks as they died, raining hot blood everywhere.

By then, the archers had run. Except one. His arrow hit dead center at practically zero range and left another crack in my breastplate. Brave, this one, so I cut his head off to make sure his bravery didn't get any of my friends killed later.

I'd just turned to continue down my newly cleared corridor when the entire world turned into a wave of dust and debris.

The blast of stone narrowly missed me, and I barely caught what it even was before it hit the ground a meter ahead and blew apart under its own speed. Flecks of rock struck my skin and armor, cracking and scraping as I stumbled away, eyes teary and senses dazzled. More orcs were coming by the time I righted myself, and then I saw him.

Guraganar wasn't much bigger than most of his men, really, and was pretty average for the handful of bruisers he'd tried to rope me into a close quarters fight with. But the magic around him was tangible. It was like staring down Corvan, almost, or close enough. Setting my teeth on edge, my skin tingling. Sending a shiver down my spine.

Rocks were floating around him, the size of my head. Magically floating. Because, of course, the orc was a fucking magus. He gestured, and the projectiles came shooting out.

I moved as best I could and dodged one pretty well. The other hit me like a trebuchet stone. My feet left the ground, and for a second, all I heard was screaming wind and all I felt was my guts trying to escape. Then I landed, sliding and scraping, rolling and coughing as I came to rest a dozen meters back from where I'd been standing. A dozen? No. More. Many more.

In one motion, I lunged to my feet, so quick and explosive I left myself dizzy for a second and came critically close to being hit by another stone. My dodge took me to the path of another, which I anticipated and blocked with a hastily conjured shield. The length of ethereal matter split open as the stone crashed into it, and for the second time I was sent flying head over heels.

Had the King of Blades hit me this hard? Maybe harder. I'd been wearing armor when I fought him, not having needed to sneakily climb a big wall beforehand, and there was less weight to toss now. But that weight was less protected, and I was feeling every impact as a strain on my superhuman body.

If I'd been a normal person, I knew, I'd be dead already. Magical armor or not, that first hit alone would have snapped me like a twig. As things were, I could barely keep moving, worried with every shuddery, twitchy stride that I'd broken a rib, a limb, or something else. And the orcs just kept coming.

I shambled away, rolled from the path of another boulder, and took off at a sprint. It was a pleasant surprise to find that my body was still capable of that much, at least, and I picked up speed quickly. Periodically, I'd dart to one side, feeling the projectiles miss, ignoring the arrows that hit. Even to this day, I barely remember what came next. An orc reared up in front of me at one point, too fast for me to conjure a weapon, so I just hammer fisted his skull down into the spine. An arrow actually came so close to my eyes I felt it pass on the wind, and a clipping blow from that fucking magus sent me spinning 360 degrees to just level out and maintain my sprint. Slowly though, surely, the distance between us increased. Their ranged attacks became less accurate, their interruptions through melee less frequent. Eventually, I had a nice gap separating us.

That didn't stop me from running though. Even exhaustion didn't. It was only the realization that I'd reached the farthest place possible from the site of my ambush that finally got me to slow down, crawl my way onto a rooftop, and pause to check my injuries. Contrary to my fears, they were manageable.

Lots of bruising, of course, and I thought, but didn't know, I'd cracked one of my lower ribs from that big direct hit. Otherwise I was fine. The fall hadn't even caused me pain in the moment, none of the arrows had gotten past my armor, and I'd not taken any real hits but that. In a way, it was comforting. Mostly, it was nerve-racking. I'd gotten used to being powerful for a second there, gotten cocky. But there were still threats in this world. Could I have taken Guraganar alone? I thought so, especially in closer quarters. But he hadn't been alone. And that had been enough to almost kill me.

Standing, groaning, I got moving again, figuring that the *farthest* spot from the point of my ambush was probably an easier hiding spot to find than certain others I might pick. The taste of my failure was salty in my mouth, tangy. Like I was sucking on iron.

Oh, no. That was just the blood. Easy mistake to make.

CHAPTER TWENTY-FOUR

Beam's POV: Day 143
Current Wealth: 712 gold, 26 silver, 14 copper

I hadn't gotten away, and the trap was closing even now. It had been a mistake to sprint where I had in the first place. That mistake might kill me.

The orcs had, in fact, figured out where I was heading, and they were a lot more communicative and coordinated than even Adannaya had predicted. It wasn't long before they were swarming around in search of me. And more than a few, of course, were scraping the rooftops.

Well, I didn't stay put. And I still had more or less all my speed despite the bruising I'd gotten, but there were only so many places to run that weren't already orc'd. And those places were shrinking by the minute.

I scrambled around like a damned rat, like Solitaire. Dodging one party only to almost throw myself ahead of another, scurrying around corners and behind stares, keenly aware all the time that a single sentry in an elevated position might spot me anyway. My heart had graduated from drum to orchestra a while ago, and my blood felt physically *hot* in my veins. But there was still nothing I could do but what I was doing.

My mistakes had been made; my situation was decided. All I had available to me now, my only choice, was whether to keep prolonging the inevitable or not. I opted to continue. The net came closer, the noose tighter, and I kept scrambling away for every further second I could. Death, it seemed, had finally caught up to Beam Belahont.

And then it backed off.

It was slow at first, almost hard to see, but within a minute or two, I saw entire forces of orcs peeling back and rushing elsewhere. Confusion followed that, and, ridiculously, suspicion. Lucky breaks just didn't happen in Redacle. A mass hysteria, right when they were about to catch me? The idea that it was somehow intentional mercy was even more far-fetched.

However I saw the cause soon enough, and it lit my face up in a triumphant grin.

The gate, the main gate, was wide-open, and people were cutting through it in a great wedge. Shields up, spears out, one or two figures among them towering over the rest. Argar was clear as day, with most of the other men falling short of his shoulder, but I saw Helena and the rest too. Not a lot, less than thirty. But my God, did they feel like a reinforcement of titans.

Of course they were a good while away from me, but clearly the orcs had recognized the threat they posed. Somehow they'd taken the gate and opened it for the rest of their forces to cut in—maybe while I was distracting everyone—and now they were coming to get their friend back. Only Solitaire wasn't among the ranks.

No, Solitaire was on a rooftop, where masses of orcs had a clear view as he performed his ceremonial war dance. Even I don't know what that means, except that it usually comes out in one of his more violent episodes. Today was looking to be very bloody.

The orcs were congealing together as fast as they could, but plenty among them—the brave or the stupid—were trying to mount defenses and intercept the attackers with their limited squads or clusters. It wasn't working. Modern steel made brigandines sturdy enough to turn away axes swung by all but the toughest of them, and our future-sharp spears were biting deep into all the joints Helena had taught the men to aim for when fighting against heavy armor. That, and the difference in unit cohesion was incomparable.

It was like watching a boulder roll over pebbles.

But that wouldn't hold long. There were a lot of pebbles, and the longer this assault lasted, the faster they'd pile up into a great enough mass to stop it. This attack had less time left in its lifespan than my metaphor. It needed someone running interference.

Someone, I realized, that Solitaire had intended to be me. Because he didn't make the sorts of mistakes that would have led to the failure I had to prevent now.

I got moving.

The closest squad to me, the one that had been just on the verge of capturing me, was the first one I fell upon. Eight orcs, in all, and pretty much every one of them was as well armed as the standard for this horde. It *might* have been a struggle, if I hadn't dropped down with surprise on my side. Two were dead before the rest even knew I was attacking them, and their counters came slowly and sluggishly. I breezed aside from lethargic swings, going low and taking another leg off at the knee before righting, backing off, keeping them from surrounding me, and pouncing the moment one started pulling ahead of the rest. Four now, and they started splitting up to get me from all sides at once.

So I picked one and ran him down alone. Then the remaining three all died one by one, cohesion destroyed by losing so many so fast. With one squad erased, I went looking for another. Then another.

Training with Helena—or rather helping her train others—had taught me something about the sorts of things that were necessary in big, coordinated group fights. Things I'd never have considered as a duelist and sportsman. For one thing, it was vital that you knew where everyone was, as much as you could. I wasn't making much numeric difference by killing off individual squads—what was twenty men in an army of thousands—but I was throwing whatever plans they might be helping out of whack.

If the enemy planned to hold Solitaire back with a few units while others combined to form a more solid defense, then killing those pinning squads off before they could do it would have an exponentially greater effect than their deaths alone.

But only if I was smart about it, so I moved ahead. I came to squads that were closing in on one another—my roof hopping giving me a great holistic view of the conflict—and moved to cut them off. With my speed, I could reach them well before they reached one another, and none took more than a few seconds to cut apart. Minutes passed before I finally realized there were no more individual lines running around.

The enemy had started falling back, and now they'd formed their mass. Not a lot of orcs, compared to their true numbers—seemingly nine-tenths were split out across the city, not sure what was happening—but those few who'd gathered together still made a hundreds-strong force to meet the Belahont crew. I moved in to unite with my own side as they charged, both forces apparently content on meeting in one of the narrower streets, a section of town with many small buildings separated by a network of crisscrossing roads and alleys.

By the time I came, Solitaire was giving his speech.

"Alright!" he snarled, a giggle to his voice. *"I'll make this quick. Fucking kill them all and if anyone doesn't get at least two before dying, I'll eat their corpse!"*

By the looks on our men's faces, they believed him. Our men formed up into a shielded formation, weapons high and defenses ready. The orcs were less restrained. They came charging in as a great mob, like watching a mountain struck by a river. The carnage was so sudden, so revolting in its intensity, that I almost tasted it.

But I got stuck right in with the rest of them. Of course I did. You didn't come through Redacle with clean hands.

CHAPTER TWENTY-FIVE

Solitaire's POV: Day 143
Current Wealth: 712 gold, 26 silver, 14 copper

I didn't like fighting, honest. Too messy, too dangerous. Too much risk of me being the one to bite it. I liked hurting people though, and I liked watching a good plan come together. On balance, I decided the first clash of our men and the orcs was a generally positive experience, though it certainly could've been better.

A club came at me, a big, mean club swung by a big, mean orc. I sidestepped, let it whip by me, and stuck a knife down to the hilt in its wielder's armpit. I felt the blade snap off against iron plating as it actually exited the shoulder and crunched up into the pauldron from below. By then though I was twisting around as I caught movement behind me and lashed back to avoid an axe. I did. Barely, and the axe kept coming right up until a spear gutted the giant bastard holding it.

There's always a temptation to waste time and watch a kill finish when you're fighting for real. I'd learned that much well since I came to Redacle. I ignored that temptation and moved on to the next enemy. A big orc came thundering up to our formation, and I splashed him with enough nitro to reverse his momentum as it blasted his chest open. Arrows spit down at us in plunging volleys, sent shooting back to hit their own charging men by Corvan's winds. Argar . . . Argar, he was having the time of his life. A giant laughing golem of meat and steel plates whipping around a pair of bearded axes in each hand, so big most men could barely swing a single of them. He took off heads, limbs. Split helmets completely in half, gouged deep into breastplates, and sent rivers of blood sizzling in cold air out of the jagged cuts.

Beside him, Helena was the opposite in every way, lacking his physicality but killing with a mechanical precision. She went for joints with her spear in short, fierce jabs that never committed too much of her weight to any one attack, while her shield staved off counters better than any of our twen's. This was the style we'd passed onto our unit, thanks to her expertise in teaching it, and with the small alleys around us, it was devastatingly effective. We'd split our forces to advance down two routes, each picking a set of thin streets to cross, both chosen to be sized just right that there was no room around us in them.

I was in the first group; the other had more of the trainees but Beam to even things out. I saw a rank of orcs forming up ahead, ready to meet our shield wall with a formed defense of their own. They had the numbers, with ranks maybe four times deeper than ours, and it was doomed to be a bloody one.

Right up until Beam's group smashed into them from their flank.

The chaos was instantaneous, and we hurried in charging over to compound it. Orc shields turned one way and the other, forced to block two directions at once and managing neither. Corvan doused the center with a fireball so potent, it killed half a dozen with that single casting, and our rocketeers managed almost as much damage with their own projectiles. By the time we came to aid Beam, there wasn't much form left to the formation, and we cut it apart in moments. Double our number turned into mincemeat and fleeing men.

It was scary, honestly, what a decent attack can do, and incredibly empowering. But we'd killed only a hundred orcs just now, and maybe twice that in smaller groups so far. They still had plenty more fight left in them. Their numbers were in the thousands.

I could tell, despite our success in winning short term, that the overall plan had failed. Beam had sent me the info needed for it, telling me everything he'd seen and learned with a note attached to an arrow. English, not any Redaclan language, so none but I could read it. I'd timed this attack to come just a few minutes after his assassination of the orc leader, and if he'd succeeded in that then it would've meant we were falling on their forces at their most disorganized. We might have killed thousands, and at worst we'd have sent a lot spewing out of the town.

That, as far as I could tell, was more luck than we'd had, but the secondary function had worked at least. We'd given Beam an opening to escape after his assassination failed, and very possibly saved his life. He was returning the favor by personally killing as many of the enemy as any three of us, and perhaps all the recruits combined.

Another arrow volley was knocked aside by Corvan, and another infantry unit got eaten alive by ours. I realized there was a lethal combination going on that we'd not even planned for. Enemies who bunched together were susceptible to Corvan and the rocketeers, their tight formations letting each fireball or rocket kill several targets at once and mount up casualties. If they spread out, the damage was limited. But they were fodder for our own infantry's overlapping shields and thick armor.

We cannibalized one unit after another, but I kept my eyes out the entire time for enemy reinforcements. We were still a force of dozens against an occupation of thousands, and sure enough, after fifteen minutes of fighting, I caught glimpses of more motion building to the side of us. A mass of bodies advancing between buildings just fifty meters from the carpet of corpses we were making.

There really were quite a lot. A wall of them, I'd say, all big and ironclad, and clearly well organized. Beam winced, and I followed his gaze to see a taller one with boulders levitating around him at the front. Their leader, I guessed. Funny, the letter hadn't mentioned him being a magus.

"Retreat!" I squawked like a majestic fucking eagle having its neck wrung by several boa constrictors and a serial strangler. Not my finest order, I'll admit, but there's really only so much coolness you can slip into what is fundamentally a command meaning "turn around and leg it before we die."

Fortunately, we'd drilled that too. If you couldn't run away from a fight then you wouldn't last very long having them. That was a lesson dear old mum had taught me very early on indeed, and it brought a prideful tear to my eye to watch my young grasshoppers scrambling away like such cowardly little rats alongside me.

We didn't flee the town of course; that would be utterly unthinkable. After today, there wasn't a chance we'd be getting through the gates again. This little blitzkrieg of ours would have made the orcs doubly cautious against attacks in the future. They knew now that our force of twenty-nine was more than equal to any hundred of theirs. Even any two or three hundred. We were no longer something to be ignored or tolerated. They'd be going for the kill now.

So our fallback point had to be *defensible.*

Good thing about having such a small force of course was that there was never a shortage of defensible places you could squeeze into. While I'd been squatting on top of that building and doing my ceremonial war dance, I'd taken the opportunity to scan as much of the town as I could and commit its layout to memory. There was a very robust-looking warehouse just a quarter mile from our current location, and I directed us toward it promptly.

Difficult to move a large group with any great speed. Particularly when they're weighed down by armor and weaponry and you don't want anyone to lag behind. Difficult for twenty-nine, but impossible for the thousands that were following us. The distance only grew as we scurried off like the mighty little rodents we were, reaching the warehouse in no time at all.

It was just barely big enough to fit everyone in with ample storage and movement room, the storehouse of a smaller town rather than the city that it was, and we wasted no time in cramming ourselves past its doors. Within minutes, the warehouse was beset by the sounds of an army of footfalls crunching around from all sides.

But they didn't get closer than hearing distance; they didn't turn into an attack. I waited a minute, until my brain started vibrating with the urge to start digging up the cobbled floor for hidden traps, and then slowly shuffled to one of the windows and peeked outside.

The orcs were there of course, and there were a *lot* of them. Three thousand two hundred, at an eyeballed guesstimate. My more concerted calculations narrowed that down by a further fifty.

"Beam," I began. "I need you to take the next opening you can find and run off to fetch something we stashed outside. This is gonna get dicey."

CHAPTER TWENTY-SIX

Shango's POV: Day 144
Current Wealth: 713 gold, 21 silver, 32 copper

It was the day of the ball, and my wife was still mad at me. That much was to be expected though. Such things tend to happen when one arranges a ball knowing that it will make one's wife mad. Honestly, I was starting to get tired of Phelia's attitude. She'd sustained it for the entire day since our last talk. If Solitaire were here, no doubt, he'd be able to explain exactly what was going on in her head. That's what empaths were good for—stupid people, angry people, and crazy people. Logical reasoning was all well and good, but aimed at human behavior, there were a lot of cases where it fell through.

Fortunately, I had bigger concerns than one person, even if she did have unfettered access to my genitals. We were soon dealing with the arrival of our guests.

And holy fuck were there a lot.

I mean of course there were; they were poor people. Growing up as a billionaire's son did give me a bit of a sheltered experience of the world, but I knew enough to know that there were always more poor people. They were like something as numerous as cockroaches but that Solitaire didn't headbutt you for comparing the working class to. And they just kept coming.

Phelia was hanging close by me—something about marital duties to be seen together in public—and she was doing a good job of controlling her feelings. Ish. They still showed on her face. Clearly she had never trained for the levels of tolerance needed to put up with so many lower-class presences at a time, and each new handful that slipped into the hall was straining her already thin patience ever more.

I was fairly sure she wouldn't snap. She was too clever and controlled for that. But I could practically feel the next few weeks of my life becoming even more unpleasant as her brain whirred away to coin some new and unusual punishments for me.

But they really did just keep flowing into the place, and poor Phelia looked like she was approaching a breaking point.

"There's so many," she hissed. "Hundreds, thousands. How can you expect to watch them all at once? They'll have the place pilfered."

"I've moved all the valuables out of the sections we'll be allowing them in," I told her. Phelia relaxed slightly.

"That's something then," she noted. "At least you can understand their tendency toward thievery, if nothing else about them."

I was actually starting to get annoyed now. I usually have a strong tolerance for casual evil and bigotry in other people—you need to where I'm from—but Phelia seemed to be doing her best to test that to its limits.

So it was a relief, then, when Arthur made his way over.

"Lady Velaharo," he breathed, eyeing Phelia and grinning so warmly that I thought my wife might drop dead from a handsomeness overdose. "I must say you have surprised me. This event of yours—allowing all these poor, impoverished souls to escape the cold and eat their fill for this night—it truly warms my heart."

Phelia eyed him, not seeming to know what to say at first.

"Oh, well, I, uh. This was actually—"

Arthur cut her off with a hand on her shoulder.

"Truly, you are a cut removed from other nobles. Too many of our kind allow themselves to remain closed off to the plight of the common man, to blame them for their own misfortunes even as they starve and die. It is wonderful to know you and your husband are not counted among them."

Phelia's face burned like a tomato, skin reddening with a flush that almost made me worry if she was going to pop something. She smiled though.

"Thank you, sir." My wife beamed. "But really, the work was all my husband's."

She drifted off at that, mood seeming lifted. It was only when she'd left our sight that I turned to Arthur and slipped him the pouch of silver.

"Nice work," I told him as he pocketed the cash. "You really do know how to lay it on thick."

"Yes, well, charming noblewomen can be as important as charming the men sometimes." Arthur smiled. He really was annoyingly handsome. Bastard.

We shared a look of appreciation though, one scumbag to another, and he made his way off to continue bodyguarding.

"He's going to be busy," Alora told me, having snuck up behind me somehow without my hearing her. Even in steel lamellar armor. I didn't jump though, used to this now.

"How so?" I asked.

Alora looked at me with a glare that made the sun seem cold.

"Because you invited hundreds of strangers into our base of operations, we're both going to be very busy. Tonight is the best chance to kill you anyone's going to have for a long while."

I winced, seeing her point. "Sorry about that," I murmured. "But it's necessary, long-term survival winning out over short-term."

Alora swore and stormed off. I figured that was about as close to an accord as I was going to get with her on this and headed away to see to my own business too. After all, I was the reason these people were here. I was the one who needed to win them over.

It was really not categorically dissimilar to doing the same thing with the nobility of Elswick, save for a single key detail. These people offered a lot less in terms of mutual benefit.

Which was understandable because they *had* virtually nothing. But it still meant that every deal I granted was, in some small way, a diminishment. I'd not been presumptuous in saying it was a basic lack of altruism and decency that motivated their dismissal by the other nobles, or even that it was a tiny bit stupid for my rivals not to appeal to such a great mass of human life. But this, of course, was the basic motivator. Cost-benefit. There wasn't much profit in appealing to an impoverished underclass. That was, in fact, in accordance with their civilization's design.

Some of them, really, I wished I could have granted anyway. Most had a point; some had a purpose worth dying for. But there were far too many of those for one man to die for them all, and so I had to be careful in picking which ones I took on. I ignored the majority of them, always polite and cordial but never committing.

There were spies here, I knew it. There had to be. If I were any of my enemies, and even half my actual intelligence, there would be spies here, and so, I knew, there were spies. Best not to let them see what I was doing. Let them think this was just a search for new deals, see me spending my night whittling away the hours in attempts at finding them.

Smoke screens were important when the whole world had its eyes on you, and only just less so when a whole city did.

One man did stick out to me of course. There would always have been at least one. Henry Grimworth, visiting on behalf of the Jeleheim. He was a tall man, for a commoner, and rapier lean with skin like hard leather, dark hair, and darker eyes. He had that grim, hooded look to his gaze that I recognized from Solitaire. A mad dog, ready for violence to emerge at any moment and agitated with each one it didn't. He spoke gruffly and without mincing too many words. I could appreciate that. I was a busy man tonight.

"Lord Belahont," he began, nodding but not quite bowing. "Thank you for doing this, and for hearing me out."

"It is important to be aware of what the little people think," I told him diplomatically. I didn't miss his face twitching at that. Like Solitaire or Elizabeth.

"Yes, well, I'll be brief. I represent the Jeleheim, a group formed to combat the growing cruelties and abuses of the Dead Edge. I believe you've had a run-in with them before. We're limited, for now, but growing in power, and with a noble like you behind us, I know we could do more to help people. To genuinely make Elswick a better place, a better place for *all*."

Well, that sounded good. It sounded very good—and useful. This one had a touch of violence to him that spoke of a strong capacity for getting shit done.

"I see. How nice for you," I replied, keeping my face and voice carefully apathetic. I saw the grinding of teeth and the dropping of eyes as I did and actually felt a stab of guilt to be crushing the man's hopes so thoroughly. But it was necessary. I couldn't just pounce on this.

I knew for a fact there were spies here.

"Is there anything else you wished to discuss?" I asked, resisting the urge to throw in some banal comment about shoes or whatever else. If I ladled it on too thick, a word-for-word report would make it obvious to anyone who'd actually spoken to me that this was just a ploy. Even as things stood, Viras might see through it anyway. It still bothered me how little I knew about him.

"That was all, my lord," Henry replied, eyes dropping to the ground and, I didn't doubt, barely hiding some expression of utter fury. "Thank you for your time."

I watched as he trudged off and made a note of his name. Then I moved on to other matters.

There were, of course, so very many things that demanded the attention of a lord of my status.

INTERLUDE THREE

Henry did not stay at the ball for long after his meeting with Lord Shango. That short conversation alone had been all he'd needed to see the futility of his presence there. He left the warm, expansive halls and trod home through the frigid mists of Elswick a defeated man.

But that was nothing new. Defeat was a companion he'd become well acquainted with over the years. It was almost comforting to feel it draped around him. Better than false hope, for sure. Defeat held no further surprises for him, no treacherous twists or ruinous turns.

It was a long time before he reached his house. Velaharo Mansion was far from anything peasant related. It was far from them in nature too. Henry's house could have fit alongside all his neighbors' within the hall he'd just been attending a ball in and still had over half the space to spare. He felt no stab of jealousy at that, but the bitterness was intense as ever.

"I'm home," Henry called out, keeping his voice low as he entered, knowing the children would be asleep at so late an hour. Kat was up though and turned to stand as he entered their living room, smiling up at him expectantly.

"How did it go?"

Henry could barely stand to reply.

"Badly," he croaked, not looking at his wife's face but feeling the way it must have fallen all the same. Every word out of Henry's mouth was like a dagger twisting into his own guts. "He was just like all the rest, barely even saw me. I was lucky enough, I suppose, to have gotten the chance to even speak, but we'll get no help from Lord Shango."

Finally, he made himself look up and felt his heart break at Kat's face.

"Why did he even host the ball then?" she asked.

Henry could only shrug. "To earn goodwill with the people, just not at any expense to him I suppose. As I said, he's just like the rest in the end. Perhaps a bit more proactive and desperate for allies but nothing fundamentally different."

Silence hung between them like a condemned man, and soon it was too much to bear.

"I'm going outside for a drink," Henry said at last, taking his leave without another word. He couldn't face her. Not sober.

The air was cold, almost painfully so, but his bottle of home-brewed booze kept him warm enough. Besides, a sharp, cutting wind was just what Henry deserved for letting such stupid hope enter his wits. He was left to enjoy its tortures only for a few minutes when something caught his eye in the dark.

Something moving.

Booze was expensive, even brewed oneself, but life was more so. Henry hurled the half-emptied bottle into the dark and was gratified to see whatever shape he thought he'd glimpsed twisting to avoid it. His cleaver was out before he'd taken his first step, and he was on the newcomer within two more. A downward swing came inches from opening up their throat and forced them into the light.

Alora the Red Blade. He recognized her. Tall, lean—less soft fat and more hard muscle than was common for a woman, even if she had no great bulk—and clad now in glinting steel lamellar plates that covered most of her body. That explained the light movements. She was favoring thinner armor with an emphasis on mobility and carefully padded creases where steel would otherwise have scraped against steel. It was a masterwork, and a great advantage.

Henry wondered, at that moment, whether he might die. Then banished the thought and continued his attack. No time for worrying, not when a noble's assassin was staring him down.

She had a weapon out now too, a shortsword. It came up to stop his next hacking swing with a tremble down Henry's arm and a spitting burst of sparks into the air. Alora the Red Blade took a step back, balance strong but body weaker than his own. She was moving before Henry, more gracefully. He barely parried her next swing— though only the flat of her sword would have caught him—and was sent reeling as a boot to the gut followed it.

Clad in steel, that kick hurt. What hurt more was the smack that followed, her sword crunching into his face like an iron bar. Again, the flat, not the blade, but it sent sparks dancing in Henry's eye. He swung blindly, got lucky, forced her back long enough to recover, then swung again. Once more, steel bit into steel, but this time Henry saw a great chunk smashed free of his cleaver. Whatever this woman's sword was made of, its metal was sturdier than the construction of his own. He felt a shiver at the thought of how sharp it might be.

Henry was drunk, and she was not. He was unarmored, and she was not. He was equipped by some peasant rabble's thievery and hoarded wealth, and she was not. Every advantage was hers except for one; Henry was not a tourney fighter. He'd never risked the annual bouts, which meant he knew what she could do, and she didn't know of him.

She always favored distance and offense to defense, and Henry guessed, correctly, that she would seize the initiative again. He left an opening, saw her notice it, and met her attempt to lunge in with an elbow to her face.

It hurt him, maybe as much as it did her. But it knocked her off-balance too. Henry brought his arm back and smashed his cleaver down onto Alora the Red Blade's head.

Her helmet, combined with his strength, smashed the blade to pieces, but she dropped onto a knee all the same. Henry kicked her in the face while she was down, then again, then again.

He had to press this chance; it might be his only one. But he got off no more than two additional stomps before Alora the Red Blade's leg flashed out and caught him in the calf. An explosion of pain, then a numbness ran through the meat of his limb as all the muscles went lax and useless. He limped back as she whipped to her feet, staring at him through those perfectly crafted eye slits like a hungering animal.

"I'm not here to fight," she said just as Henry was about to start backing off again. He paused. "I'm here to deliver a message from my employer, Lord Shango Velaharo. He's interested in working alongside you."

Henry paused.

"He seemed to be falling half asleep at my words earlier," he noted. If this was a trick, it didn't matter. He could use the time to recover from that kick, maybe give the frenzy of battle a few more moments to clear the alcohol from his system. Hard to get drunk, with his strength, and easy to get sober. A few minutes might be enough to level the playing field.

"He needed to look disinterested. The other nobles have eyes everywhere. But if he didn't care, I wouldn't be here talking to you now."

Henry considered that, drink-sluggish thoughts picking through what he knew, putting the information together.

"The . . . The ball was just to gather parties interested in causes like mine, so he could sift through who to contact later?"

"That's right." She sounded slightly impressed, but it was quickly stifled. "At the moment, all eyes are on us. Nobody will touch us directly, for now, but they'll all be watching us carefully. This means they won't be watching you, even if you were to suddenly start receiving the means to grow in power and influence through us. How many are you?"

". . . A few hundred," Henry whispered, almost not believing what he was hearing. Wanting to, so very much, but not daring to. Not wanting another crushing disappointment. "But that could increase if we had better weapons, better funds."

"I know," the Red Blade replied. "And that's the offer. You in or out?"

Henry didn't need to think about it for long.

"In," he breathed.

CHAPTER TWENTY-SEVEN

Solitaire's POV: Day 144
Current Wealth: 713 gold, 11 silver, 32 copper

I'd been having a pretty stressful time waiting for the orcs to get back to us, even after Beam returned. It wasn't that I was scared, you understand. I was just aware that we had upsettingly high odds of dying if things turned into a fight.

I didn't pace though. I wanted to—fuck did I want to—but nothing in the world made a human panic more than seeing fear in someone it was following. They're social creatures, and prone to deferring out of some need for guidance. People want to know there's something bigger than them they can put their faith in, and when that fails them . . . they get twitchy.

So I bottled all my emotions up and put on a stoic face. Fortunately, I wasn't left to do it for too long. I'd sent a messenger out with word offering a parley. Even that much had felt . . . dangerous. When you had thousands in your army, the idea of a messenger getting iced was nothing big, but for us it meant a 3 percent drop in our total number of fighters. I'd sent one of the recruits for this reason. Losing Magnus, Argar, or another of our elites would have hit harder than I was willing to risk.

The poor sod didn't get killed, though, and he returned with only the mildest tremble to him. I ordered that he be given a double ration of booze for his dangerous mission, and was pleased to hear that the suggestion for a parley had been accepted.

Soon after that, I was heading out myself. Keenly aware that this might just be a ploy on Guraganar's part to get me himself. Well, when *wasn't* I aware about a potential ploy to kill me?

The orcs sent out a few of theirs too to meet me. Guraganar and his retinue I'd guessed. Beam had mentioned four big bastards guarding the orc during his failed assassination, and I saw four now. I supposed they were regular bodyguards. Either that or the number was coincidental. Funny. It almost seemed redundant to give a seven-foot magus *bodyguards*.

On the other hand, Beam might have killed him without them. Magic or no.

Guraganar was a big fellow, there was no doubting that. Taller and broader than most of the other orcs, he looked like a big statue made out of violence and meanness. He glared at me, apparently having taken my successful little opening raid personally. Within those beady eyes though, I saw . . . absolutely nothing. No glimmer of hidden intellect. He was just pissed. Funny that.

"So, you are the giant human," the orc huffed, lips curling as if I were disgusting him. "Small, still, like the rest of your kind. One of your warriors is bigger, even."

I knew for a fact I was taller than most of these orcs, at least when I didn't slouch. He was just being a cock. Well, fine, I could beat him at that game like I beat everyone else.

"Who built your technology?" I asked. "It's not that I don't believe it was you, just that . . . well, you know, you're a moron, and whoever made your equipment wasn't, so I don't believe it was you."

Evidently, Chief Unga Bunga wasn't accustomed to being spoken to like that. I almost expected his face to drop off with the fury twisting it.

"You know nothing," he snarled, then inhaled, readying himself for a speech. "I am—"

"Bwah."

The orc hesitated, eyes narrowing.

"I am—"

"Brrrr," I cut in.

"I am—"

"Bloggledy blee."

"*I am*—"

"*Dubblyshlubbles!*" I added, matching his rise in volume. Finally, the orc snapped.

"*What are you*—"

"*Slogglefloggleblorgelblip!!*" I cried, quite enjoying the sight of several orcs standing back as if they were fearing for their lives. "Sorry, I just thought since you were going to spew mindless bullshit at me, I'd follow suit. Anything worth actually listening to to say, or should we continue?"

He wanted to kill me. He wanted to tear me apart, to *eat* me. I could feel it, smell it, taste it. Orcs were people enough that I felt their thoughts slithering into my mind just as keenly as anyone else's.

It didn't take long for anger to turn into murder, and murder was a motivator for all sorts.

"I wonder, are you lying about your strength too?" I asked, adding a physical element to the insults that I figured would deepen the orc's fury at them. It turns out, I'd figured right. I practically saw the muscles bunching under his neck and worried for a moment whether his head might come bursting off its shoulders. Alas, it did not. If I wanted him headless, I'd need to do it myself.

"I am ten times your strength!" the orc snarled, closing in now, standing just a foot back from me. I backed up, an inch. Too little for his men to see, too much for him not to. He needed to get a taste of bullying me, needed to want more.

"Why don't you prove it then?" I asked, adding a slight tremble to my voice. The meat on the hook. I saw beady eyes light up as all seven of Dumbass the Barbarian's neurons rubbed together in stumbling onto the obvious. "Come on," I urged him. "Prove yourself against us, or do you think a Belahont is too much for you to fight?"

I'd slipped that in on purpose of course. A Belahont, not me. Because I sure as fuck wasn't going to fight this giant idiot, but Beam would probably take him apart. If he agreed to fight *a Belahont*, then he'd agreed to die. And I could see the orc was tempted.

"You are arrogant," he hissed. "You overestimate yourself."

"Nah." I snorted. "And you'll see how wrong you are about that soon, as long as you're not too much of a quivering pussy to accept the challenge. Come on, the strongest orc versus the strongest Belahont. Got a reason you don't want to see how that one plays out?"

If anyone asked, if anyone claimed deception, I was confident I'd now sown enough ambiguous wording that I could honestly claim to have been offering a fight with my brother from the start. The trap was set. Now I just needed the idiot to waddle into it.

He was about to, I saw. I *smelled*. Then he paused.

"Hmm. Tricky, and careful with words. Slippery like eel. No, manling, I will not fight you."

He would not fight *me*. So he'd fallen for it—even now he thought he'd have been going up against Solitaire Belahont. Which meant . . .

"I just figured out everything there is to know about your command structure," I told the orc. As I'd expected, he looked rather *fearful* for a moment and was fast in speaking again.

"You know nothing."

I sighed. It really was irritating, sometimes, how much everybody insisted on making me demonstrate my cleverness, only to turn around and call me cocky afterward.

"Tell whoever's in charge, whoever's really in charge, that if you don't pull out of our town, I'm going to gut every single one of you like a fish and play with your entrails."

Sometimes it hurt to have a reputation for violent insanity, but it did wonders for making your threats hit home.

"You would dare threaten us?" Guraganar snarled. I snarled back, hissed actually. Bared my teeth, stepped in, brought my face right up to his, and just barely resisted the urge to take a bite out of his cheek.

"No, fuck you, listen," I spit. "I'm *telling* you that you are about to find yourself in the middle of a shitstorm. I have weapons your silly little world won't see for five hundred years, and they're all pointed right at you. So grab your shit, grab your idiots, and run away before I start using them."

By the looks of things, Guraganar was actually considering it. He seemed perturbed, which was a good sign. Perturbation was a short step from worry, which was barely shy of fear, which was, I knew, prone to make idiots do any number of things that weren't in their best interests.

Our parley didn't last much longer than that, and I was relieved to be allowed to return to my little safety warehouse without having any limbs removed. An hour passed, with more tedious resistance of my body's ever-strengthening urge to pace. Then the news reached me of a change among our enemy's forces.

They were falling back. We had, it seemed, won.

CHAPTER TWENTY-EIGHT

Beam's POV: Day 144
Current Wealth: 713 gold, 11 silver, 32 copper

A lot of my body hurt, but it was the good kind of pain. The burn of muscles pushed long and hard, of fighting done without injury. On any other day, I might have found it satisfying. Today though it was hard to feel anything at all.

I'd fucked up, and my fuckup might have gotten us all killed if Solitaire hadn't been so good at tying people in knots with words alone. It might still, even, if our enemies came back for seconds. And it was all because I'd failed to kill one damned orc.

Well, the failure wasn't mine alone. I eyed Adannaya, letting my displeasure show.

"So," I began, just barely veiling my irritation. "Something went wrong."

"It did," she replied. For some strange reason, Lady Adannaya did not seem as bothered by the near deaths of me and my friends as I was.

"Do you have any idea *what*?" I pressed. "Because I don't. In fact, I'm fairly sure I did everything about perfectly. I was just walking into a trap from the start."

Her eyes frosted over, but her composure didn't seem to crack.

"I do not know what you think you are implying," she replied, in an eerily similar way to how Shango sometimes did, "but your failure was no fault of my own. If . . ." Her eyes widened, and the shift in expression came so suddenly it almost made me jump. "Oh," she whispered. "*Oh*. I . . . I know what went wrong."

"What was it?" I pressed, recognizing the sight of a quick mind exploding itself onto the right answer and wanting that shared as soon as I could have it.

"The orc . . ." She trailed off, looking ahead. I followed her eyes to see that our enemies, at last, were moving.

Moving backward.

"A . . . retreat?" I asked, glancing at Adannaya for reassurance, not quite wanting to risk believing it.

She nodded though, seeming just as surprised herself.

"They're retreating," she whispered. "With their leader intact. I . . . didn't think it was possible."

Something started fluttering up in my belly as I saw the orcs spilling off, trudging their way back through the town as a giant wave of musculature and metal. Disorganized, clumsy, slower than might have been ideal by half. But definitely moving back, definitely freeing us from the rest of the fighting.

We'd forced away an invasion and not lost even a single man. I almost started weeping at the realization.

Solitaire actually *did* weep, or rather he started twitching and convulsing so much that his eyes watered. I didn't directly ask what was wrong, but I ended up finding out anyway as he muttered something, on repeat, about the orcs "plotting" and gave me a new assignment. It was another carry-and-relocate detail, which I finished quickly if only to soothe my poor friend's near-incendiary nerves. By the time I was back, he'd calmed down a bit. And something new was happening.

People were swarming us and our men as we exited our safety warehouse, a crowd of them encircling us from the front, sides, and back, so fast I barely even realized it was happening before we'd already been surrounded across every direction by grinning, venerating faces.

"You did it!" one woman cried, gripping the hem of my shirt in a way that was more than a little disconcerting. I barely had time to even consider a response before more spoke, all saying much the same thing, men and women, children and old, gawping and cheering and touching me as if there were some secret divinity in my clothes that might rub off on them with sufficient molestation.

The rest of our men were getting similar, if lesser treatment. Known apparently as the subordinates and not the leaders, they were mere accessories to the great deeds for which I was being rubbed like a pair of sticks in a campfire.

I actually shot a glance Solitaire's way and was rather thankful to see he had not yet beheaded anyone in some screaming reflex, but his eyes were dancing everywhere as we slowly waded through the group and tried to convince them to back off for a moment and give us some breathing room.

"It was nothing," we'd say. Or, "Please, we couldn't just stand by and watch." Or the all-time classic, "You all saved yourselves by surviving so long." The problem with trying to convince people not to worship you was they tended to do it even harder the more you did.

In their defense, of course, getting this sort of reaction had been part of our reason for coming. Another big reason was, or at least I hoped it was, that they were largely innocent people, and them dying would be *bad*.

But as the celebrations continued, and the space was finally given for us to breathe and move, I started to find myself caring less and less about the strategic gain. That old feeling was back again, the one we'd gotten at Rinchester. The sensation of having done the right thing and feeling my conscience purr like a sated cat.

It was spoiled, of course, by Solitaire. But not by any of the usual quirks. This time it was raw, primal terror I saw detonating across his face.

"*Fuck!*" he screamed, gesturing ahead, then turning to our men. "*All of you, back to place, back in formation, get ready!*"

The orcs were rushing around, turning and hurrying back for an *attack*. Their retreat had been false, and was covered by so many buildings, we'd taken until they were a dangerously thin half mile away to notice.

Except they were moving faster now, charging rather than marching, and our forces were still tied up by fawning, now panicking, civilians. We were tragically slow to respond, and they were tragically fast to close in.

"*Out of my way!*" I snarled, suddenly finding myself urged to move like I never had been before. I felt bodies pressing in, claustrophobic, crushing, strangling. They were constrictors about my limbs, chains at my ankles. It took every screed of will I had not to start hitting people to carve a bloody path through them with my fists and elbows, but I was too strong to afford lapses of temper like that. If I started getting rough with humans, they'd die, period. I couldn't bring myself to allow that, couldn't bear the thought, and so I nudged and pushed and shoved hard only with great hesitation. Even that reminded me how awfully fragile they were.

And it still wasn't enough.

The orcs came closer, the bodies tighter, the panic hotter. I saw Solitaire convulsing at it, knew that with so much human fear crushing him from so short a distance, his mind must be about to burst with the pressure. Still our towering enemies lumbered on. I thought my heart might stop.

But then, I realized, they were crossing *that* section of the town, sprinting right along where I'd—

The orcs were closer still, a few hundred yards away, and arrows were flying now. They were eager, *hungry*. Hateful and vengeful, and whatever savagery they unleashed on us, it would have been inspired by my own rampage among their own ranks. I had just enough time for regret.

And then the killing started.

CHAPTER TWENTY-NINE

Solitaire's POV: Day 144
Current Wealth: 713 gold, 11 silver, 32 copper

The orcs were like a tidal wave bearing down on us, all death and mayhem. Humans, really. Less intelligent, bigger, more impulsive. But humans still. I hated them. I loved them. Just like I hated and loved my own kind.

And I would kill them today. I felt a lot of ways about that, but the end result of my emotional cocktail was a smile.

Arrows started cracking against cobbles, whipping by ears. A lucky few thudded into the meat of bodies and sent people down and screaming. Everyone was trying to move now, but there were limits to how quickly several hundred humans could disentangle themselves, and it was far easier for several thousand to charge across the same direction.

The ambush had been perfectly timed, by a genius. Shango couldn't have done this; Phelia definitely couldn't either. It betrayed a certain tactility to the mind, combined with a head for timing and figures, that I'd only ever seen exceeded by me. I wasn't left long to ponder it though.

Because the Gatling gun started firing shortly after.

Obviously, I'd predicted this backstab. I mean, I'd predicted about fifty others that hadn't actually happened, but that's just good tactics. The point was I'd seen this coming, saved the day through my preparations, and everybody should've been really impressed by how clever I was.

Except the orcs, they had more pressing things to worry about. Ten things, in fact, every second. Each one weighing about forty grams and hitting them at somewhere north of Mach speed. Iron plate armor was all well and good against arrows and spears, but it really wasn't designed for this kind of punishment. Neither was steel, for that matter.

Gatling rounds punched clean through the metal, and the flesh below. They impacted so forcefully that the sounds of bullets on armor was almost as loud as that of the gunshots themselves. Thousands of orcs were coming, but the tight streets were funneling them toward us a few hundred at a time. That was a lot, but ten dead per second was still a notable loss among figures like that.

And the orcs were freaking out.

They were slowing, though still coming on. Hate and fury doing as much to drive them forward as the snarling upper rankers holding them in place. They were weathering casualties well for a force that had never been faced with massed gunfire before, and that was holding them together through precious strides. They'd be on us in minutes. Could we uncoil our forces from the swarming civvies before then?

I had to try.

"Argar!" I called out, whipping around and soon finding the giant shoving his way through. "*Argar!*" He heard me, turned, face frantic and sheet pale with terror. But my words were getting through, and that was the first step to controlling any situation. A chink in the panic.

He was the largest of us, physically, and what we needed now was sheer bodily presence. Argar made quick work of the chaos, beating it back—sometimes literally—by weight of personality and, well, weight. In moments, he'd gotten a few more listening to us; within a minute they'd expanded to dozens.

Not easy, forcing hundreds of people at once to all fight back panic and behave properly. Maybe impossible. The trick is to turn their emotions against them. Argar was big and screaming, the people around him were following suit, together they made a collective terror that drove the crowds all away. In the same direction.

That omnidirectional scrambling ended in some scattered, clumsy form of unity. Finally, we had room to form up into a wall once more as our men were freed at the shoulders. It happened just in time.

In regard to stopping a charge from several hundred rabies-infested bodybuilders covered in iron, there really aren't a lot of easy solutions. The one we went with—standing ground, ceding ground, and blunting the impact with our own weight—proved to be a poor one. We *weren't* competing in weight.

But we had a cohesion they lacked, and our armament spoke for itself. Wave after wave the orcs crashed against us, fought, died. Pressed into spears by the charging allies at their backs and trampled by their own side as the momentum of battle snatched away any hope of retreat. I, naturally, was getting stuck in with the rest of us. Snarling, hissing.

My own spear was a big and thick thing made to withstand my growing strength, the sort you'd drive through a bear. It did orcs even better. Creaking and groaning as iron plates surrendered and rent apart, spilling vaporous innards out and wetting the ground.

It's not fun fighting in a tight formation. Not interesting, not exciting. Not even in retrospect. I wish I could tell you about our epic heroics and incredible feats, but, really, the best any of us did while the bodies remained packed was hold, snarl, and push. This was too dense a conflict for any single person to distinguish themselves.

Except for Beam, that is. Except for bloody Beam.

He was a thing. A really impressive thing, that kills lots of people but isn't one—thus making it extraordinary and evocative to have his effect on the battlefield compared to the thing in question. Orcs just died wherever he went, and Beam moved on so fast from each kill that he was making the next even before the first bodies finished falling.

Somehow though the biggest change wasn't the five or six dead cunts per second. It was the morale. I physically felt our lines hold better as Beam did his work, the sight of him like a reinforcing steel spine at the backs of our defense. With his actual armor properly equipped, and that ethereal substance coating his weapon and glinting out at the joints, he almost seemed to be glowing. The orcs seemed to pick up on it too, backing off from him as if they could taste the violence around his body.

It was probably the smartest thing I'd seen them do yet, but it didn't do any of them much good.

And we were still losing ground. Because there were more orcs coming all the time, a giant fucking flood of them that Beam could only stem so much no matter how fast he killed. We backed up, and backed up, and grew ever closer to having no more space to back up through.

From the corner of my eye, I saw the army arrive. There wasn't anything strange about this. If I didn't maintain my peripheral vision in a fight, I'd get killed about twice per altercation. What was unusual was . . . well, the fucking army arriving.

There's a weird sort of awareness that hits you during a fight. Everything is rough and fast. You see movement more than texture and mass more than anything else. I didn't get the chance to do much studying of the new arrivals until a lapse came in the orcish attack, and even then I barely believed what my eyes told me.

A thousand men—1,108, to be exact. All were decently armed, gambesons and proper spears for the most part, bowmen unfurling around the rear flanks. They were ordered and well moving, and . . . absent. Held back, waiting. They weren't engaging us, and they weren't engaging the enemy. I caught a banner flapping in the wind and sifted through my memory for its owner.

Lord Viras, just fucking brilliant. The vultures had arrived, here to wait and see how the fight panned out and either fuck off or finish whichever side came out weakened. That was low. Unsporting, underhanded. Exactly what Shango would've done, and maybe what I'd have done if you ignored the absence of any pyrotechnics. Was that Lord Viras himself I saw standing at the head, or just the overactive imagination of a paranoid with too much adrenaline poisoning his conclusions? Given that I'd never met or seen the man, probably the latter.

Oh, and there went my lapse. The orcs crashed back against us, and I was back to killing.

CHAPTER THIRTY

Beam's POV: Day 144
Current Wealth: 713 gold, 11 silver, 32 copper

Rockets took to the air, screaming wheels of death cutting bloody tunnels through the space between humans and orcs and blowing apart multiple bodies at once. Grenades rained down on the enemy and erupted amid them to send blood, scrap metal, and limbs spitting into the skies. All the time, there were more attackers. More dangers, more chances for death. One of our men went down, helmet taken off by one blow and skull split apart by another. He wasn't the last to die.

Our solidity was starting to give as the orcs continued their endless onslaught, stepping over the bodies of their own men to reach us. I did what I could to stem them. What I could do though wasn't that much.

My hearing was just about gone, so intense was the killing frenzy. Everything in the world was near-monochromatic light and adrenal heat. My weapon was so fast even I barely saw it as a blur and tracked its motions more by the bodies splitting open in its wake. There was no counting the kills I made, so I studied their effects on the battle instead. I had no clue how long I spent fighting. Five minutes? Maybe ten. It was a long affair in any case, too long.

Our neat formation broke just as the final wave of them stopped its advance, and fleeing orcs barely made a dent in the terror of what came next. The dregs of the battlefield were all we had to kill, but there were hundreds of dregs against dozens of us. I steeled myself for it and backed up.

They were surrounding us now. This fighting would be more intense than any we'd done before. And I had no clue if we'd all survive.

Well, some of us already didn't. Another of the men went down as a spear slipped the gaps in his armor. One more fell and was trampled to death. A third retreated into our back ranks as he took a nasty wound to the leg. We held and stabbed and battered and thrust. Every moment, more orcs dropped, but nowhere near as fast as before now that our munitions of rockets and grenades were dried up. The Gatling gun continued pounding away, and Corvan's periodic fireballs kept blasting several new corpses into being, but even still we were losing ground.

The formation broke clean at the middle, and from it came . . . Solitaire. Solitaire moving fast as ever and plugging the gap with his own body. He was a terror, reared up to his full height—taller than most of the orcs—and swinging around an oversize meat cleaver of a weapon that took limbs and heads off in one swing. The enemy backed up from him as if his violence were emitting heat that pained the skin. But only for a moment because then another orc came forth. Bigger than Solitaire, just as strong, almost as fast. I started trying to barge my way over to him. Too slow.

He was being swamped with orcs, attackers pressing in from all sides and actually bowling him over like he was trying to stand in a riptide. My brother disappeared from my sight, and as I closed to catch him, something smashed into the side of my head.

I went down, lights dancing in my eyes. Everything was loud and bright and frenzied, thoughts scattered and mouth tasting of blood as feet stomped around me. I blinked, gathered myself, stood, snarling and hissing. Animal noises that came from some deep part of my psychology long buried by the calm of modernity. Now it reared up and bared its fangs.

Orcs fell back as I shot to my feet, swinging and punching. Kicks, fists, everything I had at my disposal went in every which way I could throw it, thoughts not even on the fighting anymore. I was killing with gut instincts alone, and I couldn't do it fast enough. Ten orcs dropped dead around me in two seconds, and there were still more blocking my path.

Ahead, I saw Solitaire raised up from the mass of bodies around him. They were grabbing him. *Carrying* him. My guts squirmed as I saw him taken farther from us. My time was running out.

Something slammed down in front of me, a towering orc who had the look of some champion. He might have been a brother to the one Solitaire just fought. One mountain range of muscle convulsed as he brought his weapon around, and I ducked, hacked up with my own, and took his arm off at the elbow, then cut again and again before he could reply. He was dead in a heartbeat, and I smashed his falling corpse aside to close on Solitaire.

But more orcs flooded me, more. I realized it was deliberate. Solitaire was their prize, and they were sacrificing everything they needed to to secure him.

I headbutted one, stars dancing in my vision as the iron helmet caved into orc bone and killed the enemy instantly. Something grabbed me from behind, then went flying as I moved and landed hard. I killed, killed, killed. Broke out of the mass and screamed as the world turned into shrapnel and pressure at the impact of something too fast to catch and too big to avoid.

My feet left the ground, and I flew. Landed, rose, sprinted. There was another magus among the orcs, levitating stones around himself just like Guraganar had and staring straight at me. Solitaire was dozens of meters back now, almost at the main mass of orcs. My heart was beating so hard I thought it might burst out of me.

Where are you? I desperately asked, turning my thoughts inward. *Please, if you're listening, if you're there, whatever I did to fight the King of Blades, I need it now. Please.*

But no answer came, and more orcs did. I screamed. A long, feral cry that seemed to give them pause before I carved into them. Solitaire was still moving though, and they just kept on fucking coming. My friend disappeared from my line of sight just as I buried my sword deep into a spine, twisting it out and staring into the churning horde of retreating orcs to find . . . something. Anything.

But there was nothing. He was gone.

I stared, as if staring might bring him back. Orcs moved around me, slow as ever. I had all the time in the world to stand and do nothing as my friend disappeared. But then more sounds hit me, the fears of a failing formation. I turned to see our men were on the back foot still, defense crumbling as the orc dregs pressed it. I swallowed, mastered myself, and got to work. There wasn't time to mope about. I'd been given more power than anyone else on our side, and I was going to fucking use it.

Even if I couldn't save the one person I needed to.

Argar stumbled back with blood gushing down his side, a spear tip having bitten between armored plates. I cut its wielder in half. Elizabeth was hiding behind an increasingly battered shield as two orcs pounded it, neither of whom survived a moment longer. Several of our men were already dead, recruits who'd never turn into veterans. I couldn't know for sure I'd avenged them, but I killed nine or ten orcs for each one who'd fallen. With the enemy already in retreat at their main body and a mere hundred engaged now, the cleanup didn't last long at all.

The air smelled of blood and defeat as they started pulling away, and it was all Helena could do to bark back a few of our more enthusiastic members into place rather than letting them give chase. We watched the enemy forces peel back.

Solitaire was with them, still. Alone, captured. Again. For the second time, my brother had been taken from the rest of us, and this time I'd been there to stop it. I screamed, kicking a dead orc and watching the body roll several paces away with the impact. It didn't do anything to mitigate my rage, and certainly not to bring back my friend.

Looking around, I saw plenty of dead enemies and a good few dead friends. We'd accomplished nothing else today. Just death.

CHAPTER THIRTY-ONE

Beam's POV: Day 144
Current Wealth: 713 gold, 11 silver, 32 copper

The orcs had backed off, for now, and they'd left us with death and absences. The ground was carpeted by their corpses for hundreds of feet out from where we were, a great ocean of dead and dying things that thickened in density as you drew closer to us.

Of course, we had our fair share of corpses too. Six of our twenty-two recruits had bitten it during the fighting, and four more were injured badly. A single conflict had almost halved our strength. If Solitaire were here, he might've given us an idea of how many orcs we'd killed. Probably he'd have known with just a single glance at the battlefield.

But he wasn't. He'd been snatched off by the enemy while I watched. Everything was blank and quiet. Sound eaten by the shrieking in my ears, the beating in my chest, the constriction of arterial blood in my body. Someone was talking to me, but I couldn't hear them, only stare at where I'd last seen my brother. I screamed, slamming a fist down into the ground and watching as a few cracks spiderwebbed out from the point of impact. The vent of fury did nothing to calm me. But it did give me my hearing back after a second.

Well, that and being slapped.

"This isn't the time to shut down, Beam," Elizabeth snarled, glaring at me in a way that brought back unpleasant memories of mean old schoolteachers. "Solitaire's gone. You're in charge. What do we do next?"

I blinked, mind slowly working through the avalanche of information to realize that she was right. I'd only just gotten to my feet though when another voice came out, this one angrier and grimmer. Corvan.

"Army approaching," he spit. "Looks like Viras."

I turned and felt myself gutted by the sight of just how right he was. What looked like hundreds of men were closing on us. Us specifically, not the orcs. And they were already in the town.

From our elevated position, I could make out a few details about their armament, which was impressive, and their cohesion, which was very impressive. It wasn't until they were just a minute or two away that I recognized the sight of Viras himself at the front though.

He was in some kind of lamellar armor built under a set of robes, like the sort Corvan wore, and carrying a ludicrously thick scroll of coiled paper. Not smiling, never that, but looking more than a little pleased as he made his way over to us.

"Good evening," he said, voice like steel on ice. "I'm pleased to see all of you are alive and well."

Something about that sent a chill down my spine, and I was actually glad for a moment that Solitaire wasn't here. A surefire way to escalate anything into violence was giving him the creeps.

"What do you want?" I asked, eyes flicking to our dead men, and his very much alive, well-armed ones. A decently sized army with this equipment could have cut the orcs' flank apart with how they moved. The enemy might not have even known they were coming before contact. But they'd pulled back.

Viras soaked up my hostility the way Shango might have, just swallowing it like debris in the ocean and moving past without another word.

"With respect, Belahont, I am not here on matters of your family, but rather the town of Swanhen itself." His eyes moved over to Lord Appleberry, who was panting and gasping beside us. I hadn't even noticed him joining the fighting, but he was covered in plate armor, blood, and more than a few nasty dings. I was almost surprised he was still alive, and more so that he looked so healthy even now.

"You want to speak with me?" Appleberry frowned, rightfully nervous and growing more so as Viras' scroll was unfurled.

"Lord Appleberry, I am here to inform you of my family's claim on the land you are currently holding as your own. That land being the town of Swanhen, its mines, and its surrounding territories." Viras spoke slowly, but somehow it was still almost hard to follow him. "This town was loaned to your ancestor some fifteen decades ago following the death of the last heir of its original owners, the Devenar family."

Appleberry's face was tightening like a garrote wire, but he nodded.

"Correct," the man whispered.

"Well, you may be surprised—and perhaps understandably disheartened—to find that my own family has distant ties to the Devenars, dating back almost two centuries. Very distant, of course, to have only been discovered now, but . . . well, strong enough to contest your claim to it, I'm afraid."

Appleberry stared, aghast, as Viras continued.

"I am afraid that I have decided to make a press for my land, all legal under the king's law and, naturally, all to be resolved between our own families and their heads. How you choose to respond is entirely up to you."

I must have been slow from the battle, or exhausted. Maybe I'm just dumb. But it only hit me then what was happening. Swanhen was crippled, Appleberry's forces in tatters long before we even arrived, and Viras was suggesting they settle the matter between their families alone. If Appleberry accepted, things would become martial. He'd lose Swanhen, and we'd have gained nothing from this escapade.

If Appleberry didn't accept, it would turn into a contest of influencing the powers that be for preferential judgment. Appleberry was obviously not as powerful as Viras, and Appleberry himself was clearly not as driven. I had no doubt that that would be an even harder win.

"This is . . . This is outrageous!" Appleberry snarled, face turning beet red, hands turning to fists. "You . . . You can't do this. It—"

"Is quite legal," Viras replied calmly. "But I understand, of course, that we find ourselves in extraordinary circumstances. It would be cruel to expect you to engage in a clash of armies at such a time as this. So, I intend to offer you an alternative. A contest of champions. You may pick a warrior to do battle with me, and the victor will determine how this conflict is resolved."

Appleberry hesitated, and I stared, waiting for him to shoot *that* idea down too. But he didn't.

"You . . . have offered generous terms," the noble—the moron—replied, as if he were not suggesting a fight with one of the deadlier magic users alive. "And so I shall accept. Who here shall be my champion?"

I stepped forward, obviously, and felt the fear washing through me in dense waves as I did. This wasn't good, not good at all. It . . .

This might be how Shango ended up alone in Redacle. Solitaire gone and me killed. Alone in Redacle . . . I couldn't imagine a worse fate. But what else could I do? Our men had died here. Our brother had gone missing. We needed this win or we'd be dangerously weak after. I had no choice.

"If I might interject?"

The new voice surprised me. It was lighter, calmer, and rather more out of breath than anyone else on my side. I turned to find Adannaya standing at my back, looking over the conversation with cool eyes.

Lord Viras eyed her, head tilting.

"I do not believe I have had the pleasure," he began, but she breezed past him to study the document.

"Hmm," Adannaya noted. "I was not aware these champion duels of your people would pit peers of the realm against mere step-nobility. Are there not injunctions against that scenario?"

As she said it, her eyes flicked back up to Viras and lanced him with an accusatory stare.

Viras, for his part, didn't seem very rattled. Only met the stare.

"That is tradition, not law. And I am afraid I take the rule of our lands too seriously to disobey its legal precedents on the whims of cultural pressure."

Spoken like that, with all the big words and stuff, it sounded perfectly logical. Or at least smart. Adannaya wasn't done though.

"And you believe it would suit the rule of your lands to endanger yourself in a bout with the man who almost bested the King of Blades?"

A shudder ran through Viras' men, but not Viras himself. I saw muttering, shifting gazes, disconcertion. Evidently, Viras saw it too. Adannaya kept going.

"History is full of young rulers with something to prove, but it is novel to meet an old one."

With that single sentence, the tumors she'd sewn among the confidence of Viras' men calcified.

Viras picked up on it, or at least I think he did. With a single glance back at his soldiers, his mind changed instantly, and he eyed Adannaya like some barricade to be dismantled.

"You would not object, then, to my sending out my own champion instead," he noted. Adannaya hesitated, clearly trying to think of some way she could get out of that as well, but then shook her head.

"Of course not."

Viras smiled, like a cat with a rat between its paws.

"Then I shall call forth my champion."

The champion in question was one I remembered. Nine feet tall and covered in so much plate armor that every footstep sounded like a trebuchet impact. His shoulders were well over a meter across, and his curled fists were like anvils. The last time he'd fought, it'd been against the King of Blades. But Xerght the Giant looked healthier now.

And certainly more confident.

I was aching everywhere, exhausted. My head throbbed, and my mouth tasted of blood and puke. I was weakened, tired, closer to death with every scrape I got in. Could I win?

Yes, probably. But it was hard to tell myself that looking at the guy.

INTERLUDE FOUR

Adannaya felt a chill run through her wits as she watched the men form up into a circle, standing around and waiting, practically drooling, as they stared eagerly into the ground where one of them would win and another, in all likelihood, would die.

It was a barbaric custom, but then she'd had to grow used to barbaric customs since she'd first fled Illeade for this nation of savages. At the very least, this custom gave her a chance to salvage some advantage from the situation. If only a chance.

"He's bigger than you," Adannaya noted, surprising herself as she spoke to Belahont while he prepared. His was a lengthy prefight ritual, consisting of strange motions where he extended limbs, tested joints, moved in slow and fast trajectories as if he were rehearsing the battle before it began. He didn't look at her as he did it, or as he replied.

"Lots of people are bigger than me" was all he said.

Adannaya fancied that an exaggeration, at worst. Six feet and one inch was a good deal taller than even most nobles in Illeade, and it was taller than this land's norms too. Still, he was right in that he was no giant. The man he'd have to defeat was.

"What do you think your chances are?" she asked him.

He still didn't look at her, just continued his bizarre routine.

"This feels like a bad time to be asking that, compared to right before you set up the fight."

Adannaya buried her annoyance. Men, she knew, were creatures of emotion. Simple and direct, and soft inside. Probably, he was using that petty wit to distract himself from the fear of combat. If so, then his odds were not good.

"We are ready to begin," Lord Viras announced, eyeing them coolly. There wasn't a whiff of victory or condescension to him, no smugness or arrogance. He seemed the perfect political creature. A thing seeking victory with so detached a cognition as to barely even yearn for it. A being with no mental faults to be chiseled into in a counterplay.

Perhaps that made him the better enemy. Certainly, this was not a noble to force their own niece from her homeland through malice and bitterness. If Adannaya bested Viras, he might deem her a future obstacle, but he would not chase her across the world out of spite alone.

She would have to beat him, first, to decide.

"To ensure all present are familiar with the rules, I will explain them now," Viras called out. "The bout has no time limit, nor any illegal attacks, though each fighter must aim to spare their enemy. It is, however, single combat. The winner can be determined by incapacitation, surrender, a successful removal from the ring, or, of course, accidental death. Let us begin."

He timed it well because Beam Belahont was ready just as he finished speaking. The man stalked into the arena clad in his curious plate—armor he had not worn when infiltrating the town—and aglow with his curious magic. Adannaya hadn't asked about that, not directly, but she intended to find the secret of it. It was a power she'd not seen before, and she'd seen every power there was.

A mystery, that family. First the invincible killer with the impossible might, then the snarling animal in the skin of a man who made weaponry even Illeade had yet to produce. Mysterious and potent allies, thus Adannaya's cooperation with them so far. They would, she imagined, go places.

But only if they survived today.

Beam Belahont was hopping, almost dancing. Foot to foot like a traveling gymnast rather than a man clad from head to toe in steel. His enemy was slower and more massive, every footfall a battering ram against the dirt. Neither spoke.

Xerght was the first to move.

He came like a rockslide, arm twisting sidelong with more speed than Adannaya would have imagined possible. At its tip was a great big meat cleaver of a weapon almost akin to the one swung by Solitaire Belahont in the previous bout, though exponentially larger. Belahont ducked, then whipped back ahead of the boot that came to catch him low. He skidded back to the edge of the circle—entire thing a mere fifty feet in diameter—and skirted along its perimeter as he darted just beyond his enemy's reach.

Beam Belahont was so fast, it was almost hard to see him move. The giant was slower. But reach and strength meant that he didn't need the impossible flitting speed of his enemy. Only luck and perseverance. The latter was there already; the former would come with time. Another swing came fast, and this time Belahont opted to block rather than dodge. Adannaya winced as his plate armor shivered and his feet left the ground. He landed just a yard shy of the opposite end, rolled almost out of the ring, and hastily scrambled back in. He was up well before Xerght came down on him and lunged in with a deadly quick stab that scraped against the steel of his enemy's thigh plate and sent metal etchings wisping out amid a spray of sparks.

It did not penetrate, and Xerght swung again. Beam Belahont backstepped, reached the edge, and was pinned for the next attack, which came crunching down and smashed him into the dirt. He bounced high, spinning and landing *behind* his enemy with a groan. He was fast, truly fast, but even he hadn't finished clambering up to his feet before the next blow came. Belahont barely rolled from its path before springing up and backing away. Cautious now. Fearful.

Adannaya saw the great buckle in his breastplate where the enemy's cleaver swing had bitten deep, plate split open, mail below ruined, and . . . something glowing under. She blinked, found the light still there, and dismissed it as a concern. Because something more pressing had just happened.

Why did the giant not take his chance to hurl you from the ring?

The thought didn't take long to find an answer as Xerght lunged again, and Belahont kept backing away. Slower now, body left enfeebled by its new wound. He was hurt, badly. The giant noticed too.

Beam Belahont sidestepped one falling-meteor swing that struck the ground hard enough to send flecks of dirt exploding out like sling stones. Adannaya hissed as she covered herself, feeling the impacts sting her skin even thirty feet back. Another swing missed high, and she heard the wind of metal passing through air as if it had whipped by her own ear with less than a fingerbreadth of clearance. The strength on display was perhaps more than in any other man she'd ever witnessed. Almost like watching the whipping tail of a dragon.

A small one, at least. And any dragon was one too many for this bout. Fire or no.

Finally, luck was on Xerght's side for a second time. Beam Belahont was clipped by another swing, sent stumbling as a pauldron was torn almost fully off. By the time he righted himself, there was no way to avoid the coming swing save by blocking. He did, downward stroke driving his feet perhaps a half yard into the dirt. Knees bent, body folding, he did everything right to disperse the impact. Still, the cleaver's edge came down on his exposed shoulder and chewed through into the gristle and meat. Blood ran like a stream down his chest, bright and terrible.

It was then that Adannaya understood.

The second hit, landed at the edge of the ring, would have been a winning blow if the giant had struck Belahont head-on to send him back. From the center, this one would have ended the bout too if he'd been pushed back properly. But to do either would mean to send him flying from the ring and gain a victory by that method.

Doing that would end the fight with Beam Belahont still alive, and Adannaya knew now that their enemy intended to see him killed. There was a vicious logic to it. What was better than a bested enemy? A bested dead one. With Solitaire Belahont missing, the death of Beam would cripple his family's potence.

Adannaya started turning over cards in her head. A family in that position would be extremely eager for help, and grateful for any who provided it. She could win incredibly generous terms of alliance by rescuing Solitaire Belahont after Beam's death.

The giant swung again, biting several chunks from the back of the man in question and spurting blood down into the dirt again. Adannaya winced.

No, in that condition, the family would be too risky an alliance anyway. She needed to find out how to stop this disaster before it finished happening.

Could she step in directly? No, unthinkable. This was not Illeade or even Akanite. Adannaya's nobility—even her royal relation—would go only so far. In fact, if Viras had deduced her plan to ally with the Belahonts more permanently than her bad luck of being in Swanhen during the siege would imply, he had a vested interest in using any excuse he could to kill her now. To interfere directly would only provide that.

Another blow came directly and sent a piece of truly magnificent steel exploding free of Belahont's armor to leave a nasty cut across the brow of a spectator.

What could she do then? Declare an injunction? On what basis? Adannaya's mind whirred just as Beam Belahont finally fell, and his enemy loomed over him. Weapon raised.

In the end, it was not she who helped at all. Lord Appleberry himself cast his body below the weapon, glaring up defiantly.

"*Stop this!*" he roared. Everyone was silent; everyone halted. Except the giant. His blade kept falling, impeded only by a hardening of the air into physical substance durable enough to stop it. Even still, it continued long enough to bite through steel and leave a small trickle of blood running down Appleberry's arm. He didn't even blink at it.

"You were meaning to have your champion kill mine, were you not, Lord Viras? And empowering him too. I saw Xerght the Giant fight against the King of Blades, and his physical might was not so great as now. Not even close."

Viras ignored the latter remark entirely, as would Adannaya whether it were true or false, and focused on the first.

"My champion was merely fighting to win," Viras replied, voice like a serpent slithering down her spine. "If Beam Belahont was at risk of dying in that process, the fault is his for not conceding."

"Your champion could have won several times. He was able to toss him the length of the ring and landed many blows from less than half that distance removed from its edge. He was even about to land a blow upon a downed opponent before I intervened."

Lord Viras hesitated, and then his face grew terribly hard and angled.

"Are you willing to make an enemy of the Virases over this town and a mercenary?" he whispered. "Because if we part today with the contest unimpeded, I will not give you another thought again."

Appleberry's glare was like roaring fire to match the misting ice of Viras.

"You already made an enemy out of *me* by attempting to murder my ally," he declared. For a moment, Lord Viras said nothing. Adannaya found herself stepping back, anticipating some explosion of rage. She'd heard of him, of course. There wasn't a magus alive who'd not made a study of Azelis. Adannaya's memory was better than most, and so she still recalled each one of his students. Their names, their faces—from the portraits known to her family—and their power.

Could every man and woman in Belahont's coterie have defeated him if they pooled their efforts? She doubted it. Even with Beam Belahont uninjured.

But there was no volcanic wrath, only a mild irritation and deep sigh.

"My greatest weakness, even after all these years," he sighed. "Stupid men." Viras turned and started to leave.

Lord Steeblitch and Lord Elzar were not at the top of Phelia's admittedly short list of desired acquaintances. Unfortunately, her desires had very little to do with what needed doing. And so she was in her office, and so were they.

Both men were mirrors of each other, and neither was pleasant. Handsome and well groomed, they were often mistaken for brothers. Not least because of their indescribably foul attitudes toward any not within their own circles. Phelia had never had direct dealings with them before. She'd lacked the political influence for them to engage her in such a way until now, but she'd made a study of them. As with any man, they both had weaknesses. Soft spots, vulnerabilities, and blind sides.

The issue today was that both were such dull creatures, she could hardly be sure using such things against them would be of any actual advantage.

"I thank you for attending this meeting, my lords." She smiled sweetly. Some men were charmed and disarmed by a woman smiling at them; others would respond with hostility. When that woman had the power Phelia did, the latter reaction became far more common. And she saw it now.

Flared nostrils, narrowed eyes, curling lips, and forced exhalations to vocalize a contempt too strong and instinctually raw for mere words to convey. Steeblitch, always the stupider of the pair, made the mistake of spoiling their effect by trying to vocalize it anyway.

"Believe me, neither of us would be here if we had anything better to do."

It was the sort of childish remark that bounced clean off a truly adult negotiator, and that he had tried it at all told Phelia a lot about the order of incompetence she was dealing with now.

Bless him, he looked quite pleased with it. Doubtless he was asserting some form of power in his mind. Well, Phelia would have to see what she could do about that.

"I have called you here," she continued, ignoring the little outburst entirely, "because I have a proposition that may benefit the three of our families. The two of you have a well-known monopoly on the supplies for alchemical arts in this city. I would like to arrange a standing order for those supplies to my household."

A pause, which was hopeful. Then sneering laughter, which was less so. Elzar spoke now, face a mix of falsified amusement and very real contempt.

"You want to deal with us?" He snorted. "You, who whored yourself out to a commoner? What in the world makes you think we'd want anything to do with you?"

A great many things, all of which you are too stupid to have noticed for yourself.

So help her, Phelia almost said it. But that would have been *undiplomatic*, and so she bit her tongue, forced a smile, and threatened him instead. It was, in many ways, the more satisfying retort regardless.

"It's funny you should ask that, my lord. Because I recently intercepted a few letters you might find rather interesting." Phelia sat back, eyes flitting between the two. They already looked concerned—a bad move. She could have been lying, testing them. She could have been saying this purely to confirm from their reactions whether there were any letters the two ought to have been worried about.

She wasn't, but still. They really were awful at subterfuge.

"What letters are those?" Elzar frowned, swallowing and licking his lips in that delightful way men tended to when their facades of masculine bravery were at the point of breaking.

"Ones between each of you and a certain Mistress Kiyana, I believe," Phelia told them.

The room froze over as fast as rain falling onto ice, and Phelia saw the delightfully sluggish rise of horror and fear upon both men's faces. Their skin burned crimson within moments, mouths gasping in silence for the right words. She'd already have confirmed her suspicions, if they were still only that, but with the letters securely in her position, this display was just an enjoyable indulgence before the final move was made.

Finally, speech came from Lord Steeblitch. Choking speech, mind, of the kind that a man might produce while staving off a strangler.

"I'm sure I don't know what you're talking about," he snapped, standing, almost knocking a table over in his haste, and suddenly appearing to be propped up on shaky legs. Phelia smiled again.

"Oh really? Then let me elaborate." She paused a moment, sifting through her memory for the carefully imprinted information. "Quote, 'Oh Mistress Kiyana, I yearn for your cruelty like a starving man does food. I beg you, please fill me up like you did the last time. Hurt me like the little pig whore I am.' One excerpt of many. All rather distasteful, isn't it? And taken from letters found in your quarters. Both of them. Would you like me to read some more?"

She actually worried, for a moment, whether the men would die right in front of her, hearts giving way and bodies bleeding as vital veins ruptured beneath the stress of her revelation. Fortunately, nothing so inconvenient as that occurred.

"This is outrageous!" Elzar snarled. *"How dare you—You—I have never—"*

Phelia stopped listening, sitting back and waiting for the man's rage to exhaust itself before, gently, reminding him that she had merely quoted letters found in his home, which were now in possession of her family. She then offered to quote some of that Mistress Kiyana's own letters in response.

He had paled like an exsanguinated man and become suddenly, remarkably docile. They both had.

"Now then," Phelia continued at last, "I hope this has made it clear to you both where we stand with each other, hmm? I would recommend that the two of you become more polite in conversations with my family from now on, given that the letters in question are signed with your names and written in your handwriting."

In a bizarre and inexplicable turn of events, they *did* become more polite. And Phelia walked from the room with a rather lucrative new arrangement securing her brother-in-law's required materials to sustain further weapons' production. She wasn't left to feel smug for long, however.

Phelia headed for her husband next, finding that increasingly strong flutter of anticipation in her chest as she did. He was in a meeting with Grimworth, or at least she had thought he was, and yet entering the room revealed only Grimworth himself.

"Good afternoon," she greeted him with a nod. "The meeting I had with lords Steeblitch and Elzar were rather lucrative, thanks to your efforts. It seems the peasant class' penchant for gossip and thievery can come in rather handy at times."

For some reason, the compliment didn't seem to please the man. Phelia hesitated, tapering her words off and sighing. She decided a moment later to merely give up on trying to charm this one. He seemed intent to interpret everything she said as some slight or another.

"Do you happen to know where I might find my husband?" she asked at last. Grimworth shook his head at that.

"I'd expected him here," he grunted, and Phelia scowled. That man couldn't keep a schedule to save his life. He was royalty elsewhere, she expected. Or some equivalent of it. Accustomed to the world warping itself around his whims and not the other way round.

"Progress has been fast," Grimworth added, snapping Phelia from her thoughts. "Belahont funding has been carrying us a long way. We're recruiting more, arming them better. Our numbers have increased by half already, and we hope that the difference will widen shortly."

She nodded, tucking the figures away.

"And your fighters?" Phelia prodded.

"Fifty-three in all," he replied, and Phelia felt a surge in her gut. It really was quite a lot. More than the Belahonts' own standing force, even, though certainly less well equipped. And if it was projected to grow even more along with the hundreds of non-combatants now swarming his ranks . . .

She smiled, speaking fast. "You should leave soon before people suspect a connection between us, but I would recommend that you work to begin preparing for an assault by the guards. They would be the most natural avenue of attack on you. Whether by people who hate you or people who wish to weaken us through you."

Grimworth nodded, getting up and heading for the door in one fluid motion. He was gone a moment later. Phelia headed down the hall herself, stopped mere paces into it by a frantic servant.

"My lady," the woman breathed. "There's . . . Please just come quick."

A new girl, most of the servants were now. Phelia had insisted on getting at least a few around the house for when nobility visited to further their signs of, if not wealth, a lack of abject poverty at least. This one looked on the verge of tears, the poor dear. Phelia hurried after her as she led them both to the courtyard outside.

To Shango.

Her husband was unhurt but concerned. Surrounded on all sides by bruised, cut, and beaten mercenaries. Brigandines were mangled and gashed, faces bandaged and bleeding, bodies shivering with cold and desperate gasping of air. Exhaustion hung over them, thick as winter snow. The worst was Beam.

Beam, her poor brother. He looked like he'd been savaged by dogs, his armor warped and buckled where it lay beside him, body littered with deep wounds. The sight was so dreadful that Phelia didn't register the most notable fact until long moments had passed.

"Where is Solitaire?" her husband demanded, voice like a vise. "Where's fucking Solitaire?"

CHAPTER THIRTY-TWO

Solitaire's POV: Day 151
Current Wealth: 663 gold, 17 silver, 46 copper

If I got captured one more time, I was going to go fucking insane.

Well, there was no dungeon the second time. Yet. Because I'd been captured far from enemy territory, I guessed, so I was just marched off with the rest of the orcs. I'd figured out pretty quickly that they'd decided not clashing with Viras' army was the better part of valor, which meant we were probably retreating to a stronghold of some kind.

Big brain time: How does one create one or more outposts able to support a thousands-strong army when one is a rising power consisting of orcs with several times the caloric intake of humans, fueled by barely advancing agriculture?

The answer is one doesn't. Which meant, in all likelihood, I was being taken to their home city. It would've been exciting, where it not . . . you know. Me being dragged to the fucking home city of a pack of orcs.

For about a week we moved, orcs crossing great distances thanks to sheer stride size and strength. I didn't have a hard time keeping up, even shackled, and within those seven days, we crossed well over a hundred miles of terrain. I kept an eye on the night sky, memorizing the layout of the stars the first night and then using that as a reference to figure my bearing for the subsequent ones. It was something to do, at least. And then we arrived.

I'll admit to being surprised by the city, and yes it absolutely *was* a city. A big one, almost Elswick's size and with a composition of towering stone. There was a mountain at its back, a great many hills around it, and it seemed to have valleys for streets. Inside there was an impressive density of people, probably a good few tens of thousands in total, I'd guess, *maybe* close to a fraction of a million. All orcs. It was slightly disheartening to be around so many towering forms and certainly didn't bode well for escape. But then I'd never have been forcing my way out anyway. The chance would come. I just needed to pounce on it.

For now, water was all I got.

They dragged me into some bathhouse, quadrupled my guard, and removed my shackles. The skin around them itched slightly, but it wasn't nearly as bad as some of the other captives I'd seen. There was no flaying, no blood and festering wounds. I guess that was the benefit of supernatural durability. I'd felt another surge of that power we leveled up with after leaving Swanhen, and though Shango wasn't here to quantify it, I knew it was significant. I'd given myself improvements across the board to my physical abilities, with an emphasis on toughness. With luck, that'd come in handy whenever I made my move.

Well, if I didn't mess up, physical abilities would be irrelevant, but still.

Bathing as a captive was, I learned, an exercise in self-control. They didn't clean me as much as hose me down, bucketing gallons of water over me, then calmly scrubbing me while I snarled. They ended up reshackling me after the third time I punched one of them, and the whole affair took about forty minutes in all. Not my record, of course, but I suppose I could work on it. Once that was done, they marched me elsewhere.

Interestingly, I was far from the only human here. Even discounting other captives from Swanhen, there were quite a few of my own supposed kind wandering around with the demeanors of people who'd been there for a while. All wore similar clothing, simple woolen things, and all kept their eyes carefully downcast. Some sort of servant class? Well, no surprise there. I made a note to learn more about the city.

But there was no chance for that now. Now I was being hauled off to . . . somewhere. Through big corridors, which got broader and higher ceilinged as I progressed. The decor improved too. Less gold and pomp than in places like Elswick, more dead animals and proof of feats. I figured out I was heading to this place's equivalent of a throne room long before the door opened to reveal it.

A big room. A very big room, bigger than I'd have expected for a throne room even. At the end was a great seat that looked all regal and impressive, holding the uncomfortably familiar Guraganar. Beside him, kneeling at his feet, was a short redheaded woman with skin pale enough I thought she might combust in the sun.

Leading up to them was a thick rug made from something very big and very dead. The walls were adorned with banners, more stone coated with more hide, and the room was lit by a great many bonfire-sized fireplaces burning away. Awfully wasteful, I thought. But then, build your castle out of solid rock into a mountainside and you'd end up going through a lot of firewood.

"Leave," Guraganar ordered, and the orcs behind me hesitated only a moment before turning on their heels and disappearing out through the door. I looked around again, walking forward idly as I did.

There were no other exits, of course, not even if I were willing to test the limits of my resistance against falling impacts. They'd not have left me unguarded otherwise. I took the sights in, bundled them away in my mind, and then turned to the leader.

"Get up," I ordered her. "We're alone now. There's no point in keeping the act going."

The woman at Guraganar's feet didn't hesitate even an instant before climbing up and facing me, grinning. Guraganar himself lifted his body from the throne, which she took a moment later.

"Impressive," she noted, eyeing me like I was some master-crafted weapon she was figuring out the best use for. "Very impressive. I see the stories about you are true."

"Not even close," I told her. "The words for how clever I am aren't featured in human language yet."

She laughed, apparently thinking I was joking. "I'll be the judge of that," the woman said at last. "My name is Adravigi, and I am, as you have already noted, the true leader of this city. Welcome to your new home, Solitaire Belahont."

I didn't wring her neck.

CHAPTER THIRTY-THREE

Solitaire's POV: Day 151
Current Wealth: 663 gold, 17 silver, 46 copper

Barbed Point was not a nicely named city, but I had to admit it was more than I'd have expected. Adravigi was pretty eager to show me around the place. Guarded, of course; she wasn't stupid. That much was remarkable in and of itself. Do you have any idea how many people *aren't* stupid? You're more likely to find someone over seven feet tall than a person fitting into that category, and I couldn't deny Adravigi was an example.

She was sneaky about having Guraganar order her to show me around, one slave teaching another. Apparently that was what I was now. A slave. She was careful to stress that it was only so far as public appearances went, and I didn't miss that she was a little strained as she did.

"So that's your cover then," I noted, earning a nod and a quick smothering of her distaste.

"The Machinator's favorite slave," Adravigi confirmed.

"Smart." I thought about it and found a lot of advantages jumping out. "You can go anywhere or nowhere. You're invisible when you want to be but can command authority just by claiming to be carrying his orders. In a lot of ways, you have power that you wouldn't even if you had his position openly."

She eyed me, suddenly on edge.

"It took me a long time to work that much out," the woman said at last. Oh god. Had I pricked her ego? If I had to tiptoe around her being offended by every reminder of her own stupidity, I was going to nose-dive off a fucking mountain. It was bad enough doing that with the average morons—they couldn't really help themselves— but I wasn't taking this from her.

"I've had a lot of practice with this sort of thing." I shrugged. "The moment I arrived in this country, I had to think like that just to stay alive."

Thankfully, the moron accepted my olive branch with barely a feather ruffled.

"Swanhen," I said abruptly. She looked at me, looked confused, and I elaborated. "You were at Swanhen when you met the orcs, right?"

"That's right," Adravigi replied after a second. "That was where Guraganar first took me as his slave."

I thought about it.

"You were just passing through and got unlucky," I ventured. She stared at me again.

"You're a very good guesser," Adravigi grunted at last.

That much, at least, was true. My reasoning had always been more intuitive than Shango's. Less reliable, but far more explosively, inconsistently powerful.

The story Beam had been fed to lure Guraganar into that room—the room that hadn't boasted a rape victim at all—seemed specific to me. Adravigi was a slave, one Guraganar had taken a liking to as far as most were concerned. I doubted that circumstance had been engineered by her from the start. More to the point, she'd had business in Swanhen sometime in her past. The place meant something to her.

It really wasn't much, any of it, but together it formed a thin pattern-shaped mist that I'd tried building a theory around anyway. Empathy, intuition, and a well-aimed guess had saved me the trouble of deducing an answer more scientifically. But only after she'd been nice enough to confirm it.

"You're an infiltrator then," I guessed, more confidently this time. "You head into towns as a human, scope them out, gauge the best way to . . . Oh."

She'd lied. There'd been no history between her and Swanhen. It was a mining town, with iron veins under it that a growing technological power like Barbed Point could use. She didn't have anything like their regional accent—and certainly hadn't adopted the one local to where we were now—and using her own story in her own former town would've been needlessly risky.

"What?" Adravigi pressed, smelling of concern suddenly.

"Nothing." I shrugged. "Just realized you need to feign total loyalty to Guraganar too to not be questioned when you're sent independently ahead into these places as a scout. Limits the information you can get among your own people if they all think you're blindly tied to him."

It obviously hadn't been what I was thinking, but letting her know that I'd caught her in a deception had no advantages and a good few drawbacks. If she thought she could fool me easily, maybe she'd ease up slightly and become easier to see through. I'd certainly be watching more carefully now that I knew how well she lied.

Moron. She was a fucking *slave*. A female slave. Of course she lied well. Darwin told me as much from her continued respiration.

Adravigi continued leading me around, which told me quite a lot about her plans for my future in Barbed Point. Her words confirmed it all.

Orcs were, overtly at least, the dominant species here. Fighters, but builders too. Adravigi, through Guraganar, had been feeding them all information on construction, city planning, and the works. Smart woman. *Literate* woman, which actually was quite the feat in this world. Hell, I wasn't literate yet. I'd not even started learning.

The population of Barbed Point was generally supported by a series of rivers running through the hills and mountains they called home, all of which boasted oddly large populations of fish. Really oddly large, actually, to the point where I made a note of investigating later because there had to be some ulterior explanation to how such a place could support so many.

"What do you do for winter?" I asked abruptly. "Mountains, elevated terrain even around that. I almost froze to death sleeping in human settlements a few months ago."

She smiled, taking some measure of relish in the question.

"We distribute our resources. Everyone is given firewood and housing, and if that isn't enough, we have several communal areas to weather the cold in together, where it's easier to heat more generously."

That was a lot of relish, smugness, and, I thought, relief considering the question. Was Adravigi impoverished before she was taken to Barbed Point? I'd be surprised if not.

I was shown more of the place because this was, after all, an attempt at recruitment. Most notable to me were the training grounds. Adravigi seemed to have been preparing her military expansion for a while because orcs were sparring and practicing intently all in the iron plate they'd worn to Swanhen. That sparked an idea.

"How do you get so much iron?" I asked her. I actually hadn't been expecting a response and was sort of right in that regard. She looked at me and arched an eyebrow instead.

"You're the genius." She shrugged. "Why don't you tell me?"

A test. Well, no surprise there. I gave it a thought anyway.

"The orcs," I guessed. "Obviously, you have decent amounts of iron in these mountains, but more than that, I'd imagine you can process it better thanks to the orcs. Their size and strength make actually extracting it easier, and then you can process the ore into usable metal too . . . Probably by just smashing the fuck out of it until you get smaller, purer, more easily smelted pieces."

She looked pleased, which I decided was *not* a good thing, and smiled at me.

"Half right, which is half more than anyone else has gotten so far. You really are worth the risk, aren't you?"

I smiled back but didn't feel much of anything regarding the expression inside.

"You're going to hurt me if I refuse to help, am I right?" I asked her.

Adravigi's smile grew, but only by a few millimeters.

"You're getting the picture." She nodded. "Yes, Solitaire Belahont. I will do what I need to. I won't enjoy it, but I won't hesitate to do it if you force my hand."

I nodded. It was refreshing, being honest, to have someone be so up-front about their intent to put me in the dick skinner. I almost felt grateful for it.

Almost.

CHAPTER THIRTY-FOUR

Shango's POV: Day 152
Current Wealth: 664 gold, 5 silver, 29 copper

It was just chemistry. Chemistry and engineering. And I wasn't even sure if it was advanced.

Solitaire was the cleverest man I'd ever met, seen, or even heard about, but he wasn't a god, and he had his limits. The difference between us was that of a modestly smart man and an average one, not a genius and a simpleton. If he could do it, so could I.

Yeah. A few problems with that line of thought.

The first was that Solitaire and I had different strengths. My mind was narrower than his, more focused. I excelled in the things I did well. Even he would, while puking in his mouth mind you, admit that he couldn't balance deception, advantages, and countermoves in his head the way I did as a matter of course in negotiations. But that specialization was biting me here. There were just too many things that needed juggling, too many skills to lean on. I was good at all of them, brilliant at a lot.

But not *all*. And that was my main concern. I wasn't sure I'd ever understand everything here the way Solitaire did. Which meant, given that this was a workstation, that I may never replicate his technology. He'd explained black powder's creation so we wouldn't be deprived of that. Otherwise though?

Our advantage as technological pioneers in Redacle might have been dead in the water.

So came my second problem; I didn't *know* what Solitaire did. For all his brilliance, Solitaire was only intuiting, at most, maybe half of what he did. All his work was built around a reinforced spine of tangible knowledge. Knowledge gained from his lunatic mother, sure, but still practical experience that didn't exist in this world. I couldn't compensate for lacking an entire childhood of having bomb-making techniques instilled in me, even if I were twice his intelligence.

I could tell that I was fighting an uphill battle, but I kept going. The frustration that had gnawed at me early on was gone, drained away like pus from a boil. All that was left was the knowledge of what needed doing and the will to do it.

The air was acrid, smelling of imperfect combustion and Solitaire's typical brand of near-suicidal chemistry. Reactants and products tinged my nostrils with every inhalation, and the inside was cramped. Musky. I pushed through it, making notes of what chemicals did, trying to compare my deductions with the remembered details of my youthful chemistry lessons.

I was actually good at chemistry, maybe as good at Solitaire when comparing talents alone. I didn't have an issue piecing together what would do what based on atomic composition at least. It just made sense to me. That was a far cry from success though, and my efforts were interrupted by a knocking on the door.

"I'm busy," I called out, then another knock rang, and I realized ignoring it wouldn't make it go away. I paused my work, turned, and made for the door. Opening and making way for Phelia to step in.

She looked concerned, I thought. Face taut and worn, eyes sunken slightly with worry. As usual she didn't waste time—at least no more time than she already had—mincing words.

"I'm worried about you," Phelia told me, meeting my eye as she said it and moving farther into the room.

"Not there," I told her abruptly, gesturing to where she was about to step. "That's one of Solitaire's traps. You'll be instantly killed if you stand on it."

Phelia didn't *scream*, but she was barely short of it. "And your answer?"

Of course she hadn't let me distract her—it would've been uncharacteristic if that had worked—but I'd given it a try anyway. Might've gotten lucky.

"Solitaire's gone." I shrugged. "We need someone to pick up the slack. Our entire model of growth was built on the premise of further technological discovery or, at worst, maintaining the technologies we already had."

It had been pure idiocy not to have him take exhaustive notes on it all. We had the paper and ink now. I supposed none of us believed any of us could truly be killed. We'd gotten through so many scrapes that it had turned to delusion.

When I next glanced over at Phelia, she was staring at me. But not just with concern anymore.

"Your brother has been captured," she whispered. "Captured by . . . savages, animals. *Orcs*. Your other brother is an emotional wreck with guilt. How can you be focusing on lapses in production now of all times?"

I didn't bother pausing or pretending to think about it. There was no time to feign the usual emotions.

"Because that's what's most important," I told her. "That's what we need to focus on long term to maximize our odds of success here. Everything else is a distraction. I'm doing the only practical thing."

"Beam needs you," Phelia shot back, making an accusation of the statement.

"The world needs me," I told her. "And they outnumber Beam billions to one."

Phelia took a step back, staring at me with . . . yes, disgust. Horror, betrayal, and disgust. I might have given some thought as to why under different circumstances, but I had no time to play petty gardener for the emotions of those around me. There were things that needed doing, and only I could do them. Maybe not *even* I.

She left me soon after that, heading out of the room in a storm of rage that, thankfully, took her too far away to be a continued distraction. I focused on my work, though the conversation had left me with a few idle thoughts.

Solitaire was, in all likelihood, still alive. This wasn't hope talking, just the basic facts of his capture. That he'd been taken at all, while posing such an obvious threat in battle, was evidence that he was recognized by the enemy as a potentially valuable asset. I doubted they'd go to all that trouble just to kill him in captivity—it made no sense at all. So Solitaire was alive.

And probably being either persuaded or, soon enough, forced to work on improving *their* technology too.

Something struck me then. A foreboding—or as close to one as my pathologically calm mind could register. Solitaire had been making progress. Slow, steady. But progress. He'd been getting better. Healing.

This might set all of that back, might turn him back into the feral monster I'd arrived with.

I thought about that and waited for the rush of emotion to hit. It didn't, so instead I turned the idea over in my head. There were problems with a violent insane man being on your side, obviously, especially one with his creative intellect. But there were advantages too.

How many times had we cowed someone with the threat of Solitaire's violence? How many *more* times could I use that as a redirection? And then there was the simple fact of his effectiveness as a killer. Solitaire had a way of understanding people—of truly getting inside their heads—that I could never replicate. A technique of emotion and intuition relying on equipment my brain didn't seem to have come with. The ways he used human fear were almost arcane.

But no, Solitaire was more useful to me sane. He was more useful to the world while in control of himself.

And I couldn't deny that I preferred to see my friend healthy and happy.

[Appraisal]
Class: Emperor
Level: 22
Condition: Fine
Modifiers: +11 Toughness, +9 Strength, +8 Speed, +6 Alertness
Statistics: Strength 15, Speed 14, Dexterity 6, Stamina 5, Toughness 15, Alertness 14, Charisma 9, Intelligence 8
Inventory: Local wear, plate armor, repeater, shortspear

Class Abilities: Appraisal III
Current Experience Points: 143/660
Unspent Skillpoints: 0

Combat was marginally less of a concern now. My statline had gotten a nice boost from my recent successes in Elswick, and, last I'd checked, Beam's had been upped by his time in Swanhen too. Between the two of us, we'd probably gained more power than we'd lost by seeing Solitaire taken and several of our men killed. Direct power, at least, not counting his inventions.

Which meant expansionism was our best move, to leverage the temporary surge before we could feel the lack of our long-term growth. Time was against us now, not for us, and if we didn't adjust strategies, it'd eat us alive like it did everyone else.

CHAPTER THIRTY-FIVE

Beam's POV: Day 152
Current Wealth: 664 gold, 5 silver, 29 copper

Training was, usually, a practice in relaxation for me. Soothing in its familiarity, keeping the mind calm and still by pushing the body through a great enough extreme to distract by association. It wasn't working today though. There was no extreme great enough.

I put everyone through their paces, even as I found my own to be increasingly impossible for them to match. If there was one problem with my constant growth, it was that I was finding it ever harder to actually get myself sweating in practice. Arthur still helped with that much.

That, and I had a lot more people to train alongside Helena.

For the past few days, we'd been getting a slow, steady trickle of new recruits. Some from Swanhen—those had been with us since we saved the town—and some from Elswick, spurred on by stories of our crushing victory against the orcs. It hadn't happened like that of course, but pointing that fact out hadn't seemed like the sort of thing that got us additional subordinates, so I kept my big mouth shut.

Training wasn't going as smoothly as before, for a few reasons. I was among them. It was hard to stand there and look heroic when I knew my brother was missing because of my own failing. The more obvious my lie became to me, the harder it was to tell. It didn't matter that I was hurting us by not selling it. I just . . . couldn't. Helena compensated of course, but that was still compensation at its core.

With more than a dozen men who'd already gone through training and fought with us twice, we were progressing slower than before. And it was because of me and my inability to fucking get over myself.

Well, bitterness wasn't helping any either. If it were, I'd already have saved Solitaire through sheer volume. Perhaps then Shango would actually be speaking to me instead of barricading himself in Solitaire's lab just to get out of it.

"It's not your fault."

I jerked around, reflexes fraying every nerve I had as the unexpected voice rang out. My fists were already balled and ready to fly by the time I finally looked up to recognize Argar's face solemnly gazing down at me.

"Thanks," I told him. "Thanks, Argar, I know, but . . . That's still good to hear, thank you." The lie came easily enough. At least this one, I knew, would be sparing someone else a bit of grief instead of causing it. I headed off without much pause to train alone after that.

Difficult to train now. More difficult to do it alone. I'd started swinging around big blocks of lead and steel. Thick, heavy things that each weighed about as much as a small child. They'd have been hard enough to bicep curl when I'd first arrived, but now they made perfectly workable training weapons to build all the muscles that went behind a sword swing. More particularly, the ones that went behind a sword swing you were trying to kill a man in armor with.

These last few months, my arms and back had gotten bigger than at any other point in my entire life. I'd probably gained one or two dozen pounds even with the drop in my nutritional quality, and I was only packing on more muscle as time went by. No point in cutting weight and focusing on mobility now. I was fighting to kill.

And there was no help for me, of course. Not from that fucking monster in my head, not unless I was doing something pointless like winning a shitting tournament. I'd have to rely on my own body. Even when it didn't serve the monster's own interest to ignore me.

Hold on, there was a thought. What did Solitaire always say? *Everyone who even slightly glances at me is trying to kill us.* No, not that, the other thing. *Don't listen to what people say. Look to what they do.*

The entity had been very overt about how powerful and scary it was, but it also had a clear interest in me . . . doing things. Fighting. Winning. Using its power. That last part was a contradiction clear as day. Why the hell would the thing that wanted me to use supernatural powers not give me those same powers? Why would it cheer me on for throwing myself at the King of Blades like a one-man wrecking crew, then fail to give me advice or help or whatever my next fucking class ability would be when my friend was being dragged away and taking all our munitions with him?

Look to what they do. Well, this one wasn't doing anything. What did that tell me?

My mind must still have been slow from the exhaustion and mental batterings I'd taken over the last few days because it took me a good long while to figure it out.

Are you there?

No reply, so I asked again. And added a few flavorful coaxes onto the words, remembering how easily the entity's ego bruised.

I know you've been lying to me. I know you're weaker than you've been pretending. I know you can't do half the things you've been pretending not to want to. The jig is up. Deny it.

If you dare, I liked to think my tone had added. Truth was, I didn't have the faintest idea how well sarcasm made the leap across one mind to another. Mental-only communication was still new ground for me.

Fortunately, I wasn't left to aimlessly ponder for long. A familiar voice racked through me.

You goad me.

I didn't let the sudden presence in my thoughts unnerve me, though it was bloody unnerving. Just replied.

Yes, I goad you. Do something about it.

Silence. I spoke again. Thought again. Whatever.

I'm not going to stop bothering you until I get an answer. Am I right?

Another silence rang out, long enough that I almost kept going before, at last, I got my answer. It wasn't a long one, wasn't a complex one. But it conveyed everything I needed to hear and more.

Yes.

CHAPTER THIRTY-SIX

Solitaire's POV: Day 153
Current Wealth: 667 gold, 14 silver, 32 copper

Walls, that was my major contribution to Barbed Point. Walls. Nice big walls, made with a halfway decent understanding of mathematics and engineering. Walls with angled sections to deflect projectiles, their weights distributed and supported properly. Walls that might last a good long while.

But still, fundamentally, just walls. Because if I was going to help the town of giant angry rapists, it would be with as little overtly weapons-grade technology as I could manage to give them. Even this much stung, knowing how well it would perform against magi or siege engines compared to the shoddier architecture they'd been making before.

Funny thing was, I actually didn't know how good the walls even were. I had a basic knowledge of mathematics and engineering, and I could intuit things well enough to fill in the gaps my actual understanding had, but that just meant I had no clue about the relative advancement of what I was having them do. For all I knew, I'd given them architecture able to weather cannonballs. I suppose I'd find out if I ever attacked the place.

"You really are clever," Adravigi said abruptly at my back. She was sneaky, very quiet when she walked. Quiet enough that she was risking her life every time she let her presence be known by speaking within arm's reach of my back.

This time, I resisted the instinctual, reflexive urge to spin kick her in the head.

"I told you." I shrugged, not enjoying the acknowledgment as much as I usually would have. It was soured slightly by knowing that every flourish of intellect I demonstrated would only make me a more enticing and useful ally. I was keeping myself safe by feeding the orcs information, but I was tightening my chains too. It was a balancing act. Freedom versus security.

And that was without considering that Adravigi was, no doubt, having me followed subtly on top of the overt bodyguards accompanying me all over the place. Cunning bitch.

"You're holding back, however," she noted, thankfully not taking pride in having noticed the obvious.

I just shrugged again. It irritated her, which was both good and bad. An enemy who was irritated was more likely to make mistakes, but mistakes could include hurting a person who was useful to them. I decided it was worth the risk. Barely.

"I heard about the weapons you used against us," she pressed. "The magic ones that spit fire and metal. You could make those for us, couldn't you? You could arm us with tools of war to overturn this very kingdom and make us the greatest military power in the region." She stepped in closer, eyes intense. "You could rule us alongside me if you did."

That was a lot of offers. In fact, it was so many offers that it made that little paranoia bit of my brain start frothing at the mouth, rolling around on the floor, and shrieking about killing John Lennon. I kept as much from showing on my face of course, making sure to be polite and calm as I replied.

"First time I've gotten an offer like that. What makes you think I care about ruling?"

She smirked.

"I've never seen a man half as sure of his own intelligence as you, nor one half as impatient with the world's stupidity. Do you expect me to believe you *don't* want to rule?"

Well, she had me there.

"One of the stupidest things about humans is how many of them think they should be calling the shots." I shrugged. "Kings, emperors, prophets, Reddit moderators, cops. They need control, and they think they're the ones to bring it about. It's pathetic. No, I don't want to rule. I'm better than the rest of you by such a wide margin that it's not even worth calculating. Why would I be stupid enough to want infinite power?"

I almost had myself convinced, and certainly had her. That's the issue with clever deductions. They're only worth anything if you can keep your confidence in them.

"What do you want then?" she pressed. "There must be something. You and your brothers were working for something. What is it?"

Interesting question. I'd barely even thought about it myself. Was I doing this to genuinely help people? To prove I could? Because I was, deep down, a violent person, in search of excuses to justify my destructive behavior and in desperate need of help to drag me out of my self-cannibalizing ouroboros of psychotic annihilation? Nah, that was lame.

I was doing it because some people needed killing, and I just so happened to have been dumped into a whole world of them. If the universe didn't want me to be a terrorist, it wouldn't have made everyone such a cunt and me smart enough to see it. Maybe I was a bad man—with my upbringing, I hardly had a choice in the matter—but I could take out plenty of other bad people to make up the difference.

Of course that wasn't the sort of thing you could just *say*. Unfortunately, wanting to kill most of the people you met tended to give you a reputation for being unstable or dangerous. Not great when you were at someone's mercy and a known manufacturer of, from their perspective, weapons of mass destruction. I didn't think Adravigi would preemptively kill me rather than keep trying to make use of my knowledge, but I couldn't know for sure and wasn't in a position to survive taking more chances than I absolutely had to.

"How about my freedom?" I asked with a smile.

Adravigi didn't smile back.

"You think you'll find more freedom out there than in here?" she asked. "You'll still be a prisoner to the laws that put you below every noble brat with half your guts and a tenth of your brains."

Right, of course. That was the same as my literal imprisonment here. Note to self: Arguing with slavers is an exercise in futility.

"I'd have my family," I noted, deciding to take a different stance altogether than the one that required moral insanity to not already agree with. Maybe I'd actually get somewhere that way.

By the look of her, Adravigi was at least *slightly* moved by the appeal. Though her eyes were still hard with resolve and contradiction.

"I see." Her voice came out tight and reluctant. I knew then that she'd not bother continuing to convince me. Not for a while at least.

And I wondered whether I'd made a mistake. I already had to be sneaky with my plans, knowing she was keeping track of everything I introduced to Barbed Point and watching my every move. That was when she'd thought—or hoped—that I was aimless and stuck in my ways. If she believed that I had something serious holding me elsewhere, she herself would be more diligent about keeping me from leaving.

That was the problem with smart people. They drew a lot of conclusions from a little information.

"What were you actually here to ask me?" I hurriedly added, wanting to give her as little time for conclusion drawing as I could get away with. "Or was that it?"

I added a hint of a sneer to the inquiry, to see if she'd pick up on it and feel overestimated. Most people *hated* falling short of expectations, and I was willing to bet someone who ranted about cleverness as much as this one did would be even more inclined to.

I was right.

"Your loyalty hasn't been accepted by most of the orcs yet," she told me matter-of-factly enough that it was almost tempting to believe that she *wasn't* just giving an excuse for whatever she personally had decided to do next. "And we need to fix that. Every day you stay here, with the memory of what your weapons did to our forces fresh in their minds, the odds of you being killed by some overeager moron remain unacceptably high."

"And let me guess," I began. "The only way to reduce this is to be more helpful."

Obviously that wasn't what she was going to say, or what she wanted me to think. But if she thought I thought she was trying to needle me into offering more technology, instead of justifying more surveillance, it might convince her that I was less suspicious than I was. Rarely a bad idea to let yourself get underestimated. At least by your captors.

"No, you need to prove yourself. To me, to them." She was, at least, up-front about having a stake in what I did too, but the tone in her voice . . . It had me worried.

"What will I be doing?" I asked, sharper than was probably wise.

Adravigi met my eye and responded with a voice that sounded like something dead was speaking to me.

"We will soon be going on another raid, and this time, Solitaire Belahont, you shall accompany us."

CHAPTER THIRTY-SEVEN

Solitaire's POV: Day 154
Current Wealth: 668 gold, 4 silver, 35 copper

The town wasn't far from Barbed Point, and it wasn't very big. The orcs knew ways through the hills that local humans didn't, and with their stride sizes and robust bodies, a single day of marching was enough to bring our group to its destination. I wished it'd taken longer.

Nice place, and with decent defenses. Walls made from what looked like entire tree trunks, circling the whole thing and with enough guards to man them lightly. It seemed like a logging town. Rather, it had to be one because I doubted any crops would grow for shit on land like this, and there was a great big woodland next to it.

Someone knelt down beside me, and a quick glance showed me it was Adravigi.

"Any thoughts on invading the place?" she asked. I blinked at her.

"You're aware I'm not a tactician?" I shot back.

"Could've fooled me, with the mess you made of our Swanhen occupation."

"That was different." I shrugged. I knew people, and panic, and I knew the basic logic of moving things across distances, delaying around corners, the simple mathematics our world was based on. Outside of tactile reasoning and emotional intuition though I had no real background in command or tactics.

Still, I supposed neither did she.

"Why should I tell you?" I asked after a moment. "If I want to, I can choose to just not help you. You can try torturing me, but that won't work. Torture in general doesn't work. Whatever I end up saying could be the truth, or a lie, or something I only *think* is the truth because having all my pubes torn out left me frothing mad."

To her credit, she met my eye with as cool a look as I'd seen anywhere and replied with words that were even cooler. This wasn't a woman to be easily thrown off. Unfortunate, that. My escape would've been easier otherwise.

"This is your chance to prove yourself," she noted. "To them, the orcs, not even just to me. How much easier will escape be for you if you have half the settlement convinced you can be trusted not to try to do it? More than half even. Let's be honest here, orcs aren't the brightest."

My blood ran cold. Of course she knew I was thinking about escape. She was clever. And of course she'd timed telling me until now, where I was staring down a town I knew was doomed and left weary and irritated by hard travel. My face slipped and gave away my reaction before I could cover it, and that instant's lapse was enough for her to confirm whatever she'd suspected.

Clever bitch. She'd been right, on many levels. My choices were being made for me by sheer practicality. When were they not?

"Obviously they're aware of how close Barbed Point is," I observed. "Or some orc settlement at least. Those walls would've been hard to make, expensive. Which means they've probably gone to the trouble of at least drilling on how to use them since they're too well maintained to be some generational inheritance of long-dead paranoia."

"So you think they'll put up a fight?"

I glanced over to Adravigi.

"Definitely, they'll be terrified and have their backs to the wall. And that defensive structure will be a force multiplier for them."

If ever there was a kind of fight for me *not* to pick, it was this one. Then again, we had the advantage in sheer force. We had that ten times over.

Huh. Numbers were on my side this time. That was a nice feeling, almost. Spoiled of course by the fact that I was now on the side of massacring innocent people instead of protecting them. My mouth tasted foul, like other people's misery. But then when did it not?

"I was thinking the same thing," Adravigi replied, glancing at me and reeking of suspicion. Funny smelling that from the other side, and also not unexpected. This one glorified intelligence so much it was a wonder she didn't distrust me for not revealing the secret of immortality to her. I wondered how she'd react to finding out about my hilarious ignorance compared to an actual engineer.

"Why are you doing this?" I asked abruptly, finding the curiosity all too overwhelming to resist satisfying suddenly. "Surely you're just as capable of escape as me."

More capable, really, considering she didn't need to worry about her escape attempts being overlooked by a person with considerable intelligence and completely reasonable paranoia.

Adravigi stiffened at my question, and I smelled, instantly, a cocktail of emotion I'd half expected. One didn't make the life choices she had without a very strong motivator one way or the other.

"Once upon a time, there was a woman," she replied, eyes suddenly distant and unfocused. "A clever woman, but a poor woman. And a *woman*. This world wasn't kind to her, for obvious reasons, and she found her gifts going to waste. People didn't care about her head for sums or her mind for estimation. They only wanted to know how well she could scrub floors, clean dishes . . . suck cocks. But this didn't stop her from trying. She believed, you see, that she could get somewhere, could make things better for herself. And you know what? She was right. It took her years—fucking years. But one day she'd succeeded in stealing enough spare hours in her master's study to have taught herself to read and write. She'd gotten somewhere; she had *options*. And then the orcs came."

I saw her stiffen, and suddenly that distant emotion was twisted back with rage. With hatred.

"She'd been in town on business, you see, sent to deliver a message by her master. And she'd taken that opportunity to spend the coin she'd been hoarding and find the bargains she'd been studying and finally set up her own, small shop. The orcs burned that shop. They took her. They raped her. They dragged her back to Barbed Point. And the ridiculous thing was that, over time, she found more opportunities there than she had anywhere else. You see, this world isn't kind to its people. It doesn't care about your abilities or your potential. It just wants you to surrender for whatever arbitrary fate it's decided for you." She spit on the ground. "Well fuck that. I'm not going to listen to it, and I'm not going to limit myself to what some fat, stupid old men have to say about the way my life should go." Her eyes came back around to me now, burning with passion and belief. "Can you imagine what it's like to have the whole world tell you you're worthless while seeing it exclusively populated by idiots?"

Of course I could, insofar as my limited experiences allowed. And of course, then, Adravigi was so desperate to do what she was doing. She'd found her path of least resistance, and not moving forward was simply unthinkable for her.

Could I blame her? Perhaps, everyone was fundamentally in control of their actions—barring those who deserved *help* rather than hatred—but plenty of people did worse than her, and without a tenth of her justification. Adravigi had been forced to pick between herself and the world. Was that any different than what anyone else did?

Yes, it was. Because her self was being threatened with a far worse fate than most would ever even come within a whisper of. By all metrics I knew, whether I liked it or not, I had no choice but to give her the label of *more moral than average*. That should tell you a lot about my average view of humanity.

Should get you thinking about the relative merits of serial murder, while you're at it.

I looked out at the town. From our distance, there was no way to actually hear children playing, but I could imagine it easily enough. The weather was warming up, but the snow was still there. About as perfect a day for fun as little kids might get. Doubtless the day of our raid would be just as perfect.

But I was being forced to pick between myself and them. Was that any different than what anyone else did?

Most anyone else wouldn't tell you they were better than other people, evolved, intelligent, moral. But then, most anyone else wasn't constantly being force-fed so much of everyone else's humanity that they forgot what their own tasted like. Maybe fewer people meant fewer people to suffer, fewer people to hurt others. Maybe the dead children of today were the absent killers of tomorrow. Maybe enough rationalizations would make it all go down easier.

"We'll need siege engines," I whispered. "Those woodlands will produce a lot of lumber. I can think of a few designs to make use of it."

INTERLUDE SIX

Elizabeth was getting used to sneaking around. It seemed to come with the territory of working for Shango Belahont.

Well, that was unfair. She'd been a thief long before they met. The only difference now was she was sneaking around with messages rather than loot. That, and she had an actually safe place to hide if the guards ever decided to break her legs. All in all, however much of a nob the bastard was, she had to admit he was a good thing for her. A good thing for lots of people, she thought. Her mind moved to Solitaire, captured again, and everything positive about her reflection evaporated.

Today Elizabeth was just doing an information dump, simple and low-risk. People cared about a million things, but so few of them bothered with *information*. That was another thing separating the Belahonts, she thought. They had minds for abstractions that most of the material-obsessed nobles standing against them simply lacked.

Viras was the natural exception, as well as a few others, but the brothers had always had a funny way of regarding things, and through her time working with them, it'd rubbed off on Elizabeth. Information was about the most valuable thing she'd been asked to move around.

Henry Grimworth was waiting just where they'd arranged him to, a nicely overlooked and nicely alienated warehouse on the edge of the city surrounded by enough poor people that the guards rarely bothered to patrol. There were drawbacks to meeting in places as dangerous as that, but they'd gotten a lot less severe since the Belahonts began building their own urban army. One of the infinite benefits of power.

A tall man was Grimworth. And about as happy looking as his name would suggest. He never did seem pleased to meet Elizabeth, though that may have just been the shape of his face. As far as she could tell, it had been chiseled into his permanent frown on a skeletal level. Might have been funny were it not aimed at her.

"You have the money?" he asked, cutting right through the pleasantries as usual. Elizabeth hid how pleased she was at that. She'd never been the most patient of girls even at the best time. Now was certainly not that.

"I have the information of where you can find it," she replied. "Best not to have noncombatants moving around with that sort of money."

He grunted, either approving or disapproving but not caring enough to make it clear which.

"Dead drop is . . ." Elizabeth trailed off, sensing, suddenly, that something was wrong.

To his credit, Grimworth was almost instantaneous in picking up on it and responding. Stance lowering, weight spreading, legs coiled and ready to go taut with muscular contraction at a moment's notice. It was like watching a bow drawn back. And Elizabeth had a feeling it would be necessary.

"Were you followed?" Grimworth snarled, voice suddenly wrung out and sharpened like the talons of some feral thing. Elizabeth was so taken aback she became stupid for a moment, question bouncing off her mind. He repeated it, angrier.

"No," she snapped, thought, blinked, then swore. "Maybe."

She'd gotten cocky. One of the few detriments of power.

"Looks like you've fucked this up good and proper," the man growled, drawing a long knife from inside his clothes and hurrying to a far wall. Elizabeth did as she saw him do, figuring that there was probably a good reason not to stand so close to the room's center and plenty of even better ones to be as close to the only nearby killer on her side as she could manage.

"You need to make a run for it," Grimworth hissed, cursing as he glanced out through the window. "There's guards, dozens of them. They seem to have cudgels and disabling weapons rather than edged steel, so . . ." He cursed again, putting away his grisly knife. "With luck, they'll fight to take us alive unless things escalate. Still, you need to run. I can fight my way out, but you'll need to jump on that distraction if you want to escape. Either of us being captured is a risk to the other."

Elizabeth didn't like the implication—either of the two there. That she would sell him out or, conversely, that he would her. There were particular times for arguing, however, and this certainly was not among them.

The door shuddered, cried out. Grimworth was backing away from it, so Elizabeth followed. Another impact rocked the entrance. It was a sturdy thing, easily two inches thick and seemingly made to resist a troll. Whatever force was on the other side though was larger than a troll in totality. A third blow came, then a fourth, and more followed. Elizabeth had lost count of the rest by the time the entrance fell apart.

Men surged in ahead of those six wielding the battering ram, and Grimworth threw himself at them. It was like watching a wolf smash into a nest of rats, a sheer physical disparity that almost tricked Elizabeth's eyes into seeing the man as a towering giant. He smashed several of the guards off their feet, forced several more back, and had broken out of the warehouse within moments.

Elizabeth was scurrying after him before she even knew what was happening. Tiny, without greatly disproportionate strength or resilience, saved only by her small stature making a difficult time of grabbing her, the confusion of those she was slipping by, and, of course, her speed.

Everyone save for her and Grimworth seemed to be moving through molasses, and even he was sluggish to her eyes. She slipped out of the first row of guards and took off at a run, daring to look back only when she was sure no grasping arms were within reach of her.

Amazingly, he was still fighting. Still winning, even. Either the guards had been more surprised by Grimworth's emergence than even he had anticipated, or the man was a great deal stronger than Alora's report had led Elizabeth to believe. Watching him barge through them was like watching an adult manhandling children. A club came from his blind spot, caught him in the temple, and sent him sidelong a step. A killing blow. It didn't kill. He shrugged it off, responded with a vicious punch that sent the offending man back in a spray of blood and teeth. Two grabbed his arm at once and were dislodged with a contemptuous flex while a third swung with a strike so slow Grimworth was able to duck beneath it and counter before it had even reached where his face *had been*.

Movement caught the corner of her eye, guards heading for Elizabeth. She cursed her own stupidity for pausing—for even considering holding back and trying to help Grimworth—and got back to running. Elizabeth was fast. Before anything else, she was fast. Always fast, always the fastest. But today she wasn't just running from a few men. The guards had known what they were doing in preparing this ambush.

More were pouring in from ahead of her, half a dozen. More. They were spaced well and with their arms splayed, making a net of limbs that she had no choice but to sprint for. She twisted, weaved, slithered around them, and sent the oafish thugs stumbling, falling, swearing. Then fingertips snagged her clothes, and it was Elizabeth's turn to surge away on uneven footing.

Something smashed into her from behind, sweeping her clean off her feet, and she went down with a great deal more than just her own weight to pin her.

"You, my dear, are under arrest for colluding with known criminal factions."

CHAPTER THIRTY-EIGHT

Fatigue was a luxury I didn't have the time to indulge, so I beat it back from my mind with a club. I was pacing the mansion, thinking, using one of my rare breaks to continue the arduous process of planning out our next steps. When I wasn't doing this, I was back to emulating Solitaire's creations. With mixed success, to say the least.

My pacing today was interrupted by Lady Adannaya. I looked up as she approached me, mentally switching gears from long-term planning to short-term manipulation. I still hadn't figured this one out yet. She was smart, that much I knew, but she was a great deal more slippery than even Phelia. I didn't know her plans or ideals, and yet I couldn't afford to keep her at arm's length and risk driving her off before I could figure them out. She had to be drip fed points of intrigue to hold her around us while I worked on the problem.

Always another layer to the lies, wasn't there? Always another.

"Good afternoon, my lord," she said without smiling. Good. A smile would've been too obvious, too easy, too tempting. That she'd resisted it showed a knack for lying most didn't possess.

"Good afternoon," I said back, smiling myself. Because when one *did* possess that knack, it was often a good idea to convince others one didn't. Particularly when they might be working against you.

"Forgive me if this is forward, my lord," she began with all the hesitance of a woman who didn't give two shits how forward she was being, "but I simply wish to express my condolences regarding the loss of your brother. I was there when he fell, and I saw firsthand how . . . bravely he fought."

If I knew Solitaire, he'd probably invented several new war crimes before being captured, but that wasn't the most concerning thing here. She spoke as if she thought he was dead. I could use that, at least when hiding Solitaire's absence was no longer an option.

"Okay," I replied, realizing I ought to say something at least and knowing that how I responded to banal pleasantries didn't really matter that much.

She stood there, eyeing me. Suddenly the woman seemed awkward, unbalanced. That might have been useful ordinarily, but now she didn't really have any information I needed. At least none I could get my hands on with a little unbalancing of this caliber, so I just sighed.

"I'm sorry but who are you, and what are you doing in my house?" I knew the former, of course, and suspected I knew the latter, but it was rarely a bad idea to be underestimated.

"I am Lady Adannaya," she said slowly, patiently. "Your wife, Lady Phelia, welcomed me into this mansion as an indefinite guest."

She was being polite, not abrasive. Not having her interest in me shrivel, which meant she was probably playing an angle. A woman looking for partners would be worried to see how abrasive and cold I was being. That she was playing things so calmly told me she was just after our technology.

Well who wasn't?

"I don't have time for this now, sorry."

I breezed past her, not giving much thought to the genuinely stunned look upon her face, and headed for Phelia. It was time for the other part of my job—the part that *should* have been my only job. And would have been, if my brother hadn't gotten kidnapped again.

Phelia was where she usually is, in her office and, as with increasing frequency these days, working. Solitaire's absence was keenly felt in our long-term plans, which had been undergoing a frantic rearrangement on her behalf as much as mine. I'd come to lean on her a great deal more since. The fatigue upon her face, I supposed, was better proof of that than my own word.

"Morning," I told her, closing the door just as I said it and starting into the room. "I think w—"

The door burst open, and I whipped around. Time in Redacle hadn't left me as paranoid as Solitaire—I didn't think anything could do that—but I'd certainly developed a jagged edge for surprises, and it was bared as I turned to find Alora storming in with a face that sent shivers down even my spine.

"Elizabeth's been arrested."

I froze, thought, then gestured her on. Alora told me everything we knew—everything Henry had seen before extricating himself—and I forced myself to slow down and work through everything piece by piece. Panic was the last thing I needed now. The only thing that could worsen bad luck was a stupid decision made in response.

Fortunately, as far as bad luck went, this . . . could definitely be worse.

"The charges won't stick to Elizabeth *or* Henry," I said at last, confident about that much at least. "We've been careful not to have anything that indefensibly ties them to what we've been doing, and once we start leaning on the guards, they'll have no choice but to release Elizabeth. Particularly once we start making some pointed suggestions regarding our own household guard."

Alora's brows arched, but she, at the very least, didn't seem intimidated by the prospect. The city guard probably outnumbered our soldiers a dozen to one, but they were poorly armed and equipped. Made for beating up poor people, not actual combat. Batons didn't go very far against spears, even ones not made from tool steel. Which only left one other factor. A big one, however.

"Everyone knows now that the Belahonts and Jeleheim are working together," Alora observed, and I stiffened. I'd known of course—I'd been about to say this—but it still made me wince hearing the fact given voice. I glanced over my shoulder and found Phelia looking suddenly green.

"It will be harder to use them now," Phelia noted, not letting her own disquiet slow her thoughts. "But not impossible. Progress will slow, but it will still be progress."

True enough. There was a bigger concern though.

"It won't look good," I noted, taking a seat, mulling it over. "Not a lot of nobles are sympathetic to them. This was the reason we wanted to avoid a public connection in the first place."

"That was always a risk." Phelia shrugged. "It's no strange thing to have a gang in your pocket, for a powerful family. Even several. The coalition has the Dead Edge, and we have the Jeleheim."

That was, in fact, what I was worried about. Now that they knew we existed on that level, they might engage us on it. What was one gang wiping out another, after all?

"How did this happen?" Alora cut in, seeming to follow everything well enough, I noticed, but with her own set of priorities. Well that was no surprise. Her job was keeping us alive.

"Viras, I'd guess." I shrugged. "I doubt it's a coincidence. He probably found out right before he tipped the guard off."

If he'd found out significantly earlier, he'd have waited until leaning on them to press us. It would have gotten him more. An actual conviction—as far as that concept existed in this legal system—or far more complications in freeing our ally.

"But how did the guards know where to go? Do you think Elizabeth was followed?" I considered that and then realized . . . No. Elizabeth wouldn't have allowed that. I stood up slowly, heading from the room and searching for Beam. He was training of course, lashing a boulder with punches and kicks, ripping chunks of stone from its body with every impact of his iron-hard fists. He paused as I approached, stiffening. Awkward and half worried. I ignored it, having more important things to focus on right now.

"Shango." He smiled, forcing it with as much exertion as he had any of his strikes. "What are you—"

I came in close, lowered my voice, made absolute sure only he would hear by seizing the air around us and thickening it into a muffling, distorting wall to obliterate the sound. Then I spoke.

"There's a spy in the house," I told him. "One of our crew. We've been betrayed."

CHAPTER THIRTY-NINE

Solitaire's POV: Day 155
Current Wealth: 670 gold, 13 silver, 6 copper

It wasn't hard, making the siege engine. We decided on a trebuchet in the end, simply because it was the best pick. Maybe others would've been limited by the difficulty of actually getting a working design laid out with so many moving parts and extra factors to account for in the flexible pulleys. Maybe I would have myself, normally. Not today. Adravigi was at least my equal in engineering, and if she lacked my knowledge generally, we were both about on par when it came to matters like this. The two of us had a working design laid out within minutes, and we spent the next hour improving on it until we had something I was semiconfident actually exceeded whatever the local humans' own king could bring to the field.

Working with Adravigi was an exercise in . . . well, not much really. It was laughably easy. She had a way of intuiting things that made communication simple enough to be done monosyllabically, if I really wanted to, and every so often she'd surprise me by improving on one of my own suggestions. I didn't think she was generally as intelligent as Shango, not even close, but in the field of tactility and mechanisms, she was unbelievably ingenious. I actually caught myself enjoying the work.

Of course, those little bouts of enjoyment never lasted long. It only took a memory of why we were doing it—to kill people.

At last the weapon was done, which left the creating of the day finished. Now we just had the destroying. I felt gutted as I looked at it. A towering thing, maybe triple my own height and made with a surprising lack of ramshackle clumsiness considering.

Orcs were unexpectedly good with their hands, and more so at larger-scale construction. Having several times the individual strength of a human, I supposed, was convenient for all the heavy hauling that people in my world had had to start making use of leverage to overcome. I wished these ones could have been a little worse. Could have bought the town a little more time.

I watched the trebuchet fire.

Counterweighting stone came down, ropes tightened, torsion built, and finally the projectile was whipped through the air like a sling bullet. Two hundred pounds of rock spinning and hurtling at our target like Satan's own fist.

It missed, of course. I'd certainly never fired a trebuchet, and none of the idiots with me had either. I considered letting them flounder around failing for a while longer but steeled myself. I could curry more favor, help more people, by aiding more, and an extra hour of terror was hardly worth buying these villagers. I tracked the trajectory, eyeballed its path, made a few guestimates, and ordered some readjustments. The next shot hit just a few meters in front of the wall, rolling and bouncing to slam into it.

The wood held, but now I had the range and the angles. A few more adjustments—tiny ones this time, in the order of single degrees—and the trebuchet's next stone struck the wall directly.

It broke apart like kindling, and then it did so again and again. Every boulder the trebuchet loosed from that third one was another hole in the walls, and within half an hour, we'd left a section dozens of paces wide collapsing and crumbling.

My heartbeat felt louder than the bombardment, thudding in my ears, almost making me dizzy. I tasted acid in my mouth, felt fingernails cutting into my palms as I curled hands into fists, shivered and quivered with the adrenal twitches of . . . What? Impotent rage? Bitterness? Guilt?

If these people were in the orcs' sights, they were dead already. By helping to kill them fast, I could both save them suffering and better my position in a way that would let me help more. It was logical; it made sense. But I couldn't do it. I couldn't *bear* to do it. My fucking stupid human emotions were screaming in protest.

I almost leaped out of my skin when the hand came down on my arm, despite the obvious friendliness of it. I almost pounced the speaker and started mauling him, biting and ripping with teeth, fingernails, fists. For just one moment, I was the animal. Then I calmed myself.

It was Guraganar touching me, far from the most convenient person to savage to death. I restrained the urge and met his eyes, and waited for the dull, vicious murderous dog to speak.

"You did well," he told me in his garbled half speech. "This attack is going faster and safer than without you."

You stupid fucking ape, I'm going to eat your tongue.

"Obviously" was all I said, deciding to settle on a subtle reminder of what I'd said to him when we met about his intelligence. The tone, the expression, everything except the words—which a slave couldn't get away with. By the flash of hurt in his eyes I saw it had landed. Lovely.

"Are you ready?" he asked.

I blinked at him, taken aback, stared. Realized what was happening, but asked anyway because I didn't *want* to.

"Ready for what?" I croaked. Guraganar grinned now, a nasty look that exposed all his tusk-long teeth.

"For raid," he pressed. "You will fight on the front lines, to earn your place and prove yourself."

"I'm not a front liner," I replied, looking around for Adravigi to find support. She was nowhere to be seen, and I knew even before glimpsing that she'd set this up. Guraganar wouldn't be given the chance to hurl me out into a fight without her explicit say-so. I'd been fucked over.

"Front lines," the orc repeated. "Get ready." He gestured to his side, and I saw a set of armor. Clumsy iron, thick and heavy. It was orcish, but it was sized differently. Similar height as the others, but thinner by far. It was sized for a human as tall as most orcs were. It was sized for me.

I realized a lot of things very quickly there, and I buried all of them. There was nothing for it, no clevering my way out of this one. The only person who'd be susceptible to my reason had disappeared into nowhere, perhaps to avoid being on its receiving end. My mind was of no use now, just my body.

Slowly, with limbs that felt like they were made of lead, I put the armor on. There were slaves there to help me dress in it, to arm me with my choice of thick and heavy blades—of which I settled on a nastily weighted machete. I watched as the orcs stood around panting and roaring, beating their chests, hopping and swinging at the air. I felt the salty brine of their bloodlust, excitement mixed with rage, mixed with fear, mixed with that most special of emotions that came when one person saw another and failed to realize it.

The orcs started downhill for the humans, and I came along with them. I could easily keep up of course, even in armor much heavier than my tool steel set and competing with orcs. We came down like a plague because we were. Arrows rained upon us, mostly missing and a few finding their marks. One orc went down with a shaft sticking from his neck. I saw one about to hit my own and moved at the last moment to send it bouncing off my pauldron. The run continued, the death came closer, the battle reared up and snarled at us, foaming at the mouth and with eyes red and aglow.

And then, at last, we hit the village.

CHAPTER FORTY

Solitaire's POV: Day 155
Current Wealth: 670 gold, 13 silver, 6 copper

Everything was messy, a clotted compression of flailing limbs and terror. I wasn't one foot through the breach before a spear came for me, barely batted aside with my machete as orcs behind me drove my body forward into the row of meat blocking my way. It gave, mass and momentum proving more than a match for the people trying to stave us off. There was a pressure, crushing and painful, but my enhanced body weathered it just long enough to survive being driven through the row of bodies and out the other side.

There were enemies, a dozen, more. All of them were armed but not armored. Simple spears and frightened faces, eyes wide and half of them fallen straight on me. I lunged forward into the thick of it, waiting for a spear to come at me, then beheading it with one swing. Its wielder didn't even have time to scream. I was on him a moment later and swinging again. He split open, guts and gore filling the air like worms bursting from the ground. I rolled under the coiling entrails and came up slashing, took a foot off at the knee, and saw something coming at my head from one side. Ducked again, felt a blade snag my shoulder, swore. Slashed, punched. Slashed again.

Men fell around me, bodies landing hard, limbs landing soft. The air was filled with a shrieking that I took a moment to realize came from me, a deep, animal snarl born in my muscles and bursting out through my lungs. I chased after it, going wherever the roar took me and killing whatever waited there.

Orcs were bursting through now, spilling into the town like toxin from a syringe. I was ahead of them, cutting my way deeper in and watching the defenders melt away from me. Everything around me was a sea of hatred, fear, horror, disgust. I was swimming in murder, drowning in it. It seeped into me, through the skin, into the muscles and bone. Urged me to move, demanded that I add to it. It made me sick. It made me dizzy. It made me forget about everything except killing and being killed.

I wasn't killed.

The defenders were falling back already, their front lines crushed, mutilated, and eaten alive by the waves of orcish iron. They had others of course, and the trick would be running them down before they got to them. There'd be no conveying that order though, only leading by example. I rushed ahead and split the nearest one's skull in half. Orcs aren't quite as sharp as humans, but even they got that message. Or, at least, got excited enough to sprint forward and keep killing. It didn't take long for another half dozen or more defenders to be mopped up while they tried making a break for the rest of their side. Then our own forces were bolstering cohesion again, ready for the real advance.

It was a quick affair, but bloody. Bodies came apart beneath my swings and those of the orcs, my allies for this fight. Blood wet the air and made the cobbles slick and dangerous. Limbs fell, and I stared into the faces of people as I killed them. It was no different than what I'd done already in a lot of ways. The simple mechanics of it were unchanged. The practical facts were identical. But the weight on my back grew heavier with every life taken, the urge to turn around and start hacking apart my own side almost irresistible. I resisted. I had to.

Someone came at me, almost orc big and moving fast. He swung his spear like he'd spent a lot of time with it and almost took off a bit of my ear as I whipped back from the thrust. My counter missed too, whipping by him. The two of us circled each other for long moments, testing the other's guard and looking for an opening. It became clear in moments that he was better than me, overcoming speed and strength with skill. I hurried back, struggling to keep ahead of the flashing spear, then seizing my chance as he slipped on the blood I'd lured him over.

My machete took his arm almost off with one swing, and I backed away to let him bleed out rather than risk finishing him.

The battle was ending, if it could ever have been called that. Maybe that asshole was one of the resistance's leaders, or maybe the orcs had just gotten a lot of killing done while I was tied up with him, but everything was tapering off and slowing down. People were surrendering, discarding their weapons and raising their hands, weeping and begging, kneeling and flinching. I caught more than a few looks from the human settlers as orcs rounded them up.

All of them were hateful, confused, bitter. All of them had a point, I supposed. Even if it struck me that they'd be so concerned with species now of all times. What did I owe them?

Not a damn thing, not based off something as arbitrary as genetic similarity. But that didn't make me feel any less wretched.

Something touched me from behind, and I whirled around before my brain even fully registered it. The orc stumbled back with his face gushing blood where I'd dragged the blade across it, metal still cutting deep despite the constricted field of motion. He looked up at me and grinned.

"Fight is over, Wrathful!" he roared, thumping me on the shoulder all friendly like and grinning like a moron. Others were crowding in now, all looking as thrilled as the first.

"Fought like a demon!" one declared.

"Like ten demons!" agreed another.

"Like feral beast!"

I wanted to spit out an answer, to let them know that it was just being force-fed their own violent savagery that had left me in that state. I didn't, partly for the pragmatic reasons of not alienating myself . . . and partly because that excuse already rang hollow enough in my own head.

The orcs were closing in on me, great walls made out of giggling moron. My head was spinning, throat tightening so much it hurt, hands balling into clawed fists, and heart thundering in my ears. My mouth tasted acidic, tanged with iron. I wanted to fall on the nearest one of these murderous animals and bite out his fucking heart.

Instead I mastered myself, letting them swarm me and burying my volcanic hatred while they cheered and sung my praises. Wrathful, they were still calling me. It seemed like I'd gotten a new nickname. I didn't hack them to pieces, I didn't.

Now the fighting was over, but not the killing. The killing, I knew, was still ahead of me. More killing than I'd done now, more killing than anyone had ever done. The world didn't listen to reason, it didn't care about morals, it didn't take suggestions. It fought you tooth and nail. Try to do good and you were making yourself an enemy of every person in it.

Fine. I'd kill my enemies, crush them, and force them under my power. Then, finally, good could be done without being dragged back by the dug-in heels of all the world's grunting animals insisting that they had better ideas.

I'd been letting myself get soft. No longer. The world didn't need another soft idiot following everybody else's rules. It needed someone to play solitaire.

CHAPTER FORTY-ONE

I was pacing through the mansion, feeling the grinding gears of my own anxiety turn away inside me. I hated that. Hated this situation, and everything like it. A spy among our numbers was something I just . . . wasn't suited to handle, and Shango knew that. I could fight ten men and win—hell, I could beat fifty now—but in this I was no less helpless than the rest of us. Not for the first time, I felt the absence of Solitaire. How long would he have taken to find them? Days? Hours? Minutes.

There wasn't much use thinking about it, but I couldn't help myself.

Solitaire, what would Solitaire do?

No, don't do what Solitaire would do. Nuclear terrorism is wrong. What could *I* do? That, at least, was something that would lead to results, that would get us somewhere. As far as my skill set went, I had to admit it was a fairly limited one. It was hard to get more specialized than me, and though my ability to erase entire squads of people at once had certainly come in handy lately, I was having a tough time thinking of how I might apply it here.

The answer, of course, was that I couldn't. Not to the spy. But we had other issues than just that.

At the end of the day, there was a single crux to our current situation that escalated it from a problem to a life-threatening disaster in the making. Viras. His raw power was more than we could handle, much more. In our actual book, magi weaker than him had obliterated entire buildings with waves of their hands and reduced armored men to puddles of gore and molten steel.

I wasn't killing him. Even I had to admit that. I wasn't even coming close to killing him, and with Solitaire suddenly gone, we'd now lost our ability to overcome any given threat by just breaking a new term of the Geneva convention.

Which left me, and my powers. I couldn't just bomb Viras, or build us an Abrams tank to blow him in half from a kilometer away. I had to do things the old-fashioned way, and to do that, I needed to tap my powers more.

I didn't stop walking, but I wasn't aimless in it anymore. I had somewhere to be now, or rather I had something to do. The mansion was big enough that it was rarely hard to find somewhere conveniently out of the way and isolated for my practice, and today was no different.

You wish to speak with me.

The creature—the entity—didn't ask; it told. Observing my intentions with the sort of certainty even I didn't feel regarding them. I nodded as I replied, more to myself than anything.

"I do. I have things to ask you. The most important one is what you actually want."

A pause followed, then stretched long enough that I realized I wasn't going to get an answer. I pressed the issue, not content to just be ignored. Not now of all times.

"This is your chance to work with me, to get my cooperation," I pushed. "If you ignore it now, you're telling me that you can't be reasoned with."

It was the sort of thing Shango would do, simply tell a person where their best interest was and how their current course was jeopardizing it, then let them decide to stop all on their own. As usual, it worked.

I wish for you to do my bidding.

That one threw me for a loop. So badly, in fact, that I actually took a good long while to respond. Blinking, actually scratching my head, I waited for the words to sink in . . . then found myself bafflingly irritated when they finally did.

"Seriously?" I snapped. "That's it?"

A pregnant pause followed that, sitting between us like a mine separating battle lines.

That is all, the voice repeated, sounding, of all things, suddenly uncertain.

"And it didn't occur to you to just fucking *ask*?" I pressed. "Holy shit, doing what you say gives me superpowers. Why would you not just ask? Are you stupid?"

I was not aware you would be so . . . willing, the voice replied, actually sounding slightly defensive now.

"To get superpowers?" I snapped.

Super . . . powers?

"To become capable of ripping people's arms off," I translated. "Point is, yes I am. I . . . Okay, maybe not at first, maybe not before seeing what I could do in this world, and probably even then not before having Viras force the issue. But now I need strength above all else. And serving you will give it to me, right?"

There was no pause this time.

Right.

I nodded again, more to myself than anything, and tried to thread as much steel into my spine as I could.

"Right. Then yes, I'll do your bidding. So long as you can promise me I'll get the power I need to save my family."

I can promise you that times a dozen, she answered, sounding triumphant now, her voice suddenly a war cry. *Times a hundred.*

I'd be lying if I said the thought didn't strike me. My current situation aside, having that kind of strength at all felt . . . magnetic. And if you think it *wouldn't* to you then you're either a damned saint or deluding yourself.

"Then I'll do what you say," I told it truthfully. "Whatever I have to."

That's what it came down to in the end. I wasn't selling my soul here because I wasn't making a decision. The decision had already been made for me when we were sent here. All that was happening now was my adapting to it. The choice between living and dying was no choice at all. The choice between watching my friends die and stopping it was even less of one. So I'd damn myself with whatever kind of bargain I had to if it meant preventing that.

I would do what had to be done, and fuck anyone who tried to tell me otherwise.

The entity didn't respond to that, but I got the impression it had heard me and understood. Was that a trick of its own devising? Letting me know with instinct rather than words? Maybe I was just overthinking things; regardless, it still left something unsaid. Something important.

"From now on," I told it, "no more of . . . this. This roundabout way of trying to hint me toward things. If you want something done, you tell me. I don't have time for your bullshit, not with my friends' lives on the line. Give me my jobs, I'll do them, I'll become powerful."

I could tell it wasn't entirely pleased—something about that arrangement still snagged at it—but it didn't vocalize the fact.

Very well then, Champion, the creature said at last. *Then seek out powerful warriors so that I may give you a worthy challenge with them.*

Ah, right, I'd be doing a lot of fighting, and probably a lot of killing. I waited for the feeling of disgust at that, but it never came. Just a hollow readiness. It was what I had to do, so it would be done. Mission, soldier. Feelings didn't come into it, not until I'd already done enough winning to give us the luxury of useless sentiment.

"What's my first target?" I asked. "Or should I just go wandering around to find you some candidates before even asking?"

The latter.

Looked like I was going out for a fight then. I hurried out, packing my equipment—sword, unrestrictive leathers, and a black powder/mercury grenade just in case—and looked for someone suitably impressive to fight.

Fight and, I knew, probably kill. But then that was Redacle all over, wasn't it?

CHAPTER FORTY-TWO

Shango's POV: Day 155
Current Wealth: 670 gold, 13 silver, 6 copper

It was one of our recruits who informed me we had a guest. You might find that strange, having them do more work for us, including messaging and fetch-and-carrying within the mansion itself, immediately after finding out about the spy. Not the case. I couldn't figure out who it was if I didn't keep them all busy. More work meant they had less free time, which would make it more likely that any one of them would pick a bad moment to slip out and give whatever messages they were clearly conveying. It also let me examine their behavior for any attempts at information gathering alongside their typical duties, and I'd reinforced that by adding particularly unpleasant jobs around more sensitive areas. If someone ended up getting themselves assigned to clean the area around Solitaire's workspace a lot, I knew there was a heightened chance they wanted in on its contents.

Finally, it was just convenient. There were only so many hours in the day at all, and they became a lot rarer when you started trying to emulate the work of an exaggeratedly rumored-deceased chemistry genius while simultaneously running a noble house. Such is life I suppose.

Anyway, I got my heads-up about our visitor nice and quick thanks to this. Unfortunately, the visitor in question was about the last one I'd have wanted to see. I made my way through to him all the same because frankly anything he wanted to speak about was too important to ignore, but I felt my blood chilling as I headed for the guest room.

Lord Viras was waiting for me inside it, eyeing me expectantly as I stepped through. He dressed about the same as ever and had that same calm, sharp look in his eyes that made me feel like I was lying on some metal slab to be surgically examined.

"Good afternoon," he said. "You look well."

"Fuck off." I had the sudden, ridiculous urge to grab a fistful of his hair and pull it out. I did not, of course. One did not live as a black African in Western countries without learning to control one's temper. Viras seemed more amused by my remark than anything else.

"Shall we skip the small talk?" he asked. "I fear it's rather redundant. The both of us are guarded enough that neither will learn anything from the other regardless."

I was already seeing what I could learn from that out of sheer reflex, and sure enough the answer was nothing.

"Fine. What are you here to say?"

Viras kept his voice even as he replied, even sounding pleased.

"I would like to, once again, extend my offer for you to join me as an apprentice."

I actually found myself disappointed at that, like catching a professor in some mistake. This probably said something very interesting and disconcerting about my psychology, but for the time being, it wasn't strictly relevant, so I ignored the fact.

"You think I've changed my position on that?" I asked, genuinely perplexed.

"Of course not." Viras sighed. "But I think it is within my power to convince you now."

Ah, I was going to get the recruitment pitch.

"I have killed one brother," Viras told me with no more emotion than if he was observing the decor. "It will be no great exertion on my part to kill two more. Already, I consider the loss of Solitaire Belahont to be a waste. I have heard that his talent for magic is not far beneath your own, and Beam Belahont is something I would much enjoy to study for the peculiarity of his powers. That is why you remain alive, because you interest me. The greater a problem you make yourself, the less time this will last. Solitaire is dead. Next, it will be Beam. What will you fight for then?"

He would've made me go cold at that, if I weren't already a talking ice sculpture. This kind of threat was far from unexpected—I'd have made the same one in his position. The sad fact was . . . it wasn't hollow.

"You killed my brother," I answered him, deciding not to waste my enemy's misconception. If he thought Solitaire was gone for good, then I could use that. "When the time comes, you're going to die. I'll be the one to stop your breathing. It won't be revenge or retaliation. It will be because some people just need killing."

For a moment, I felt Solitaire's hand on me because that had been the most him thing I think I'd ever said. Viras didn't notice the torch of misanthropic violence passing from one fist to another though. He merely leaned back fractionally in his seat and examined me.

"I'll take that as a no then. Thank you for your hospitality. You really do have a lovely home."

He got up, heading for the door with all the grace of a gliding lizard. "I can see myself out."

I watched Viras leave, processing what had just happened. Nothing he'd said was wrong, and not one of his threats had been idle. We'd beaten Corvan, and he was certainly a moderately powerful magus, but compared to Viras . . . Well, he didn't compare to Viras. This was our first experience of the world's truly strong magic users, and it wanted us dead.

That seemed pretty on-brand for us, being fair, but it didn't exactly take the edge off. As things stood, Viras would win. When we'd challenged him, I'd been banking on Solitaire's help. I could make black powder in his place—we'd even figured out the secret to his rockets and grenades—but that wouldn't do for this kind of fight. We wouldn't be surprising Viras with artillery or, ideally, a stealth bomber. It was more or less just us.

For now.

Well, getting into a losing fight wasn't something I had any intention of allowing. I paced as I thought, twisting my cerebrum into knots as I tried to work out what our options might actually be.

More power. I kept coming back to that, and for obvious reasons. Back home, money was the source of happiness—or at least all the things that made you happy. That basic premise didn't function exactly the same way in Redacle, but only because there were now more factors involved. Feudal inheritance and state-influencing monarchy were extra factors, competition for currency to control the finite scraps of power that existed in a society. Another was . . . well, power. Literal power. Magical power.

The idea that one person could physically force states or nations to do what they wanted seems laughable and silly back on Earth, because the strongest people there are just four-hundred-pound athletes limited to exerting a measly few times more force than the bodies of average people.

In Redacle, the strongest people were magic casters and non-humans. Beings who'd been sharpening their power for longer than a human lifespan. That, and the more primitive technology, meant there was a far more inherent, tangible threat to an individually strong person giving orders than had existed in my world for a good long while. Maybe if we had a modern attack helicopter or ten, Viras could be taken lightly, but we didn't.

Power. In the end, it all came down to power. Ethics and ideology were nice, as a treat, but they were second fiddle to that. Everything was. But we'd known that from the beginning. That was why we'd started amassing influence and kept at it long after the point where starvation wasn't a threat anymore. Why I'd kept up my magic studies, Beam his training, Solitaire his bomb making. That's why we'd keep going still.

If I joined Viras, I'd have power. But I'd also be under the thumb of a man very well served by the current status quo, and my opportunities to upturn it would vanish. Further, Viras very likely didn't plan on keeping me around forever. He knew I was a threat to him with Solitaire gone, and in his position, I'd probably use the new impossible prodigy to get whatever clout I could before conveniently disposing of him, ideally on some suicide mission to make a nice dent in my enemies.

No, joining him wasn't a real option. Not while I had options at all. The question, then, was did I?

Phelia was spending a lot of her time in the library of late. It was hardly something to complain about, of course. For several reasons. The library was where she found herself easily relaxed most days anyway, and, if she were being honest, there were far worse tasks a woman recently married to an ambitious man might have expected of her.

Her hand moved up to rest upon her belly absently, and she felt her lips dry a second. Shango had said that he wouldn't make her . . . But then, men could be fickle about such things. Particularly desperate men, and it was hard to find one more desperate than a Belahont was currently.

And he's been acting far from normal.

Phelia stopped the thought before it could swell further, making her way deeper into the library and searching for the book on Elswick's genealogies. It was one she'd gotten a surprising amount of use out of lately, albeit not to any great results. Family histories were an excellent place to start looking for sordid affairs, embarrassments, and, at best, potential claims. The only reason she didn't fear the same being done to the Velaharos was that her imbecile father had already brought them to ruin himself.

She found the book, taking it out of its place and straining slightly at the weight of it. One day, Phelia thought, the heavy, leather-bound tome would need separating into several other volumes. Each new generation of Elswick's nobility just added additional mass. Her own family had long since surpassed that critical point, but then that history had availed them nothing in the end.

It wasn't a moment after Phelia even cracked the book open that she heard footsteps behind her and turned, surprised to find Lady Adannaya entering.

A year ago, Phelia might have been struck by the woman's dark skin, but marriage to Shango had let her adjust to the foreign oddity. She supposed Adannaya must have found her own coloration just as peculiar. She was taller than Phelia, but not by much, and her wear was clearly selected for convenience more than aesthetics.

Then again, Phelia couldn't judge in that department. She was doing much the same thing. She walked too often for anything else.

Adannaya smiled, and Phelia answered it in kind. She also raised her guard. A smile could do many things, and her own were used to disarm people all too often. Adannaya was a stranger in this house still, and one Shango believed was attaching herself to the Belahonts out of political ambition. Phelia happened to agree. With their precipitous situation, that ambition could easily turn her against them.

There was a spy among their numbers . . .

"Am I intruding?" Adannaya asked. Phelia was quick to shake her head.

"Of course not. Please make yourself at home. I was merely searching for . . . Well, this." She held the book up, keeping her smile in place.

"I see," the woman responded, hesitating just long enough to be polite before she continued.

"To tell you the truth, I was actually coming here to seek you out in particular. I had a conversation with your husband lately and was left rather . . . uncertain by it."

Phelia felt a sudden tension at that.

"In what regard?" she inquired, perhaps a shade too sharply.

Adannaya told her, speaking clearly and cutting all the right corners to compress her account as much as was feasible. Phelia felt herself catch a chill as she listened.

"I apologize," she said once Adannaya was finished. "My husband has been . . . under a lot of stress recently. I will have a word with him about this."

The woman just nodded, not commenting one way or the other. That told Phelia more or less everything she needed to know about her thoughts on the apology. More, actually. That she chose to hold her silence rather than offer a false acceptance and mollification said that she either had a high view of Phelia's ability to see through deception or a low one of her own ability to deceive.

"I adore your library, by the by," Adannaya added abruptly, actually succeeding in stunning Phelia by combining her non sequitur with a sudden and intense study of a nearby statue. "Some of these decorations are extraordinary. This is Organdae masonry if I'm not mistaken?"

Phelia actually found herself modestly impressed. It was one thing to have the origins of every piece in one's home committed to memory. That trick was among the most fundamental and simple ways by which any imbecile could pretend themselves an expert of history by pointing them out and providing assessments. It was another entirely to walk into the home of a stranger and do so.

Even if Adannaya had merely researched the Velaharos' possessions after arriving, to do so in just a few days spoke well of her mind. Very well in fact.

"It is," Phelia confirmed, realizing she'd paused for quite some time. "Two centuries old. Actually one of the younger pieces here."

It was true. Her family had been great. Once. Like so many other treasures, her father had tossed that greatness to the side, but the relics of it still remained. Phelia dared to say that if she sold off her family's remaining collection, they would be among the wealthiest families in Elswick overnight.

And one of the most mocked. Prestige could not be bought, but it could easily be sold. Was that why she had refrained? Perhaps she was just clinging onto the past. Clinging tightly enough to not have even told Shango at that.

"So I see." Adannaya hummed, continuing her walk and drawing Phelia along behind her. They soon came to the largest portrait in the room, scaled to actually feature a depiction larger than the man it was modeled on. Handsome, proud, clad in plate, and of course with hair as blond as gold.

"I do not believe I recognize this figure," Adannaya observed, actually sounding like she considered the fact novel. Well studied then. Given how she'd avoided even mild deception before, this reaction of all things was most likely sincere.

"He's a controversial one," Phelia admitted. "Sir Etron, a young man who sacrificed himself some hundred years back to save my great-great-grandmother from a necromancer's wrath."

Adannaya did not shudder, as most Eregaran nobles would have. Phelia remembered then that she was of Akanite, of Illeade in particular. Phelia had heard plenty of stories of her people—not all pleasant, and most of the unpleasantries stemming from their rather liberal view on the necromantic arts.

Then again, she'd heard whispers that the clergymen of Elswick were rather displeased with her new family's inventions too. No Witchfinders, not yet, but . . . well, a concern for later.

"I'd like to hear the story," Adannaya replied, sounding rather sincere in her eagerness. Once more, Phelia found herself unable to see through any deception that may or may not have been there. The knowledge was disquieting.

"It's a long one." Phelia shrugged, a deliberately unladylike gesture that tended to unguard those who'd experienced ostracization among the nobility. Adannaya, she thought, was receptive. "Over a century ago, my ancestor was threatened by the Dread Necromancer Khar. Sir Etron, courageous and powerful both, was merely passing by, a hedge knight of no particular influence or prestige. Nonetheless, he risked his life to fight off the necromancer and thus save my great-great-grandmother. She was grateful, and he renowned as a hero. But dark casters are not to be slighted lightly, and this one bore a grudge for the knight's interference."

Her father had always told it in almost the exact same way, relishing his pauses. He'd been a fun man, with a strong sense for the dramatic. When sober.

"The necromancer came for Sir Etron in the night, and by the time its grim magics had been worked, there was nothing handsome or noble left of him. He was a grotesquerie, a shambling beast. An undead. And he was loosed upon the very family he'd fought so valiantly to save. His will was strong, and yet the frenzy of a recent reanimation stronger. By the time Sir Etron came to his senses, he had already run my ancestor through, and the last thing he saw, so it is said, was her dying moments. Then the Velaharo household guard fell upon him from all sides, and put him out of his misery."

Phelia realized only once she'd finished her telling that she was decrying necromancy to a woman for whom it was as mundane as fire magic. She glanced nervously at Adannaya but found no hint of offense in her face. Though, once more, it could merely have been that she was so adept at hiding it.

Shifting her fingers, Phelia felt two of the rings scrape together. That reminded her of another feature of the story.

"These," she said, holding them up. "They are a good deal older than one century and would have been worn by my ancestor almost all the time. She would have been wearing the very same stones upon her death." A smile hit her at that, unexpected and warm. The anecdote had been a distraction from her faux pas but had turned into an unexpected reminder that not *everything* her family had once controlled was now lost.

Adannaya looked impressed, though, of course, social proprietary demanded Phelia beg her pardon still.

"Forgive me." She smiled. "That story is a morbid one. I should have warned you before telling it." It was, in fact, only the second most disturbing version. The other held that Phelia's own ancestor had been the one to reanimate Etron, that she, a woman by all accounts unnaturally focused with power and magic, had flirted with the necromantic arts herself. Most considered that to be nothing but slander of the time, but even slander could do its harm. Phelia's family had carefully suppressed the tale thusly.

Adannaya smiled. "I've heard worse from my own family, believe me. We *are* the necromancers in most tales."

The remark stunned Phelia for a moment, then she found herself grinning. The unexpected stab of irony punched clean through the tension and let a giggle leak out of her, which Adannaya clearly reciprocated. It was Phelia who spoke first once their laughter subsided, eyes turning back to the tall portrait of Sir Etron.

"You must think it improper for such a controversial figure to be displayed so brazenly." Adannaya shook her head with what, Phelia thought, was actually a degree of passion.

"The opposite," she began. "I must praise you for displaying such a divisive visage upon your family's wall. Your people's church holds that those reanimated as undead can never enter paradise, if I am not mistaken, and yet here you venerate a fallen hero reduced to their ranks."

Adannaya took a step closer to the painting, reaching out to caress the air in front of it, examining it closer. "Many would dismiss its themes here, I imagine," she continued. "But I find them invigorating. That a man could find himself even after being reduced to less than a corpse, that he might have the will to retain his humanity even against the magic of a necromancer and the destruction of everything there is about him . . . Yes, it is a good story. If the painting is controversial, then I can only admire you all the more for displaying it here to do justice to its history and the themes of its story, despite the disapproval of others who care not to hear them."

Phelia nodded. "I am pleased you like it." She beamed, deciding not to mention that her motive for leaving the painting up was that she thought Sir Etron looked handsome.

CHAPTER FORTY-THREE

Shango's POV: Day 155
Current Wealth: 670 gold, 13 silver, 6 copper

I was in an office, and I had to say . . . it was a nice one. Actually smaller than mine, thanks to the historic wealth of the Velaharo family, but far better furnished and maintained. The rug was thick and warm, the entire room heated by perpetually crackling fires. Despite the large windows, which must have been vacuuming in cold from the frosty air outside, it was actually pretty toasty. That was much appreciated when you happened to be from Nigeria instead of one of those deranged, frozen fantasylands like England.

Of course it wasn't my office, and it wasn't Phelia's. Its actual owner returned after I'd already been waiting there for a good half hour, and the look on his face was priceless. It was shock first, then anger, then recognition. The fear came next. Blunted, I thought, by word of Solitaire's death, but still there. All too many people remembered Beam's performance in the tournament even now.

"Good afternoon, governor." I smiled, leaning back in his chair but deciding not to go so far as to put my feet up on the desk. Too much contempt and he'd feel the need to assert some measure of authority, and I'd lose the effects from whatever sleight of cerebrum had him sweating so much in my presence if he actually exerted his influence.

"What are you doing in my office?" The fear was giving way to anger again now, which was more or less expected. Putting aside that I'd invaded his personal space . . . We were in his personal space. His domain. He could probably have a team of big, impolite men barging in here within sixty seconds to start brutalizing me. So I talked fast.

"Sorry for the intrusion." I smiled. "I'm just here to talk. Stealth and subterfuge are quite important for me these days."

"Here to talk you say," the noble spit. "And why should I believe you? Your family's gained quite the history in so short a time, Shango Belahont."

Well, zero points for successfully recognizing one of two black people in the entire city.

Still, he was growing hostile. Worse, he was perceiving a threat. I had to kill both those unfortunate developments with a single stroke.

"If you know of my family's recent history, then you'll know that when we want someone dead, we kill them. Instantly. I'm here, waiting for you, because I want to talk, because I think we have a mutual benefit we could enjoy from each other. If we had anything ill planned for you, you'd be meeting my brother here instead. You've seen him fight, haven't you? Yes, you have. I can tell. You look nervous."

The threats did their work, and the governor plopped himself down in the chair opposite me.

"Thank you." I smiled, deciding to lay a bit of sugar onto the pill. "Now, I'm here because I'd like to form an alliance with you, or at least to work together toward our mutual benefit . . . Is something funny?"

He was laughing already, the mean and shrill laughter of a man witnessing an execution he found particularly amusing.

"I have no intention of crossing Viras, boy," the governor spit, looking at me as if I'd drooled on myself. "And you shouldn't either. Do yourself a favor and just join him. Accept his offer. Save your wife and remaining brother."

I wasn't sure if he'd intended to piss me off with that, but it didn't work either way.

"You're the only one who can," I pointed out. He was sympathetic of course, or rather he was trying quite hard to *seem* sympathetic. It was almost offensive. Phelia could lie. Solitaire could lie. What this idiot was doing was . . . I didn't even know what. A series of muscular spasms in his face, perhaps. He was about as convincing as the metaphorical red hand itself.

"I am sorry. Truly, you have my sympathies. But I can't help you. It is simply too dangerous to cross Viras. I must look to maintaining what I already have."

That, at least, gave me an idea for my new angle of attack.

"I understand." I smiled at that. My smiles tended to creep people out when I was in the mindset I was now. I'd never known why but had a few theories. Uncanny valley, the instinctual recognition of a danger. Human interaction was all emotion and intuition—Solitaire existed on one extreme of that spectrum, and my pathology, whatever it was, was planted firmly on the other.

I think when people saw me smile, they also saw that there was nothing of a smile going on behind my eyes. I think they realized that whatever they were, I wasn't one. The governor seemed to realize it now, and he grew ever so slightly more nervous. Good.

"If I join Viras, I'll give him everything. All our technology, everything we know. Slowly, at first, but I'll give it all the same. I'll need to make myself indispensable to him, to ensure I don't get killed. I need to make sure the risk of me taking revenge is outweighed by the benefits of me being alive. Understand? I'll need to make Viras unstoppable, not just in Elswick but in the entire region. Maybe the kingdom."

The governor couldn't have gone paler even if I'd slashed his throat, and he suddenly seemed terribly weak. It was satisfying to see a threat land so perfectly and with so much weight.

"I see . . ." He took his time making a decision, formulating his response only after several long and deliberative moments of thought. That was fair enough. This was hardly the sort of deal to be made lightly, and unlike me, he hadn't expected this meeting. I'd gotten the advantage by dropping in with a plan, my actual reason for sneaking to his office.

"Then . . . Then I have no choice," the governor croaked, sounding defeated. Well, he was.

"It seems neither of us do." I nodded, studying him, making sure he wasn't having any sudden spasms of regret that might complicate things. It didn't seem he was.

"My help comes at a steep price however," the governor added. "I'll need insight into your technologies, the steelmaking for one."

No surprise there. His family's dislike of Wilskasai's was old and well-known. I just shook my head.

"You're not in a position of power here," I told him, making sure to explain it simply and slowly. "You're not in a position to make any demands at all. You will offer me your help because both of us will be fucked if you don't. I will do the same with you for the same reason. Don't overreach here."

He swallowed.

"What is our relationship then?" he asked. "Just allies of convenience?"

"Just allies of convenience," I confirmed.

I hated this man. He was in charge of Elswick, he employed the guards, he directed them. He set the laws, and he was the owner of the streets in which people were freezing and starving. Everything we'd seen here, all the casual, everyday suffering you couldn't go ten feet without glimpsing, could be tied back to him and the status quo that he was content to leave as it was.

But I needed him for now. He might not pay for what he'd done—might never pay for it at all. That was acceptable. It was a condition I was willing to allow. Because we had bigger problems at the moment, and though he may have been a sack of shit, he was a giant, fat solution-shaped sack of shit.

CHAPTER FORTY-FOUR

Beam's POV: Day 155
Current Wealth: 670 gold, 13 silver, 6 copper

I'd been having a very Solitairish afternoon. Which was to say, I'd been listening to a voice in my head and going where it told me to with the intent of hurting someone. In this case, it sent me to some fighting ring, not a proper amphitheater like the one I'd competed in though. A smaller, more derelict, and shittier place that smelled of grunge, blood, and sweat. I'd have called it underground, except it actually wasn't illegal to horribly injure people for recreational purposes in this society. So it was just a sea level arena.

So this is where I'll find my . . . worthy opponent, feat?

Just watch.

Putting aside how chatty the voice was being today, perhaps a direct consequence of my cooperation, it had at least been giving good intel. I found my place in the grounds, paid for my position, and shouldered my way up to the front ranks just as a new fight started. A champion's bout this time, though the challenger was actually bigger. Neither was particularly large by Earth's standards, and both were decently armed and armored. Good steel, chain mail rather than plate. I figured that was a feature of the arena itself—these people seemed more interested in blood than sport. The bleeding began.

They were both good, actually. I tried to remember if I'd seen either in the tourney but couldn't. If I had, they'd probably have gotten to the second round. Or the champion would have, at least. The other guy . . . Well, he was a cut or two above average. Just not enough for this fight.

It lasted maybe half a minute, and in that time easily fifty swings were exchanged. Sparks spit off the steel weapons. Links of chain sprayed out like shrapnel from exploding shells. Both of them did their darndest to dismantle the other, but there could never have been any doubt about the outcome.

The challenger went down in a spray of his own blood and mangled armor, and the crowd went wild. I just watched as the fallen man hit the dirt and scrambled back, weapons discarded, defense forgotten, completely at the mercy of his opponent.

"I forfeit! I forfeit!" he cried out, hands held high and limbs shivering as he gestured for mercy.

"He forfeits!" The champion laughed, looming over his beaten enemy and raising his weapon high. It was a nasty thing, a big, barbed mace that looked too heavy for most men to wield with both hands. This fighter had it in just the one, with his shield taking up the other. It came down like a guillotine blade, caving in the wounded man's helmet and making a grizzly puddle of blood and brain matter all around him.

The crowd seemed to approve.

Fucking prick. I'd seen my fair share of executions—come to think of it, more than half had been done by one of my best friends—but this one still made my blood boil. It was the fucking pointlessness of it, the mindlessness. When Solitaire was a crazy psycho frothing at the mouth, it scared people. It got results. This was just . . . This was just madness.

You hate this man, the voice noted. *You wish to hurt him.*

Yeah, I do. No point hiding it. It would know even if I tried.

Good, that will make what comes next easier. Fight him. Defeat him. Claim his spine for a trophy.

Jesus Christ.

Well, as Solitaire used to say . . . Uh. Actually, I didn't think even he had a saying that applied to this specific situation. I guess it just goes to sho—Oh, no, he did. "People with strong spines lose them once the vertebrae start coming out." Weirdo. Anyway, I hopped into the ring and started beating my chest to let the idiot know he was being challenged.

He took umbrage with this and began circling me. The crowd was thrilled of course, thrilled at first to see him fighting again—then, once a few recognized me, the thrill took on an altogether different note. I decided to strike fast. If the idiot realized he was fighting the guy who came in second at the tourney, he might deny me a fight altogether.

My first swing was caught by his shield, which surprised me by surviving the effort. But then, I'd promised not to use any of my weapon conjuring, and that included armor. I was doing this practically uncovered. There *was* a risk here, of some kind. His mace came swinging to exploit it, missing me by a mile and countered as my heel crunched out for his gut. It hit a hip instead, almost breaking the bone and launching him back. His feet slid and scraped at the ground, his footing almost gave, and I was on him with another swing before he fully recovered.

He blocked this one too, but the physical force of it blasted him off his feet. I lunged before he even landed, sword coming down hard and splitting through chain mail like it wasn't even there.

His blood spurted up high just as the ground caught him, and he rolled back. He'd landed a good few meters from where he'd been first hit, and now it seemed even standing was a struggle for him.

The crowd had gone silent, and I stalked toward the killer with the blood turning to slush in my veins.

"I forfeit," he croaked.

Well, of course he did. That's what you did when you feared death. This whole situation was reminding me of a similar one I'd seen, just a minute or two ago in fact. How had that ended again?

"You didn't spare your opponent. Why?" I asked. I was surprised by how quiet my own voice was, how soft. I was practically murmuring it, but he heard me well enough. The question terrified him, left eye widening, mouth gaping, body trembling. I gave him a good few seconds to respond.

Then I swung my rapier down. The light blade wasn't made to hack through armor, but sheer strength and speed gave it the energy to cut through the man's mailed shoulder and leave the corresponding arm completely useless. I tore it out amid another squirt of blood, then mangled the other limb. Then, while he was screaming, I kicked him over.

My knife wasn't exactly a surgical tool, and I wasn't exactly a surgeon. Real life isn't *Mortal Kombat*, and if you try to tear a human spine out—even if you have the strength to do it all at once—you're just gonna rip chunks off. So I extracted his more carefully, cutting around the bone and finally pulling it out amid a shell of sliced connective tissue and dripping nerves.

It was one of the more disgusting things I'd ever done but . . . honestly, at this point what did that even matter? You can only spend so much time hacking off limbs and watching cocks get bitten off before your stomach toughens up a bit. I straightened, standing tall and hoisting my gory prize high.

"Beam Belahont killed this man!" I roared. "And this trophy is mine now!"

A silence ran out across the room, and I waited for the inevitable backlash. The explosion of disgust and scorn, the devastation of whatever reputation I'd been building. Part of me looked forward to it. I was tired of being glorified for all the worst things I did.

Then the cheering started.

It stunned me at first, and I just stood there frowning, confused, waiting for everything to make sense. But it never did because more and more people picked up the momentum. Soon my name was being called, fists were pounding the air, laughter was ringing out all while I stood there proudly displaying a dead man's spine like some house cat with a dead rodent. I didn't know what to say, think, or feel. So I stayed silent and still while I took it all in. My hands were still dirty with blood, ichor starting to crust and congeal, nostrils flooded with the reek of iron and life.

And they were praising me for it, almost venerating me.

You have won, my Champion. Victory is yours. Drink in the glory, feast upon it. Let it strengthen you.

Even the fucking voice in my head was agreeing with them. But somehow, as I held that mangled bit of tissue, I found my spirits actually lifting. There was something infectious about this, about seeing people cheer for the right *person* at least. If nothing else, worshipping the guy who ripped out a psycho's spine was better than worshipping the psycho, right?

And it was necessary for my family. It was necessary.

CHAPTER FORTY-FIVE

Solitaire's POV: Day 156
Current Wealth: 675 gold, 11 silver, 24 copper

I liked sitting in the town's ruins. Reminded me of what I'd done. Built character. See, if I didn't actively feed my emotions then they'd weaken and die. That's what emotions do. They get smaller and more manageable, until they're almost fizzled out entirely, and the next thing you know you're *complacent.* Doing insane things, like calling police officers sir instead of ramming your car into them, or making sure to maintain your credit rating instead of hanging a banker from the ceiling and lighting him on fire.

There were lots of things I regretted since coming to Redacle, but, if anything, I regretted more from the days before. I regretted that it took me being starved and beaten in some fantasy world to finally behave like a rational person and start slotting all the pricks who needed slotting.

So there I sat in the town, inhaling the smell of smoke, blood, and terror. Fueling myself with it. I'd need to do a lot more killing, and I needed to make sure pesky things like empathy or prosocial conditioning didn't get in the way.

"Basking in your victory?" asked a voice from behind me. I turned around, ready to bite out the offending person's throat and jump up and down on their carcass, but paused when I recognized Adravigi. Killing her would be inconvenient, now at least.

"I don't think I've ever seen a person be less correct about anything in my entire life, and I spent the last few years talking to Yanks about health care."

She paused. "I . . . don't know what that means, but okay."

"Just say what you came here to say." I sighed.

Adravigi smirked at that. "Well, first I'd like to congratulate you on—"

"FUCK YOU, CUNT, I'LL FUCKING EAT YOU."

She shut up instantly, face twisting with shock and fear as she stumbled back from me. I calmed myself a moment later, drawing the anger back in.

"Sorry about that." I sighed. "I'm in an emotional state at the moment. Stop wasting my time and talk about what you're actually here to discuss."

For a few seconds, she studied me. But not many seconds. Clearly she'd taken my outburst to heart.

"I want you to know that I had nothing to do with your involvement in the fighting. It was Guraganar's—"

I sniffed the air, letting the reek of her deception hit me. The sound and motion cut her off.

"I don't like liars," I told her simply. "You told Guraganar to divert me into the fighting and then stay quiet about it. You've worked with him for too long and too carefully to let him do anything impromptu like this."

Adravigi eyed me, then nodded.

"I did," she replied at last. "I'm . . . sorry about that, but I did what I needed to do. To survive. Just like anyone did—just like you would—and now you and I are the same."

The same as me? That was hilarious. I'd only ever met two other people who were the same as me, Shango and my mother. Going by that sample, it seemed to me that being an absolute fucking psycho was almost a prerequisite.

Doing what she had to do to survive. It made me want to start biting fingers off. What she had to do to survive was sit around and keep being reasonably useful for Guraganar. This was pure ambition. She had no great plans for the world—just to rule as much of it as she could.

"Wrathful!" came a new voice, booming and deep, powerful and enthusiastic. I turned to see Guraganar himself strolling over, dull face as slack as ever and the ground almost trembling beneath him.

Wrathful, my new nickname. Orcs were so very creative. Well, that was unfair. It's not like humans were either. Case in point, the name Solitaire for a deranged misanthrope.

"Thanks," I replied, not biting out either of his eyes and starting to walk briskly in his direction to lure our conversation away from Adravigi. "Though I could've done better, if I'm being honest. The entire fight was . . . underprepared."

That got a thoughtful look from the orc, which was, I thought, the literal only thoughtful look I'd seen from him anywhere.

"What do you mean underprepared?" he asked.

God, it really was easy to lead people around in conversation. Just hitting prompts.

"Well, your weaponry was lacking." I shrugged. "Could've used a few tweaks. Armor too. Really there were a lot of things that were just . . . off. Mostly in small ways, of course. Adravigi really is clever, but that sort of thing adds up in large numbers."

Guraganar rewarded me for that with the second thoughtful look I'd ever seen on him. The expression still looked weird on his face. Not because he was an orc. Just because he was Guraganar. It was an oxymoronic configuration for his features.

"Why did you not make these adjustments then?" the orc asked me, suddenly intense. "Did you not have the time?"

"Well, that was part of it," I replied, nodding quickly. "Yeah, it was the time."

"There is more," he growled. "Tell me what it is."

People always trust information more if you make them push you into giving it, as if the extra effort somehow makes them better at seeing through bullshit. They're wired to put more stock in things that are harder, maybe because the alternative is realizing just how unfair the world is to those who work hard.

So it was no surprise when my next response got a lot of nodding and dawning realization to shine back from him.

"I . . . did suggest a few tweaks, but ultimately all the final designs had to go through Adravigi, and I suspect she either disapproved of most or had a hard time . . . understanding them."

Guraganar's eyes narrowed at that. His nostrils flared. The conversation didn't go on much longer, which was good. Because I'd already exerted most of my willpower to go this long without removing any of his body parts and throwing them very, very far away.

I was left alone once he departed, and I used that alone time to walk and think.

The town really had been beautiful. Had. Past tense. We'd ruined that nicely, of course. Charming houses were now not-so-charming piles of burned wood. The people were either dead or enslaved. Everything reeked of smoke, and anything valuable had been hauled off as if the British had come to visit.

Oh wait, I'd been in the attack. We had.

One good thing about the dereliction was that it helped me think and straightened my priorities. One good thing about Adravigi was that she mirrored my thoughts and made them honest. The ends justify the means. Her end was, supposedly, survival, but that was bullshit. What about mine?

My end was to save the world. Huh. Also bullshit.

No, my end had been to hurt people. Why was that? Because Mummy was mean to me, taught me bad things, and hit me. Obviously that meant that everything I did to everybody else was justified and that I could do as much of it as I wanted. What a fucking joke.

What was I doing here then? Helping people? Not really, certainly not directly. So what was my end for these means?

That's the tricky thing with means and ends. You can more or less just make up whatever the fuck you want about either. Sometimes you do need to do something for the greater good. Some people really do need killing. Sometimes. But not every time, and, looking at history, certainly not most of the time.

I was totally pursuing a justified end here though. This time was one of the rare exceptions. My goals were actually worth killing a shit ton of people over. Honest. What?

You don't trust me?

Henry closed his eyes and inhaled, cycling the air through himself, using it as a focusing agent. The air was his emotion, and his control over it exerted control over the turbulent thoughts rocking his mind. There was a fight coming up. People would die. Henry might be one of them.

Despite it all, he kept calm, held himself orderly and still. He was precise, mechanical. Tending to his weapons, stretching, going through all the routines that he'd acquired over the years. Probably, they didn't help much. But they soothed him. They brought order.

That was what it was to win a fight, to be the most orderly. Idiots took this to mean uniformed armies looking miserable and marching in neat formations. People who survived their first few bouts learned that it really meant being able to give an order and know that men with enemy arrows raining on them would still leap to obey.

It was a lot of arrows raining down, these days. Ever since the Dead Edge found out about the Belahonts and Jeleheim's alliance, they'd been carefully targeting them. Escalating things, dragging the violence onto a scale the Jeleheim didn't have the numbers to match even with their growing list of recruits and improving equipment. Today was looking to be one of the worst.

They were holed up in a safe house, or something that was meant to have *been* a safe house, when the enemy first made their presence known. Close to a hundred of them in a single attack, dwarfing the few dozen Jeleheim present and making it clear how things were likely to go. Henry had stayed though, restored order to the panicking men. They'd needed to hold together and avoid scattering to be picked apart. And odds were made for defying.

Henry was seated up in a top window of their two-story safe house, waiting, watching as the enemy came closer. He held, felt the tension of his men boiling. Raised a hand just as the doors were smashed in and the boots flooded inside. The attack came.

They'd all been trained for ambushes. It was half of their success. With fewer numbers, one had to learn to use them better, and there were few better ways of using numbers than attacking an enemy who didn't know they were being attacked. These ones did, but the particular moment of violent explosion still caught them unawares. Henry dropped down from the top floor and landed hard, twenty-foot fall barely straining his legs. He was straightened up fast enough to have cut two throats before a single reaction came.

Screams cut the air, and knives cut flesh. Long knives, blades made for brawling and killing. Henry was a blur of motion disappearing into the enemy's ranks and dragging his own steel through every slab of meat within the reach of his arms. Legs gave in, arteries emptied, eyes rolled back, and jaws slackened. For a few moments, there was nothing but madness in the room, one hundred and something men screaming and moving, thrashing around like they were all a part of the same body dying messily and spasming out its pain.

But the enemy's commander wasn't an idiot, and he'd clearly stumbled through more than one fight alive. He started giving orders, and they started being obeyed despite the rain of arrows coming down on his men.

Order asserted itself piece by piece, men fighting their way around, encircling the defenders and trying to leave them trapped. So Henry gave his own order—he sent his side back and up through the building. They hurried to the top floor, leaping down through windows and shoots, dropping a dozen feet to the ground below. He made sure to send the strongest first, the ones whose bodies were empowered and trained. Those weaker than them—the majority—had the luxury of landing on soft human pillows. Henry himself was one of the last out, killing another seven men before he finally extricated himself from the carnage and traded blades for gravity.

It was snowing again, cold. They were all going to die around snow and cold. The moment Henry dropped out, his heart lurched as he saw their safe house was surrounded. Men with shields, with spears, with crossbows and hastily arranged palisades. A cavalry charge couldn't have forced its way out of this kill box, and twenty wounded men with knives was certainly no cavalry charge.

From the building, the initial assault force came out. Henry took a moment to consider his actions. He could flee. He could escape. That barricade wasn't made for a man of his power—it was virtually impossible to erect a blockade that could stop him and was larger than a dozen yards wide in such a short time. He had an out.

Henry didn't take it. He was sick of running. If he had to die—and he knew his days were numbered now; there'd be no recovering from this—then he'd die in solidarity with his allies. He thought to his wife and smiled a moment. Felt guilty. Then screamed, ready to unleash a new crescendo to the killing.

It was only a sight down behind the barricade that gave him pause. A large sight, men approaching. They were all armored in thick wool and cotton, all walking in line. They wielded large clubs and quarterstaves, came in an orderly column of twenty, thirty. Sixty.

His despair doubled in an instant because Henry knew that only Lord Viras or the city governor could have dispatched so many guards for a single affair. They were violent thugs, the guards, but well trained and well equipped. Any two of them were probably worth three of either Dead Edge or Jeleheim men, blunt weapons or no. There wouldn't be any victory with them joining the enemy. There'd barely be any fighting.

They came to the barricades and then surprised Henry by butchering the men at them. Clubs came down; shields came down harder. Bones broke, lives were changed, and in moments, the great wall keeping Henry's men from freedom was nothing but a carpet of cripples. He stared, taking a single long second to overcome his shock and piece together what had happened.

He realized, and that realization hit him harder than any blow could have possibly approached. Hope was a heavier thing to feel than anything else. He gave the order, and the Jeleheim swarmed for the barricades to join the guards.

Their new allies. Shango Belahont, Henry had to remind himself, was a scary man indeed.

Everything that was good about the Dead Edge's position turned bad. They were the trapped ones now, and they had the inferior strength. Henry took no small amount of satisfaction in seeing their forces bludgeoned and battered by the guards, in no small part due to them being almost hesitant to fight back.

The Dead Edge didn't get into a lot of brawls with the guards. That hesitation— that instinctual fear of authority—dulled them even further. There wasn't much doubt as to who would have won when the fighting started, but there was none at all by the time it was half done.

Henry watched as one of the guards took off his helmet and stalked over, walking as if he were single-handedly carrying the law on his shoulders. It must have been heavy. The law was drenched in an awful lot of human blood.

"Henry Grimworth?" he asked, stopping before him and getting just close enough to be uncomfortable. Big man, and not just tall. Well-built, broad. Henry had seen him take a man's head completely off with a cudgel swing during the fighting. It wasn't often he stared down a man with cause to fear him. This thug might have been a rare exception.

"Yes," he replied, staring him down anyway.

"Well, Henry Grimworth, you have a great lot of thanks owed to Governor Elkatin. We're here on his business, helping you on his orders."

It almost didn't feel real, and Henry found himself scrutinizing the man for some hint of deception. There was none—not that he was the perfect judge of faces required to be sure.

"Thank you," he said at last, finding the words tasting sour. "You saved our skins."

The guard eyed him, scowled, then kneed him in the balls. Henry doubled over, puking.

"We're on the same side for now," the guard snarled. "But that doesn't mean you're not scum." He turned away from Henry, disgusted, and called out to the others. "Alright, boys, into ranks. We're done saving the street rats." The guards began their march away.

I t's a bloody disgrace!" Varder roared, his temper forcing a level of volume from both lungs that tested their very limits. He didn't care, barely feeling the burning at his throat. It was nothing. Not compared to the burning of his heart. Not compared to the revolting injustice his family had weathered.

"Quite right," one of Varder's household guards agreed. Tony. Always enthusiastic, Tony, so long as he thought he was agreeing with a Byror. Always.

"Shut up, Tony," Varder snapped, in no mood for his sycophantic drivel today. He had to think, and to do that he needed to hear his own thoughts *without* the damned echo.

"They can't get away with this." Varder sighed. He was seated with some of his most trusted men, all of them veterans of the Byror household guard and all of them confidants of his father. His dear father, who still couldn't eat solid food and still woke up four times a night shitting himself and crying. His blood was boiling again with just a few moments of the memory.

"Maybe they won't," one of the men, Irig, suggested.

Varder looked up at him, expectantly.

"Maybe," Irig began, "we should teach them that there is a line and show them what happens when it's crossed."

They'd all been drinking, and such suggestions were far from uncommon among slightly drunken men. But Irig was always the levelheaded one. Indeed, even now, there was nothing of a boast about him. Just an icy calm and a burning intensity. It was that very same nature, the cohered violence, that had taken him so far in his work.

"What are you suggesting?" Varder asked, feeling himself sober as he studied his guard. There was something tangible about a suggestion of violence from Irig that got his heart pounding and body working like it was in a fight already. The alcohol perished in his veins, quickly giving way to lethal-sharp focus and explosive strength.

"I'm suggesting that these little bastards need to have a taste of their own medicine. They . . . attacked your father, hurt him. And now they're strangling our income with this damned embargo. So we hurt one of theirs. An eye for an eye." He took a long swig of his mug at that, but his face never wavered. His fury was a palpable force at the table, drawing everyone in close and simultaneously warding them back. Like a bonfire in the frigid winter's night.

Every man at the table paused and shared a look. Within the hour, they'd left their drinking behind them and moved out together. Arming themselves, armoring themselves, warming up, and marching off. They'd sent feelers out to see about the Belahonts, and their wait began. One day passed, two. On the third, they struck gold.

Beam Belahont, the youngest of the Belahont brothers as far as Varder could tell, was a man of routines. Among those routines was a fondness for jogging. Every day, along the same routes. Varder had his opening, he had his opportunity, and he had his men. Wearing his armor, he set out along the path and waited. There were twenty of them in all, and any one of them could have dispatched three of the city's guards at once. They were the elites of the Byror family's household. They would not fail him.

It was a long road they'd picked for the site of their ambush, to make sure that Beam Belahont was possible to see from as far ahead as possible. Sure enough, he was. They first caught sight of him at the end of the street, jogging . . . ludicrously fast. It had to be two hundred paces from him to them, yet he'd cleared half of them within seconds. Moving faster at his barely exertive long-distance run than most men could in a flat-out sprint. Byror felt his worries grow a shade and quickly buried them. They had twenty-to-one odds on their side. And their enemy was running right into their own ambush.

"Everyone ready," he hissed, crouching down and taking comfort in the sound of master-crafted steel creaking around him. He peered ahead through his eye slits. Then froze.

Beam Belahont was gone.

"Where the fuck is he?" one of the men gasped, while others started shuffling around, nerves suddenly coming unwound. Varden worked quickly to restore order.

"Calm, all of you, calm. He can't have gotten far." He was, after all, only out of sight for a moment—perhaps a three-yard span where their view to him was blocked by something. What could he have done in that time?

Beam Belahont dropped down into the alley they were hiding in, evidently having scaled a roof and sprinted one hundred yards across several more in the time since they'd lost him. He landed hard, right on top of a man who was promptly crushed down beneath him. By the time any of them had even turned, he'd already swung his weapon twice.

Two more men fell to the ground in four pieces, their blood filling the alley with steam as it touched the freezing air. Varder screamed, thrusting his halberd out and finding Beam Belahont gone from the point he'd been aiming at.

He was *fast*. Impossibly fast, and it took another man being hacked into bits for Varder to even find him again. He lost him just as quickly.

They were screaming, scrambling, smashing into one another, and swearing as weapons caught on allies and allies died on Beam's.

What is he? What the fuck is he?

This wasn't a man, no matter what he looked like. Varder saw the way this thing—this creature—was killing his men. He saw Tony's jaw ripped from his head, saw Irig's entrails wrapped around another man's throat and pulled to neck-snapping tightness. It wasn't just Beam Belahont's strength, speed, or resilience—though any one of those would have made a dangerous man alone—it was his *brutality*. He was making sport of them. Making art of them.

He was acting as if every kill was something to be proud of, a sacrifice made to the world itself.

Varder screamed, swinging his halberd in a wide arc, suddenly too scared to care about anything except life and unable to think of any way he might keep himself from losing it save by taking Beam Belahont's first.

His enemy did not dodge the swing; rather he simply countered it with his own. Varder's halberd was magus forged, as strong a steel as he had ever seen and resilient enough to behead stone statues without a dent. It broke apart where it hit his enemy's weapon, debris scattering across the alley. Then a boot crunched into Varder's breast-plate and blasted him from his feet.

By the time he was up, his men were already dead. Dead and butchered. Limbs lay strewn about, blood had painted the alley walls in arcs a dozen feet long, and he found brain tissue spattered across his own armor.

Beam Belahont was looming over him like a headsman, blade gripped loosely at his side, head cocked over. There were a few nicks on him, some cuts and scrapes where steel had opened up his skin, but the man looked like he might have wounded himself worse by shaving. Varder screamed, scrambled to his feet, and ran away.

For one minute—one entire minute—he thought he might actually escape. Beam did not seem eager to give chase, simply allowing Varder to gain ground. Then he came after him. It was like trying to flee a horse, like trying to flee an arrow. It took him seconds to close in, bowl Varder over, and launch him skidding and bouncing along the street to stop heavily with a wounding impact against a wall.

A strong arm grabbed him, tearing him away from the ground and hoisting him high. Varder screamed, kicked, punched. None of it did anything. His enemy's grip was made of steel, his arm of muscle. He held him suspended a yard from the ground, plate and all, without even exerting himself, staring into his visor with eyes like a starved tiger.

"I was wondering how long it'd take you people to try attacking me while I was jogging," Beam Belahont said, as if he were merely remarking upon some idle fact about the world. Discussing the weather, appreciating a pleasant landscape. Crushing an insect.

"I can pay you," Varder gasped. "I can. I'll promise never to work with Viras again. I'll withdraw from the coalition. You'll never hear from me for the rest of my life."

Belahont snorted.

"Yeah, you're right about that. I won't."

Varder felt the fingers digging into him, and he started screaming as his flesh came apart.

Not like Father, please not like Father. But it was beyond his control now, how he ended up looking. He was nothing but prey in the jaws of the predator. Before long, even his petty struggles were beyond him, and his body surrendered to Belahont's ripping strength and crushing grip. Blood soaked the ground, appendages came free, his vision failed him.

And yet, he did not end up like his father. Belahont had the scant kindness needed to kill him for good.

CHAPTER FORTY-SIX

Shango's POV: Day 156
Current Wealth: 675 gold, 11 silver, 24 copper

There was one good thing about a citywide embargo and political shit fest, and that was that it made more or less all our goods a *lot* more valuable. The steel especially. We'd more than doubled our selling prices in Wilskasai's deal, and the extra funds were piling up nicely in our family's coffers.

One hundred and seventy-five gold and counting. Roughly six a day. Another month of this and we'd be over 350 gold. Another five months, and we'd be over one thousand. We weren't *rich* though, obviously. Rich in Redacle was inheriting several generations' worth of assets, and there wasn't an easy way to replicate that overnight. "Income rich, asset poor," I think the saying was. Oh god, I was applying sayings designed to demonstrate economic nuance to myself instead of just making the generalized statement that I had more money than whomever I was speaking to. What had this world done to me?

Well, given me a lot more fucking work for one thing. I was making my way out through the governor's building with a bundle of tension the size of Denmark slowly forming in my chest. The shit was officially hitting the fan, and now there was nothing we could do except see how effective our umbrellas were. A meeting had been requested between us and one of the seemingly inexhaustible number of pissed off nobles who'd decided their declining wealth was our fault. Well, in fairness it was. The embargo—several embargos at once really—had been my own suggestion. And I'd actually agreed to the meeting too, seeing it as a useful opportunity to scope out the requester's mood and, in general, not wanting to pour fuel on the fire by showing contempt.

Lord Wessin was not an extremely powerful figure in Elswick, but he was an old one. Or, rather, his family was. No surprise there. Most of the city's nobility had been saving themselves from the horrors of genetic diversity for over a century.

The meeting was at Lord Wessin's own mansion, which had me on edge by itself. What was worse was the fact that he'd explicitly invited Phelia as well as me. It was only slightly reassuring to see how much Velaharo Manor dwarfed Wessin's. Dick measuring aside, what mattered was how many men he had here.

I didn't get much of a chance to scout that as our carriage took us to the foot of his house, and we were soon ushered inside. It was a nice place, well decorated. I hated it. Too exposed, and without Solitaire here, we were left on our own to spot any elaborate attempts to kill us.

Wessin was fat. No surprise there. In this world that made him handsome, though it would've been doing a fair amount of heavy lifting. He wasn't bad looking, exactly. Just sneering enough that I thought his face might fall off.

That sneer intensified by the step, until it was an outright snarl as we finally came to hover just beyond arm's reach.

"I know your family is behind this all," he spit, face turning so red it might have been drenched in blood and not looked any different.

It appeared I had been summoned here specifically to be yelled at by a whiny, entitled old man.

What else was new?

"My family is behind our profits by *weeks*," the noble shrieked. "Weeks! Can you fathom what that means? Do you even have the ability to imagine the sort of money you've cost us? I had a life-size marble sculpture of myself scheduled for today, canceled. A sword of solid gold to give my youngest as a gift—on hold! I was going to get a giant room, fill it with one billion dollars, and light it all on fire, and now I can't! Waaagh waaagh, rich person want money, waaaagh!"

He probably didn't say most of that, but I actually wasn't listening to even half of his rant, and this is more or less all I remember of it. Unfortunately, I let the boredom show on my face. That seemed to agitate him somewhat, in the same way that a Molotov cocktail tends to agitate a mosh pit.

"I don't care," I told him, saying a rare honest thing. Despite my emotional bluntedness, despite the unbroken icy calm I'd spent the last weeks wrapped in, I derived no small amount of pleasure from seeing searing rage twist into stunned surprise. It almost made me giggle, almost.

The noble didn't find it quite as funny. Lord Wessin was charging at me in an instant, rage back across his face, fury overcoming him. That wasn't such a surprise. What was was the sight of flashing steel as he drew a dagger from his side and brought it lunging for me.

I just froze, even now. Even after weeks—months—of being in Redacle, surviving a dozen death matches, hardening up and adjusting to my new world. Even after it all, I fucking froze. I have no idea why. The sheer surprise of it, I think, just punched the movement out of me. But not Phelia. She was moving just as fast as the noble, faster. Lunging ahead quickly enough that by the time the knife was closing in on me, her flesh was between it and mine.

Blood, opened skin, a cry of pain, and wide, hateful eyes. I unfroze. My body moved.

Phelia was falling, falling in slow motion. My senses were at full speed now, mind racing and watching the world trickle by at a fraction of its typical pace. Wessin didn't even begin to react by the time I'd taken the knife from him and shoved his chest. Shoved, not punched. And even that, I thought, might kill him. His momentum was reversed, and the fat man shot away at a downward angle to land meters back from me. The wooden floorboards actually trembled under his impact, rolls of blubber rippling with kinetic waves at a fascinatingly sluggish rate.

By then, Phelia had almost hit the floor. I caught her and slowed her fall just in time to keep it from catching her too hard, gently setting her down on the wood and studying her injury. It was a deep cut, but not one in a fatal area as far as I could tell. It was far from the wrist, with all the big veins, and had mostly hacked into the back of her hand. That still wasn't great—there were tendons there, ligaments. But we had Corvan. A nonmagical cut wouldn't cripple her . . . probably.

I stood up, turning my gaze back to Lord Wessin. By now, though it had felt like I'd spent a good few seconds examining my wife, he'd barely even *started* to sit up. He didn't make much more progress before I crossed the few paces separating us, tightened my hand around his head, and hauled him up off the floor and off his feet by the skull.

Wessin was struggling, if it could be called that. A while ago—six months—he might've actually matched my strength. I'd never been a physically impressive person. Beam had changed that with his grueling training, and Redacle had changed that even more. Now I barely even felt his resistance. He tore out fingernails failing to scratch my skin, strained ligaments attempting to pry open my grip. Face turning purple, eyes turning red, he was terrified and growing more so by the second. It would be quite easy, I knew, to just squeeze harder. A quick exertion, maybe a sickly crack. Then he'd be dead. His life was quite literally held in my hand.

But there were consequences for everything. I gave the potential ones here a bit of thinking while I held him.

There weren't that many, but all were huge. Impossible to ignore. Impossible to miss. If I killed him, I was killing a noble. I was starting the process of nobles being killed. People would panic. They'd freak out. It didn't matter that he tried to kill me first, didn't change anything that my wife was hurt. All it took was a few idiots to believe I was lying despite the evidence, or react too quickly to check, or do any number of other dumb things. Then everything would escalate.

It doesn't matter how right you are if everybody else is too stupid to realize it, and nobility was, if nothing else, stupid. I raised my arm, gripped his by the elbow, looked him in the eye.

"You hurt my family," I told him, then twisted. The bone broke like a breadstick, and his scream of agony actually made my ears sting. I let him drop, moving back to Phelia.

"Drag your idiot lord out," I told the man's guards. "His presence is annoying me." They hurried to obey, perhaps worrying that their arms would be next. Then I was beside my wife. She was up now, conscious, and my senses were slowing back to conversational speed.

"I'm okay," she told me, flexing her hand, wincing, but not showing any great impediment to her mobility. Phelia hesitated a second as she looked at her moving hand, then continued. "Do you know what you're doing, Shango? Are you really accounting for all these enemies we're making?"

Was I?

I supposed I'd find out if any of them managed to kill us.

CHAPTER FORTY-SEVEN

Beam's POV: Day 156
Current Wealth: 675 gold, 11 silver, 24 copper

My first ambush of the day hadn't been too much of a surprise, thanks to Solitaire's "readiness training" (read: randomly jumping me while I jogged to make me as close to his paranoia as he could), but even I was taken off guard by the second one.

Two ambushes in one day was just *excessive*.

This time they actually managed to get the drop on me, and they opened the fight up with arrows. I heard the bowstrings snap through air, realized what I was listening to, and turned to dart aside. I actually managed to dodge the projectiles, somehow, seeing them move from the corner of my eye like . . . well, something faster than me. But not arrow fast. Not imperceptible, not near instant. They were more like thrown darts than anything.

One caught me though, digging into my thigh before I could conjure my armor. I winced as I felt the steel cut through skin and muscle, landing and rolling, springing to my feet. I looked down and saw the arrow had sort of bounced off me, but not before opening up a shallow cut. Well, there were benefits to a body that could withstand dozens of times its weight I supposed.

No time to dwell on that though. The rest of the ambush was coming and coming fast.

Four men, at least four attacking at the moment. They moved with the superhuman speed I'd come to expect of the tourney, and all of them had fancy armor and weapons. Steel came for me, bouncing off my rapier as its wielder stumbled back and his three friends tried to circle around. My armor was up a moment later, my sword sheathed in ethereal matter the moment after, and my next swing cut clean through chain mail and took an arm off at the elbow.

I felt pretty smug about that, right up until the polehammer smacked the back of my head and sent me stumbling. In an instant, I was surrounded.

Doesn't matter how fast you were: Three attacks coming from three directions at once meant that one would hit. Probably more. I didn't have eyes in the back of my head, and it was just touch and pain that let me know I was being battered from all sides. I swept my sword out in a wide arc to try to force one of the men back, but these killers were good. The target backstepped, but he focused more on guarding and, at the expense of sliding a foot or two away, held his ground. Before I could lunge through the gap, he was attacking again, keeping me caged, keeping me trapped.

My armor was tough stuff, but it had its limits, and currently I wasn't wearing a thick layer of tool steel plate to supplement it. I felt the blows coming down, lucky ones hurting bad and others just adding up anyway. I couldn't take this forever.

And I didn't need to because salvation came just moments later. By salvation, of course, I mean that Elizabeth sprinted up behind one of my attackers and stabbed him in the neck. She surprised me, she *certainly* surprised him, and by the look of things, she even surprised herself.

Most importantly though, she gave me my moment. While the poor guy was still reeling from receiving a new neck ornament, I stepped in and hacked off his head entirely. I lunged forward, darting past his falling body, rolling, getting to my feet. Elizabeth was nowhere to be seen—which was good. I'd fight better without her to worry about.

Arrows plinked off my armor, annoying but no real concern. What worried me was the two men closing in now. They were nervous, and I didn't blame them. With half their numbers gone, my abilities must have felt a lot more intimidating all of a sudden. Time to see if their worries were justified.

We came flying at one another, and our weapons moved like blades in a blender. Blood trailed after my sword like smoke from a burning ember, and though I took a few more hits, the fight didn't last much longer after that.

I want the tall one's heart.

The voice almost cost me a blow with how sudden it was, but the moment after I registered it my body was moving faster, more powerfully, more sharply. I felt the throb of my wounds fading, and the burn of my fatigue disappearing altogether. I felt like I could've kicked around the King of Blades.

Asshole Number One overcommitted on a stab, and I let him know by cutting one of his fingers off with a clipping blow. While he was busy screaming and spasming around, my boot caught the other's chest and sent him to bounce off a wall some paces back. By then the first was swinging again. This time I just stepped into his reach, let his arm catch my shoulder, and hit him with the Solitaire special. My headbutt caved his helmet in. Not enough to kill him, but he went limp in my arms for a few moments. Just a few though. Long enough for me to grip his head, not long enough for me to finish him. He started wrestling, snarling, punching. I tightened my hold on his skull, jerked sharply.

The neck broke with a noise and a vibration I actually felt through his scalp. It was just in time too because the other man was swinging his poleax, and if I'd been tied up for even a second longer, he'd have connected dangerously cleanly. I twisted aside as things were, letting the blow glance off my pauldron and retaliating with a punch. His helmet surrendered to it, a fist-sized buckle covering one temple and forcing him to a staggering retreat.

He was still moving though. Tough bastard this one, tougher than the other—and the other was already superhuman to a modestly impressive amount. I punched him again, and again. His skull must have actually been more durable than the helmet around it because by the time he finally went down for more than a single second, the steel shell had been misshapen to the point of more closely resembling a polygon than a piece of headwear.

His heart, came the voice, almost shaking me off my feet with the shock of hearing it. *I want you to eat his heart. I want to taste arterial blood. I want to feel muscle burst and tear between grinding teeth. Eat his heart. Eat his heart. Eat it.*

It was disturbing how tempted I found it to obey that. Somehow the thought actually seemed appealing. Not just as a means to an end. I found myself imagining all the things the voice in my head was describing and agreeing. Why not? They were small, weak, fragile. Barely human—like rodents more than people. I was the predator; they were they prey. I snapped myself out of it quickly enough.

"Nice going there." I whirled around, ready to find another enemy and rip them in half. Instead I saw Elizabeth, just in time to keep from attacking her. She seemed to realize how close it'd been too because she was stepping back warily as I mastered myself.

"Thanks for the help," I grunted, blinking back the pounding in my head and turning to the man now trying to crawl away from me. I grabbed him, but not to eat his heart.

The man was wearing moderately heavy armor, but compared to the tourney fighters he didn't weigh a thing. I hoisted him up over my head with one arm and didn't strain myself to hold him there as he started kicking and scrambling for freedom. I left him just enough leeway to speak as I gripped his neck.

"I'm going to ask you a few questions. Some of them I already know the answer to. Lie to me and I'll rip a piece off your body. Tell me the truth and I'll let you go when I have everything I need."

He nodded so fast I thought he might concuss himself.

After making sure of his compliance, I hauled him over one shoulder and started the run back to Phelia's mansion. Elizabeth really was fast. With my own sprint slowed by the added weight of a concussed idiot, she was moving almost as fast as I was even after all my level-ups. We made good time in reaching our home. I was half surprised to find no signs of an attack on the mansion's exterior, and entering it showed that the insides were still unbreached too. I quickly found Shango and felt the stomach drop out of me as I saw him next to Phelia.

Her hand was bandaged, but even beneath the linen I could tell she'd been badly cut across the back of it.

"Fuck, what happened?" I was rushing to her side before I knew it, letting the asshole drop off my shoulder and land hard. Shango, fortunately, had his eyes on the man.

"A noble tried to stab me," Shango replied calmly. "Phelia took the knife for me."

She winced, as if the very reminder made her hand hurt again.

"Who's this?" Shango asked.

"Funny story," I replied, once satisfied Phelia would live. "Part of a group that tried to kill *me*. Elizabeth didn't take any knives, but she did stab one. I guess Viras is sending people to kill us now."

Phelia spoke up at that, and if anything I was surprised her voice was so strong. Stronger, actually, than it was normally. Pain seemed to bring out the best in her.

"No, that can't be it. This is too uncoordinated and chaotic to be the work of a single mastermind."

Shango understood before I did, nodding in agreement.

"This seems like idiot subordinates acting without orders," he concurred. "Which is good, since it shows Viras' commands aren't absolute, but . . . Hmm. If they're so pissed with us that they'd lunge into some ambush in the streets, then they might even . . ."

His eyes widened.

"Fuck. Beam, you need to get to the governor as fast as you can. He might be the next one in danger. Hurry. Fucking hurry."

There was no time to think, so I didn't. Just hurried.

CHAPTER FORTY-EIGHT

Solitaire's POV: Day 156
Current Wealth: 675 gold, 11 silver, 24 copper

Guraganar surprised me by calling on me to ride with him as we made our way back to Barbed Point, except not really because I had a cerebral cortex the size of a small universe, and he was a giant ape-man orc who thought in the most predictable and simplistic patterns I had ever seen. I'd dangled some keys in front of him and jangled them, and now his brain had done the inevitable and motivated him to draw them back in front of his eyes. Like clockwork. Well, it still worked fortunately for him. Being stupid didn't make him any less able to kill me, and my plan needed this little heart-to-heart in any case.

The orc didn't mince words as my horse came up beside his. He had, I learned, developed quite a fondness for getting conversation over and done with fast.

"What can you do that Adravigi is not letting you?" he asked.

Well, that was quick. Almost painfully direct too. If he asked me a straightforward question like that, I had no choice but to give a straightforward answer. No slithering around and tricking people for me. I'd have to put my opinion out in the open. Unfortunate, but there was nothing else for it.

Looks like I'd have to just wait a while.

"I'd rather we not be seen discussing things together," I said after a tactful few moments. "There are some things I'm better at than her, but she's still an extremely skilled inventor."

There it was, the spark in his eyes. Eating away like poison already. The brilliant thing with human emotion—or more specifically humans feeling emotion—is that most of them, somehow, have worse control over their feelings than me. Orcs even more so. It barely even took the slightest whiff of doubt to have someone's worldview twisted in knots, so long as you were willing to just . . . be patient.

Then again, I was about as skilled in patience as a millionaire producer was in keeping both hands off his coworkers.

"I have the power here," Guraganar snarled, his fury suddenly intense enough to make his voice wobble, suddenly intense enough that I was left regretting my main tactic of trying to make him go insane and attack me in a murderous rage when we first met. Fortunately he didn't seem to be dwelling on that. "Not Adravigi, understand? She is just a slave, nothing. A bed warmer without me. I use her for her mind, but she *needs* me for everything else about her."

Dear God, a man who felt insecure about a woman's intelligence? I was stunned, baffled. I felt my entire worldview crumbling. I'd never even thought there could be such a thing. This world truly was an alien and disturbing place.

Still, however predictable and bland this response was . . . it was still the response of someone who had all the power here. In theory. I wouldn't be doing myself any favors to mock or dismiss him. If I was going to weasel myself out a niche here it needed to be by working *with* the local idiots, not against them. So I let my eyes fall a bit, clamped up. Gave all the signs of a loyal person pressed into an uncomfortable situation.

For several reasons.

The first, obviously, is that there was always the outside chance Adravigi had put Guraganar up to this as a way of testing who she worked with. It was what I'd do, the smart, obvious thing. Which didn't necessarily mean it was what she'd do—she was only human after all—but again, she *was* smart.

My other reason actually lined up nicely with this. It was just the best way to ensure Guraganar remained invested in working with me. Give someone something too easily, and they stop caring about it.

People need to feel like what they have is something they worked for. As my mother always used to say, "A man doesn't want what he can have. He wants what he needs to take, what he needs to win. It's all about the contest for him, and he'll put a lot more cash into winning than he will into enjoying himsel—" Was my mother a prostitute? No, Solitaire, not right now. That's a thought for later.

"That is all you have to tell me?" Guraganar asked. He was pissed, I could tell, but . . . not a threat actually. He'd been much, much more so during our little meeting before and managed to restrain himself from attacking me—albeit at Adravigi's explicit instruction. He actually had pretty good self-control, and my abilities made me one of the most useful things in Barbed Point. One of the least killable, to put it more practically.

"I'm sorry." I sighed, still leaving my gaze low. I wanted to castrate him with my bare hands rather than defer, but then I wanted to do that to most people. I was a mentally ill working-class man, and I'd paid my way into surviving until my early twenties. I had good self-control too, by necessity.

"You can go," the orc grumbled. I took the change eagerly, rather liking the idea of not being within Guraganar's limb-detaching range. My horse shuffled away as erratically as ever, horrible fucking animal that it was, and I was soon riding alone again. But not for long. Perhaps expectedly, another mount pulled up beside me. This one was being ridden by Adravigi.

"What were you and Guraganar speaking about?" she asked. Trying, I thought, to seem calm and only mildly interested. Trying a bit too hard. The strain on her face was clear, and I got a strong whiff of caution and uncertainty as she neared me. I'd gotten her scared it seemed. Lovely.

"Nothing much." I shrugged. "He just had a few questions about how your siege engines work and what I can do. I think he's hoping to find some new world-destroying weapons in the two of us."

A plausible enough lie. It was so very close to the truth. Adravigi had, however, survived for several years among a town of giant angry rapists who actively looked for excuses to kill most of the people they spoke to. She was justifiably paranoid, and I saw the suspicion blooming behind her eyes before I'd even finished talking.

"What are you playing at?" Adravigi asked me, throwing the question my way like a burning piece of shit. I sidestepped, as one better with such things.

"Survival?" I shrugged, as if it was a nonissue. "Believe me, I don't like being approached by pissed-off orcs either. If you could stop this from happening again, we'd both be happier."

"I could arrange that," she replied, a dangerous note to her voice. "I could arrange all sorts of things. Do remember that, Solitaire. I hold all the cards here, me. I've been friendly and understanding because I do value you, but if you keep pushing me, that can change the moment I want it to."

I didn't reply, just kept my silence and let her read whatever she would out of that. Adravigi walked away, shooting glares back at me all the while. She'd certainly given me a lot to think about.

CHAPTER FORTY-NINE

Beam's POV: Day 156
Current Wealth: 675 gold, 11 silver, 24 copper

I was running faster than a horse, faster by far. The wind was a hurricane in my ears, and the houses flitted by me. Most of the people I passed didn't even have time to react until I'd already shot down along the street and left them far in my wake. The governor's mansion was a fair distance from the Velaharos', almost the city's radius away. More than a mile of straight movement even without counting the winding streets and obstacles.

I made it in three minutes flat, thanks in no small part to my willingness to send anything in my way flying and hurl myself over a wall instead of wasting precious strides going around it.

At any other time, I might have found it surreal to be sprinting toward my destination. For so long, places like that had been distant things, beyond our reach. The homes of unseen forces who knew nothing of us but decided every facet of our lives through their decisions about the world. Now I'd be forcing my way in and quite possibly saving the life of its owner. The world was a funny place sometimes. Right now though it was just terrifying.

The gardens whipped past, then the entrance, then the corridors. I realized then that I didn't know the building or its layout. No problem, I'd just need to sprint faster. I did, and in another minute I stumbled onto the butchery I'd been fearing through sheer chance.

Fortunately, the governor was still alive. He stood in the middle of the room, panting and gasping, sweat clinging to his face in a thick sheet, hands trembling as they held some humming, probably magic sword. Around him were his household guard, and at the forefront of them was . . .

My stomach clenched. Aja the Pit Hound. I recognized him. Big as ever, mean looking as ever. Around him were no fewer than a dozen dead bodies in over twenty pieces, and not a wound on him. Well no surprise there. He was one of the few people in this city I wouldn't want to fight.

Or at least he would be, if he hadn't done what he'd done to Helena. And yet he was an ally, a servant of the governor. Off-limits. It infuriated me, but there was no time to dwell on that now.

"Belahont!" I turned to the sound of my name and realized the governor was staring at me, speaking between heaving pants. "Took you long enough, eh? If it weren't for my guard, I'd have been dead long before you arrived."

I was about to apologize, but he spoke over me.

"You were bloody useless for this assassination, but the assailants are escaping. They went that way." He nodded to a far wall, broken through and presumably the enemy's means of escape. "Chase them down while we secure the area."

Do the work while I get over my panic and hug my bodyguards, I translated but kept it to myself.

More running wasn't exactly what I'd been looking forward to—I had just sprinted an entire mile—but I got to it all the same. What did surprise me was that outside the broken wall, I was awaited by a very, very long drop. Fifty feet, maybe sixty. It would've killed or injured me if I hadn't gotten those endlessly convenient superpowers from my time here. As things stood, it was really more of an unpleasantry, necessitating a bending of the knees before I picked my run up again.

Now, I could see the enemy. And if I could see them, I could catch them.

We were in a courtyard, a wide thing—but not wide enough to keep them more than a few dozen paces ahead. I took off like one of Solitaire's rockets and saw that distance shrink with remarkable speed. They, apparently, saw it shrink too because every step I took seemed to leave them more terrified than the last.

There weren't that many of them left. After the massacre I'd seen left in the governor's hall, that was hardly a surprise. Five men, none of whom were running with more than the barest level of superhuman prowess. I guess the tournament had left me with an inflated sense of people's power.

One of them did the smart thing, raising a pike and bracing it against the wall—hoping to skewer me with my own momentum. It was a nice idea, foiled, unfortunately, when I just beheaded their weapon with a single swipe of my own and smashed into them instead. The wall shivered as my body crushed theirs against it, breaking bones and squeezing bloody drool out from gaping lips. Before they'd even fallen, I was whirling on their allies.

Four of them now. They had me surrounded. That wasn't a problem.

Kill these ones and bathe in their blood.

I could do three, sure, but killing the entire group would be inconvenient. I still needed information from them, after all. The first one was brave, and possibly eager to die. He swung at me and fell down with one less arm than he'd had before. The others closed in as a unit to put me down together. It didn't work. The fight was brutal, fast, and intense, but in the end there could never have been any doubt about who'd come out on top. I was standing amid a pack of gasping, scrambling men, each of whom was drenched in their own blood and nursing at least one serious injury. That would be a victory, I decided.

"Ah, I'm late." It was Elizabeth who spoke, and I turned to see her practically trembling with a knife in one hand. Good old Elizabeth. No good at all in a fight, but always willing to, if not join one, then briefly visit it and leave something pointy in a person's back.

"It wasn't much trouble." I shrugged, heading for the governor. "You're actually just in time. Can you babysit these four?"

She frowned. "Babysit?"

Right. Redacle was more of a "let the kids eat gravel" kind of world.

"It's a common saying from my land. Basically just keep an eye on them, and if they try to escape, hit them until they stop."

I reached the governor again soon enough, actually opting to leap and climb the wall to get into his hall through the hole in it rather than waste time on stairs. As I straightened up, I found him pacing.

"You killed them?" he snapped. Lovely temper, this one.

"I incapacitated them. Figured we might need to ask them a few questions," I corrected him. That seemed to improve his mood.

"Where are they?"

I told him, and in a short while a new pack of guards were hauling the beaten men up for a stern talking-to. None of them looked happy to see us.

The governor was about to start talking when I cut in.

"If you don't mind me making a suggestion," I volunteered, "why not ask them all separately?" He paused at that, and I turned to the men. "We're all going to give you the same questions, and we'll be expecting the same answers. If we get different ones, we'll know at least one of you is lying. The situation will escalate from there."

I smiled and saw them all cower back from it. They probably still remembered me disarming their friend. Good, that sort of fear would lubricate the wheels of this interrogation.

We got our answers, and we got them fortunately quickly. Ten minutes of enhanced interrogation had everybody suddenly becoming very chatty, and a few more minutes to verify what they were babbling about let us know that none of them had risked lying after being informed we could cross-reference their deceit. Either that, or they'd all agreed on telling the same lie in the first place. We'd done that a few times, but then in Solitaire's words: We were smarter than everybody.

Regardless, the interrogation was finished, and one particular name flopped out of the captured assassins. Gilbert Raelig. The governor looked like he might rupture, such was his rage, and I took that to mean he recognized the name from somewhere.

"Raelig," he hissed, face turning beet red as he began stalking around the room, trembling. "Bloody Raelig."

"You . . . know him?" I asked, almost jumping with how quickly and violently he replied.

"Yes I fucking know him! That treacherous, simple little worm. I want him brought to me! You hear?! Bring him to me now!"

For a second, I thought he was giving me some new errand and thus putting me in the awkward situation of reminding him that Shango didn't work for him and telling him to fuck off. Fortunately, he was speaking to his own men. Half of them peeled off out of the room and disappeared.

The governor paused as they left, turning to me and frowning.

"Do you have a reason to still be here?" he asked irritably. I shrugged.

"Shango said to make sure nobody kills you, so I'm going to keep doing that."

He seemed to consider arguing, then decide against it. That I was capable of turning squads of men into piles of limbs was definitely unrelated to this fact. He was probably just struck by my charming personality. Regardless, we waited there for a while as he calmed himself down—apparently by stuffing his face with things covered in fat and chocolate—until the men returned.

They looked a lot less happy than when they'd left and were hauling a small man behind them as he struggled impotently against their grips. Lord Raelig, I imagined. The real surprise was when Shango walked in just after them, greeting me with a nod.

"Saw your men dragging this one to the building, and I thought I might help," he explained, stopping just shy of the nobles and watching the affair unfold. He turned to the governor. "What you're about to do," Shango said slowly. "Don't."

I was confused, and the governor hardly seemed to notice him. Just rounding on Raelig with a face like thunder.

"What the fuck did you think you'd get from this?" he snarled. "A new patron? Protection? You thought you could cross *me* and get away with it?!"

He would have gotten away with it, I observed, if I hadn't shown up. Raelig didn't say that, didn't meet the governor's eye.

"It's Viras," he whispered. "Apprentice of . . . How do I cross him? How can you?"

The governor roared, drawing out his big, stupid-looking magic sword and raising it high.

"This is Viras' plan!" Shango snarled, voice suddenly edged and wild. "You can't play into it—"

"Fuck off!" the governor roared back. "I'm in charge here, and I intend to deal with my problems like a damned man. Any last words, Raelig? No? Good, then die, you stupid fuck."

The sword came down in a single stroke, and Raelig's head fell down at his feet.

Alora entered just as the man's head came off, and she felt her guts twist themselves into knots at the realization of what was happening. To put it briefly: They were fucked.

To put it less briefly . . .

"You've fucked us," Shango said, voice a terrible unbroken and still monotone. He didn't seem to care in the slightest what had happened, save on a tactical level. It felt bizarre to hear the events described like that, wrong. Alora was watching her life slip away from her, chaos grip an entire city, and Shango felt the affair was suitably described in three measly words.

Apparently, the governor agreed. Though he seemed more confused at the understatement than disagreeing with it.

"What do you mean?" The oaf frowned, still not getting it. What must it have been like to go through life like him, she wondered. How dull was he? How empty was that head that he could see this and still ask a question with that face. Perhaps she should have been jealous. How much worry could really plague a man too stupid to even recognize danger?

"You just beheaded a fucking noble in the middle of your own home. A noble prisoner, by day, after countless people saw him dragged into your mansion by your guards, plus however many saw him being captured in the first place," Alora explained, her frustration escaping as a tone of pure vitriol. "You fucking moron, you just gave Viras all the excuse he needed to stage the coup he's been drooling over since he got to Elswick. He can call you corrupt, call you a murderer—call you whatever he wants. It's not like anyone will contradict him. He can bring his army over here and *take* the city by *force*."

The governor seemed to take the better half of a minute to even comprehend what Alora was telling her, frowning only at her gender when he did.

"Who are you to lecture me, whore?" Alora was moments away from striding over to punch him when Shango cut in.

"One of my finest soldiers, and someone who, clearly, has a far greater understanding of nobility than you." His eyes flicked her way at that last part, and she carefully avoided them.

Damn. That was the problem with Shango. He didn't miss much. Not as explosively, erratically focused as Solitaire, sure, but vastly quicker than most all the same. That little slip of hers might have already gotten him suspecting the *source* of her knowledge. She couldn't exactly ask him to confirm.

"So what if Viras has an excuse to attack me now?" the governor sneered. "Let them come! I'll take them all on if I have to." As he said it, he lifted his broadsword in one of the more pathetic displays of masculinity Alora had ever seen. The weapon was clearly sized for a man far larger and stronger than the governor himself, an ancestor perhaps, and it trembled in his arms as he hefted it up.

The thought that she would die because of this drooling imbecile actually hurt more than the thought of dying itself. Not for the first time, Alora prepared to walk over and hit him.

As usual, Shango was the calm one. Too calm, icy calm. Unnaturally calm. It sent a chill down Alora's spine as he kept talking regardless of the obvious pointlessness of trying to say anything at all.

"Viras is not just some traveling noble." He sighed. "He's a student of Azelis. *Azelis.* If he's one of the weakest of them then he could still . . . fucking . . ." He looked around, frowning for a second before finally gesturing at a far wall. A big thing, maybe twenty feet high, twice as wide, and probably close to a full foot thick, solid stone all the way through. "Destroy that. He could destroy that in seconds."

It seemed quaint to Alora, but she realized that the comparison must have made a lot more sense to the governor. He was in charge of his city—and a man. Walls and their ability to resist siege weaponry would have been well within his purview to know all about, which explained the way his entire face seemed to drain of blood in two seconds flat.

"Dear god," the governor croaked. "Dear fucking god. I . . . Oh no, I need to . . . I'll apologize, that's it, I'll apologize, and explain what happened, and—"

Shango interrupted his hysterics with the same tone he'd used for everything else so far.

"No." He sighed. The closest thing to emotion Alora had heard from him thus far. "There will be no apology, no recompense, and no forgiveness. Viras won't attack out of offense. He'll attack because he always wanted to and has now been given an excuse. This is war, governor. We're in a war now."

On the losing side, Alora thought, but knew better than to say it out loud. The mood was already grim enough to extinguish candlelight. That sort of remark would do nothing but worsen their morale. They'd need that, and any other advantages they could snatch.

"Fuck." The governor was pacing, trembling. Alora thought, several times, that he might lose consciousness already. She hoped he did. It would make the world around her a great deal quieter and less infuriating if the simpleton would just drop and stay down for a bit. Alas, fate was not so kind. "Fuck, I can't die, not like this, not like this . . ." He rounded on Shango. "You, this is your fault! You dragged me into—"

Shango hit him. Alora actually couldn't believe it, the motion came so unexpectedly and with such abrupt strength. The governor was certainly surprised, stumbling back, almost falling, whole body reeling with the force of it. Easy to forget, with his lanky frame, but Shango was Belahont. His body was strong.

"Have you gone mad?!" the governor asked, then flinched back as Shango took another step forward.

"We don't have the choice to surrender," he explained. "Which means you don't either. Give up and I'll find out. If I find out, I'll surrender myself and make my condition for doing so that Viras kills you no matter what."

Alora gasped just as much as the governor at that. Even she barely believed her ears. She knew Shango was cold, but that was *damned* cold. And . . . effective.

"Y-You wouldn't," the governor whispered.

"Try me," Shango replied, his gaze as still as a chirurgeon's hand.

The governor challenged his gaze, and for a moment the two men just stood there locking eyes and testing each other. Obviously, it was Shango who won. The governor looked away, trembling still but with more control now. He seemed . . . defeated.

"You will call on all the guards you can," Shango told the governor. He spoke so confidently Alora almost failed to notice that he'd transitioned from giving suggestions to orders. As of that moment, as of the instant his eyes remained still and the governor's dropped, Shango Belahont had become the ruler of Elswick. It was a shame it wouldn't last much longer. "Guards and mercenaries, and any other hired toughs you can find. We need every set of arms we can get, and if Elswick is in debt afterward, then that's a price we need to pay. Once you have them, bring them all to Velaharo Manor in preparation."

It was that last part, and only that last part, that spurred the governor back into speech.

"Why?" he asked. "We can hold them here!"

"No we can't," Shango corrected him, leaving no room for argument. "We probably can't hold them at all, but if there's any one place we can, it's Velaharo Manor. That place has been protected in ways you can't imagine by the most violently deranged man I have ever personally met, seen, or heard about."

Soon enough, they were all hauling the governor's things to Velaharo Manor.

CHAPTER FIFTY

Solitaire's POV: Day 158
Current Wealth: 682 gold, 14 silver, 31 copper

Guraganar liked his new toy, which was fair enough. Because it was, I was fairly sure, ahistoric. It was a bow. Orcs liked bows in Redacle. Their giant ape-man arms made the weapons fairly effective for them. Strength to manage a heavy draw weight, length to yank it back farther. The end result was recurves able to put arrows clean through chain mail and, with more limited success, through steel plate.

That was *normal* orc bows, or normal for Redacle at least. Mine had added a bit more complexity, and a lot more power. I'd spent a while fiddling with pulleys and gears, and it'd taken me some time, but eventually I'd managed to coin a setup that took a lot of the physical strain out of yanking the thing back. A normal human could fire this with about as much power as a normal orc. A normal orc . . . more so. Guraganar though?

The arrow hit a wall, and it went in *deep*. Steel, this one, piercing centimeters into the solid stone and sending spiderweb cracks running out from the point of impact.

"Amazing." The orc gasped, face actually slackened from his own surprise and disbelief. He liked it, obviously. Loved it. That was good. Provider of loved things was a very good position to have in any situation, and especially when you were actively trying to avoid being dismembered and eaten.

"It's hard to make," I warned him. "But you should be able to churn them out semiregularly. By my estimates, it's about twice as powerful as the bows your men are using already. This one's scaled to their strength, not yours. I could make a better one, but it would take more work."

Eventually we'd run into hard limits like the speed at which a bow's limbs could snap back when the tension was released, at which point the only way of upping power would be to use heavier arrows. I'd already started experimenting with iron ones anyway. The wooden projectiles had a nasty habit of hitting their targets as clouds of splinters with stray broadheads spinning somewhere in the midst.

"But you can make these for all of Barbed Point?" Guraganar couldn't have looked more eager even if he was literally drooling with his tongue lolling out. At the risk of inducing premature ejaculation in the giant orc, I confirmed with a nod.

"Eventually, yes, it should even be replicable for everyone else. The components involved are a bit different from most of what you make, but not enough that your craftsmen can't pick it up eventually."

He got a distant look at that, seeming awed.

"We might have entire armies using these one day," the orc whispered, face twisting with ambition. I could practically see the crippling victories he was imagining his forces bringing him.

In fairness, that wasn't such a far-fetched wish considering the capabilities of these weapons. Accuracy wouldn't scale up as fast as raw killing power, but they'd still have better ranges, and *far* better lethality at the same ranges. Light armor was a thing of the past with things like these. Even the low-level superhumans who usually cut apart entire units in this world could be brought down fast if caught out in the open.

It'd taken me some time to land on the perfect invention, but I was pretty satisfied with this one. It might have been the perfect choice for making me as indispensable to the orcs as quickly as possible. At least for a while, as I continued helping their craftsmen learn to replicate it. Wouldn't want my contribution to end *too* fast, now would I? That was how you became expendable, and expendable people were invariably expended.

"For now, I'd recommend you pick out a handful of your most accurate bowmen and get them equipped with copies," I suggested, noting Guraganar's good mood remaining strong through the advice.

"You have done a great service to Barbed Point," he told me, so serious I got the sudden ridiculous urge to start dancing purely to water down his absurd severity.

"Consider it a favor." I smiled. "And, I hope, you'll repay me by doing me the favor I mentioned . . .?"

Just then the door burst open, and Adravigi stormed in scowling and glaring.

I smiled at her. That wasn't a particular tactical decision one way or another. It was just that in my experience angry women tended to get much angrier when you grinned at them, and for reasons that were no doubt related to my horrible upbringing, I always felt the overwhelming urge to antagonize them whenever I found one already in a bad mood. It worked in this case, maybe a bit too well.

"Adravigi." Guraganar grinned, seeming not to notice that he was currently standing before one of the more pissed-off creatures on the planet. "Look at what Wrathful gave me!" He showed the bow off like a little kid with his favorite toy. In a way, I supposed, he *was*.

"Leave us," she snapped at the orc, turning the full intensity of her glare on him. Even I felt a shiver at that one. Clearly Adravigi was not used to disobedience, and I'd seen already that she didn't shy away from much. Perhaps wisely, Guraganar took his leave.

But he hesitated, and he was bitter about it.

Not good, Adravigi, not good at all. You don't want to go around pissing off your subordinates. That's how you get a knife in the back.

"Give me one good reason," Adravigi hissed, "why I shouldn't kill you right fucking now."

She phrased it like an order, all domineering and forceful. It gave me one hell of an erection—and if I hadn't been so preoccupied, I might've spared a thought for why it was that women caused that when reminding me of my mother. Instead, I had to concern myself with not . . . you know, being killed right fucking now.

"Because Guraganar likes me," I told her, making sure to keep calm and avoid matching her rage. Doing that would make her angrier, and possibly scared. Scared people were stupid. Stupid people did things like kill me when it wasn't in their best interest. "He probably can't stop you from having me killed, but do you want to do that? You saw how much he liked that bow, and I've already promised him more. Slot me now and you're making a rift between the two of you. That rift might never heal."

There were other elements to it too. I was a warrior, and a man. Among these orcs, that counted for something. For a lot. I'd already gotten the name Wrathful. I collected grins and praise as I walked past the orcs. One day I might not need to pose as a slave to wield power here. I could just do so openly.

That was probably what Adravigi had been planning to come of our partnership, and I felt a stab of guilt at that. I crushed it fast.

Sorry, bitch, shouldn't have made me kill those people.

Adravigi trembled, actually trembled at that. Not good. Fortunately she didn't lose her shit, remaining calm and collected as . . . well, as a woman who'd spent years of her life surrounded by orcs and ended up in charge despite it all. When she spoke, there was a terrible calm to her voice that activated my fight-or-flight response, and now it was my turn to desperately will myself out of doing something rash and violent.

"You're right," she said at last, smiling now. Well that wasn't good. "I can't kill you, Solitaire, not right now. But I can hurt you."

Adravigi whistled, and the door opened again. Two orcs came in, two very, very big orcs, and then several more behind them. A retinue, I realized. Probably one she'd prepared the moment she started to suspect betrayal from me.

The first one came in slow and cocky, probably expecting me to curl up. I made like I was going to, lowered his guard, then lashed out with a punch that cracked him across the jaw and snapped the bone entirely. Three hundred pounds of gray-skinned cock sniffer left the ground and landed hard back down on it. The blow was satisfying, but it spurred the other ones on and dissipated their lethargy. They came hard.

I did my best to guard and soak the damage, and to some extent I was successful. Any one of them was far bigger than me, but none were actually a match for my strength. Still, superhumanity only went so far in the helpings of it I had. Their fists came down like sledgehammers, gnawing away at my endurance and beating me down. I hit the ground, and they started stomping instead of punching.

"You were right about why I can't kill you, Solitaire," Adravigi said, as I was busy trying not to shit out my own intestines. "But you overlooked one thing, an important one. Know what it is?"

At the moment, I didn't even know how many teeth were in my mouth. Fortunately her question was rhetorical.

"I can't kill you because I actually *like* you. I *choose* not to kill you, not while I have a choice in the matter at least." Her voice got hard, shaky. "I really, really didn't want to fucking do this, Solitaire. But now you've started fucking with me, with my life, and putting me in danger. I don't have a choice in the matter anymore. And that's your doing."

A heel came down like a blunted guillotine, and that was where my memory cut out.

CHAPTER FIFTY-ONE

Beam's POV: Day 158
Current Wealth: 682 gold, 14 silver, 31 copper

I wasn't a scout, and a lot of the finer points of the job were lost on me. I couldn't read tracks very well, didn't know how to turn weather to my advantage, and in general just found myself out of my depth in the whole affair.

However, I'd been given the job of scouting the woodlands and plains around Elswick all the same. There were certain things that running faster than a horse's gallop just couldn't be substituted for, and getting ahead of enemy marches, it seemed, was one of them. I'd suggested sending Arthur instead, but Shango wanted him at the mansion in case things went sideways.

Fair enough, honestly. I still couldn't beat him even one time in ten.

Running through snow and woodlands wasn't nearly as hard when your body weight didn't even register to you as a felt mass. The slight sinking of my feet was overcome virtually without effort, and I crossed over a dozen miles every hour all without significantly pushing myself.

Not being trained or practiced in scouting was a problem, but it was compensated by the fact that what I was looking for was an *army*. Probably a very big one, at that. Shango and I had never done the hard figures for our worldbuilding—obviously, Solitaire existed—but we knew enough to know that we'd be looking at somewhere north of ten thousand if Viras sent any sizable fraction of his own forces after Elswick.

Redacle was larger and had higher populations than Earth ever had at similar technological levels, thanks to magic and a small helping of fantasy bullshit. That wasn't good for us. Viras controlled a respectable slice of it, after all. Perhaps a thousand or fewer magi in the entire world could match his power, and maybe even fewer leaders.

The literal only advantages to this were that armies of that size took a long time to move anywhere and tended to be pretty obvious when they did. So there I was, running through the woods like a sword-wielding werewolf and desperately searching for some sight of enemies that may or may not exist.

Dear God, I was turning into Solitaire.

Putting aside one of the most harrowing thoughts I'd ever had, I continued the hunt. I wish I could say it lasted a while. I wish I could say it proved to be a waste of time. But, of course, it didn't.

The arrow missed me by an inch, sloppy shooting. I moved before realizing what was happening, leaping a dozen meters in one pounce and rolling behind a tree. I came up with my back flat against it, limbs tucked in, fingers closing around the hilt of my sword. Cool, calm. I inhaled, went still, emptied my mind of everything.

Will you be sparing these ones?

The voice was bitter, angry. It considered itself cheated. Fair enough.

No, I won't.

I lunged out of cover and leaped again, this time watching the arrow fly below me and turning to get a good look in the direction it'd shot from. Two men, one coming at me. The other, the bowman, was in a tree, already nocking another arrow. His eyes were narrow, focus unbroken. He wasn't even looking at his ally.

Trust, then. I'd encountered an enemy scouting pair. That wasn't good. Scouts in Redacle were picked with the same logic we'd used; they were physically powerful to the point of pulling far ahead of horses in movement. Two-on-one might be too much even for me.

Scout Number One, the bowman, loosed his latest arrow from maybe fifty feet. I smacked it out of the air contemptuously as I closed on Scout Number Two. He went for me with a shortspear. Feinted, saw through my own feint, and went low at my feet. I stumbled away. He was very good, and clearly had more experience against swords than I did against spears. I came in for another swing just as he backed up and started circling me.

To get my back toward the bowman. That was a losing proposition right there. However fast I was, I wouldn't be blocking arrows I didn't see. I moved away and broke off at a sprint, putting a few strides between me and Scout Two, then veering around to charge at his bowman ally.

Normal men would've panicked, but not these ones. They remained cool and professional as Scout One readied another projectile and Scout Two cut ahead to bar my path. The arrow was spinning for me, but I realized too late that it was turning, its wielder having flicked his bow at the last second and added a few degrees of tilt to the trajectory. It cut my cheek but missed otherwise, and the moment of pain gave Scout Two his opening.

I could've tried to dodge but didn't. My armor was up now, and I let it soak up his thrust, rolling to send the steel sliding off and slashing for his arm. This time it was my turn to score a glancing blow, sending a few globules of blood drizzling down into the snow and scaring the fucker back.

This one is brave. Eat his heart.

Lovely.

Scout One's next arrow was tilted as well, and timed. Scout Two lunged forward so that the projectile actually curved *around* him, and there was no seeing that one coming. It thudded clean into my breastplate, bouncing off but hitting with a surprising amount of mass that actually left a light crack in it. The spear struck that same spot, widening it.

And then my sword removed all its wielder's fingers. Everybody went into a fight with a finite amount of luck. It seemed this guy had just used up the last of his.

He scrounged a bit more to avoid losing the top of his head from my next swing but fell down. That was when *my* luck ran out, as not only did his friend's next arrow pass by just as his falling body cleared the way, but it caught me right between the plates of my ethereal armor and hit nothing but flesh.

This wasn't a normal arrow either. Its construction was far sturdier, and I doubted a regular human could've even drawn the damned bow that fired it. It went deep, threading agony through me and setting my nerves on fire.

Nine meters, maybe. Thirty feet. That was all that separated me from my enemy. I probably could've dodged arrows without fail from that far normally, but this bow was launching them a great deal faster than I'd come to expect. There was no helping it.

If I stayed where I was, I was dead. If I ran for cover, I might make it, but I was bleeding now, and that'd just give Asshole the chance to relocate. I'd die that way too. I had to rush him.

Bracing myself, I took off in the fastest sprint I could manage. Was I slower already? I felt slower. The arrow came, and two more. That stunned me. The bastard had fired a trio at once, each one off-kilter and awkwardly flying from having so many projectiles balanced on a single bow, and yet his odds of getting lucky and hitting a gap in my armor were tripled.

They slammed into me. Luck was still against him, but he was already nocking another three as I continued my sprint.

If he'd been on the ground, I would've made it. As things were, his height in the tree made me leap and climb for a few more precious seconds and let him fire off another volley. The odds finally added up to score in his favor—a second arrow found its way past my armor.

My arm, the left. The arrow had snuck in right beneath the pauldron and found its home in the muscle of my limb. Every motion made the pain worse. I kept moving. Death would worsen it even more. The archer was already lunging back, and he almost kept himself from feeling the tip of my saber as it ripped through his boot and opened up the bottom of his foot. Blood spurted out, but not enough. Both of us fell from the tree.

It was the first time in a long time that I'd felt myself hurt by gravity, my injured arm jarred enough by the fall that I let go of my sword somewhere and lost it in the snow. The archer's bow was discarded too, but he'd replaced his weapon with a more suitable one. I leaped back just as he lunged with his knife, actually hearing the steel whip through air inches from my face. My punch landed better, but not by much. It grazed his cheek shallowly and sent him growling and thudding off to land beside me. I rolled away, darting back, scrambling to keep the space between my skin and his steel as wide as I could for as long as I could.

But scouts were quick, and he had two fewer arrow wounds than me. He was closing fast. New plan then.

I came forward, turned to let his knife slide off some of my armored plates, and smashed into him with all the speed I could manage. He got bowled over, landed hard with me atop him. The blade came up, but I kept it from me and twisted him into a lock all on instinct alone. His arm gave a moment of resistance, then snapped like a twig wrapped in paper. The knife was mine, and I left it jutting out of his neck without a moment's hesitation.

He went still, and I was the victor. Now . . . which heart had the voice asked me to eat?

CHAPTER FIFTY-TWO

Beam's POV: Day 158
Current Wealth: 682 gold, 14 silver, 31 copper

With my injuries being what they were, and the delay needed to hide the two dead scouts, I took quite some time to make it back to Velaharo Manor. That wasn't good. Time was one of the few things we still had, and it was running out second by second.

By now, even I was feeling wrung out, my body pushed further than most of my training had ever delved and aching with each new step I forced myself to take. I took them anyway. My news was worth too much not to. Elswick's gate guards let me in easily enough, and I was among the streets moments later. They weren't much changed, physically. But the difference in atmosphere hit me like one of the arrows had. The city's districts were less crowded, and when I did see people, they were invariably moving in larger groups than before, shuffling along fearful and edgy. There were fewer guards—typically a good thing, but currently a sign of just how stretched our new ally had been in concentrating his forces on defending Velaharo Manor.

Everything felt . . . dangerous. Imminent, incendiary. It felt like the buildings, cobbles, and gutters were all slathered with gasoline and just waiting for someone to drop a match. Good thing Solitaire wasn't here then. There were many times where a violent lunatic came in handy. The *absence* of a fight was probably one of the most extreme cases where that wasn't true.

It hurried me up to see the city like this. In my wounded state, I could still kill ten average soldiers, and I'd probably do so easily. But Viras might send *a hundred* average soldiers, or he might send ten tourney-tier superhumans, or God knew what else. Best not to take any longer than was strictly necessary. I continued my jog, despite my body asking me in no polite terms to stop, and soon enough Velaharo Manor was within sight.

I rushed past the gate, dodged the *defenses*, and made my way into the mansion. Shango and the others were before me within minutes.

"What is it?" He knew something was wrong, obviously. What disturbed me was that he didn't even ask about my injuries. I'd not exactly bothered to conceal them, and despite neither one being serious, the bloodstains from where arrows had sunk into me were clear as day. They'd stung all the way back home, and they stung even more, somehow, now that I'd finally come to a stop.

"Scouts," I managed, spitting the words out between breaths. My lungs hurt. Neither had actually been hit by the arrows—I'd checked that—but the exertion of fighting and running felt like I was gargling acid. "Two scouts, killed them both. Went ahead and . . . An army is coming our way." I'd checked that much after taking care of the ambush, and the memory still made me shudder.

Shango had his priorities straight of course, at least in his own head.

"How many?" he pressed.

I paused before replying, not deliberately. The words just hurt coming out. A sting born from reality itself. Nothing hurt like the truth. "Thousands," I told him, watching the faces of our friends and subordinates fall, terror sprouting across the whole room. "Maybe more."

Shango alone kept calm, like always.

"I see. Well, thanks for bringing us this information." He was speaking as if I were his subordinate, not his brother—not his friend—and it was pissing me the fuck off.

A time and a place though. This was neither. Even if that weren't the case, Shango was speaking again so quickly that I'd not have gotten the chance to yell at him anyway.

"There's been a development," he told me, speaking with a gravitas that almost felt at odds with his new lack of emotion. "You'll want to hear it." He stood aside, as did the others, to reveal a table. On the table was a letter, opened, and in the letter . . . Well, I took the slip of paper into my hands and read the opening words four times in a row before finally letting myself believe it.

From Bernard.

Hello, idiots, it's me—the cleverest person you both know. I'm guessing this note being written in English instead of the local grugg-speak has already tipped you off as to who it's from, but in all likelihood you've also both become slightly more paranoid since coming here (good progress on your part) so I signed it with my other name to let you know who it is. I'm alive in case either of you were dumb enough to doubt me, and if you weren't then know I'm in a mountainous settlement called Barbed Point and have not yet been mutilated, molested, or otherwise inconvenienced by the local dumbasses.

My heart felt like it was going to burst out of my chest. Weeks without Solitaire, and his absence was like a bonfire blistering my skin. This wasn't the sound of his voice, or the sight of his smile, but I could *feel* them both between every word. I was grinning as I read it.

You're probably still fighting Viras, since you don't have my incredible mind to create new weapons for you. And Shango has probably been torturing himself trying to intuitively guess his way into a high-level understanding of chemistry, since you don't have my incredible knowledge to create new weapons for you. Sorry about that. Shango, this next section is for you. I've guessed a bunch of the things you'd probably try to do, as well as the parts that'd most likely confuse you. This list will either be me putting my foot in my mouth all the way up to the hip, or it'll help lubricate your process a bit. Let me know which if we both survive to meet again.

True to his word, there was a list below, which actually took up most of the page. I couldn't make sense of most of it and didn't spend much time trying. Like Solitaire had said, it wasn't for me. All I needed was to know that he was alive and where he was. With that . . . Well, with that, I could do what I'd promised I would. Protect him. I kept reading.

Right about now, Beam, you're probably planning some half-cocked suicide mission to kick down doors and kill your way through Barbed Point until they hand me over. Don't. For one thing the doors aren't locked, so kicking them down is wasteful. For another, soon enough they'll probably be my doors—and I don't like people breaking my stuff. Also you have more important things to do, like protecting the brother who's actually in danger. Viras is the most dangerous thing any of us have ever encountered. Shango needs you.

I really did hate how he read my mind sometimes, especially when he had a point as well.

This is where I say goodbye. Urghla slachtmu voigrabta seehsnt fifpomo derretima.

What?

Sorry about the gibberish. It's how you say, "I know you're reading my mail, you dumb cunt," in orc language. That part isn't for you, but this part is. Good luck, guys. I'll see you soon. Or not. Try not to die I guess.

The letter ended.

I looked up at Shango, eyeing him and not bothering to give voice to my question. He knew what it'd be already. He always knew.

Of course he did.

"So," he began, "Solitaire is alive. He's well. If anything, he's probably safer than we are—no need to rescue him at the moment. He's given us peace of mind if nothing else. Let us focus on what actually needs doing—"

"What needs doing is saving our brother," I growled, resisting the surprisingly strong urge to crumple up Solitaire's note and risk smudging the precious terrorism instructions as I did. That would be unforgivably stupid of me. Fatally stupid.

Other eyes turned to Shango at that, all looking stern and accusing. It seemed I had the room on my side. If that bothered him, it didn't show on his face. He tilted his head slightly, like he was examining some strange peculiarity, and continued to speak calmly.

"We can discuss this later," he told me, not looking remotely surprised when I lost my temper and snapped back.

"No, fuck you," I growled. "We'll discuss it now!"

He met my eyes. Again, cool as ever. Shango paused a moment before, at last, nodding. And then he spoke again.

CHAPTER FIFTY-THREE

Shango's POV: Day 158
Current Wealth: 682 gold, 14 silver, 31 copper

B eam had the look in his eyes that people got when they'd found a cause they were willing to smash their head against in perpetuity, which wasn't good at all. I'd seen that expression on him before, of course. When he was fighting, risking his life, erasing entire squads or tossing himself against a superior opponent for our own sake. Seen from the other side, it became far less inspiring, and far more . . . inconvenient.

This is going to take up a great deal of your time, my brain told me, and I happened to agree. One did not defeat Beam easily at anything, even when the outcome was never in doubt.

"Remind us what you saw during your scouting mission," I told him, sending a wave of cautious jittering through Beam's face. He did, and I was pleased to see that most of the people present—all our handpicked recruits from Argar to Alora—were stiffening at the news. Not all of course—some, like Argar himself, were as fear immune as Beam. But it was a start.

"We can't afford to divert our forces from here," I told him flatly. "This is where Solitaire's lab is, where our weapon production happens, where we make our money. If it's not defended constantly, and defended well, it'll be taken almost instantly."

Most of our men were reconsidering at that, seeing the logic. Beam, of course, remained stubbornly unconvinced, but he didn't actually argue. I took that as a concession—or the closest thing I'd get to one—and moved on to more important matters.

"Thousands or more, you said," I began. "So let's call it ten thousand. A worst-case scenario. How do we handle that?"

"We die well," Argar suggested, not seeming at all bothered by how useless it was. As Solitaire would say, the only good death is one that isn't your own.

"I think we can do better than that," I replied diplomatically. "I think, if we play our cards right, we can either delay Viras long enough for Solitaire to come over here and bring help . . . or kill him ourselves and rush in to save Solitaire once he's taken care of. Or does nobody here like the sound of watching that smug prick have to thank us all for a rescue?"

Despite the situation, I saw a few smiles at that. Solitaire was everyone's friend, more or less, and some far more than others—Elizabeth and Helena were extremely close with him. But that didn't mean we hadn't all felt his ego rubbing against our faces more than once. Bringing that up, framing it all comedically, injecting some levity to everything—it'd make a crack in the severity of the room.

Now came the chisel.

"We have a serious shot at winning here, but we need to play things smart. If we use our advantages—mobility and a high number of individually powerful fighters—then we can harass Viras' forces as they try to approach. There's several roads moving up to Elswick, and he won't be able to funnel all his men down a single one without costing himself speed, so his army will be fractured on the march. That gives us the chance to launch surprise attacks at the smaller units while they travel. A few of those will buy us time, and bleeding off some fraction of his troops never hurt either."

Truthfully, the latter part was unlikely to matter much. Even if each of our elites killed a dozen, we'd still only be knocking off a percentage point or two of Viras' forces. Still, we needed any advantage we could get.

I looked around and found that I'd managed to restore some semblance of cohesion to the group, minus a few who were smart enough to know how screwed we were and not loyal enough to ignore it. Corvan in particular had that look in his eyes, like he'd bolt at any moment. Finally my gaze came to rest on Beam.

He was glaring at me but doing his best to hide it now at least.

"Alright then," he said, reluctant and not quite managing to conceal the fact. "You have a point. Fine, we'll focus on Viras first, and we'll help Solitaire when we have the chance."

It was surprisingly compromising of him. Beam was usually a pretty agreeable person, of course, but not when he was seriously invested in something. Getting him to pause a training session was like pulling teeth. Getting him to abandon a rescue mission for his friend . . .? That *should* have been like pulling bones, but here he was going along with it.

I had the feeling I'd hear more about this from him later, but I put it aside for now and got back to giving out orders. Fortunately there still weren't that many to be handed out, mostly delegation between which elite would be in charge of which attack force, and the difficult decision of who was remaining in the mansion to guard our base.

No surprise, once I was done with that, Beam took me aside with a concerned look upon his face.

"You shouldn't have disagreed with me in front of the crew," I told him, touching on the most important point first. "We need solidarity now. We need to be a united front. If they get the impression that there's friction between us then there'll be friction between them too. Our leadership needs to be consistent."

That wiped the concern from his features and replaced it with rage.

"You've been acting really fucking weird lately, man," he snapped. "Like a robot, like you don't give a shit about anything. Your friends included."

I blinked. This wasn't exactly unexpected, I had to admit. I knew I could creep people out—did, invariably, creep people out, rather—unless I actively made sure to keep myself from doing so. I'd come to falsify my expressions and reactions so naturally that I didn't even think about doing it anymore, most of the time.

But then Solitaire had been captured, and I'd had to break down all those walls of humanity. To do what needed doing. Well things still needed doing, and yet here Beam was asking me to distract and shackle myself all over again?

This would have to be handled gently.

"I do care—" Beam exploded, like the muzzle flash from a gun, the eruption from a volcano. Like the response from a Solitaire.

"Then start showing it," he spit, cutting me off and actually stunning me into silence with the unexpected savagery of his response. "Because if you keep giving me reasons not to trust you, eventually I'll take the fucking hint." He turned and stormed off, leaving me by myself.

At the risk of sounding callous and cold, I actually didn't care in the slightest that Beam was mad at me because I had more important things to worry about. Like answering Solitaire's letter. I headed for the messenger we'd received it from—a human, surprisingly. And a slave of the orcs.

It was an innocuous-looking man who only revealed himself as an outsider to Elswick by talking, which was probably why he'd been chosen to carry the message here. I called him over.

"I'm going to write up a response for my brother soon. Take it to him and tell your leaders that if anything happens to him, I'll come for them with the finished version of weaponry he'd still been working on before our assault."

A complete and total lie obviously. At best I'd have a few new tricks following his advice. Still, it never hurt to try. Particularly with things that were somehow dumber than average humans.

The slave looked sufficiently frightened at least, and I headed to a desk for some paper and a quill. It was then that the governor's summons came.

I could've ignored him, of course. That would certainly have reinforced the authority I'd snatched out from under his nose in our last meeting. But . . . No. Sometimes reinforcing your authority was a *bad* idea. What I had over the governor was the deference of an uncertain, scared man in a bad position. I didn't want to mix my contempt in with that because uncertain men tended to cling to what was familiar. He might try to reclaim his lost power over me and put his foot down. If he did that, I'd have to get Beam to cut it off. That would not be politically useful, however satisfying I would find it.

The governor was not happy when I entered, as you might have expected. Worse, he was with his family. A wife, a bunch of children—one or two adults who *looked* my age but, I would guess, had about as much going on upstairs as Charles I. Postdefeat.

"Twenty thousand?!" the governor shrieked, squealed, really, like a pig being sodomized.

"Ten thousand," I corrected him calmly. "At most. More likely a good deal fewer."

"Thousands nonetheless," he snapped. "On top of the men Viras already controls in this city and Viras himself, yes?"

I paused. Should I have just lied to him? No, he'd have ended up finding out. I didn't trust our elites to be completely airtight with information like that, especially with people like Argar and Magnus. And Alora. And . . . Hmm.

Note to self: Deal with the rampant alcoholism among the people tasked with guarding your family.

"We have certain advantages," I assured him. "This position is the most fortified one you will ever see, for one. And we're waiting on assistance from an ally for another."

"You have a few hundred men at most," he snapped. "More, perhaps, if we start levying peasants, but we can't possibly match the coalition's speed at that. We're dead. We're—"

"Father," one of the women among his family began. "I think Lord Shango has a point here. Certainly, the Belahonts have a history of beating odds like this, yes?"

I saw something bizarre then. An old man actually paused and listened as the young woman talked. For a moment I was stunned, then I became less so, remembering I was in a fantasy world rather than real life. And then I looped back around to being even more surprised when I remembered we'd made Redacle even more misogynistic than our birth countries.

"My daughter Amira seems to have faith in you," the governor said after a moment, still glaring at me. "Is it misplaced?"

Probably. We're hanging on to this situation by a single pubic hair, and it's about halfway snapped already.

"Of course not. As she said, we have a history for overturning these odds. And we have new weapons prepared specifically for this situation."

That mollified him enough that I could take my leave. What surprised me was his daughter Amira took it with me, following me out into the hall.

"You're interesting," she told me. I turned around, eyed her for a moment. Didn't find myself reciprocating.

"Thanks."

She studied me a second longer as we walked.

"Did you want something—" I began. She cut me off.

"You don't feel things the way other people do, do you?"

I froze. That, at least, made her . . . interesting. I turned back to examine the woman.

My age, maybe a bit younger or older. Dark skin by Elswick's standards, maybe Helena's shade. Tall and healthy, without a trace of abnormality in her face. But then, mine didn't have that either.

Strength 2, Speed 2, Dexterity 4, Stamina 4, Toughness 2, Alertness 5, Charisma 6, Intelligence 7

Well, holy shit, seven intelligence. She was as a step below being as smart as Phelia, more or less. Almost as smart as me. I'd scanned her father a while ago, of course—four Intelligence, mid-wit—and this was like a punch in the gut by comparison.

Perhaps it shouldn't have been. I'd crawled out of my only reasonably intelligent mother with an eight, and my other genetic donor had been my father with his petty-but-unremarkable cunning.

"You don't either, do you?"

I wasn't sure why I said that, a gut feeling perhaps. Interesting. I didn't have those as a rule. My brain either thought of something consciously or it didn't. What was happening here?

Intuition. That was almost disturbing. Perhaps I was finally knowing what it was like to meet my own kind. Amira smiled.

"Your guess was easier than mine," she told me, turning and making her way back down the hall without another word.

INTERLUDE ELEVEN

I know you're reading my mail, you dumb cunt.

Adravigi's blood boiled at that, and for far more reasons than just the petty concern of being insulted. It was the *rejection*.

Her whole life, she'd been surrounded by morons. Simple, arrogant pigs who didn't give a damn what she was capable of, only what was between her legs. Solitaire Belahont had been more than just a kindred spirit. He'd been one sharp enough to see past her sex and realize it. And this was how he treated her? This was her payment for offering her friendship to him?

It was unforgivable.

She stared at the letter in her hand, eyes slipping across the insulting note one last time as she tried, and failed, to glean anything more from it. The entire thing was written in gibberish. Or, more likely, some sort of code language known only to the Belahonts. It was just the sort of clever trick she should have expected from her new enemy, but being foiled by it still stung.

Her rage was growing so rapidly and so hotly that it almost blinded her, then literally blinded her. Tears welling up, eyes contracting past the point of admitting light. She just barely kept herself under control.

Fits of uncontrolled rage were satisfying, but deadly. To her more than her enemies. Years of pulling the strings in Barbed Point had almost made Adravigi forget that, but she needed to keep the knowledge tight in her mind now more than ever.

"Here you are." She smiled, handing the letter back to Solitaire's messenger with a smile. The man seemed relieved as he took it, hurrying out. Adravigi would kill that man. She had no choice. He needed to die.

The messenger was gone only a minute, but Adravigi knew by then he was dead. She'd made her orders explicit—kill him before he entered the city proper, here in this outpost, and ensure that the return message did not reach Solitaire. Make it look like some impulsive, overeager thing. Make it look like the work of Guraganar. She wasn't sure how hopeful she could realistically be that the move would work and actually sow enough distrust between the two to leave a rift separating them. At this point, Adravigi was past the luxury of being picky about which possible moves she chose to make. Anything that might work was something she had to try.

I've lost my handle on him.

Whatever hold Adravigi had managed to secure on Solitaire when he'd arrived was rapidly crumbling. She'd isolated him in knowledge and connections, and he'd exploited his forced battle to make up for both. She'd kept him without political authority, and he'd cut straight to the source of hers to offset it. Everything she'd done to limit his ability to move against her, it seemed, he'd recognized and overturned. It was impressive. It was *damned* impressive, and it may well end up killing her.

Would she have taken him in still knowing he was this diabolically clever?

Yes, instantly and without hesitation. It would have made her want him more. But not knowing he'd be this hostile. A man with his brains made a more powerful enemy than Adravigi could tolerate, even without his connections to the other Belahonts.

Solitaire had to die.

It hurt to acknowledge that, but not on any deeper emotional level. Adravigi felt a sense of hurt when she saw damaged weapons discarded and beyond repair. It was a practical loss, a feeling of waste. She buried it.

Her options were few, but several of them were hopeful. Among these, the most hopeful were the most drastic. The decision practically made itself. Solitaire had killed her chance for moderation and subtlety when he'd subverted her authority. He'd pushed her into this, and she could do nothing to damage herself more than hesitating.

Adravigi made her way from the outpost and back into Barbed Point, seeking out Chenca the Decimator.

Chenca was often thought, based upon his name and title, to not be a very nice man. This was rather far from the truth, as he was actually among the more vile and monstrous creatures Adravigi had *ever* encountered *anywhere*. Controlling him would always have promised a finer grip on Barbed Point than Guraganar. And it had always promised a far more tenuous grip on the locus of her power too. He was far less predictable, stable, and *safe* than the orc now known as the Machinator, and so Adravigi had passed him over in Guraganar's favor. Because she did not like taking risks.

Fuck you, Solitaire. Fuck you for making me do this. Her temper was threatening to boil all over again as she entered the great orc's abode.

It was not the equal of Barbed Point's primary castle, a monstrous citadel built upon the backs of Adravigi's decade-long contributions. But it was surprisingly close. Chenca had been among the orcish city's greatest luminaries before her arriving all those years ago, the greatest in fact. He still commanded a respect for his raw strength that Guraganar would never match through cleverness and magic alone. Fitting, as that was very much Solitaire contrasted to her. As Adravigi entered, she walked past displays propping up great stuffed beasts, seized trophies, and enough skulls to stack into a pyramid.

All, she knew, had been seized by Chenca's own hands. He had always been one to prefer the personal touch.

Chenca himself awaited her in a throne room. It was a blatant challenge, she knew, to Guraganar's own. He had mentioned it to her. If Adravigi sent men after Chenca, he would fight back, the conflict would escalate to an open civil war, and thousands would die. If Guraganar challenged him personally, for the disrespect, he would die. If the fact were brought up openly, Chenca might assess these facts and hold his ground or, more realistically, refuse to change out of stubbornness, either way causing a loss of face for Adravigi and Guraganar. So the throne remained. Not discussed, not challenged. Tolerated. One of her countless sacrifices to stability.

"Whore," the orc said, as if it were some declarative statement. An observation of fact, a reminder, perhaps, to Adravigi herself, lest she forget. It was about as creative as Chenca ever got. Maybe she should have felt honored for so great a volume of his mind to be exerted on her behalf.

"I will work with you," she told him. "Lending you my mind from now on, whispering in your ear, feeding you strategies and ideas and machinery, making you the new Machinator and ruler of Barbed Point. Your strength and my mind will be a combination Guraganar could never have matched, and our reign will be unrivaled."

He was practically salivating by the time she finished. Adravigi was not a fool. However much slower than humans the orcs were, she knew they—or at least those few in the highest positions of Barbed Point—had long since deduced her true relationship with Guraganar. But power had a wonderfully self-preservative effect. She had helped push their city into a new height, and all of them were enjoying the stability and freedom from constant internal skirmishing it had brought. She had, quite carefully, made herself the linchpin to it all.

Orcs were stupider than humans, but not *that* stupid. Not enough to cut off their own feet in so blatant a way.

"I accept," Chenca told her, eyes threatening to burst out of his sockets with their abundance of eagerness.

"No you don't," she replied. "Not yet. You haven't heard what I'd be asking in turn."

Chenca's lips peeled back, revealing a row of jagged orcish teeth. There were few sights in all the world as fear inducing as that. Predation made manifest, violence given a physical form. But that was what Adravigi needed now.

"What are you asking then?" he snapped. The air seemed to shiver at his voice, as if the very room around them were scared of it. Well, it and Adravigi had that much in common.

"If we do this, then I will not be a slave any longer," she said, feeling the words slop out of her like guts from a disemboweled man. Almost willing them taken back but knowing they couldn't be.

"Humans do not live free in Barbed Point," Chenca hissed. "The manlings are beneath us."

"Not me," Adravigi pressed him. This was the largest point of failure in her offer, she knew, and the one she would least compromise on. Solitaire had taught her the dangers of ruling from the shadow. Power that was purely illusory in nature could, at any moment, crumble. It only took a single clever bastard to make people stop believing in it. Never again.

Chenca's face betrayed nothing. Orcish features were too robust and blunt to generally give much away in terms of fine expression and nuanced emotion.

"You think you can demand this?" he growled, standing now. God, he was big. Like a sculpture come to life, towering taller than a doorframe and disproportionately wide despite the fact. Adravigi had no doubt he could have plucked the head from her shoulders like it was the cork from a wine bottle.

But he didn't, merely glared at her. So she glared back. In the field of conversation, she was the better armed between them. So long as she remained calm.

"Yes," she replied simply. "You can't give up this opportunity, and neither can I. Do you want to take Guraganar's place or live in his shadow forever?"

It was perhaps a shade too much needling, but she couldn't afford half measures now of all times. If he killed her in a rage, then so be it. At least she'd be spared the humiliation of losing everything she'd worked for. Adravigi had no chance here if Chenca couldn't be predicted even that far anyway.

But his fury didn't come, or rather it didn't come without control. Beady eyes practically vibrated as they met hers, and she focused on ignoring her every instinct to turn and flee. She wondered if doing so would trigger some pursuit response in the man before her.

She would never find out.

"Very well," Chenca growled, spitting the words as if they burned his tongue.

And it was done. Adravigi felt the uncertainty hit her like a flash flood.

Why the fuck couldn't he just have worked with me?

Solitaire's face was there in her mind's eye, a mocking, leering ghoul. Just like the real man, she supposed. Could she not still have him killed? Of course she could, and it would, if anything, be simpler than trying to stage her coup with Chenca's forces.

And still she spared him; still she gave him that kindness. What she would have achieved with half the liberties he'd been allowed . . . Not that he'd allow her them in turn. Adravigi didn't want to waste Solitaire Belahont's intelligence, but she wasn't a fool either. He wouldn't hesitate to end her life. She knew that now.

No, there would be no going back. This was the only way. The only way. And God would need to have mercy on her if she didn't win.

Because Solitaire certainly would not.

CHAPTER FIFTY-FOUR

Solitaire's POV: Day 159
Current Wealth: 684 gold, 30 silver, 15 copper

I was completely sure that the diplomatic situation around me would devolve into an uncontrollable, chaotic bloodbath as people desperately frenzied to kill me specifically. This time I was actually right though. It was inductive reasoning.

We were in some big meeting room in Barbed Point, apparently an ancestral one going back a hundred years. Which meant primitive as shit. Basically a cave that, I suspected, may have been hollowed out via headbutting and could barely fit the fifty or so orcs now packed inside it with me. I didn't do well in crowds at the best of times. Crowds that had me boxed in though?

Well, I was only human.

Guraganar seemed to be dominating the meeting, him and some other, even bigger orc who I'd gathered was called Chenca. They didn't like each other. I could tell this by observing finer details in their body language and gesticulations. Flaring nostrils, narrowed eyes, literal fists beating chests, and verbal threats. That sort of thing. Truly, I was a master of deduction.

Honestly, it was almost embarrassing to watch. I kept expecting one of them to sniff the other's genitals.

"How about you two hurry this up before I get bored and start sniffing genitals?"

I don't really know why I said that, didn't even notice myself say it if I'm being honest. Good thing about everybody thinking that you're an unhinged lunatic though is that when you say weird shit, instead of getting judgmental and mocking, they take you *extremely* seriously and start listening to whatever orders you're barking out. Things became graciously faster from there.

We weren't alone of course. Besides me and the two grunting morons, there were a good few *silent* morons. They were lining the walls, all glaring in at the disagreement as menacingly as they could manage. Which would've been pretty menacing a while ago, to be fair, but had somehow lost its edge of late. Maybe it was my newfound ability to bench-press a hundred-kilo biker, bike included. It was probably just one of life's mysteries.

The guards were each flanking one of several elders, another orc of some higher importance, none quite as prominent as Guraganar or Chenca, but all of them influential enough. If there were any room in all of Barbed Point that contained more concentrated power than Adravigi and me, it was this one.

Speaking of Adravigi . . . Where was she? Alarm bells, she wasn't here. The literal only possible explanation for that was that this was an imminent attack planned by her specifically to kill Guraganar and capture me so that she could seize control of Barbed Point without a large-scale conflict. The bitch!

By the time the closest elder had drawn his knife and started for Guraganar, my flying dropkick was already landing in the asshole's temple and blasting him clean out of his chair.

Everything exploded into chaos in an instant, and for once it wasn't my fault. He who struck first wouldn't be striking last today. Not unless I lost.

The guards were closing in, great machetes and spears raised as Guraganar drew his own maul and several elders made the decision to freeze (the ones who weren't expecting this), instantly flee (the ones who'd agreed to the coup but were pussying out), or attack. For a moment, everything in the room was converging in on Guraganar and me while Chenca rose and grinned.

Then the first of the guards skewered the first of the hostile elders, just as we'd agreed beforehand.

What, you thought I threw a dropkick on the basis of Adravigi being absent in a single meeting? What am I, insane? What if she'd just been taking a shit or something? No, I'd figured out long beforehand that she was trying to pull one over on us. This big a meeting this quickly with someone you distrusted this much? Only reason you'd want to risk that is if *you* were the one turning it into an ambush.

So I returned the favor. Speaking of ambushes, the floor tile I'd mined caught one of the larger elders' footfalls just perfectly and went up like the Fourth of July. He disappeared in a smog of half-burned black powder, filling the room with that sulfuric rotten-egg stench and obfuscating most of the fighting even from the fighters themselves. Suddenly we were all trapped in the world's pointiest mosh pit.

I wasn't complaining about *that* of course. I'd have felt right at home with a bit of acid.

I was leaping around, snarling. I felt movement beside me and knifed it through the face. An orc stumbled back. He wasn't screaming like any of the ones I'd allied with—an enemy then. I stabbed again, again and again. Knife's butt pressed against my palm, fingers curled in. Punches with a point on the end, each one sending the metal deep and dragging out a squirt of blood. Bulging muscle convulsed and went slack as the orc dropped, then something grabbed me from behind.

A scream burst out of me as my skull swung back. Human heads are big and tough, cranial bones measuring thicker than most and with plenty of mass behind them. The back of my head made a nice and functional hammer as it found the offending party's face, wetting my hair with what I hoped was blood as something went *crunch.* The grip slackened. I squirmed out, turned, and bit down blindly. This wasn't my usual finessed combat chomping, just a frenzy of teeth and jaw muscles. I made a nice mess of something all the same, and soon enough I was free.

Then a fist caught my face and sent me into the table, nonexistent lights spinning in my vision. I stood there for a moment, blinking in confusion, as one tends to do when one's brain is currently busy coming unstuck from the inside of one's skull, and by the time my head had cleared enough for me to remember I was in a fight, it'd taken a turn.

Powder smoke was beginning to disperse, revealing at least three days' work for whoever cleaned this room already. Aside from that, we were winning. I had of course managed to secure more help than Adravigi, thanks to my bulging brain muscles and not at all to Barbed Point's cultural misogyny and warrior lionization, but Chenca was . . . Well. He was like the orc version of Beam.

Guraganar clubbed him across the face, knocking a few teeth out but *not* killing or incapacitating him. Chenca laughed and punched Guraganar in retaliation. This didn't technically incapacitate him either, but it was a near thing. One of the guards slashed at the orc's back, and his machete seemed to slide against the tough flesh like he was cutting stone. The Decimator whirled around and backhanded the offending orc without even looking his way, and I knew he was dead before he even hit the ground. His neck was bulging with displaced vertebrae, head turned at an unnatural angle.

There comes a point in life where every man must either shit or get off the pot, and now was shitting time. Ordinarily I might try to find some clever way to link that back to my excrement-based explosives, but I still had a concussion. I started condensing nitroglycerin between my fingertips and introduced myself to Chenca with a nice spray of droplets.

Miraculously, ridiculously, they barely seemed to even hurt him. Little cuts and tears in the skin, points where a Mach 20 shock wave had scoured square centimeters away, maybe some mild damage to the soft tissues beneath. But he was, notably, neither flayed nor bleeding to death. And now I had his attention.

I thought fast, separating hydrogen from oxygen in the air and cooling it to liquid form. Another droplet of nitro set the mix off, and Chenca the Decimator was nice and surprised by the kilogram of burning rocket fuel going off in his face. That didn't do much damage, mind, but it bought me a few moments to widen the gap and make something more complex than a single element.

Nitroglycerin, I made more nitroglycerin. If it ain't broke and all that. Unfortunately Chenca wasn't broke either, so I got to work on fixing that. A good few ounces of the stuff caught his face and went off nice and cleanly, sending him stumbling, swearing, throwing punches into the air so hard I actually felt his fists sending out wind from ten feet back. Obviously, I didn't go anywhere near that. Backing off, readying another serving of violent explosion. But Chenca didn't come to get it.

With a frustrated roar, he turned for the exit. I realized instantly where this was going and cried out a warning.

"Stop him! He's getting away!" Some of the guards listened; others were too scared to even do that. And none succeeded in impeding him. One orc was sent flying, another just killed outright with a punch. Soon Chenca's route was clear, and he sprinted through it with me in hot pursuit. But he was faster as well as stronger, and widening his lead with every stride.

I needed him caught. We'd known—I'd known, rather—that Adravigi had gained a new ally among one or more of the other elders to try to replace Guraganar. That ally was Chenca, had to be. He was by far the most influential of the ones present, and the one most desperate to flee now.

Which meant that if he got away, our plan to cripple Adravigi's faction in one swoop would fall through. Chaos would emerge, large-scale fighting. It would be messy, bloody, wasteful. Most of all, it would be *time-consuming*.

Viras was probably rubbing his nuts against the back of my brothers' necks as we spoke. I didn't have time to waste.

How did I catch Chenca? Speed up. How do I do that? I got halfway through hastily made and poorly considered plans for some kind of improvised nitro propulsion before deciding I had better options. Slow Chenca down. So how did I do *that*?

The nitroglycerin rained down ahead of him as we burst outside, going off and turning his run into a stumble. It let me close the gap before he'd finished righting himself. I was ready to start biting chunks off, perhaps try shoving a bit of nitro into somewhere nitro has no business being, when a spike of pain hit me in the neck and sent *me* stumbling. I glanced at the direction it'd come from and found Adravigi's terrified face staring back at me.

Bloodied knife still held in her trembling hands.

My neck was wet. Dangerous, deadly. Wet and warm like blood, so I clamped a hand down around the wound and squeezed like I was giving myself a strangle wank. The blood kept coming, but slower, barely trickling. If she'd hit an artery, I was dead. Assuming she hadn't, I might make it.

If I was clever. Adravigi was leaving, and so was Chenca. I could go after them. I *couldn't* fight without both arms though. As tempting as it was to heroically throw my life away purely to kill one more native, I defied my British ancestors and focused on treating myself instead. Wincing, I got ready.

Ice sizzled as it flash froze across the wound, in the vein, around the cut. Filling it out and sealing my circulatory system off as best as I could manage. It was dangerous, careful work that I had to focus on entirely. There was no good enough with major blood vessels. If I expanded the ice too fast, I could rupture something. Which would kill me. Don't control its shape and let it form pointy bits and I might nick something or block circulation entirely, which would kill me. Do any one thing on an endless list of fuckups and it could kill me. So I stayed still, focused, watched my enemies fleeing, and ground my teeth.

And braced myself for the damned war.

CHAPTER FIFTY-FIVE

Beam's POV: Day 159
Current Wealth: 684 gold, 30 silver, 15 copper

I wasn't enjoying my new company. It wasn't that they were all bad people; uncomfortable to be around, poor at conversation, a bit too fine with their jobs of killing, and a bit too proud of how good they were at doing them . . . Wait, yes, it was that. It was exactly that. I was hanging out with a pack of murderous sociopaths, and they seemed to be taking a shine to me.

There were six of us, me and Alora included. The Usurper I knew already. Though we'd never spoken, I still remembered his performance in the tourney and, I had to admit, felt reassured to have someone of his caliber on my side for a change. He was up there with Aja, more or less, and another example of someone named after perhaps-misplaced confidence in his defeating the King.

Aja the Pit Hound though did the opposite. Every moment I spent around him was a moment dedicated almost completely to controlling myself because if I let up for a single second, I'd fall into a spiral. Remembering Helena's fight, her torture. Remembering her long weeks of recovery afterward. I actually caught my mouth watering as I imagined hacking the giant bastard's arms off for what he'd done, twisting his head off, thumbing his eyes out—

But no. For one thing, we needed him. He was a valuable ally. The governor's war hound. For another, I still wasn't quite sure how a fight between us would go. Whatever magic I'd called on in the tourney's final round, whichever miracle had let me give the King of Blades a bit of trouble. I didn't know when it would reemerge, if ever. For now I was just Beam again, and he wasn't a guaranteeable match for Aja.

Not yet.

The other two men were strangers who'd joined up with the Belahonts a while ago. I didn't remember them from the tourney and had only the Challenger's word to go off regarding their abilities. I'd been told they wouldn't embarrass us. That was, I realized, high praise. Relatively at least. Soon enough, I'd see it put to the test.

We were tense on the road, journeying by foot and moving with the most balanced combination of speed and stealth we could manage. Aja, I realized, didn't say a single word, at all. He didn't ask for names, he didn't communicate turns, he didn't say anything. The rest of us were far from chatty, but him . . .

"Mute." I glanced over as the Challenger spoke, realized he was nodding in Aja's direction. "The savage is mute, and not particularly smart even when you understand him. But he's good for killing."

Given what I knew of wealthy white aristocrats, I decided to take that stupid-savage sentiment with enough salt to exterminate the slug population of Washington. The fighting one though . . . That I'd seen verified myself.

The snow was mostly gone now, melted more after just another day or two. The world was warming, our footsteps more silent and our journey . . . Well, all of us were too superhuman to actually care about the cold anymore, but it was a nice change at least. It'd probably make the blood harder to see too.

Our task was to delay the army, as we'd planned. We were to attack its split units, the smaller ones. Not the whole thing, of course. Fighting ten thousand men with just the six of us was unthinkable.

Somehow, it hadn't dawned on me until we came within visual range of our enemies that we'd *still* be taking on about one thousand. They were moving in a sort of scattered, zigzagging column. Covering about three times the area they needed to, unformed and more vaguely herded than marched. Figured. I wouldn't want to stay in neat ranks for a hundred-mile trek either, and it was certainly good for us.

That kind of sloppiness only went so far though. Attacking by day would be a mistake, so we tailed them, keeping far away and out of sight as we waited for night to fall. Most of our group got shifty at that, fidgeting and twitching as boredom set in. Aja was still as a statue of course. I liked to think I was too, but realistically I was probably shifting around like the others. Everyone else would probably have been yelled at if they'd been poor enough to serve under a sergeant.

But then discipline only went so far when you were a group of six, and killing power a lot further. Our wait continued, and we started sleeping in shifts to ensure at least some of us had a bit more gas in the tank for when the fighting started. When it was my turn to rest, the Challenger and one of the men whose name I didn't know was on watch.

That turned out to be a huge mistake. I woke up to a strange warmth and the smell of smoke. Bleary-eyed, I frowned, rubbed my face, and looked up to see . . . a fire.

There was meat on it, strips of pork sizzling beside the flames as the Challenger grinned into the inferno. He looked up at me.

"Ah, you're up. Fancy a cut? We got hungry waiting—" I was on my feet instantly, kicking the fire apart, desperation moving my legs faster than they ever had before.

"We're on a stealth mission, you fucking idiot!" I hissed, not fully believing he could have been so fucking stupid.

He didn't get the chance to respond before the enemy's attack came, a great, long swarm of bodies tearing toward us like a tidal wave. I spun around, swinging before my brain even registered what was happening and splitting one man from shoulder to hip. But more were coming. Always more.

Say one thing for the Challenger, say he was quick. He'd kept his plate armor on, despite being insanely lax in every other area, and that gave him a nice edge as he threw himself into the fray and started swinging that broadsword around. Aja was joining a moment later, as were the two Belahont elites. Six on however many dozen, score, or hundred were attacking seemed like ridiculously long odds.

But we weren't normal men.

Standing shoulder to shoulder, the six of us made a wall that took more than a little doing to get past. Every second, another dozen of the enemy died, if not more. Armor like wet tissue, swords like lead pipes, bodies like malnourished children. My ethereal armor rattled as arrows thudded into it, but none of them had the speed and draw strength that had made the scouts' so dangerous. And I had help this time. We actually started to *gain* ground rather than lose it.

Then the enemy began encircling us, and everything turned to chaos as we started fighting all the more desperately to keep them from managing it.

It's hard to describe how this fight felt, but the best way to put it is probably likening it to a blender. We were the blades. Everywhere around us men died, coming apart, sending blood in all directions. There was no grace to it, no precision or aesthetic. We didn't have that luxury. We just killed as fast as we could and hoped to God that they couldn't come even faster. In moments, I was standing in pooling blood that had to be an inch deep, and it was growing thicker by the second as more and more of them fell apart around us.

Something broke of course; something always broke in these conflicts. That was one of the little lessons I'd picked up from spending so many months flitting between them.

A Belahont man was dragged down by three, six—more—of the enemy. He was screaming, and smart. Discarding his spear to switch in his knife, stabbing and slashing, freeing himself fast but cut off even faster. I had moments to decide and was halfway toward lunging for him when I heard another cry. The Challenger, this time threatened by a great deal more.

Whoever was fighting him, they weren't a normal person. Fast enough that they didn't seem to be moving in *slow motion* at least, and with plenty of help. He was losing ground, panic swinging, fearful. Another Belahont was separated from us, moments to live.

I was needed everywhere at once, too many places demanding my attention. Too many allies facing death. Who did I save?

The answer was a no-brainer of course. The Belahonts were my men. I owed them my protection, my loyalty. But the Challenger was the governor's family. If he died, our little deal fell through and there wasn't a thing in the world that could save us. I fought my way to him.

Despite his disadvantage, the Challenger was still one of the deadliest things I'd ever met. Naturally, he held his own for the few moments I needed to reach his side.

The man fighting him was among the best of the enemy's little assault, so I did things the Solitaire way rather than the Beam way. My sword came down hard on the back of his knee, biting through the mail protecting his vulnerable joint and hamstringing him in a single messy impact. Blood ran down his leg, which buckled. The man didn't have a chance to recover before the Challenger's sword came down hard on his neck joint. That was all she wrote.

I turned back to see both Belahonts' struggles had stopped, and Aja was regrouping with the Challenger and me. I'd made my choice. Now to live with it.

Which wouldn't be necessary, actually, unless I managed to live at all.

One side of the enemy was thinner than the other, a weakness in the wall of flesh caging us in. We hit it hard. Swords came down, blood came out, bodies went away, and the path was cleared almost before I knew what was happening.

I was running with wind in my ears and screams at my back, drenched in gore, smelling hot iron and feeling it sting my nostrils. Arrows whipped by us, sling bullets, then *spells*. A fireball hit a tree and pretty much killed it, throwing a spray of burning splinters in all directions. Still we ran.

We ran until Alora's leg caught on something and she went down hard, crying out as she landed, gasping and splayed out in the dirt. Men came up around her, spears raised and ready to kill. I was too far to help.

But Aja wasn't.

It took him one swing to clear two men from Alora's side, and another got rid of three. They fell like confetti to the ground. His body smashed into the few still standing, leaving just enough of a gap for him to grab Alora and haul her over his shoulder. Then he was running again, arcing over the ground in long, bounding strides.

We were off, into the woods and far from the enemy. We didn't stop running until we'd put miles between us, and even then we only slowed down to a pace brisk enough that normal humans would still have struggled attempting it. Battered, beaten, down two men. But alive at least. For now, we were alive.

CHAPTER FIFTY-SIX

Shango's POV: Day 159
Current Wealth: 684 gold, 30 silver, 15 copper

I was busy, and Solitaire's instructions were about as helpful as a pair of clamps on my nuts. Every screed of my focus was needed just to make sense of them. Sometimes they'd be coherent, clear. At others they . . . babbled. Perfectly balanced chemical equations and clinical descriptions of methodology were spliced between deranged lunacy, rantings on the Tree People, whatever those were, and conspiratorial predictions for the future based on God only knew what.

Honestly, I was impressed by how good a job he'd done in dialing his usual insanity back. But that didn't make it much easier to sift the nuggets of gold from the river of shit. Particularly the parts where he just copied the King James Bible, word for word, from memory. Backward. Not sure why he even did that. Solitaire was an atheist.

"I've been looking for you." I turned to the voice and found the governor's daughter was its source. Leaning near the door, smiling knowingly. Knowing of what, mind, I did not actually have a clue, and I also didn't care in the slightest. Unfortunately telling the daughter of a valuable ally to fuck off would be . . . Politically inconvenient.

"I'm somewhat busy at the moment," I told her, being as polite as I could.

"Oh that's fine, I won't be long." She smiled sweetly, missing the point as if . . . as if she were stupider than I knew she was. So, intentionally then. Why?

"Do you mind if I watch you work?"

I answered her on autopilot, far more concerned with what she was playing at here than the small talk. It was probably just a distraction anyway.

"Feel free." If she was trying to get some idea as to what I was doing then it was a waste of time. Even Solitaire couldn't pick up modern chemistry through imitation and observation alone. I thought. She didn't seem disappointed though and didn't grow frustrated as she waited there watching me.

"Do you want to hear a secret?" she asked after a minute or two. I bit back my annoyance, plastered on my most convincing smile, and nodded.

"Sure!"

She giggled, but at what I wasn't certain.

"Lady Adannaya is trying to run away."

I stared at her. "What?!"

She giggled again, as if she were *trying* to piss me off, and stepped aside to give me a wide berth as I barged out of the room and took off down the corridor at a sprint.

Velaharo Manor was a big place, and I had a lot of damned ground to cover. If I'd not become so much faster than I used to be, I wouldn't have cleared even half of it. Fortunately, I just barely managed. I found Adannaya halfway to the main hall, her modest belongings already packed and her pace fast. She'd clearly anticipated that she might be stopped.

"Your wife already tried convincing me to stay, my lord," she said, not looking at me, just heading for the door. "I'm afraid there is nothing you can say that will persuade me. I'm sorry, believe me I am, but I must do this."

"No, you have options," I pressed. "And you're better served staying with us than leaving."

"Am I?" she snapped, actually sounding exasperated now. "Really, you can keep your silver tongue between your teeth with me. I've seen you work too much to fall for it, Shango Belahont. Your family is doomed. You have no escape and are in the sights of the strongest magus within a hundred miles. An army ten times the size of your own forces approaches, and you have nothing up your sleeve."

Clearly, she'd thought this through. That would make it harder to sway her, but not impossible. I wasn't actually *doomed*. We were facing long odds, sure, but not impossible ones. Which meant there was a way I could spin this without even needing to lie. Good thing too. I wasn't sure this one would've fallen for it.

"Solitaire has been in contact with us," I told her. Waited, not very long, for that to sink in. Her eyes were quivering masses of emotion, and I fancied for a moment that I could hear the sound of synapses screaming at one another beneath her skull. She answered me with a simple nod though. Keeping her cards close to the vest. Also smart.

"He's given me some consultations, helped me to make progress in creating a few new weapons. Ones that, we think, might turn the tables against Viras. More, now that Solitaire isn't here."

She thought about that.

"Because Viras won't be accounting for new weaponry, thinking your brother is dead?"

"Yes," I confirmed. That much I was sure of. Viras played a deep game, but he'd tried to needle me by reminding me of Solitaire's death. Which only reinforced my conviction, due to him being *alive*. Would he have done that intentionally, just to make me more confident my weapons wouldn't be anticipated?

No, I decided. It wouldn't have made a difference, not a big one. He thought Solitaire was dead.

"And you think this is enough to lure me back?" Adannaya wasn't hiding her skepticism, using the genuine emotion as a bludgeon to press me harder, get me to give more away. So I did. What choice did I have? We needed a magus of her caliber. We needed a magus of any caliber.

"My brothers and I all have a . . . particular ability. We grow stronger, rapidly. Faster than others. We do this by winning, achieving objectives, managing goals." I felt my guts twist with every word, that instinctive aversion to giving away information for nothing. But there'd be no half measures here. We needed her. And if I thought she'd run off with the knowledge instead of being swayed by it . . .

I could always just kill her.

"That's an interesting thing to *claim*," she said after a moment. "But can you verify it? Can you *prove* it? You're far from the first to make an impossible promise."

"You've looked into our history, and I've no doubt you heard about Beam's performance in the tourney."

"Where he hid his power in order to lengthen the odds against him and made you more money through betting as he fought to the final round?"

I sighed. She really was . . . clever. I tried my best to appreciate that, but it was truly quite hard considering the circumstances.

"When Beam became more powerful by the match, resulting in us losing several bets because we couldn't afford to bank on him overturning the odds."

That did faze her, but only a little bit. I could still see that fog of distrust in her eyes. It was like talking to Solitaire, except less explosively violent.

"We both know that isn't enough." Adannaya sighed.

"Then just wait and see," I hissed. "Don't march out of here and leave us to die because you didn't believe that the family producing more powerful magical prodigies and weapons than you've ever heard of are exceptional in other ways."

She was considering it, I could see that much. But she was cautious. I needed more.

"If you stay now," I began, hesitating, preserving. "If you help us . . . I'll offer you a marriage to my brother Solitaire. You'll be part of the family proper, privy to our secrets, benefiting from our rise."

And Solitaire will get nobility in a nation whose view of class and hierarchy won't send him into a murderous rampage.

Adannaya was tempted, I saw, but like most smart women, she knew better than to chase after her temptation blindly. These initial moments after hearing the offer were when she'd be most malleable, and she knew it.

"I will not be subordinate in marriage," she said at last. "That is not how my people do things."

It was, actually, just not with men above and women below.

"I'm aware of Akanite customs," I answered her. "And so we're clear, Solitaire won't be subordinate to *you*, either."

She hesitated at that, which almost had me laughing out loud. She had no right to be as indignant as she'd been, not with this kind of response to having the same request made of her.

"That is different," she said quietly. "Your brother is . . . unstable."

Was he?

"He isn't," I said at last. "Violent, yes. But he's fully in control of himself, and he doesn't hurt family."

Her eyes were intense, searching me for deceit.

"And the cannibalism?" I actually almost had a coughing fit at that, surprise coming like a punch in the gut.

"Cannibalism?!"

"I've heard stories," she snapped. "Don't pretend you know nothing about them. Everywhere I go I hear the same: Solitaire is known for biting men, chewing them apart. For devouring their flesh."

"Jesus fuck—he just fights by biting!" I groaned. This was ridiculous. Cannibalism? That sort of rumor . . . I didn't even know what to do with it. "He doesn't fucking eat people. He . . . It's just how he fights. I've seen him bite off an ear, chew out a throat, maybe . . . Uh, he took someone's balls off once, but he doesn't eat anything."

She stared at me, saying nothing. For the first time in a long time, I actually felt self-conscious.

"Okay, yes, it's fucking weird, but he's not a cannibal."

Adannaya relaxed somewhat, exhaling, nodding.

"Very well." She sighed, chewing a lip in thought. "Very well. Fuck, fine. I will marry Solitaire as an . . . equal."

I sighed in relief, then paused. I had one of those moments. You know the ones, a gut feeling. Solitaire practically lives his life jumping from one to the next. For me they're a rarer thing, more of a luxury. I actually have to micromanage my brain. Maybe he was rubbing off on me. Terrifying thought.

"This was your plan from the beginning," I realized. Adannaya's shock, and total lack of confusion, gave away that it was. "Threaten me with leaving, coax me for information about Solitaire being alive . . . Coax me for information about our family and . . . then secure yourself a place in it."

Dear fucking God, I was glad this one was marrying into the Belahonts now. I tightened my eyes and examined her.

Strength 3, Speed 3, Dexterity 4, Stamina 5, Toughness 2, Alertness 6, Charisma 6, Intelligence 8

She was as smart as Phelia. Definitely, definitely glad this one was marrying into the Belahonts. No wonder she'd almost pulled one over on me. I'd been an idiot to ignore her.

"You wanted the inventor," I said, thinking aloud. "But . . . No, hang on, you didn't even ask about that." I eyed her now, feeling suddenly cold. "Lady Adannaya, were you hoping to get yourself an insane cannibal?"

Adannaya met my gaze without flinching away from it, swallowing and remaining dignified despite it all.

"I can see why Phelia married you now," she said at last. "Now, how can I help our family?"

CHAPTER FIFTY-SEVEN

Shango's POV: Day 161
Current Wealth: 688 gold, 36 silver, 27 copper

Beam looked like he'd just dragged himself across ten miles of broken glass, by the teeth. Could've been worse, of course. He had fought a thousand people after all. But it could've been a good deal fucking better as well.

"Dumbass lit a fire," he said, glaring daggers at the Challenger who, for his part, did actually look a little bit chastened. Granted that was far too little, in the same way that the famous genocider involved in World War II—Winston Churchill— saying he was awfully sorry would have been too little.

"I see." I could've yelled at the Challenger, but what would that achieve? Make my throat tired, maybe get him to learn his lesson. More likely, it would just piss off either him or the governor. Trouble with powerful allies was it made one of your top priorities ensuring that they remained allies, no matter what.

The worst of this wasn't that the Challenger had gotten two of our men killed though. That was *bad*, but they'd been expendable from the start. Everyone who mattered to the bigger picture—Beam, the governor's killers, and Alora—had gotten out. The loss here was our chance to do real damage to an enemy advance. One hundred or so dead was a nice figure normally.

And about 1 percent of the forces heading our way.

Our odds had been better a few days ago, much better. Everything seemed to be worsening them. Time had been our ally, and with every hour, it turned inexorably to the enemy's side. Slowly waiting to pounce on us, knife raised and ready to meet the meat of our backs. Could we win this?

I was becoming less sure by the day.

I kept it to myself of course. If there was one thing that would reduce our chances from almost zero to completely zero it was letting everyone else know how slim they really were. We needed the dumb, arrogant certainty that we'd prevail. And I had to admit the Belahonts' brief history in Redacle had given them all . . .

Wait, back up. I was twenty-four. My birthday had been sometime last week. I'd . . . I'd been here since . . .

That thought was too big for the time being, so I shoved past it and turned my attention to more productive ones instead.

"Both of you focus on recovery and training the troops." I sighed, standing and heading for the door. "It seems there's nothing more to add here."

I headed out, enjoying the freedom from my job for five long seconds. Then headed toward my other job in Solitaire's lab and, exerting all my monumental will, did not kill myself. When I reached the workshop, I found it already occupied. Amira was seated in my chair, smiling up at me like she always did.

"You kept me waiting." She hummed.

As if we'd agreed to meet here, which we hadn't. I didn't like how she did that. Assumed things, pretended things. Made remarks for seemingly nobody's benefit but her own. I knew she was lying, and she knew I knew. So why say it, just to make me uncomfortable?

It was working.

"I need to work," I replied, letting myself be a bit less polite this time. If my good manners were only encouraging her, then there was no point in them anymore. Sadly, Amira was as immune to that disincentive as all the others I'd tried.

"Do you want to hear another secret?"

Oh fuck off. What the hell even is this? Do you just enjoy pissing me off? Is that it? Are you trying to get into an emotionlessness contest and win or something?

"I'd love to!" I smiled and did not say anything mean or untoward. Rather, I matched her energy joule for joule and threw the suffocating positivity like a javelin. A new tactic.

She actually did seem surprised, pausing for a perceptibly long moment before her smile was back in place and hardened to keep from any further lapses.

"I know that we're going to lose." She beamed.

Once more, she won. She might have kicked me in the balls and not caused so strong an effect.

"You should flee," she pressed. "Run, take your wife, take your brother, and leave here. Make your stand somewhere else or simply run longer and gather strength far from Viras' grasp. There are opportunities in the world for a man of your talents, no? Surely you must know about them. You seem to know all sorts of things."

My first instinct was to debate that, and I resisted it. What sort of man would focus on her question about the source of his knowledge over what she was suggesting?

The sort who had cause to hide it, which, I suspected, was exactly what this flanking question was meant to discover. So I focused on her suggestion instead.

"I'm not leaving Elswick," I replied, forcing anger into my voice to cover up its total absence. More habit than anything. This one already knew it wasn't there. "My friends are here, my people. I won't leave them to die."

Amira moved in close at that, bringing her eyes to almost touch my own. The intensity of her gaze felt strange. Like Solitaire's, though without any of the manic instability or creeping violence that came with him staring at something so dangerously hard. Amira simply . . . cared, a lot. Fascination, not suspicion. Infinitely less disturbing . . . and infinitely more.

"Viras will find you, you know," she murmured. "But he'll find you here faster than he will anywhere else. You're cutting down the time you have. I don't want anything to happen to you . . . Really."

No, it wasn't her eyes getting closer. It was her lips, leaned forward, moving for mine. What was this? She was trying to seduce me? If she thought something this blunt was going to get the blood rushing away from my brain, she had another thing—

The door opened, and I glanced over to see Phelia standing just outside and looking in. Her lips were thin, face tight. I realized several things at once.

The first, of course, was that I'd given instructions to be told if any new developments occurred, and that her presence here probably didn't bode well. The second was that Amira was actually very close to me, almost pressed up against my body. Breath hitting my face, hands beside my waist, faces inches apart, and one leg between both of mine.

My wife looked about as pleased as Solitaire being told not to manufacture military-grade explosives next to your bedroom.

"Shango," she said, speaking in that special "you are going to be very unhappy for an extremely long time, dear" voice that women seemed inherently born with the ability to put on.

"Phelia." I smiled, shoving Amira off as hard and pointedly as I could manage without actually causing a political incident. "I—"

Phelia spoke over me, crushing my explanations under her heel. Clearly she wasn't in the mood to hear them.

"There is something outside you ought to see," she told me, voice crisp and cool as the grave. It gave nothing away, and suddenly my wife's displeasure felt like the *second* most pressing issue around me.

I followed her quickly, steeling myself for what was to come. The list of potential revelations wasn't exactly long, being honest. And I got ready to see the army that was no doubt waiting outside Velaharo Manor to come and kill me.

What I found instead though was . . . Well, it was certainly army *sized*. Easily thousands of people, mostly men but a few women among them. All were . . . peasants. Yes, they had to be. Dressed in commoner's wear and with none of the excessive flab that boasted of comfort in this world. They were surrounding the mansion, but not forcing their way in. Only a few were ahead of the others, speaking with our guards.

Henry was making his way toward me, a wide grin splitting his face. That was only slightly reassuring, and I hurried over, desperate for answers.

"The people heard about Viras' army." He grinned wider. "They're here for *you*, lord. They're here to fight for *you*. You funded the Jaleheim, provided food, gave decent wages to your men, freed towns, accepted low rewards—I don't need to list it all. You've made it clear to all of them where your loyalties lie, and it's with them. So their loyalties lie with you. They want to fight for something—everyone does— and you've given them something worth fighting for."

I looked away from Henry, back to the people. They were scared, I could see, and most weren't armed with anything more advanced than farm tools or hand-me- downs. These people would die. I knew that almost without question. They'd be going up against career soldiers, outnumbered and fighting a magus of ridiculous power to top it all off. This would be the only time I ever saw so many of them because there wouldn't be this amount left once the fighting started.

But maybe it was better to die like that than keep living under a bootheel. Maybe it was, or maybe it was just convenient for me, the one they'd be fighting for, to tell himself that. Either way, I didn't have the luxury of turning down their help.

Solitaire, where are you?

The stair creaked, and the boy heard movement beside him a moment before its creator uncoiled. He spun, raising a guard just in time for vicious, quick knuckles to rebound off his forearm and deaden the muscle. He was too slow for the following lower punch that caught his belly head-on.

He wheezed, coughed, then felt hands grip him. Some bizarre magic done with his body weight left him twisted over a protruding hip and landing hard. He rolled with it, failed to fully break the impact, and a heel came down on his chest.

That was all she wrote. "She" being his mother, of course.

"You were slow," she snapped. "Noisy."

Bernard groaned, as much as he was still able. He rolled and convulsed on the floor, waiting for his breath to come back. His mother wasn't a big woman—tall, but not exactly well built. She had a way, though, of putting all her strength exactly where she wanted it, and in the twelve years of his life, he'd never known her to pull a punch.

"I . . . I just wanted a drink," he wheezed. Anger was boiling up in him now, but he bit it down fast.

"And do you think they'll relax because you *just want a drink*?" his mother snapped, her face twisting, eyes wide, lips curling back to expose jagged teeth. She'd cut her hair lately, blonde locks now closer to the scalp. Harder to grab in a fight, to pull. The result made her look wilder than usual.

But her eyes made her look wildest of all. Bernard had to be ready, had to walk quietly, react fast, and fight well. If he didn't, *they* would kill him for his lack. He lay there while his mother took her leave, wasting what breath he could muster on silent sobs. Trembling with rage.

Weeks passed, then months. Bernard wasn't a child anymore, not in his own head. If he was old enough to make his own ecstasy, then he was basically an adult. His mother didn't seem to agree, though. Nothing had ever made her relax an inch, nothing had *ever* loosed the tension that animated her through existence. Nothing that happened was unprecedented. It was all familiar. But she was raising her intensity.

Bernard was fast enough, some days. He did fight well, but she was never happy. He always ended up beaten down or hobbling, she was always sneering and chastising. He could smell the reasons for it, could inhale her fear and horror. His mother still saw him as her little baby boy, a delicate bird she could only watch torn apart by the world. As horrible as that world was to people like them, nothing could have equaled the phantom threats she readied him for.

It was the day of his thirteenth birthday, and he came down the stairs. A board creaked, but this time Bernard reacted faster than ever and caught his mother with a punch clean to her temple. He had no idea how he'd known she was there—he had felt more than seen her—but she went stumbling back and fell hard.

He was on her before she got up. In his head, he saw the fight that was about to happen, the pain. On his *birthday*. She couldn't let up, could she? Could never *let him* let up either. He saw all the old lunges and felt all the past strikes, and he returned them now as she covered up and tried to break out of his mount.

But time had brought size and strength to Bernard without him even realizing it. He had thirty pounds on her now and most all of it was muscle. Sheer strength compounded his advantage on the first blow. He who struck first usually struck last.

Especially if he also struck second, third, fourth . . .

Bernard went long beyond the fourth blow, lost count of how many times his fists came down like guillotine blades, battering the woman below. He continued after her guard broke, snarling, hissing, smashing her. He inhaled, smelling the fear and pain, the *weakness*. Felt it set his teeth on edge, boiling his blood, flooding his muscles with strength.

His mother was limp now, slack beneath him, and Bernard raised his fist, held it there for a second. Let the moment drift by him, running it over his tongue and studying every broken line of her pulped face. Then he punched.

She did not die, but it took her some minutes to reawaken. When she did, he could see the damage was beyond terrible. A cheek had caved in where his knuckles proved themselves the sturdier plane, her lips were split, eyes swelling shut. Every inch of her that he could see was either cut or bruised.

And still, she smiled.

"You did it," she hissed between bloody teeth. "I knew you had it in you. You're a man now, my Solitaire. They'll never be able to hurt you again. You're *ready* for them."

And he was.

CHAPTER FIFTY-EIGHT

Solitaire's POV: Day 168
Current Wealth: 702 gold, 14 silver, 44 copper

Barbed Point was a ruin, and it was my fault. I waited for the guilt to hit me as I cast an eye over the place. Trashed buildings, mangled streets, corpses everywhere. The fighting had been brief—a mere week—but bloody. More than a thousand had died on each side before it'd come to its end. I'd unleashed a bigger ruin than perhaps any I'd seen in Redacle so far, and it really was all my fault.

But the guilt never came. I had a mission, something that needed doing, and these idiots had stopped me. It was what it was.

Adravigi had made a fight of it. Or tried to, at least. Truth be told, she'd had more or less everything working against her. We'd had the numbers, and though she was easily my equal in intuitive understanding of all things mechanical, she just lacked the modern context I had that let me cheat my way ahead of this world's technology. And that was to say nothing of her head for tactics. I wasn't a strategist myself of course, but in what was essentially a contest of amateurs, I had a way of guessing around what the enemy had done that left Adravigi's forces trapped more than once. It hadn't taken long at all.

Now the killing was just about done. My body ached, muscles burned, bones shivered. I was littered by small cuts, crusted with blood—most of it not mine. I'd killed about sixty people today. Now I just needed one more.

Adravigi had fled from her side's last defensive position in the fighting, but I'd seen where she was headed. I took off at a run.

My strength was drained from the exertion of all my fighting, but I was still faster than any normal human and still crossed the space covering almost ten meters at a time with every bound. It took me less than a minute to get back within visual range of her.

She was tired too, stumbling and almost falling with each stride. Maybe two hundred meters ahead, a couple less with every passing moment. The chase didn't last much longer. Or it shouldn't have, at least. An orc jumped out at me as I passed a corner, swinging an axe that missed my head and was answered by one of my daggers punching through his chest. I twisted the blade, then left it in him and ran rather than wasting precious moments to retrieve it. More soldiers were up ahead, and I dispatched them with a spray of nitro that left the air shivering as I ran into it. Arrows rained around me, thudded into a hastily frozen block of ice that dropped down heavily at my side. Still, I ran.

It seemed the universe didn't want Adravigi being caught because it kept on throwing more enemies at me. Well, the universe wasn't the boss of me, and I wouldn't be listening to it. I just killed whatever impeded me, killed and killed. I'd already caused a maelstrom that ended hundreds. What was a few more?

Nothing, that was what. Not in the bigger picture. Whatever my horrible little fucking nostrils told me, whatever my pathetic brain *felt* as it smelled the reek of fear and pain, they didn't matter in the grand scheme of things. And some people just needed killing. This bitch had caused all of this; she'd die before it ended.

Adravigi ran out of orcs eventually, and she was slowing down faster than I was. I caught her moments later. A single shove sent her flying forward, feet out from under her and body hitting the ground. She rolled another few meters, stopping in a heap then turning and scrambling back as I approached. The hair was clinging to her face, glued down by sweat and grime. Between frayed strands I saw wide, fearful eyes quivering as they locked on me. I came closer, remaining knife clutched so tightly I thought the handle might break. Waited for her to beg.

But she didn't. Adravigi was terrified, trembling, staring up at me like I was some giant animal. But she didn't beg, just waited. Silent—save for the slight whimpering—and remaining as steady as any woman with so much adrenaline in her blood could be expected to manage.

That was a damned shame.

I remembered being dragged off by orcs, remembered the forced march. I remembered all those people I'd cut to pieces on Adravigi's orders. Felt the rage rising in me, felt myself *salivating* as I imagined killing her. How would I do it? Even I didn't know. Maybe I'd gut her like a fish; maybe I'd wring her neck like a chicken. Maybe I'd eat her alive. Bite chunks off, swallow, bite some more. I took another step closer, heart pounding in my ears. This was it. The woman who'd imprisoned me, beaten me, left my brothers to die, set me on a village of innocent people like some fucking war goblin. Shango wasn't here. Beam wasn't here. It was just me.

It was always just me. The Solitaire, playing alone, winning. My head was so quiet now, so, so quiet. Brain finally doing without all the noise of other people's cognition. There was just one needling irritant still left.

Adravigi's fear, Adravigi's thoughts. Clogging up my nose with the stink of them. Another step, and I felt myself close to giggling.

I was always alone, and now I was alone physically as well. Nobody here could see me. Nobody could judge me. I didn't need to *pretend* for anyone. The nail that stuck up got hammered down, but the hammers were all off busy getting killed elsewhere. It was just me, Adravigi, and my knife.

I could finally be who I'd always been.

Closing in, I brought my face up to Adravigi's and roared. She screamed, leaning back, looking away, sobbing as she waited for the end. But I just roared louder.

"I hate you," I croaked, finding *myself* close to tears now and biting them back. Men didn't cry, not ones raised by my mum. "I really, really fucking hate you. I want . . . I want to . . ." God, I didn't have the words for what I wanted to do. I just wanted to *do it*. So why the fuck couldn't I? What was *stopping* me? I'd carved my way through a dozen people to get to her, but I couldn't end one single, petty, insignificant life more?

Maybe a thousand people was enough. Right. Now a few dozen more had died for nothing.

So, was that it? I needed to ritualistically sacrifice her so I could pretend they'd died for *something*?

I called on some of my own orcs and had them seize Adravigi without hurting her any more. I didn't so much as glance at her all the while, couldn't bring myself to. It wasn't that I felt bad for anything I'd done to her. It wasn't that I felt ashamed. I didn't really know *what* I felt when I looked her way.

But I didn't want to keep feeling it.

CHAPTER FIFTY-NINE

Beam's POV: Day 168
Current Wealth: 702 gold, 14 silver, 44 copper

The army was here, and there was no more time left to prepare anything. Whatever we'd done was all we'd get done. Whatever we'd managed was all that would be managed. All we had left was victory . . . or a last stand.

For miles, it seemed, the columns of men stretched out ahead. We'd slowed them as best we could, a few more harassing actions, another two levels for me. But there was a limit. We'd gotten tired, stretched thin. We'd had to cover ground, and the enemy was getting more alert with each attempt. In the end, we'd retreated back home, and now they were there with us.

"Ten thousand," Shango remarked, eyeing the masses as if they were ten thousand ants rather than men with the conviction and orders to kill him. "Looks like less."

I realized then that I might never see anything get to him again. And maybe that was a good thing.

"Viras is coming." We all turned to see Phelia as she stood nearby, face paler than usual and body seeming to keep itself from trembling only by a constant exertion of her will. It was impressive enough considering how little time she'd spent being attacked.

"Thank you," Shango replied, still calm despite it all, then glanced my way. "Well, this is it."

"This is it," I echoed. The words sounded like they were coming from someone else.

You there?

Always.

I hesitated.

Can we win this?

The voice answered fast as ever.

I want the magus' fingers.

It actually comforted me slightly to hear that, which was probably not a good sign for my mental health. The familiarity though, the sheer certainty in the voice's request . . . That put me at ease.

Shango headed out to meet with Viras of course, buying time with the conversation. Time, and anything else, was in short supply. I came with him just in case the magus tried to kill him and a person to ineffectually squirm at him for a few moments was needed.

"I'll make this quick, since, frankly, you've eaten up enough of both our time already." Viras was calm. He couldn't exactly have gotten *calmer*, but now his state of perpetual easiness was bolstered by some measure of . . . good mood, I realized.

That much made sense. As he saw it, he'd basically won. We'd hidden a lot of our aces in the hole—though there was no obscuring the peasants whatever we did—but in his head, this was still a terribly skewed match that could end only in one way.

And hell, maybe it actually was. I suspected Shango was banking on Solitaire showing up at the last minute to aid us, or perhaps a convenient meteor strike killing Viras.

He didn't say that of course, just played the defiant hero resigned to his fate.

"We're not going to let you win this without a fight," Shango replied, keeping as calm as fucking ever. I knew now it wasn't just a poker face. Somehow the emotions of everything—of death itself—just weren't registering to him. He was like Viras in that regard, I realized. Two peas in a pod, except they were trying to kill each other and I was going to be one of the weapons they threw into the resultant violence.

Viras sighed.

"You truly are making this harder than it needs to be, you know," he told Shango. "You could be *great*, Shango Belahont, perhaps the greatest magus to ever live. By your age, I'd spent my entire life training, and I could halt the flow of a river or fling a boulder too high in the air to see. Picture what a creature of your talents will manage in ten years. In twenty. You'll be my equal in five, I suspect. Do you think anything in this entire world could stop you should you complete your training under me?"

Shango looked at him like a wolf staring at the flock.

"How powerful would Solitaire have been?"

Viras' face fell slowly, eyes twitching with irritation.

"I thought you were bigger than that," he replied. "I thought you would be beyond letting such a petty grudge tie you down. Apparently not."

"I guess not, yeah," Shango answered back, pausing a moment. "What even are your plans for me, anyway?"

Viras opened his mouth, then faltered.

"You're playing for time." I felt the wind go out of me, but Shango kept his face neutral.

"Now you sound like my brother." He shrugged, not denying it. I wasn't sure why, but Shango always played a deeper game, and Viras seemed less sure for a moment.

"No, you *are* buying for time. I won't give it to you." He turned, heading back to his army as the air shimmered around him. A shield. He seemed to think that we would have pounced on him without it.

I mean . . . fair enough. I might have. He was quite literally a third of our enemy's total strength just by himself. If I could take his head off with a swing from behind it'd be worth getting a reputation for violating parleys. Surviving today was worth problems later. Viras disappeared back into his forces, and I turned to Shango as we headed for our positions.

"You remember the plan?" he asked.

I swallowed, nodded.

"Yes. Good luck, man."

Shango nodded back. "Good luck." We went our separate ways at that, and I headed to my position. I moved better, with more strength and ease, than before. A few levels from the raids had come my way, and though the differences felt slighter than I'd have liked—certainly slight compared to Shango's gain of four from winning over the peasants—I was grateful for any bit of help I could get. In this case, that'd been two points each to speed and alertness, with one each to strength and toughness. Still not on Arthur's level, still not quite. Still far from the army I'd need to be to protect my family.

I couldn't do anything right.

Stop that. It is pathetic.

I stopped it, but only because I had bigger humans to fry.

Within moments, I was at my vantage position high in Velaharo Manor, looking down as all the ant-sized soldiers began their march across Elswick. They were met with resistance near instantly by both the Belahont guards and the city's guard, arrows and sling bullets flying through the air and smacking into their ranks. Wooden shields were raised at the front of course, doing a fine job of absorbing the worst of it, where those in ranks behind held their shields up higher and defended from plunging fire.

But nothing could help against the gunshots.

We didn't have a lot of gunners, a dozen maybe, but they were doing a fine job of messing up the enemy offensive. One shot every second or two, per shooter. The enemy was splitting their forces up, coming on in numerous lines rather than tight shield walls—probably because Viras had heard about how devastating our weapons were against people who bunched up—but that still left a lot of them to be mangled by the supersonic slugs.

I watched body parts come entirely off, heads explode, blood litter the ground. Waited for the attackers to be disheartened and flee. Instead I saw the air start to fucking shimmer all over again.

Bullets stopped in the air, exploding into lead debris and sparks. Men marched past, their shields of air remaining just a few feet ahead of them. It was only ever in one place, only ever shielding a single line of maybe a few hundred men at once, but the magical protection shifted to wherever our gunfire did. I looked across the battlefield and saw Viras, hands raised and eyes tight with focus.

Fucking magus. Fucking *powerful* magus. We'd been warned he might manage something like this by Corvan. But there was nothing we could do either way. Just hope the kills added up despite him.

I heard a familiar telltale screaming sound at that. Sharp, shrill. The rockets were in flight for barely a second before smashing into enemy ranks, some spinning off-kilter and missing entirely, others turning in the air to slice through lengthwise and kill all the more. One of them hit Viras' shield, perishing uselessly. The rest killed about a dozen each.

Within a single moment the battlefield was hot and bright, then flooded by black smoke the next. It reeked of rotten eggs. I saw men stumbling from the debris. *Then* the next wave of shooting started.

I realized the true benefit of the rockets only when men started dying properly again. Viras was using his magic from afar, by sight. And the smoke was keeping him from seeing where our gunshots were landing. For long, wonderful moments, nature was at peace, and the bullets were dropping ten men a second. Then Viras started moving again, hands clearly visible to my eye from my high vantage point. The smoke was dissipating, great winds ripping it away as every particle within hundreds of meters tore upward into the sky.

His line of sight cleared, Viras continued shielding everyone. By now we had a new strategy—split our fire, target multiple units at once. Without the massed focus of shooting the same one there was no slowing our enemies, but the kills were racking up at least.

Despite that, they were almost past the gates.

By now, arrows were coming back at our side. We had far superior cover—barricades and shelters set up in the courtyard to give us decent firing positions—but even so the sheer volume of arrows meant that a few were getting lucky. I felt my muscles quivering, instincts screaming at me to leap from my vantage point and start helping. But it wasn't time yet.

An arrow caught Alora between armored plates, digging into the muscle and drawing a scream from her as she was carried off. More were coming, and more accurately with the shrinking distance. Soon, inevitably, the sound to retreat was given, and our forces started falling back into the mansion proper.

Save for the gunners still plugging men from the roof, that gave the enemy free rein to close in and barge through the gates. Minutes had passed. We'd killed maybe a few hundred. Ten thousand or so still remained.

I got down from my perch as they started coming and dropped into the mansion, sprinting through its halls faster than I'd ever sprinted before. Praying that despite it all we still had a chance. In moments—moments, not minutes—I was at my ambush site, waiting by one of the main doors to throw myself at the enemy as they barged in. There were barricades set up all around, archer's perches, and covered stockpiles of black powder grenades ready to toss down a few dozen feet and let off among their ranks. Everything was as primed and ready as we could make it. So I headed to the window, watching them come.

Better to watch a tidal wave than that many bodies. I prayed again.

CHAPTER SIXTY

Shango's POV: Day 169
Current Wealth: 702 gold, 14 silver, 44 copper

My calling was violence now. I didn't feel any particular way about that. For the last few months, I'd been the administrator, the leader. The emperor. Now I needed to fight. It was how things were. My first days in Redacle had cured me of whatever aversion to violence might have once interfered. Now there was nothing left but the knowledge of what had to be done and the knowledge of how I had to do it.

On the first day, the enemy didn't attack. This wasn't due to any kindness on their part, or any masterstroke of strategy on mine. They'd just found the minefield.

Solitaire was insane, and I'm not going to pretend otherwise just because one of his innumerable synaptic spasms actually came in handy this time.

He'd planted a minefield around the house. Remember how we made Argar jog farther from the fence? How cautious we were with our lawn? It was because the most unstable man I'd ever met had surrounded the entire thing with a ring of what I could only describe as flintlock mines. Stones, pinching flint, surrounded by black powder and sealed to keep them dry. Some of them were duds—a lot actually. But plenty went off as intended, and Solitaire had filled each one with his usual abundance of . . . enthusiasm.

To call what happened to those unlucky few death would be to downplay it. They were obliterated, almost liquefied. Bodies torn apart, limbs sent spinning through the air, and blood turned into a shower staining their surrounding allies crimson. More than once, a mine would kill several men as great craters suddenly appeared in the dirt. Phelia watched it all from the same window as me, staring wide-eyed in horror.

"He's insane," she croaked. "He . . . He's insane."

Honestly, I wasn't complaining. Not now of all times.

"He's useful." Useful, and not exactly wrong. People were coming to kill us. Come to think of it, Solitaire's paranoia was right a lot more often than I'd have typically admitted. His absence made me realize that, made it heavier in my mind. The only man I'd ever known who was even smarter than me.

Solitaire, please come back to us. Don't leave me alone with these fucking animals.

Hours passed. The sky darkened. We watched as our enemy set up camp outside. Now, I realized, I knew what the boys stuck in that building had felt while Solitaire, Beam, and I lurked outside as the gangsters encircled them. Except we were the ones trapped now, and I wasn't sure we'd be finding any rescue.

They came again, more cleverly. Compressed into little lines and aiming their assault through paths already marred by mine explosions, limiting their exposure to the remaining traps. This had a benefit for us of course. Those rockets and grenades we had the chance to fling at them from the roof were all the more fatal with their men forced so tight. I actually wondered whether that'd been Solitaire's design.

Hundreds more perished before the first of them were at the front gates. But that left nine thousand more to rush in and get killing. Velaharo Manor really was huge, ridiculously so. It had housed all five thousand or so of our defenders—peasant volunteers included.

But we were still staring down almost two-to-one odds, and they were sending actual soldiers against cops and hobos. This wasn't going to be pretty.

I was needed at one of the front gates, where the worst of the fighting would be. I was waiting when the enemy managed to barge it down and started flooding in. *Magi* were among them, naturally, fireballs slinging through the air, stone torn from the ground and sent spinning at us. Living artillery—in the medieval era, at least. And they immediately consumed most of my focus. I smacked one stone from the air with my wind, cursing myself for not focusing more on it instead of the larger-scale strategic advantages of technology and allies. Another almost incinerated me then and there before I stumbled out of the way and just before I countered him, the top third of his head . . . disappeared.

A gunshot—I didn't ever see who'd fired it. The tide of bodies was continuing, fewer magi and more metal now. Our defenders did their best. The wooden barricades we'd erected had been perforated by magic within the opening moments, but they still served to box the enemy in somewhat as flashing spears—or pitchforks, in any case—kept them at bay.

All that to buy time for the grenadiers up top, who were raining the cast-iron explosives down like they were going out of fashion. Each killed no more than a few men, but the panic of those who survived turned into attempted flight, which drove against the momentum of those still flooding in. The attack was losing its teeth.

Or it was, before the giant man in even more giant plate barged in, and a whole host of others followed.

Giant men, which was to say men who were of the giant race. I thought so, at least. They may have been hybrids. Either way they were all about ten feet tall, and . . . yes, I recognized one of them from the tourney. They made a mess of our defenders quickly, demolishing one barricade as if the inches of wood were tissue paper, then mangling the poor sods behind it. My magic came smashing into them with all the force I could muster, a jet of air strong enough to cut stone. It knocked one down, sent another stumbling back, drew flecks of blood from both. The giants behind them just kept going.

At least until Beam dropped down to land in front of them. He screamed, but not like any human I'd ever heard. Like an animal, a wild monster sending his sword out in front of him like he meant to kill the world itself. Glowing, ethereal light met steel plate with an explosion of sparks. I actually heard the impact, even over the sounds of men screaming and dying around him. One giant fell, guts slopping out through the new jagged rent in his plate. The other swung for Beam and found him miles gone by the time his blow landed.

Beam was behind him, leaping. He drove his own sword down through the back of the giant's neck and twisted, twisted again, dragged it out. The neck was almost gone, connecting head and shoulders with only a thin strip of meat. Beam didn't even watch the enemy fall, just moved on to kill another. He wasn't short on them. Trolls, somehow. They'd gotten tamed trolls in on this, and they were sending them—and all their other heavy units—in first to break the first lines of defense. I remembered what it'd felt like, fighting these creatures.

Apparently Beam didn't. He headbutted one, smashing its skull in and dropping it like a stone. A few swings took limbs and heads off others, then another grabbed him from behind and started biting at his neck. Beam wasn't the man he'd been five months ago though. He shrugged the grip off like it was a child's and twisted around, digging his sword through the thing's guts, twisting, tearing it out.

I watched, stunned for a moment. Then the messenger's words caught me.

"My lord, the eastern gate is being pressed hard. Sir Arthur requests your help."

I hurried over without another word, for several reasons. Arthur, I thought, was staying before he'd have the option of joining Viras even if he fought against him and lost—he was just too valuable to kill out of hand. But if he thought he might be overwhelmed and slain in battle . . . he'd bug out. Instantly. It was just the sort of character he was.

Beam disappeared behind me as I turned a corner, and thirty seconds later I was staring down a new wall of carnage. More men, far more, and the barricades were in tatters this time. That wasn't what caught my eye though.

"A steel golem."

It was everything you're imagining, and more. Twice as tall as a human, three times as wide. Steel, mostly, with a few capillaries holding liquid mercury and other magically conductive fluids. It moved with all its weight and more. And it was fighting Arthur.

"Fighting" may have been the wrong word. "Bullying" came to mind sooner. He was light on his feet, Arthur, and his sword—as strong and durable as we could make it even using modern steel—was wielded by arms that could hack chunks out of an anvil. But this was a completely solid-steel body. A few nicks and scrapes littered it where he'd hit already, and I saw the sparks of another impact as he swung. Otherwise . . . nothing.

I called on my magic, shouted out a command, and stepped in to try to turn the tides.

Beam leveled up twice, then thrice more, as they fought the day away. He kept achieving things, killing monsters, taking hearts and livers, lungs and spines, even a brain stem once. He threw himself into the fighting without fear or hesitation because any less than everything he had would be a death sentence for everything he loved. He became so familiar with the feelings of metal sliding through meat, of steel surrendering to his sword, or eyes popping under his thumbs, that he started to feel phantom sensations even while they rested and he caught his breath.

And the killing never stopped.

He was everywhere the fighting was thickest, everywhere the most men in need of killing lurked. Not even connected to it anymore, not even feeling it. He came, he saw, he cut apart. He was too untethered from the physicality of his work to appreciate anything of it, the growing speed and strength of his limbs, the marvelous way in which he was barging past his physical agony, the idea of using captured magi to heal him and keep his strength as close to its maximum as was possible.

To him, to Bloody Beam, he wasn't even fighting. He was simply cutting meat. Until the twins at least.

They were fast, and strong. They fought as if their bodies shared a nervous system, covering each other's weaknesses and testing even him. The first time he almost died instantly, the second, after glutting himself on more dead men, it was still a hard bout. Beam watched as numerous allies fell to them. Not fighting, simply cutting meat. Like him.

All of them were butchers, and the butchery was far from done.

Argar screamed and actually pissed himself. He did not, however, remain still because if he'd done that the giant's hammer would have found his head, and that'd be all she wrote for jolly old Argar. He hit the ground, rolled, came up swinging and screaming. The old man's lessons were in his nerves, not his brains, and he let his body lead him around like a puppet on the end of strings. The sword came up fast, aimed for an eye slit, twisting down and biting into the joint exposed by his enemy's flinching. A spurt of blood exposed the success, then the boot hit him. Argar flew back, and a wall caught him nastily.

The hammer came down, finding Helena's shield with a meaty crunch as the Vit flung herself into its path. She buckled under it, ending her block in a squat, audibly grunting with the exertion of locking her body and remaining afoot. Argar circled around her, swinging his sword downward for the giant's wrist. It hit home and bit deep. More blood sprung out of this leak, a river rather than a trickle. Crimson muck pooled at their feet, and the enemy stumbled away. Argar chased him, swinging again and again—like chopping down a big metal tree. By the time it fell, he was almost sure the giant was dead already. It certainly didn't move upon landing.

"Tha—" Argar was hit by something big and heavy, blown off his feet, and went down, sword lost. He scrambled against it, whatever it was, and realized he was wrestling a troll only moments later. Claws as long as his thumb came scraping for his eyes, teeth as big as his knife joined them. His knife?

Argar stabbed the blade deep into his enemy's guts, felt it squirm atop him as they rolled around and vied for the superior position.

Helena didn't have time to help Argar before the men were coming for her, all swinging and stabbing. Her shield ate the worst of it, but she had to back off just to hold them at bay, stabbing with her own spear as an incentive not to get too courageous. Whoever did would die, but that wouldn't help her much when the other two fell upon her and hacked her apart.

One fucked up, and she rewarded him with a spear to the neck. While he was gurgling and dying, she turned on the others, rushed one with her shield and floored him, then cracked the shaft of her weapon across the other's head. It caught his helmet, not his face, but he was nicely stunned anyway. More were coming now. Helena's decision practically made itself. She turned and retreated. Her side were holding a line—at least the tenth they'd fallen back to today alone—and she wouldn't last seconds outside of it.

Argar, where was Argar? She couldn't see him, couldn't worry about him. He'd be fine. He had to be.

Alora was a good distance from her enemies, and that was just fine by her. There weren't enough yards in the world to put between their weapons and her skin. She fired. That was the word, fired. Set afire. It was certainly descriptive. The magic powder caught flame, burned, screamed as it erupted like a magus' fireball and spit an ounce of hot metal out of the weapon to smash into her target. The man had a breastplate covering him, which did nothing against such a devastating hit. He went down messily. Alora was reloading before he even hit the ground, looking around. She saw Argar holding a troll back with one arm while searching the ground for his knife with the other. Men were closing on him, closing fast. She swore.

The bullet ripped through one enemy, then her kyoketsu half beheaded a second. It really was excellent steel, with an edge sharper than any normal metal could hold for long. But it was still making its way back when the next man reached Argar and stabbed down for him.

She watched the blade come down into her ally's throat, gasped. Then Argar, being Argar, kicked out and broke the attacker's knee. He rolled to his feet, sending the troll falling onto the wounded man and leaving the two of them to confusedly fight each other. His neck was still bleeding, but lightly.

The glorious son of a bitch, his flesh was so tough he'd avoided a death blow. Steel skin indeed. He wasn't out of the woods yet though. Something smashed through a wall behind him—the damned golem. Magnus was on its shoulders laughing, smashing a big fucking hammer down on the thing all of three times before the steel weapon head split in half and he discarded it.

"What are you—" Alora's warning cry to the sea raider was cut off as the golem reached up and closed its fist around his head. When the thing's arm dropped down, nothing remained above Magnus' shoulders. Just a bloody, jagged stump ending midway up his neck and a grizzly rain of cranial matter.

Arthur should have run, but it was too late now. He twisted around the men around him easily enough—outnumbered a dozen to one, then zero to one after a brief second of exertion. Before the bodies had even fallen, he was the focus, once more, of that damned golem. It was, he realized, searching for him. Fair enough, he was the single biggest threat to Viras' offensive. At least unless the King of Blades joined in.

The golem's arm came swinging for Arthur, forcing him to remember every lesson he'd slept through as he parried. It was a rare occasion on which he found his own strength wanting. Not since the King of Blades. This creature was not quite so strong as that, but sheer size had a magic of its own. Arthur stepped back as he deflected.

Golems move by controlling their own weight, by pitting it in one direction or another.

Not good. The construct was double a man's height and thrice his width and thickness, solid steel all the way through. Arthur wasn't sure exactly what that turned into, but apparently that much weight generated a good deal more force than his own musculature.

That musculature was quicker, at least. There were advantages to weighing however many times less than one's enemy. Arthur darted back from one swing, another. He countered, blade practically bouncing from the solid steel of its enemy and leaving dents barely an inch deep to show it had even connected at all.

He swore, leaped back, and felt a giant club arm clip one of his pauldrons. Arthur was spun almost fully around, righting himself, darting back away, and swearing again. That time the golem's foot had almost come down on him, and the sight of it bursting through tiled flooring like it wasn't even there was a dark promise of what would have happened if it had.

Arthur took one more step back, flashed a grin, and used the technique that had kept him alive so many other times. He turned and ran.

Elizabeth just ran and threw, skirting around the rafters and depositing grenades as fast as she could manage. Any moment an arrow might catch her, kill her outright, or knock her down—which amounted to the same thing. And not once did she consider fleeing.

Stupid girl, this place is a death trap. What are you doing here?

What *was* she doing here? It wasn't even that Elizabeth could claim to be upholding some vital function. She certainly wasn't. She was a thief, a spy. Not a fighter, not a killer. And yet here she was.

Maybe a woman just got tired of running one day. Maybe she'd just realized she wouldn't be finding more than one place worth dying if she went on living and figured she'd stick with this one. Maybe she was just nuts. Another grenade went off, and this time one of the limbs it removed almost hit *Elizabeth* despite her placement some dozen feet above the shoulder it came from.

He made good stuff, that Solitaire. If he was still alive, as Shango insisted, then she'd have to tell him that one day. Have to tell him all sorts. Stop staring at her tits, for one, but . . . thanks for another.

Well, that settled it. Elizabeth couldn't die because she had to tell her friend thanks. And she couldn't run because letting her friend's family get slaughtered would just be a bitch move.

Henry backed off, snarling and hacking, punching, kicking. He was fighting a tidal wave of bodies that came unrelentingly as the rising sun. Fists and blades seemed a petty barricade before such a force as that.

But they were all he had. All he'd ever had, and they'd never failed him before. He refused to let them fail him now that he was turning them to something he knew was good. Henry kept striking, watching dead and dying men fall, cursing as more took their place. How many of Viras' bastards had they killed by now? Another thousand since they broke into the mansion, surely?

Not enough. Not nearly enough.

A scream escaped him, then a wheeze as something heavy thudded into his chest. A war hammer. Henry hit the ground, feet thrashing around him, gasping and shivering as he desperately fought to drag more breath into his spasming lungs. The killing was still ongoing, his own men fighting back the tide alone now. They were losing without him. Tears streaming from his eyes, he fought up to his feet and skewered a man, felt the touch of hot entrails worm out over his hands and forearms. He twisted his knives free, then got back to killing.

But it wasn't nearly enough. They were losing ground.

Beam was coughing, spluttering. He was pale from blood loss and fatigue. Corvan worked on him, repairing as much of his body as he could and forcing their captured magi to bolster his efforts. It would have taken half an hour for the man to be truly ready to get back into combat, at best. Instead he halted the healing after five minutes, sat up, and started for the door.

"You need to wai—" Corvan's voice tapered off as the boy turned and eyed him. God, those eyes. Like the pits of hell, darker than the sight of him killing. And Corvan would *never* forget the sight of him killing. He held his silence and watched as Beam Belahont disappeared back into the battle.

When did he become so powerful? he mused. *When did he become able to bully me?*

The defense was still collapsing, falling farther and farther into the mansion as their lines were pushed back. Now they were close to their final fronts. Corvan had considered fleeing several times now but hadn't for one simple reason. The Belahonts were a growing power beyond any he'd seen. Perhaps by the end of this, Beam Belahont would have gorged himself on enough life to slay a dragon.

Or become one.

Phelia heard the sounds of killing and dying, and they made her shiver. She was no warrior. War, as her father used to say, was a man's game. But then he was a drunken moron who'd pissed away her family's fortune, so maybe she should give it a chance regardless. What would Shango say?

Another explosion interrupted *that* train of thought, and this time the room she was in shivered. Phelia was not alone. The governor's family was taking shelter with her, including . . . Amira. Ridiculously, she still thought of catching that whore with her husband whenever she looked at her. Even now. The mind seemed to have a funny way of coping with danger. In Phelia's case, that way was scattering itself and snagging on every stray thought it could find.

She glanced over to one of the governor's sons, who was still retching into a bucket. Phelia's method was better than some, at least.

The door burst open. No, not open. Apart. Splinters of it reached halfway into the room as the thick oak split, and Aja the Pit Hound strode into the room. He looked around, beady eyes like candle flames, and Phelia felt herself go cold. A betrayal. Of course. The governor had sold them out to Viras. She should have—

Aja moved, crossing the room and raising his blade. It came down. The governor's son lost his head, then another, then his wife. Then his daughters. The entire family came apart like meat on the butcher's block, and Phelia could do nothing but watch arcane metal slide through flesh as easy as air. None of them even had time to make a sound.

Except for Amira. Amira was smiling as she watched it all, not surprised, not disturbed. If anything she seemed satisfied, a woman seeing her job accomplished. Aja the Pit Hound's slaughter didn't take long, a few moments at most. And when it was done, he turned to Amira and knelt down before her.

Phelia felt the guts drop out of her as Amira glanced up, still smiling.

"Thank you, dear," she hummed to the murderer. "Now go and rejoin the battle, if you please. I think you're needed at the new lines of defense."

Aja stood, and Phelia's instincts took over as she fled from the room. Amira watched her go, calling after.

"Relax, you're in no danger."

Phelia was past listening.

"What the fuck?!"

"Solitaire! It's Solitaire, the dark wizard! Back again!"

Solitaire was not back again, but Shango saw no reason to let the *enemy* know that. Not when they'd worked up such a sweat about it. No, he just lit the second cannon barrel and watched as the blast of projectiles—cannister shot, his brother had called it?—tore through a rank of them. A tin container was durable enough to survive light handling and rough loading but too fragile to last long in supersonic propulsion. It broke but held the lead balls contained within together just long enough that they remained somewhat grouped up.

So all of them slammed into the mouth of the corridor his enemy was now charging down. For one moment, the air was bright red. Literally turned crimson with the violence, bloody mists staining walls and ceiling and blocking sight. It dispersed slowly, revealing dozens or more dead. Maybe a hundred. Then the second cannon fired, and it all started over again.

By the third shot, the enemy had gotten better ideas than attempting to charge a third time. And Shango had come to appreciate, in some *very* minor way, his brother's love of defensible positions.

It was all for nothing though. Just more grains of sand in the hourglass, more minutes, maybe a half day, before the inevitable crashed into them. Death was a Sisyphean boulder, and they were downhill of it. The steel golem must have heard his pessimistic thoughts because it helpfully chose that moment to prove them right.

"Solid shot!" Shango roared, watching as the steel balls—steel, not iron—were loaded into the cannons. Each one was only about the size of his fist, but deceptively heavy. He covered his ears and tried not to wince in sympathy for the people *without* superhuman durability trapped inside the corridor as the cannons went off.

The golem was only halfway to them when both shots struck home.

He didn't see the impact, and he only even saw the effects once the golem was on the defenders. It sent both cannons—each a thousand-pound slab of iron itself—flying as it smashed into the line and crushed men underfoot. Its chest was damaged, deep dents pressed into the steel where solid slugs had impacted faster than sound. But it was all superficial.

The damn thing was near invincible.

Shango's magic was next, a jet of wind accelerating a volley of lead darts that didn't even stick into the surface. Gunshots bounced off, spears snapped, hammers . . . snapped too. There wasn't really much room for mundane weapons to do anything else for the most part.

Until Aja the Pit Hound's scimitar came down. Enchanted metal held together better, and the thickness of his weapon—made to accommodate superhuman strength—left it durable enough to bite a chunk out of the golem. But not a big one. It lashed a fist out, missed him. Its next blow landed just a moment after Aja's, steel scraps flung into the air at the same time as the bronze warrior. Aja hit a wall hard, bounced from it, and landed amid a rain of mangled mortar.

More men were flooding in behind the golem, all of them eating arrows and gunfire, grenades and everything else the defenders could throw their way. The mouth of hell might have opened up in the corridor and not made it any deadlier, but still they kept coming. They knew how little ground there was left for their enemy to fall back in. They could smell victory, and its proximity was coaxing them forward and flooding them with strength.

Shango screamed and for his part threw everything he had into the killing just as everyone else did. His cry was raced to the enemy by another volley of darts, these ones finding soft flesh instead of hard steel and biting in deep. Men came apart, simple as. Like the canister shot firing all over again, but there were more. There were always more.

Beam flew over Shango's head, landing amid the enemies and swinging like something out of a nightmare.

Beam's POV: Day 171
Current Wealth: 702 gold, 14 silver, 44 copper

I swung once, and a row of men died. From behind them, practically weaving between drops of spraying blood, came the twins. Near identical in every way, and faster than anything remotely human, they lunged for me like arrows spit at point-blank range. I was on the back foot instantly.

One came in with a shortsword and buckler. The latter was thick enough that even my weapon—now a broad cleaver to put a lot of weight in short swings—wasn't splitting through. The other hung back, stabbing at me with a spear and scraping wisps of ethereal light from my armor each time it connected. I kept backing up. They kept closing in. The corridor was just wide enough that I had to be careful not to get circled too. Brilliant.

Steel scraped across an armor plate, slipped under another, and nicked my skin. I swore, lashed out a closed fist that missed the one responsible and left me open for a spear thrust that almost caught me through the eye slit. I parried at the last moment, twisted back from a second swing from the swordsman, and retaliated with a knee that drove itself deep into his gut. He actually lifted off the ground, reaching about shoulder height before tumbling back down. Before he landed, I was already driving his friend back. The spear shook. Lengths of wood—which must have been magically reinforced to survive even a few hits—flayed off it with every parry. I was getting closer to winning by the second.

And then the one I'd knocked down got to his feet and came at me again, spoiling my advantage.

We became a whirlwind, a sharp one. I went wherever their steel wasn't, and their steel eviscerated my wake. The sound of air rushing around us was louder than the impacts of most other fights, and I felt sixy muscles burning as magic and matter worked in conjunction to force every edge I could get. The voice was silent. Not demanding anything, not suggesting anything. Perhaps even it realized how micron perfect my focus needed to be. A dire sign itself.

One of them moved aside to reveal an arrow moments before impact. I caught it and threw the projectile into another's face. Steel scraped on my armor, bit my flesh. I screamed, swung, opened someone's leg up, and felt another stab cut into me from behind. Not good. I only had half their combined meat. I needed to carve at least twice as much as I was carved.

I got to work at it, missing with another swing, spinning, slashing again, and taking a chunk out of the wall. Something moved behind me, stumbled away as a blind elbow smashed it back, and then I was clubbing the spear aside again. Another stab, this time in my lower body, another missed swing. I started retreating, felt the burn of open wounds and the ice of blood leaching out of me. My strength wasn't going to last, and the moment it dipped, I'd be dead. It was that sort of fight.

The enemy, of course, knew it full well. They redoubled their efforts, then retripled them for good measure. I wasn't fighting now. I was practically running. The meat on the butcher's block, and each parry let the cleaver come that little bit closer to my skin.

If you retreat, you'll die. Your strength is measured in seconds. Each move will use up more of it. Use it well.

I hadn't been expecting another word from the creature—the thing—but somehow it was reassuring to hear. And, I realized, it had a point. I halted a backstep midway through, surprising one enemy with a swing that opened up their forehead and left blood oozing down into their eyes. A shallow wound, but even shallow wounds to the head bled a lot. While their vision was distorted I pressed on, ignoring a spear thrust entirely to cut into its wielder's wrist and feeling a grin sprout on my lips as I felt ethereal matter and steel sink into soft, destructible tissue.

Again, a shallow cut. But half the effect was forcing my enemies back. I chased them and ignored their hasty swings, powering on, swinging again. For the second time, a whirlwind of steel broke out in the corridor, except now it was all me. They cut in, breaking plates of armor, biting down into flesh, sinking their blades into my body, and drawing out precious bloody strength. But not before I'd managed a more substantial cut into one of their legs. Right down into the thigh, through the muscle, opening up all the big veins and leaving ichor to puddle out at our feet. It took seconds for the leak to deposit enough blood that my enemy dropped down.

Then it was just a one-on-one.

With all the skill he'd shown alongside his twin, the remaining one wasn't a match for me in a fair fight. He lasted all of one second—maybe a dozen moves between us—before I opened him up and watched his guts slop out. I was laughing as I did, adrenaline mixing with the relief of living, the triumph of winning, the joy of destroying. He gurgled, falling down to choke on his own blood and twitch on the floor.

I buried my sword down into his head, splitting the damned thing wide open. The enemy had healing magi too, after all. Couldn't have this one living to make a nuisance of himself all over again.

"He's wounded!" a voice came out behind me, and strong hands seized me by the shoulders. I jerked at the motion, almost whirling around and killing the offending men before realizing they were villagers just hauling me back from the fighting.

Relax, Beam, they're allies, good people. Just trying to save your life. But it was so very tempting to keep killing, to kill just for the sake of it. And that was what we needed now, right? That was what *this world* always needed, killing. I'd been practically worshipped for it before. Why not again?

Do it, I heard the voice calling out. *Surrender. Let my power reach your heart. You can have all the strength you can handle, all the power in the world. I can make you the deadliest creature to ever walk this land. All you must do is . . . let go.*

I was behind our defensive lines, being treated by a magus for a brief minute before he was called on to someone else. Everything hurt, except my muscles. Those felt like heaven was wrapped around my bones. As if every kill I'd managed was another angel's kiss against the meat of my skeleton.

Why shouldn't I? We need a killer now. More than ever.

The door opened, and someone burst in. Blonde, a woman. Panicked. Phelia Velaharo—sister. My thoughts were blunt, pneumatic. They moved powerfully and clumsily from one fact to another, soaking everything up in terms of danger and challenge. She was neither. Such a fragile creature. I could twist the head from her shoulders without even exerting myself.

"You're alive!" she gasped, rushing over to me. What was that in her face? Concern? For me? The bitch. How dare . . .

It's Phelia, I . . . I can't.

But cans and can'ts felt so artificial now, thin. Like barricades made of paper. Why couldn't I? Because of rules? Of honor? Those didn't exist. Only power did. And I had all the power in the world. My wounds stopped aching as I felt a great heat rise in the pit of my stomach. Phelia kept coming.

Yes. Accept me. Let go. Become the killer you are. You will be greater than any other, greater by far. Just. Let. Go.

I let go. Phelia's eyes widened. She looked down to find the sword jutting through her gut. I was a moment from twisting it when I heard the crashing farther ahead. Loud, weight. Lots of weight. I'd heard that impact before—the steel creature. Golem. Too strong for Arthur to best.

A perfect exercise for me. My sword sprang from the woman's belly, and I left her sprawled on the floor, too insignificant to even spare the moment needed to kill. There was real work to be done. Bloody work. With a smile flashing bright and wide as a sunbeam glinting on steel, I moved to do it.

INTERLUDE FIFTEEN

The creature moved through the corridor like an east wind, slithering on all four of its limbs. Moving as a shadow, as a whisper, as a promise of violence to come. Men shied back from the sight of it—from the feeling. They knew without knowing that to stand in front of it would be death. And that was as it should be. The creature *should* be feared by all life, for it was the ultimate predator of all life. And now . . .

Now it had found a great abundance of life.

Intruders were funneling down a corridor, bursting out into a hall. The hall Shango—the weaker ones' leader—had declared their last stand. The creature charged the enemy, snarling, spitting. Drool trailed behind it and sluggishly dripped to the ground in a slow arc, gravity pulling it at a glacial pace beside the bursting speed of its owner. In moments, it had crossed a dozen paces and closed in on prey.

Arrows, a spring rain. Gentle against its skin, bracing and soothing. The creature sidestepped, watching the wooden shafts in their creeping paths across the room, stepping between them. So, so slow. So *lazy*. How could any man hope to kill an enemy with weapons such as that? It was on the shooters before their own projectiles had even crossed the room, and it swung hard. A row of bodies disappeared, then the one behind. The creature threw itself amid the men, swinging in a full circle this time and bifurcating more than a dozen enemies with that single motion. The air turned red, *opaque* with squirting gore, and still it moved on.

Screams rang out and sergeants tried to restore order, spears raised to box the creature in. It beheaded the weapons, and then their wielders, then leaped over the pitiable insects to land behind them. Another swing, another row of life turned into a carpet of death.

The creature watched as men melted back from it like paint peeling about a fire, and it knew the world was right. Yet one thing emerged from among the men, charging forward as a great lumbering mass of metal and might. The golem, the very thing the creature had gone looking for. How convenient.

The golem swung for it, and it slipped by the blow and answered with its own. Ethereal magic screamed as steel moaned, and only after biting four inches into the metal giant's skin did its weapon halt. It let go instantly rather than pull it out, leaping back and conjuring another. A machete, this time, all the larger and heavier.

The golem bulled on like a landslide, but the creature whirled around it. It circled, slashed, felt the ethereal edge of its blade bite in deep and litter the ground with shredded steel. Its enemy was too tough to hack down in one go—good. All the better to demonstrate the creature's skill, the *Champion's* skill. The world would be far too boring a place if nothing could resist so much as a single stroke.

Steel chased it, and it giggled as it darted around the metal. Hacking, hacking again. Tickling the golem with little flirting touches of its blade, leaving tiny little nicks and furrows barely as deep as a handspan to let this limacine construct know where it was. The golem began to slow, structure groaning and failing it as yet more gouges were left in the steely body. Its endurance hit its limits.

The creature wouldn't end it with a thousand cuts though. That would be no way at all to demonstrate its power. The world needed more. With another rattle of mangled steel, the golem swung for it. The creature ducked low, let its blade dissipate, and grabbed its enemy in a grip stronger than the metal about which it closed. Muscles straining, veins convulsing, teeth gritting hard enough to shatter a normal jaw, it hauled the enemy up.

And the golem's feet left the ground.

It landed hard, smashed through wooden flooring, smashed down deeper into the very foundations of the mansion. Stone surrendered to steel. Dirt surrendered beneath. The floor shook, and men stared in horror as the creature raised its blade, made a halberd of it, and took the golem's head off with one final swing.

Then it turned, a grin like an axe wound splitting its face.

"Who's next?"

None were eager to volunteer, so the creature chose itself. It was a great shadow, and everything it cast itself upon died. The hall was still being refilled as men poured in, but there was only one entrance through which they emerged. And the creature's killing was so, so fast. By the time one body landed, two more had been cut down to join it. Stabs and swings followed its wake, but none even came close. To the creature's eyes, human movements were slow, clumsy things evaded with the most fractional effort. Feet separated its skin from the edged steel chasing it, and then ethereal matter separated the attackers' limbs from those torsos that controlled them. The killing didn't even slow down as a magus began to build his power.

Fire engulfed the creature, hot enough to char a normal man's flesh off in moments. It barely hurt. The creature charged through the flames, splitting the magus fully in half and rolling back to its feet. It found a new sheath of flesh for its blades without hesitating.

CHAPTER SIXTY-TWO

Shango's POV: Day 171
Current Wealth: 702 gold, 14 silver, 44 copper

Viras' army was essentially fighting on two fronts. One we were holding, if barely. The final stand we'd set out, a set of rooms, halls, and corridors near the heart of Velaharo Manor that was accessible for as many men as he was commanding only through two routes. We'd pinned one down nicely; the other had broken. Just when the enemy's flanking assault had been primed to come through . . . it hadn't. Something had interfered with them. I didn't know what, couldn't guess—didn't care to. What mattered now wasn't the specifics. This was no time for complex schemes and counted variables. I just needed to seize the advantage before it disappeared on me.

There was, of course, only one way to do that in this stage of things. The defenses weren't falling—they were *fallen*. What I was looking at now, on my side, was a headless chicken, and though its corpse was doing a fine job of running around and shitting on Viras' men, that wouldn't last much longer. So we had to even things out—cut the head from our enemies too.

With luck, Viras' distraction would be as great as his army's right now. Certainly his subordinates' ability to defend him would be compromised, which meant now was about the best opening I could hope for if I was going to assassinate him.

I put my team together quickly. It wasn't hard to decide on them: Corvan because I wasn't going to fight a magus of Viras' caliber without one more skilled than me. My second choice was harder, but I needed someone fast and strong to serve as a front liner. Beam, I'd heard, was out of commission. He'd just disappeared after I saw him hack apart that golem, and I was pulled away elsewhere before I could see what came of him after. I kept myself from feeling the sting of that, cycled the worry out of my mind, and focused on the simple practicality of my situation. With him out, the choice was limited to a handful of other picks. Arthur had disappeared, perhaps scarpering from the fight entirely, and Alora was still hurt.

Argar, I chose Argar. The first subordinate any of us had gotten. He was all I could rely on now. Everyone else was tied up fighting. Everyone except Adannaya. She surprised me by stepping forward, clad in attire nothing like as cumbersome or blocky as before. Formfitting and economic, it allowed wide movement at all the joints and, I noted, had more than a few knives strapped along it.

The remaining members of our hit squad were . . . nobody, just the four of us. We were all I could spare. I would've killed for Beam's help, or Solitaire's. Would've damned myself with a million-gold debt . . . but no, I had to work with what I had. We departed, heading through the mansion and cutting toward Viras.

Of course, the good thing about having your own home turned into a war zone was that it meant you knew a lot more about the local terrain than did your enemy. It was almost trivial to sneak past all the fighting using back rooms, crawl spaces, and, on occasion, a strategically perforated wall. Soon enough we were right at the rear of Viras' attack, staring at the magus himself. It was . . . remarkably stressful.

I can't explain how terrifying it was to look at him from our little hidey-hole just off to one side. Imagine trying to sneak up on a Tiger tank, knowing that all it'd take is for you to flicker in the corner of one eye, for the turret to pivot around, and then everything would end. I might actually have been underselling him. But fear would get me nowhere, except dead. We all fanned out, sneaky as we could, and then our attack began.

Adannaya surprised me with her *eagerness*, and then surprised me a lot more with her raw power. Up until that point, you understand, Corvan had been my basis for a powerful magus—a cut above most, but no world-renowned conjurer.

I had my reference of power quickly reassembled after seeing my future sister-in-law work.

Viras was in a very, very big hall. Lucky. She'd have destroyed the room around us if there hadn't been a dozen meters of clearance on every side. Her fireball streaked through the air, and Viras just barely twisted around and splayed his hands before impact. It hit something invisible, something powerful, and when it detonated, I found my opinion of every explosive Solitaire had made so far reduced. The concussion made my teeth clatter. The heat made hairs curl and wither on my skin. I saw carpets ignite all around him, floorboards blacken and combust.

The men around Viras, of course, were all obliterated. Dozens of them, some incinerated entirely, others merely charred into blackened, shrunken corpses. A few were actually blown apart by the shock wave. The smoke hadn't finished clearing when Viras' counter came at us.

Argar shoved Adannaya aside, then just . . . disappeared. Thrown back by the shock wave Corvan and I focused all our efforts to redirecting. I didn't see where he landed, couldn't look. Viras was sending out another blast, a stronger one. This time we pitted our strengths together and sent it upward, with help from a last-minute explosion by Adannaya. The combined energy took the ceiling apart and left several of the rooms above to fall down as rains of debris. Viras' feet left the ground as he levitated up, a fireball building between his hands.

Yeah, no. I'd seen what Adannaya could do with fire, and I'd seen how easily he reflected that with a less destructive element. I was not getting my shadow burned onto a wall today.

I sprinted forward, hurling lead darts and watching as they just came apart in the air before Viras. Bits of them hit him, tiny scraps, but with none of their speed or momentum—he had a damned barrier around him blocking the attacks. A fireball from Corvan smashed into him, dissipating easily, and then Viras' flames attacked.

It was all I could do to slide under him and smash his arms up with a jet of air before the flames fully emerged, and the guts fell out of me as I watched them destroy so much of the mansion above that a great cavity exposed our *ground floor room* to the sky above. It was like a bomb had gone off. An actual bomb, used in a war and made by someone who didn't think the government was trying to steal his semen. The room shook, splinters fell from rafters, walls trembled and let chunks of mortar rain free. Hell was emptying itself out onto earth.

The fire was building again.

It spread around the room like . . . wildfire, but it wasn't. It was worse, militarized, intentional, directed by human will and human power and magic that had nothing of humanity to it, whatever face its master wore. I saw the flames reach a dozen feet high, then double. I saw them run around the room in a circle, trapping us in. Then the air closed around me, plucked me from the ground and pinned my hands at my sides as I was dragged to hover before Viras.

Like an insect. I was like an insect to him. I shouldn't have tried to kill him. It'd been stupid. Suicidal. How could a mouse ambush a dragon? It couldn't.

"What was your mistake, Shango Belahont?" He asked the question idly, as if we were discussing things over tea and crumpets rather than locked in a fight to the death. I guessed for him this *wasn't* a death match. Just an irritation.

No. *No.* He'd had to raise his defenses before we attacked, and he'd almost failed. Magi were quick—using magic sped up synapses and improved nerve transmission. But they could be surprised, and they were fragile. If we caught him unawares—if anyone with me now caught him unawares . . .

I needed to distract him.

"I shouldn't have tried to attack the great and mighty Viras?" Obvious cheek, obvious back sass. Was there anything in the world that pissed off an arrogant old man more than someone a fraction of his age getting snarky? I'd never seen it if there was, but . . . Viras wasn't one to get pissed off at all.

"What was your mistake?" he repeated, just as the air around me constricted tighter. I felt ribs creaking, skeleton tested to its absolute limit. I almost blacked out, vomited, gasped. There was blood in my mouth, and the pressure eased up the instant before something inside me snapped for good. Snark would not be serving me well.

"I don't—ach." Blood in my mouth, like trying to speak with . . . blood in my mouth. I coughed, spit it out, tasted iron and salt. Felt sick. Kept talking. Talking was keeping him distracted, keeping my people alive, keeping us in the fight. I'd make a mistake. Now I had to cover it before he took advantage and won. "I don't know."

Viras didn't smile, but what he said next was delivered with the inflection of one. It was like his voice and face disagreed on how he felt. "Your mistake was shutting your allies out, trying to be the lone king on the mountain. Doing everything yourself, spreading yourself too thin. I do that. It is a natural inclination of our . . . kind. And yet I am me, and you are not." The pressure returned, and I couldn't even gasp this time.

There was no breathing, no moving, no struggling. All I could do was feel my body shut down, heart pounding in my ears as blood pooled uselessly with no oxygen to carry. I had moments until consciousness slipped away, and with me disabled, Viras would turn his focus to ending this once and for all.

But moments were all Beam needed.

Phelia gasped, body spasming and thoughts a scattered, frenzied blur. She felt like her mind was being shaken, as if something had reached into the very core of her being and rearranged it. Then she remembered Beam, the stab to her gut. The pain and weakness of blood leaking out.

Fear washed everything away instantly, and she sat up.

It had been stupid, instinctual rather than considered, and Phelia awaited the harsh sting of agony to punish her impulsivity. But it didn't come. Her belly bore no jarring wound. It didn't split and lance her with agony in its damage. It was . . . fine.

That was then that the webbing caught her eye. The day, Phelia had thought, could not get any stranger, and yet around her she found what looked to be the excretions of some giant spider woven around walls, ceiling, and flooring. Her first instinct was to scream. Her first *thought* was to do anything but. The room seemed to have been entirely coated by the stuff, and Phelia wasn't nearly sure enough that whatever had done it was not still there.

The creature looming over her should not have come as a surprise, but somehow it did. Phelia hadn't noticed, despite it making no great effort to hide itself. Her eyes had simply skirted over it like metal sliding off metal.

It was tall, thin. Limbs long and spindly almost like . . .

Like a spider's.

It didn't move like a spider though, more like an arrow loosed from its string.

"You are in no danger," it said, and somehow Phelia found herself doubting the mysterious, magical abomination invading her home and watching her while she slept.

"What are you?!" If she remained silent, Phelia would panic. With nothing to turn to but her own thoughts, she'd spiral, lose her wits, and be no use to anybody. The question galvanized her. Forcing herself to speak added a coherence to her mind and a direction to her will that served to blunt the fangs of terror as they gnawed upon twitching nerves.

The creature moved, which brought Phelia's attention to how repulsively still it otherwise was. Like a statue more than any living thing. Or an undead. And yet its motion was not to attack or threaten, but to *bow*. It spoke again as it prostrated itself before her, head—or what she thought was a head—lowered.

"I am . . . I . . . I was . . ." The creature sounded uncertain now, almost hesitant. As if it were picking through its own mind for the answer to Phelia's question and just as surprised by its contents as she would have been. "I . . . was known as . . . Etron. Sir Etron."

Phelia didn't laugh, and she didn't cry. Either one would have been tied for the response her churning emotions most strongly demanded.

"What are you doing here?" She was cycling through questions in order of import. Phelia needed to know what the creature—the undead, she realized with a wrench of terror—was doing in her presence because that would inform what it could do next, how long it would remain, what it intended. Deferring her thoughts to a stark descent of priorities calmed her. It focused cognition and erected a bulwark between her and the creeping panic.

"I . . . came . . . from . . . the ring."

Phelia spent all of a second working out what to make of that. The ring? Not very descriptive, but . . . there was only one ring of note near her that she knew of. The one upon her finger, the heirloom that had betrothed one Velaharo to another for generations. Since Etron's time and long earlier.

She'd never really studied it that closely before, never tried very hard to find out what the runic engravings upon its face meant. Now, seeing them glow and feeling them hum, that felt somehow stupid of her.

"Oh."

Sleep came like water to the lungs of a drowning woman, and Phelia was no more able to resist it than the tides themselves. Everything went dark and still.

CHAPTER SIXTY-THREE

[Appraisal]
Statistics: Strength 27, Speed 27, Dexterity 8, Stamina 10, Toughness 27, Alertness 27, Charisma 6, Intelligence 5

It was hard to believe I was looking at Beam. For several reasons. The first was his stats of course—they'd jumped high, impossibly high. The second was simpler . . . I couldn't actually tell what my eyes were picking up. He didn't move as a coherent image, something solid to be recognized. His speed was so great, my eyes registered him as a homogenous blob of color blurring across the room amid a whipping wind, past enemies who didn't even react until after he was long gone and hurtling toward us.

Toward Viras.

The magus' response was quick, and instinctive. His mind whipped away from me and turned to defending himself, arms raised high as the shield I now realized was passively clinging to him strengthened and thickened just in time to meet Beam's swing. I'd fallen only a few feet by the time he hit it, and the sound of ethereal matter smashing into hardened air actually ran through me as if I was standing next to some giant gong being beaten. I landed hard down below, rolled, and scrambled back, watching the fight, waiting for an opportunity to help.

It wasn't quick in coming.

Viras twisted in the air, propelling himself higher and closer to the ceiling. Beam just *jumped*. Or at least I thought he did. His motions were almost impossible to make out. As fast as the King of Blades, maybe faster. The floor around him shattered, I knew, and then he was shooting high and swinging again. Viras gestured—a sluggish man moving in slow motion compared to my brother. Fire washed down over Beam, a maelstrom of it that I felt the heat of even from dozens of feet back. For a moment I just despaired, certain I'd watched my friend die.

Then Beam burst out of the inferno and swung again. For the second time, his blade hit Viras' shield. This time it cut through, leaving a scratch across the magus' brow. Just a thin one, maybe the span of a fingernail and barely bleeding at all. But Viras felt it. He definitely felt it.

Air came next, a battering ram. Caught mid-jump, Beam was still, momentarily, or still enough to see. I got the impression even Viras' reflexes were struggling with him, but it was his face that struck me. The muscles were all twisted and sharp, lips pulled back, teeth jagged, eyes like lances. Burning hot, boring right into me. He looked like a monster. He fought like one too, and I couldn't follow his hands as the ethereal weapon in them changed faster than I knew it could, formed a grappling hook, then dug into the far wall. With one pull, Beam dragged himself from the path of Viras' magic. I watched it smash against a section of ceiling on the other side of the room, smashing wooden support beams as wide across as my body into splinters.

The grapple flew again, and Beam was shooting back. More air blasted out, hitting him directly this time. He crunched into another wall, a *stone* wall this time. I winced, watching as the rock and mortar shattered. It was easily over a foot thick, the sort of thing that even a siege engine would need more than one hit to breach. Had I just watched my brother die?

No. The rubble exploded outward as Beam came charging again, not even seeming to have been impeded by the impact. A gash bled on his forehead, but the madness was still in his eyes, the strength still in his limbs. He closed on Viras like a homing missile.

Another wall of air slammed down between them, but magic's power diminished with range, and Beam just smashed clean through this one like a bullet hitting timber. He stumbled at the resistance, delayed a precious second, and caught another blast of air that smashed him down into the floor.

The entire room shook, building creaking and groaning around us. Debris rained down from above as more of the great hall's structure gave. That one, it seemed, actually hurt Beam. But it *didn't* slow him down.

Adannaya's fireball detonated against Viras' shield, further spraying ruined fragments of Velaharo Manor across its interior and distracting our enemy for a single precious moment. Beam was on him again, swinging like his sword was aimed at everything he'd ever hated. The impact made my teeth rattle and sent Viras shooting back fifty feet or more to bounce off a far wall. His shield was intact, at least partially. But I saw blood staining his robes as he hovered out of the wreckage.

His face had shifted too. Tight with rage, eyes hot, air shimmering around him. I felt waves of heat roll over me, a warning that came just a moment before the jet of light. It wasn't fire. No fire could sustain so much thermal energy. Beam blurred aside the instant before impact, and I watched as the volley of power streaked along the ground and ran through a rank of Viras' own men.

To call them dead wouldn't have done their deaths justice. They just stopped existing. Some were clipped by the beam, half of their bodies falling to ooze out gore as the others were destroyed more completely. Others were entirely engulfed by it—they, I thought, were luckier. They just disappeared into clouds of sizzling black ash within an instant. The room was shaking still, fire running everywhere from Viras' previous attacks with yet more spreading.

Holy shit, magma. There was *molten stone* at the bottom of a trench where his beam had cut along the ground. It was like fighting in hell.

And he was far from done.

More wind, wrapping around more fire. The blast came faster this time, burning air propelled by its gaseous capsule like explosive filling in one of Solitaire's rockets. Beam leaped over it, got tossed high as it detonated a yard beneath him, and almost hit the ceiling before he turned, struck feetfirst, and kicked off. Viras lunged back, avoiding Beam and moving right into my own blast of air. It broke against his shield without him even seeming to notice. But Adannaya's fireball hit a lot harder.

Again he flew, into Beam this time. Beam sent him flying all the harder in another direction, bouncing from walls, breaking more of the mansion around him. It was like watching a pinball ricochet around—but this was a grown man, with all the weight that involved. How much fucking strength had my brother gotten? It was like nothing human.

Viras straightened out, turned his focus to *Adannaya*. The fireball was caught mid-flight by my efforts added onto Corvan's, forcibly angled away from her and obliterating another squad of soldiers entirely by accident. Even still, she cried out as her clothing caught fire and her skin sizzled. God, so much heat. So much *power*. And we'd barely even hurt him. Beam was closing again to rectify that though, face still twisted into its snarling rictus, eyes still blazing with a deathly concentration.

It wasn't enough. Viras was ready this time and smacked him down with a ram of air. Beam hadn't even gotten up when the fire came, blasting him high, then he was struck again all the harder. Again and again, an unrelenting assault delivered with a calm so still and unyielding that Viras might have been filling out tax forms rather than beating a man to death. I saw stray drops of blood in Beam's wake, lingering midair, taking so long to fall that he left them dozens of yards behind. Each time he struck a surface, his pained movements became a little weaker and slower.

Beam had been invincible for a time there, unkillable and unstoppable. He'd been everything his growing reputation claimed he was and more. But now I saw the cracks. Even this strange new feral strength of his had its limits, and Viras was well past them. Could the King of Blades have won here, even with all his armor and enchanted weapon? I couldn't imagine how. We'd simply picked the wrong fight. I didn't feel anything as I saw my brother thrown down again, just realized how inevitable the result was.

Aja the Pit Hound's throw was a good one, good enough that I didn't even realize his projectile was in flight until it'd already found its mark. Viras' shield held, and the javelin—a thick, heavy thing of hard wood and metal—exploded into pieces. I recognized the distraction for what it was just before Helena's own throw followed.

Hers was a bit different though. A great block of mercury fulminate pitched with all her mildly superhuman strength hit home, and Viras disappeared into a flash of light and a rattle of air. For one moment, I dared to hope it'd worked, then he emerged.

But not fast enough to evade Aja.

His enchanted scimitar cut low, catching Viras in a moment of distraction and opening a second wound. This one was along his leg. I saw a few flecks of blood freed from him—only a few; it still wasn't deep—but Viras was backing away now, more cautious than ever. I saw the fire building around his hand, the power shimmering in the air around him. And a new enemy was on the scene. Tall, impossibly lean. An almost insectoid thing of metallic limbs that sent barbed shadows snaking across the room to close in on Viras from all sides. They bit through his shields, barely, and scratched his skin free of a dozen trickles of blood.

Viras fell back, guarded with air and fire, but seemed unable to fully ward off the attacks. I saw Phelia striding forth behind the bizarre creature, gesturing as it attacked with her eyes edged by focus and her body billowing with magic. Was she controlling it? Men were gaping, gasping, disbelieving as she did. Viras' shield weakened, his power strained.

He slipped out right before the barbs closed on him, and another blast of blue-hot magic struck the creature and sent it blasting out of sight. Phelia was sent flying too, though not nearly so violently, and Viras turned his focus onto her.

I stared in impotent horror, readying myself to watch my wife obliterated before my very eyes.

Then the wall exploded inward.

I took a moment to figure out what was actually happening, just staring at the new jagged gap for long, sluggish seconds as the smoke cleared and the orcs powered in. *Orcs?*

Orcs. Big, burly, snarling, swinging, roaring, rearing orcs. They were funneling in just as Viras' men had, less numerous, perhaps, but charging faster, with all the weight and strength innate to their giant bodies and none of the fear inherent to ours. They smashed into Viras' already-fragile back line, and the cracks that'd been set into it by his team killing widened in an instant.

The melee was on the soldiers almost too soon for them to even realize what was happening. I might've felt sorry for them, if they hadn't come here with the express intent of killing my family and forcing me into servitude to an evil magus.

I lost my balance as a shock wave permeated the room and turned back to see Aja flying away like a thrown brick and Helena nowhere to be seen. Viras gestured again, sending a fireball streaking to where I'd last seen Corvan and Adannaya. It was just me now, the blood practically frozen in my veins, mind . . . still, despite it all. I felt a ridiculous sense of calm, amid all the sudden chaos, and readied my magic to muster whatever petty defense I could manage.

But that would prove unnecessary.

From above Viras, in one of the numerous new holes in the ceiling, something was dropped down. It detonated just a few feet from the magus and engulfed him in light and fire. Not mercury fulminate—it was far too powerful. Viras flew away, rattly and uneven for precious moments but clearly unhurt. What caught my eye though was what dropped down through the ceiling following the explosion.

Tall, wiry. Blond hair was dark with detritus and jutting out on all sides, skin hard like carapace and scratchy like worn leather. His teeth were sharklike razors, eyes big and bulging, darting everywhere. His tongue was lolling out like a demented animal, and he was grinning almost from ear to ear.

"Alright, cunts." Solitaire leered, not looking at anyone but Viras and yet speaking loud enough to be heard over the fighting. "This one's mine."

CHAPTER SIXTY-FOUR

Solitaire's POV: Day 171
Current Wealth: 702 gold, 14 silver, 44 copper

Upon further consideration, my decision to single-handedly fight one of the most powerful magi in the region may, possibly, have been somewhat miscalculated. On the one hand, I had my disadvantages: power, speed, magical knowledge, experience, flight, etc. On the other, I had a backpack full of enough illegal munitions to equip a small eastern European military, which would be a very funny fuck you if Viras was dumb enough to blow me up while wearing it, and my wits.

Both were nice weapons, don't get me wrong, but I couldn't help but think I'd have been better suited testing them against someone who *couldn't* frisbee warhorses at my head.

"You're Solitaire," the magus said, looking suddenly hesitant. Why was that? I eyed him, one wound on his leg, another on his face. Beam was lying in a crater bigger than he was, and it was still on fire. But I'd made sure he was breathing before anything else. So he'd survived the unsurvivable.

Viras had seen what a Belahont could do on short notice then, had it proved to him how quickly we could grow in power. He was cautious of me. Good, I could use that. Really I could use anything that might somehow convince him *not* to instantly eviscerate me. If I couldn't gaslight him into playing it too safe, I was fucked.

"And you're the drooling dumbass who couldn't even get me killed with an army of orcs."

Oops. New plan, piss him off into attacking recklessly. It didn't seem to be working, and a quick inhalation gave me a big old whiff of . . . nothing. Huh. Well that wasn't good. No point in being an empath if there was nothing to pick up on.

"I will give you one chance, now, to surrender," the magus told me, speaking as slowly and deliberately as ever. "I could have much use for you and would rather have you as an ally beside me than a corpse behind me."

I repeated what he said in a high-pitched voice, but even that didn't seem to bug him.

"Think this through," he urged, coming closer now. "You are a rat standing before a dragon. You cannot hope to win."

I flashed a grin at that. "You need to read up on Chinese mythology." Before he responded, I'd already thrown out a flash-bang and started sprinting in the opposite direction. *Away* from my own side. No point in getting other people liquefied if I couldn't pull this off myself.

Viras was quick about dispersing the smoke I'd left in my wake. A single gesture sent the cloud sweeping away. His eyes were still streaming tears and spasmodically blinking though. Dumbass had it coming. I disappeared through a corridor while he was still busy being blind, then winced as I heard the structure behind me start exploding. He had, it seemed, gotten over it. And now he was coming.

Plan time: Kill this guy. More complicated plan: Figure out *how*. Corvan had used an air shield, and I'd arrived early enough to see that this idiot shared that trick. So could I beat him the same way? I gave it a go.

A spike of ice congealed in the air, steam filling its hollow interior. I flash vaporized the base and sent it spinning for my enemy even as I waved a hand out and threw a dozen bomb pellets ahead. The little things were harmless for the most part, just a few grams of mercury fulminate, but they went off nice and powerfully midair and served well to distract Viras. The spike of ice hit his shield, smashed to pieces, and vented burning steam out.

. . . Which did nothing. Evidently he'd done something to fix the air circulation issues I'd exploited in Corvan.

I turned a corner just as the corridor was flooded by Viras' retaliation—a wave of fire that tapered off mere meters behind me and actually left my skin in pain. I did some quick calculations to account for thermal transfer, area, and the amount of air it'd moved through before reaching me. Dear God, I wasn't being attacked with *thermite* fireballs, but it wasn't that far off. Best not get hit then. Superhumanly durable or no, I'd be killed flat out by this no matter what.

Another corner, but this time the air was heating up and churning behind me far too soon. I wouldn't have time to turn it before being blasted. I glanced over my shoulder, reached into my bag, and hadoukened a fist-sized chunk of mercury fulminate at a wall. The wall was kill, and I slipped into the abscess within just in time to *not* find out what it felt like to practice Protestantism under Bloody Mary.

Velaharo Manor was a labyrinth, I'd found. Lots of the walls were hollow; floors had crawl spaces—the entire thing was practically a three-dimensional maze. I'd memorized all the routes within a few days of course. That sort of advantage was just too good to pass up. Granted it went a lot less far against someone who could simply erase entire walls with a gesture.

Viras demonstrated that problem by erasing most of the wall with a gesture.

Debris smashed through the air, scraping my skin. The heat hit me like a fist. I thought for a second my hair would catch fire, and by the time I was done worrying about that, I was choking on the newly made wall of smoke filling every nook and cranny of my little hidey-hole.

But I was used to that. Smoke grenades had been dear old mum's favorite way of getting me up in the morning. I used all the old breathing techniques to keep from hacking up a lung, tightened my eyes, and started moving on memory and sound more than sight. If anything, Viras was likely more disoriented than I was. I put myself in his shoes, got ready for his response.

I'm afraid it must've come as quite a shock to him when he focused on clearing out the smoke to see only for a kilogram of Astrolite to pick that exact moment for its detonation.

Astrolite, what even is that, right? Well, to be precise, I'd made a compound called Astrolite G, a very useful and cool chemical that I thoroughly encourage you to make at home. I am, after all, a role model you should aspire toward emulating in your day-to-day life. Astrolite G is one of the more powerful explosive substances around, boasting roughly double the energy density of TNT and producing a shock wave about 25 percent faster. In layperson's terms, it's the *exact* sort of chemical that corporate assholes sitting comfy behind their reinforced concrete and metal detectors don't want you to have.

Oh, and I guess it's good for killing ultrapowerful wizards too. In this case, Viras was situated perfectly to take as close to the full brunt as I could've hoped, and a wall of air smacked into him at Mach 25 mere microseconds after the detonation.

Again, he vanished from sight. Could I make some way to improve my senses so this didn't happen? Collateral damage was starting to get inconvenient with how powerful I'd become. My thought didn't go any further than that for the time being, not with my body so intently focused on hurling about a microwave's worth of high-ex into the corridor.

Something rushed down the wall cavity I was hiding in, blasting several of my own charges back at me. I would have died then and there, instantly, if I'd not been quick enough to put up a sheet of ice. And even that didn't spare me entirely. The foot-thick shield broke apart, fragments lunging back at me and cutting me deep. I'd armored myself as best I could, but even that didn't stop the projectiles entirely, and I felt a dozen lacerations open up as I shot and rolled backward.

My vision blurred, and I tasted blood welling up at the back of my throat. Overpressure was a bitch, even when you could shrug off a baseball bat being broken across your guts.

Hopefully that'd fucked over Viras too. I groaned, rolled onto my side, and ignored the feeling of my innards trying to become outards. Move. That was the trick, the secret to living in spite of everybody else's best efforts. A stationary target is a dead target. I moved, and I lived. Barely. Another jet of wind ripped through the abscess in the wall and almost clipped me, throwing me off-balance. I hit a wall, grunted, thought, and remembered that *this* section was mostly just wood. I punched it, headbutted, bit and elbowed and practically clawed my way through into the next room, then scrambled up and sprinted with every ounce of strength I still had.

Lucky, that exit. But then I was due a bit of luck. Come to think of it, I was probably due an M72 LAW and a free shot.

The wall exploded completely behind me, and a moment later the charge I'd left next to it exploded too. I heard a man yell out over the sound and glanced back to see Viras . . . alive. Healthy, unhurt pretty much. He had a few scrapes and scratches, shrapnel thrown fast enough to break through his shield but having had most of its velocity exhausted in doing so I'd guess—and other than that was entirely uninjured. I'd have hurt another person more by just *throwing* a fistful of sand into their face, as I was now. Bastard.

Well alright then, I'd just need to be even cleverer. I disappeared into another wall and started crawling, activating rat mode with every ounce of my being and hoping it didn't fail me.

It was like fighting a rat. Viras had been exaggerating before, speaking with a flourish and scorn when he called Solitaire Belahont a rat. But he damned well *was*. And like a rat, the hardest part about killing him was the simple act of catching him first.

Clearly, the rumors of his deranged paranoia were true. He had too fine a knowledge of all the passages through Velaharo Manor—passages that Viras was *also* unpleasantly surprised to find truly existed—for the familiarity to have come to him naturally. The man must have studied them all with a pathologic intensity. It was bearing fruit now, if nothing else.

Viras raised a hand and let the magic course down into his fingertips. His master had once said that the touch of arcane energies felt heavy to him, like a physical weight. Viras had laughed then. He felt it himself now. Not nearly so much, and in all likelihood he never would, but it was . . . there. A whisper of the man who had taught him. But only a whisper. The bitterness spawned by that reminder festered, boiled, then released itself as fire. The air screamed in torture, revolting at the unnatural conjuration and twisting as a great gust around him.

The house screamed more so.

Solitaire was visible for a moment, a flash of jutting hair and spasmodic eyes. Viras lanced at him with air, watched as the very foundations of the house—stone walls and floors now, with the very cellars exposed—came apart. The debris clotted the air, and he banished it with another wave. By then his target was gone again. Disappeared into only he knew what.

Like trying to catch water in a fist.

Viras *could* have pressed harder, of course. But that would be just what his enemy was banking on. His skin still stung where scraps of it had surrendered to the traps left by the madman. His ears still rang. Viras' power was great, but whatever dark magic this man had acquired—and Viras fully intended to twist and mangle his body until each and every secret within had spilled free—it was dangerously close to the line of surmounting him. Fifty years ago, the fight would have already ended. And Viras would have died.

Caution would avail him. Time was his ally. Viras had all the magic in his body, a near-inexhaustible volume kept carefully reserved throughout the attack. Solitaire Belahont though could only carry so much of his mysterious alchemical foci. Caution would avail Viras, as it had so many other times.

He fired again, and again. Venting his magic into the building, almost wincing as he did. Viras had an appreciation for history. It was virtually impossible to study as a magus and not develop one. The past was precious and could not be restored. Each attack Solitaire Belahont survived now was a priceless piece of architecture further mangled as collateral.

Viras killed his grief at that and continued. Because with each new area of the mansion ruined, each section reduced to rubble and burning timber, he had denied his enemy another avenue of retreat. He was careful now to box Solitaire in, leave his options for movement limited, and ensure he would not escape the growing net of Viras' devastation. Soon enough it would tighten around him, and then . . .

Then the rat would be caught.

A ceiling collapsed, a floor fell in, a rafter dented the ground. Viras saw movement, saw it disappear. He attacked again. Flames, air. Power in its most elemental form thrown in the direction of his enemy. He actually frightened himself for a moment. It wasn't often his full might was exerted, and the sight triggered deep-rooted simian instincts to flee rather than face the cataclysm. He didn't, just continued it, escalated it. Watched as an area dozens of feet in each direction and just as many high was obliterated into rubble.

Then blasted out more air, more widely and carefully, feeling around for . . . Yes. Movement, breathing, life. Solitaire Belahont still lived, and he was buried under the pile.

Viras' first instinct was to circle around and attack from the other side. He could see clearly enough that there was one section of rubble thinner and more vulnerable than the rest. That was the point where his magic, once focused, would eat through fastest. It was also the most obvious site to set a trap. He felt his superficial wounds stinging again and redoubled his conviction not to give Solitaire Belahont chance to score any more severe than that.

He attacked the larger side, hurling flames out in as concentrated a jet as he could manage. With the piled rubble as it was, its volume and weight, its awkward, precipitous balance, Belahont's knowledge of his surroundings was now defunct. Any memorized passages had been obliterated, and his mobility was no more than any other man of his physical prowess.

It might take minutes or more for him to crawl out, and Viras didn't need as long as that to kill him. The flames heated up. Orange, white. Blue. They struck the stone and broke apart, washing over it. In seconds, beads of molten rock formed, then grew. Then turned into streams as the stuff bubbled and burst, becoming a great wall of magma bearing down upon the solid rock, as more and more of the buried stone melted all the while. Viras didn't pause to check for movement, didn't risk it. He'd already identified Belahont. All the temptation to verify would do now would be to give his enemy more time to escape.

His trap was made. His enemy was in it. Viras amplified the heat.

It stung to know Belahont would likely perish in this attack, and he ignored that stinging as he did everything else. Victory was paramount here. Viras' plans had been for two Belahonts. The arrival of a third—and especially with the army of orcs—had ruined them. He had to defeat each of the Belahonts as quickly as he could, before the martial balance could shift against him.

More magma welled up atop the rubble, like pus oozing from a rupturing wound. Viras gritted his teeth and continued the magical exertion. Moment by moment, second by second, heartbeat by heartbeat, he was growing closer to—

The magma surged up, like a volcanic eruption.

Viras' shield caught it, caught it so fast that he didn't even realize it was flying out at him until the impact had already come. He shot back, driven through the air by the mass of molten stone smashing against his magic. Then felt it on his skin.

Solitaire had planned it all of course. Granted, he'd planned it about ten seconds before it started—but an improvised tactic could work just as well as a long-standing one. As evidenced by the screaming, thrashing magus now falling out of the air.

Viras was cautious, and just a little bit fearful of his explosives. And Solitaire had seen him melt stone already. Probably, he'd thought he was being clever by burning through the broad end of the pile. In actuality he was being predictable, and a predictable enemy was a land-mined enemy.

Or, in this case, a pile mine. The name was a work in progress, as was the process of Viras' flesh turning into a liquid. Solitaire crawled his way out and watched the ruination as it happened, giggling to himself and doing his best to shift his pants as they became a lot tighter around the crotch.

Solitaire had confirmed already that Viras' shield wouldn't fully stop supersonic shrapnel. His skin had been scratched somewhat, and though that had done no real damage, it showed a critical flaw in the man's defense. So he'd mined the rubble pile after being buried, left a carefully measured amount of Astrolite in an abscess within it, then said fuck it and dumped about four times as much. Then crawled like fuck and conjured as many feet of ice between himself and the high-ex as he could manage, even after squirming a good few meters away to begin with.

Viras had tried to burn him out. His heat had melted the outer layers of rock. That heat and magma had seeped deeper, deeper, deeper. Then it'd set off the high-ex, which, being high explosive, had found the presence of physical matter resting atop it objectionable and thrown it out in all directions.

Globules of orange-hot magma had gotten through Viras' shield with just barely enough speed to reach his skin, like the other debris. The only difference being of course that they were fucking globules of magma, so he'd caught fire.

Solitaire giggled again. Shame he hadn't had any white phosphorus. Now would be a perfect time to dump it onto the asshole and turn his remaining seconds of burning into a prolonged roasting session.

Oh shit, he was already starting to cool off. Solitaire hucked another fistful of Astrolite at him and dived behind cover. The ground seemed frightened because it trembled as he rolled behind the stony debris. Solitaire peeked back to study the eviscerated corpse of Viras, but it wasn't there. Instead he saw the intact, injured, pissed-off *living body* of Viras, followed by a blast of air.

CHAPTER SIXTY-FIVE

Shango's POV: Day 171
Current Wealth: 1296 gold, 14 silver, 44 copper

Beam was alive, and he'd snapped out of . . . whatever he'd snapped *into* before. I could tell as much just by looking at him. He wasn't snarling. His teeth and eyes were back to normal. And he clearly felt his wounds now.

Not that anyone *wouldn't* have felt them. I actually almost did just at a glance.

Bones were broken, that much was clear. Ribs. Armor plating was sloughing off his body like necrotic skin from a burn victim, and his eyes had that distant, dissociative look of a man left sky-high on the nectar of his own adrenaline. I didn't make a fuss about checking on him. If I pointed these injuries out, Beam might suddenly feel the pain hitting him fully. He'd be useless.

And Solitaire was still fighting Viras.

"Can you move?" I asked him, taking his arm carefully and wincing at the feeling. His flesh was tangibly hot, still cooking from Viras' magic. Beam didn't even notice.

"Where are they?" he growled, hand trembling as he gripped his sword with a strangler's fist. I pointed the direction out to him, and the both of us rushed off to lend Solitaire our strength.

It was a surprisingly long and hard run, but the actual search was as effortless as any I'd ever done. We just followed the trail of destruction. Halls were scorched and blackened, mortar crumbling and stones cracking. Ceilings had fallen in. Far surfaces were blasted apart entirely like our very own anachronistic cannon had been unleashed into them. A war zone in every sense of the world.

I left Solitaire to fight this.

The thought was toxic, barbed, and distracting. I put it aside for now and continued looking.

We moved past the sizzling wall Solitaire had either punched or clawed through, carried on down the corridors that had now been forcibly converted into halls by one fireball or another. Continued until, finally, we reached the great blob of lava.

I thought for a second there'd been some actual volcanic activity, then saner heads prevailed and the obvious struck me. A great pile of stone was mounted up on the floor, and Viras had blasted it long enough to melt the top.

And it was still molten, still bubbling, still steaming.

They weren't that far away. We doubled, then tripled our pace. It took less than a minute to find Solitaire, for all the good and bad. He was crawling, slowly, while Viras loomed over him. The magus was . . .

Damn, he was actually hurt. Clothes charred, body covered in gray deposits and *horrific* burns. Blood oozed from a thousand hairline fissures in his skin, and smoke mingled with *steam* as it hissed off his epidermis. It would have looked almost cartoonish, if every breath hadn't split the air with the sound of worn lungs desperately raking themselves with strained inhalations. At any moment, I thought, he might collapse on his own.

But I didn't need him to collapse any moment. I needed him to collapse at *this* moment. While my brother was still alive. Viras raised his hands. I stopped thinking, moved in accordance with those stupid simian instincts everybody but me seemed to have. I screamed. He whirled around and blasted out his air. Beam, the glorious, stupid son of a bitch, barged me out of the way and just disappeared from sight down the hall.

I hit the ground, rolled. Came up casting.

Wind hit wind as Viras countered me and . . . was evenly matched. At the last moment, his body spasmed, pain flaring up in his eyes. However emotionally dull he liked to think he was, pain was still pain. At least when it came from half your body being grilled to medium rare. It gave me just enough of an edge to be sent stumbling back instead of bowled completely off my feet. Viras was quick in adjusting, readying another blast as I readied my defenses.

This time, I knew, he'd break through. We'd lose our edge and be just as at his mercy as Solitaire.

But then the brick hit him in the side of the head. Good old Solitaire—good old Liverpool—we were fighting an elderly autocrat in the middle of a derelict building. Millions of years of evolution had perfected Solitaire's anatomy for combat in this exact situation, and Viras went stumbling.

I took my chance, hitting him with all the air I could muster. Viras guarded it at the last second, and badly. It broke his defenses, threw him back against the wall. Then something whipped past me from behind, something glowing and impossibly fast. Beam charged, screaming. A fireball detonated against his chest, and Beam just lunged through it with a swing. His sword bit into Viras' wrist, carving through his hardened wall of air like it wasn't there, and half removed the man's hand. Blood fountained everywhere before a second jet of flames sent my brother sprawling and kept him still.

That opening though, that precious moment Viras needed to focus on casting an attack, was my advantage. He wasn't in the condition to keep his defenses up even while he focused on offense, and so my next blast—a volley of lead darts—found no resistance at all. They ripped clean through his body and burst, deformed and blood slick, out through his back.

Viras remained still for a moment, trembling on stiff legs. Then he collapsed. Of course he did.

He was still only human.

I attacked again, closing the air around one arm—not quite sure how I even did that—and compressing it. Bone snapped, then more bone as I did his other. Viras' limbs lay uselessly beside him, face pale, sheeted with sweat, eyes . . .

Calm, damn him. As if his death were of no consequence at all. But then I knew how that felt, didn't I? I didn't want to die, of course, but I always knew I would someday. Viras now realized that his someday had come.

"Well, you did it," he wheezed. There was an odd *whistling* whenever he spoke, coming from his chest. I wondered if I'd put a hole in his lung. "You beat me and killed me. The only man who can understand you. Congratulations, boy."

I looked around. Beam had collapsed. Solitaire had lost consciousness. If I hadn't scored that killing blow when I did, we'd all be dying. But I had, and now it was just me and Viras alone.

"Do you really think they can ever accept you for what you are?" he gasped.

I thought about it. For years I'd hidden myself, sectioned the real me off behind so many walls I'd almost tricked even myself.

"They'll never need to," I said at last. "They won't know."

Viras looked for a moment as if he'd say something more, then just shook his head slowly. Saving his breath, perhaps. Saving his pain. "Can you kill me faster?" he asked, clearly mustering every ounce of strength left in him even for that much. I considered his request, remembered Solitaire's capture, the weeks of horror. Considered my promise to end his life myself.

"No."

I picked up Beam and picked up Solitaire. Both of them were light as pillowcases for me. Even with my injuries, I carried them easily and made my way back down the corridor. Viras remained where he was, dying.

But dying slowly.

CHAPTER SIXTY-SIX

Shango's POV: Day 178
Current Wealth: 1296 gold, 19 silver, 32 copper

The week following Viras' defeat had been spent counting our losses and appreciating our victories. There'd been plenty enough of both. Magnus' death still stung, despite it all. But . . . we were stronger now for it. I just found myself wishing he could've lived to see it, or that I'd spent more time with him before the attack.

In a shocking turn of events, the city had decided that we were heroes after defeating Viras. All the city. Nobility included. This was surely a testament to my superior moral character, which had nothing to do with all of them being abundantly aware that I now controlled the largest force in Elswick, or that stories of Beam cutting through fucking inches of steel per swing had now spread across virtually the entire place. Even I still found myself taken aback by that one. It was one thing to know my friend could take on a squad—okay, more like a company for a while now—of soldiers and win, quite another to know he could dismember a Tiger tank in under a minute with melee alone.

And he'd gotten stronger since. We all had, and that had happened enough times now that it was an open secret. The Belahonts powered up every time they defeated an enemy. Adversity only made them stronger.

On the one hand, it meant that whoever hit us next would hit us hard, and unexpectedly. They'd have to. On the other, it had made us the scariest people, and smartest long-term investment, overnight.

So it was no real surprise when the gifts started piling in. Statues, offers to help with the repairs of Velaharo Manor, trinkets and tinctures and paintings and *poets* of all things. Solitaire had found that last one quite funny, and then introduced lyrical poetry to them about five centuries early. *Romantic* lyrical poetry, at that. But then

I'd given up on ever not being surprised by him when I found out his favorite song was "Barbie Girl."

I tightened my eyes again, for perhaps the tenth time that day.

[Appraisal]
Class: Master
Level: 30
Condition: Fine
Modifiers: +17 Toughness, +15 Strength, +14 Speed, +12 Alertness
Statistics: Strength 21, Speed 20, Dexterity 6, Stamina 5, Toughness 21, Alertness 20, Charisma 9, Intelligence 8
Class Abilities: Appraisal III, Judgment I
Current Experience Points: 848/910
Unspent Skillpoints: 0

I'd split my points evenly, as usual, and I'd finally cracked twenty in everything. I was a physical peer of the Challenger now, or would've been if he'd lived through the battle. It felt . . . hollow. Not least because Beam had crawled ever further ahead of me.

He was starting to scare me now, genuinely. I'd already seen what he'd managed in his berserker state against Viras, and now his motions were . . .

[Appraisal]
Class: Wyrmfiend
Level: 31
Condition: Fine
Modifiers: +15 Strength, +15 Speed, +17 Toughness, +17 Alertness
Statistics: Strength 27, Speed 23, Dexterity 8, Stamina 9, Toughness 25, Alertness 25, Charisma 6, Intelligence 5
Class Abilities: Beloved III, Drake's Breath I
Current Experience Points: 249/970
Unspent Skillpoints: 0

Well, they were a match for Arthur already sometime during the battle. Since then, they'd left even him behind. Watching Beam fight now was like seeing violence made manifest. And we still hadn't figured out what his new power, Drake's Breath, did.

But I had a few theories.

My own new power, Judgment, had already reared its head in some small way.

Wyrmfiend: Overwhelms enemies with physical superiority, elemental manifestation, and deadly breath.

I saw the words as I studied Beam, first noticing them days ago. And I saw similar ones with everyone else. Descriptions of some class belonging to them all, hints at what they could do. Even my own.

Master: Understands others and utilizes their abilities.

It was all very vague, and if it was the only thing I'd gained from hitting level thirty—save for the ubiquitous stat increases—it wasn't a huge advantage yet. Still, it was more information. Information saved lives. Or, if you opposed us, ended them.

For the last few days, I'd played around with my powers, enjoyed them. Tested them and really just fucked about somewhat—figuring I'd earned myself a bit of fun and relaxation. I'd crushed rocks with my grip strength alone, jumped over people's heads from a standstill, sprinted a hundred meters in under five seconds, and, to my astonishment more than anybody else's, left a sizable dent in a steel breastplate salvaged from one of our enemies just by punching it. Now though, the time to play around with my superpowers had finally ended. As fun as it was to juggle boulders, there were more practical things demanding my attention.

"So we just sign," Solitaire said, eyeing the quill in the inkpot before him as if it were a log of shit he was being asked to grab. "And then it's done."

"Yes," Adannaya pressed, her lips tight and face tighter. She wasn't any happier about this than him, of course. The two had had a full week to get used to each other's company and had promptly failed at doing so entirely. Even after I'd convinced Solitaire to actually go through with the agreed-upon betrothal, he'd handled it . . . like Solitaire.

The rest of us were doing a better job of feigning enthusiasm at least. Solitaire actually growled as he finally picked up the quill and squiggled his name down, practically throwing it back into the pot. Adannaya didn't wait even a moment before turning to leave once it was done, and that left me free for my next job.

After another glance at Solitaire, at least. I did so love seeing the progress written down.

[Appraisal]
Class: Sapien
Level: 28
Condition: Fine
Modifiers: +14 Speed, +15 Toughness, +13 Alertness, +13 Strength
Statistics: Strength 20, Speed 21, Dexterity 8, Stamina 6, Toughness 20, Alertness 21, Charisma 3, Intelligence 10
Inventory: Local wear
Class Abilities: Detect Element III
Current Experience Points: 778/820
Unspent Skillpoints: 0

It felt strange to actually be Solitaire's physical superior for a change. Even though he'd gained the most levels from the actual battle, he'd been lagging behind well before then. I guessed that was the cost of not trying to juggle everyone's job at once or running around and serially executing all the enemy's most impressive fighters. Either way, he was hardly lacking in strength. Another addition to the growing list of Arthur-tier fighters, at least when one factored in his constantly improving production rate for impromptu nitroglycerin splashes.

But again, that was a matter I didn't have any more time for. Not now at least.

Phelia had requested my permission to call a meeting. Or, rather, she'd very angrily informed me that I would be having a meeting, not bothering to frame it as a question, and then left without another word. The silent implication, the subtle nod toward her catching Amira and me, had not needed vocalization. She'd already done a splendid job of shooting down all my attempts to bring the scene up and explain myself, simply focusing on managing the city and consolidating our position.

Yes, dear, whatever you say, dear. I am the ruler of our people, dear, if you insist. I hated marriage.

I headed to my office, where I found Phelia seated beside my desk and, a few minutes later, several of the city's most prominent nobles. Wilskasai, Chiran, Zogrew, and others. Half were members of Byror's coalition—it was these who'd given me the finest gifts of currency or sentiment of course—and the others looked nervous enough that I knew they were perfectly aware of how absent they'd been during our hour of need and how much it had almost cost us all.

My memory turned to the thousands who'd died defending my family at that, and the guilt was back in an instant. I didn't smother it this time. There was no need for that side of me to rear its head anymore.

"Governor." Wilskasai greeted me with a nod. It was more or less the sentiment I'd been expecting, if more directly worded.

The governor was dead, as was most of his family. This was known to everyone. Officially, it had been one of Viras' men. Unofficially, we'd done it. That was a surprise, to us more than anyone else. Phelia had explained the whole thing to me, and in retrospect I wondered whether I could've predicted Amira's murdering of her own family ahead of time. Probably not, certainly not with all I had on my plate. I was only human after all.

Regardless, it left us all in the same basic situation. There was a power vacuum in Elswick, and nature did so abhor a vacuum.

"And all of you are of one mind on this matter?" I asked, looking around the room, taking my time. It felt good, I had to say. Speaking, being heard. Knowing that everyone here was hanging on to my every word. In a few short months, I'd inverted the power balance between me and these petty nobles, and I didn't intend to stop there.

It was Zogrew who replied first, and most eagerly.

"You have proved your genius time and time again, my lord."

"And your benevolence," added another sycophant whose name I'd not bothered to learn. Then the rest of the flattery came like an avalanche following the first shifting mounds of snow.

I actually got tired of it in under thirty seconds. The illusion of progress wore off. The satisfaction of flipping my position in society dissipated. I saw them all for what they were. Idiots. Simple, opportunistic parasites born with all the privilege and wealth in the world and somehow, some fucking how, still managing to stagnate in their stations despite it all.

There was never anything to be proud of, proving myself against these people. From the moment I'd arrived here I was *owed* this power over them. It'd just taken a few months to make them all realize it.

"Shut up," I said, almost just to see how they'd react. Predictably, they reacted by *shutting up.*

"You're all flattering me. It's not working. Why are you really favoring me over Amira?"

None of them replied, and I sighed. God, this was so tiring.

"She's a woman," I guessed. "I'm a man. Is that about the size of it?"

Eyes flickered around the room, to Phelia. She was not the slightest bit bothered. I'd like to say being Nigerian had prepared me to marry a misogynistic woman. The truth was it'd just preemptively worn down my patience for the trait.

And everyone was a misogynist here, weren't they? Maybe I *should* let myself be put in charge. I was the emperor, after all. Or, rather, I was the *master* now. Should the master not rule? I could hardly do a worse job than these idiots had so far.

"I have a plan," I told them all, deciding not to fully commit to anything just yet. Amira was slippery—I'd seen that much so far—and I didn't want to publicize any hard plans that she might turn into a humiliation by disrupting. Always more conflict, always another enemy to think around.

That was life, I supposed. It was my life now, at least.

CHAPTER SIXTY-SEVEN

Beam's POV: Day 178
Current Wealth: 1296 gold, 19 silver, 32 copper

Phelia and Shango were just on their way to leave when I caught them. Or, to be more precise, their carriage was actively leaving already when I ran it down. It wasn't hard. Carriages aren't really faster than a sprinting person anyway, and I was actually quick enough now that I'm pretty sure I could sprint a hundred meters in less time than I'd fall it. Much less. I brought myself down in front of their vehicle and climbed onto the side as it stopped.

"Hey," I began, mouth suddenly dry and chest heaving. "I, uh, can I have a word with Phelia?"

Even Shango was surprised by that. Well good, he ought to be surprised more often. Give him an idea of what it felt like to live as one of us mere mortals.

Phelia stiffened at my request of course, like she was being tased. She kept her face cool and still, but I saw a sudden fear in her eyes. My fists almost curled up at that, head pounding. The guilt felt like toxin seeping through my gut, but I didn't say anything more. Just waited for her answer.

"Of course," she replied, climbing out of the carriage, walking just beyond ear-shot and, I noticed, remaining entirely within view of everyone else as she lowered her voice to a whisper.

"You want to speak about what happened."

It wasn't a question. Of course it wasn't.

"I do," I replied, searching for the right words and finding them more elusive than perhaps any others I'd tried to give voice to in my life. How did one go about bringing up the time he stabbed his sister-in-law exactly?

"I'm sorry for stabbing you."

Well, that was a start at least. I went sixth it.

"I don't know what happened. I just . . ." I thought back to those few minutes of madness, the entity's voice in my ear. It'd been quiet since then, but not in an annoyed or spiteful way. Like a sated lion sleeping off its meal. Not a pleasant thought, not even without the memory of massacring hundreds of people by myself rattling around my skull. "I lost myself," I said at last.

It was the truth, and it wasn't. I'd made a choice to give in, to fight instead of collapse. And everything else had followed. Somehow it felt wrong to make that my last word though. I scrambled for something more worthwhile to say.

"Thank you for not telling anyone," I managed at last. Clearly she hadn't. I'd not have gone a week without having the incident brought up if Phelia hadn't kept her mouth shut about it.

There was nothing of any warmth in her eyes though. Phelia just nodded sharply.

"I was well aware of how much friction would emerge in our family if that became known. I didn't keep it to myself for your sake." There was a touch of venom to her voice, which I thought was completely fair enough. She could've hit me and I'd not have had any real grounds to complain. Maybe concern for her hand.

"Can you ensure me that this will never happen again?" Phelia asked after a moment. She was nervous, I thought, almost hesitant to breach the subject. Why?

I thought I knew actually.

"No," I said softly, remembering the feeling of what I'd done, the thrill of it. How could anyone guarantee they wouldn't indulge in that again? Even if I *hadn't* enjoyed it, the sheer power had saved us all.

Phelia didn't look surprised. That was the worst part. I'd failed to fail her because her expectations of me hadn't been high enough in the first place. I felt sick.

"Then you're a danger to us all," she told me, voice like ice. "To us all." Without another word, Phelia turned and made her way back to the carriage. I watched her go, trying to think of something more I could say. Failing, of course. What more was there? Nothing truthful, that much I knew for sure.

I watched the carriage roll away and disappear from Velaharo Manor's gardens, then turned and looked back to the mansion proper. A big thing. Huge, proud. And ruined. The fighting had left almost two-thirds of it near to rubble, centuries of maintenance and master crafting by generations of magi and only a few days had been enough to mangle it. There was a message there, a parallel to what I'd done myself. I couldn't be bothered to think of it, just started walking.

Despite everything, the mood around the mansion was higher than perhaps I'd ever seen it before. Maybe that was to be expected. Two weeks ago, everyone had been sure they were dead men walking. In hindsight, that made the number who'd stuck with us all the more ridiculous.

Oh, they'd all fought. They'd gotten hurt, lost friends. We'd all drunk to the heroic dead for much of the past week. But we were all alive too. Living men who'd expected to be dead were about the happiest kind of people you'd ever meet in your life. Second, perhaps, to Solitaire after he found out how many attackers his minefield took out. Only a few of us lacked the joy of life instead of death. I was among the miserable ones.

But then I deserved to be, didn't I? Even if they didn't know it. For the last week, I'd endured one thanks after another, everyone flocking around, praising my performance, laughing—*laughing*—about how I'd scared the enemy so much even my own side had been frightened. But it wasn't something to laugh at, was it? Because that fear had been completely justified. If anyone had stood in my way, if anyone had just been closer and easier to reach than one of Viras' men, I'd have cut them open just as readily. I still wasn't sure I hadn't taken out a few of our own without anybody knowing, even now.

And I could never know. If this ever happened again, that would be another Schrödinger's box full of dead allies. And another, the next time. Phelia had been right. I was a danger to everyone around me. Not like Solitaire, who'd spent his whole life living with what his mother had done and acting as if he was in control. I was worse. I'd chosen my path. I'd dealt with the entity in my head and given it sway over me.

And when that sway came, I was the deadliest creature around. Could Viras stop me now if I attacked him again with all my heightened strength and restored injuries? Could the King of Blades? Could both of them at once?

Could all my allies working together, holding back as they inevitably would to keep from killing a friend?

I decided I didn't want to ever find out.

Without really thinking about it, I started to walk for the edge of Elswick. My feet didn't wait for instructions from my brain, and my brain didn't bother giving any. They both just did their thing. I looked at the sights passing me by, the houses, the streets, the people. All so familiar now. Home.

Home.

I was leaving my home. My horrible, nasty, dangerous, evil shithole of a home. The fact that it was all those things and more did nothing to alleviate the strange tugging at my chest as I realized. Where was I going? I still didn't know, but I was going away. Away from where my friends were, away from all the people I'd hurt if I didn't.

Where would my legs take me? I couldn't exactly ask, and I didn't want to. I'd spent enough time agonizing over my next move and throwing myself into other people's fights. I'd turned myself into a weapon already. I could hardly complain about struggling to think now.

On and on I marched, soon past the outskirts of Elswick, then beyond its walls. The air was still cold, but I didn't feel it. The wind still strong, but it didn't impede me. My body wasn't subject to the elements anymore, nor was my life threatened by the trolls lurking in local woods or the nasty men with knives and cudgels looking to prey upon those carrying fancy swords. In six months, I'd earned freedom from the savagery of Redacle.

It was a shame Redacle wasn't free from the savagery of my freedom.

CHAPTER SIXTY-EIGHT

Solitaire's POV: Day 178
Current Wealth: 1296 gold, 19 silver, 32 copper

Adravigi had asked for a meeting with me. One of the last Barbed Pointers still in Elswick, which was fortunate for the city's already fucked food supplies, she'd taken her sweet time in finally beginning the talk both of us knew was coming. At least she actually realized it had to happen. I'd need to call on the other leaders myself most likely.

"What do you want?" I asked her, not bothering to smother my anger. It was actually some of the more *dangerous* anger I could remember feeling—this woman was responsible for one of the literal worst things I had ever experienced after all—but if Adravigi picked up on my very sincere urge to chew through her rib cage and eat her lungs . . . she bore it on the chin.

Say one thing for her, say she was used to dealing with violent men.

"I wanted to . . ." Her face twisted up, and my nostrils were pricked at a cocktail of emotion more complicated than almost any I'd ever felt. Guilt, hatred, bitterness, shame, regret, fear. And gratitude. This last one was by no means the strongest, but it was the one she gave voice to. That either said good things about her nature or typical ones about her honesty. "I wanted to thank you," Adravigi finished at last.

That was a surprise.

"For . . . overthrowing you?"

She glared at me. "For sparing my life, idiot."

Oh, right. I'd forgotten I did that.

"Just forget it." I shrugged, suddenly finding myself embarrassed. Finding myself irritated to be *reminded*. I'd only spared her after killing however many other people. The whole thing had been . . . a waste. "Was that all?" I growled.

Adravigi looked more than a little put out but didn't waver. "No," she snapped. "I also want to let you know that I'll be making sure I do something worthwhile with it. My life, I mean. And . . . I'm sorry for sending you to kill that town."

The deaths flashed before my eyes again, every detail perfectly seated in my memory. They would be for the rest of my life. How I wished I could forget sometimes. Forget anything. People didn't realize how precious a gift that was.

"Alright," I replied. I didn't forgive her, so I didn't lie about doing so. But Adravigi seemed almost more relieved at that as she nodded.

"That was all. What happens now?"

I thought about that.

"Barbed Point is still yours," I said at last. "You practically built it. You're the best to run it. Any orcs who try to push you out of your position will answer to us. But you'll follow our rules too. No more pillaging, and you treat the orcs better than you have been. Feed them, house them properly. They're people."

Being dumber than humans didn't mean they deserved to suffer, but it sure as shit meant I wasn't leaving an orc in charge of the place. I had enough problems with normal human beings without adding in *below*-average intelligence to the mix. Easier to herd cats.

Adravigi nodded at that and took her leave. I took mine too, heading back to my quarters.

Where my *dear wife* was currently residing.

The bitch was yelling something as I entered, voice in a shrill sort of "you've done something to make me angry" pitch. I didn't bother replying. She'd shut up in a few minutes if I ignored her long enough. Responding would just add fuel to the fire. Better to—

Something hit the back of my head, and I whirled around. An ambush. Somehow the enemy had gotten past my defenses. No time to think, I conjured up as much nitro as I—

Adannaya was glaring at me from across the room, holding another book after already punting the first to bounce off my skull. A big book, heavy and leather bound. The adrenaline was already rushing through me, and as I carefully deconstructed my hastily made explosives, I just knew I wouldn't be sleeping properly tonight. Cunt.

"What the fuck do you want?" I growled, trying to hide the trembling in my body. I didn't manage, of course I didn't. Adannaya noticed the muscular spasms and got scared. Being scared made her angry, and that sent her another step forward and brought her hands halfway up. Magic I wasn't experienced enough to sense was probably building at her fingertips in case I came flying at her. But she used words instead.

"The bed," she told me, not adding anything else. I actually had to take a second to try to figure out what she was complaining about. Failed.

"Not enough feather pillows for you?" She threw another book. This time I dodged it. "Toss something else at me and I'll snap your fucking neck." She didn't blink at the threat. We'd both said worse.

"You put explosives around it."

That was what she was complaining about?

"Okay, and I left instructions to get around them." Very detailed instructions, which I'd worked very fucking hard on. This last week, I'd finally gotten around to learning to read, beyond the minor tidbits I'd been picking up here and there. I liked to think that matching the literacy of a six-year-old within a few dozen hours of practice was actually quite impressive, but it didn't make writing at an adult level any less demanding of incessant drafts and redrafts. Seeing that so unappreciated actually stung a bit.

"You. Put. Traps. Around. My. Bed," Adannaya replied, as if that were somehow an argument.

"You put lots of things I don't like around my room," I countered.

"*My possessions don't kill people!*" she screamed, bursting into outright hysterics.

"*Neither do mine!*" I shot back. How shit at demolition did she think I *was*?

Adannaya paused at that, closed her eyes. I heard her counting to ten under her breath, and when she looked back up at me a degree of clarity had returned to her features.

"Solitaire, why did you put deadly booby traps around our bed using that magic powder of yours?"

Correcting her that the traps were actually mercury fulminate, and thus crystalline rather than powder, would probably only worsen her temper. I chose another route.

"I rigged those up very, very well and very, very carefully. I've been doing this since I was five. As long as you know they're there and follow the instructions, *you'll be fine.*"

She didn't even blink.

"Why did you put them there?"

"In case someone tries to kill me in my sleep," I snapped. She was stunned into silence, and then the pause followed. The one that always follows when a woman needs to take a moment to process how crazy I am. After the uncomprehending rage, but before the decision to flee for the hills before I killed them. As if I wanted to. As if they'd be fucking *alive* if I wanted to.

I'm not crazy. You're all just desperate to get killed.

But it never came.

"That much is . . . understandable," she conceded. I paused, eyeing her. What was she playing at?

"It is," I concurred, scrutinizing Adannaya's features for any sign of deceit or trap. I saw none. She was hiding it well.

"I've known others who found themselves targeted less than you and responded . . . similarly," she said slowly.

Was she being sincere? Dangerous thought, Solitaire. That was how they got you.

"And my family is still alive because of that response," I replied, strangling my voice until it was less gladiatorial than conversational. Somehow, she still seemed affronted by that. Stuck-up bitch.

Her eyes hardened.

"And I will sleep better if I am not *next* to that response."

"You want your own bed?" I offered, hoping she'd take me up on it. I hated sleeping next to her as well. Blue balls aside, it was like being beside a damned furnace, and she kept rolling onto my side of the bed.

"We are married," she snapped. "We will share a bed."

"Then you'll sleep next to the self-defense mines," I replied evenly. "I don't complain at you putting things beside the bed."

She just sort of exploded at that.

"I don't hang things up in a paranoid delirium!" she snarled, fists balling, stepping forward. Mine balled too, and I stepped forward to loom over her. She didn't back down. "I should never have married you," she spit. "I should've just turned you over to Viras."

"Turn me over to whoever you want," I growled back, bringing my face inches away from hers. "I'll cut you to bits and feed you to the fucking dogs."

For a moment we just met each other's eyes. She really did look a lot like my mother, snarling like that. Darker skin, black hair instead of blonde, but not much younger than she'd been when I was growing up. And she didn't seem afraid of anything either. She leaned in and kissed me like she was trying to suck one of my lungs out, and I kissed back like I was trying to eat her tongue. I lifted her off the ground, carried her back toward the bed. She punched me as I dropped her down onto it, fist thudding across my jaw. I barely felt the impact with my newfound durability, but it got the engine roaring well enough.

Marriage did have its perks, at least.

CHAPTER SIXTY-NINE

Shango's POV: Day 178
Current Wealth: 1296 gold, 19 silver, 32 copper

Phelia didn't say what Beam had wanted to talk to her about, and I didn't ask. I figured I trusted both of them enough to know that there was no harm in letting them keep it between themselves, and they wouldn't want to do so without good reason. That did mean that Phelia and I had little to talk about in our ride to Amira though.

As a fact, I suspected Phelia's presence in accompanying me was for the sole purpose of ensuring I didn't sleep with the woman. She hadn't said as much, or deliberately implied it, but those frosty glances I'd been getting since she caught her rubbing up against me had only doubled in consistency since we'd started heading for her.

You could've just talked to me about this.

But then, being up-front was probably not a great survival strategy long-term in a world where women were generally regarded as their husbands' property.

The governor's manor was as impressive as ever, and . . . as well staffed. That was surprise number one. Surprise number two was finding out that actually, on the inside, it had even more armed men permeating its innards than it did before many of the house's guard died fighting against Viras' men.

Somehow, Amira had upped her numbers. Or, more likely, she'd held a majority of them back during Viras' attack. That was . . . concerning. If she was reckless enough to do that, to kneecap our defense purely in the hopes of surprising me once we both came out the other side of it, then she was reckless enough to do almost anything. My style of negotiation revolved around convincing people that my best interest lay alongside theirs, twisting pragmatism into conformity with my own designs.

That didn't work with idiots or lunatics. I was fairly sure Amira wasn't the former, but the latter . . . It was amazing the kinds of people—even clever people—who could turn out to be unpredictably crazy. If I hadn't known that before, a yearslong friendship with Solitaire had certainly made it clear enough for me not to take any unneeded chances.

"This could be a trap," Phelia noted. It was the first thing she'd said to me since we started for the mansion, and of course it was pure business. And the most important thing she could've said.

"It could be."

If it was a trap, I wouldn't be able to bank on catching Amira unawares anymore. The days of Belahont power growth being an unknown factor were long behind us. She'd have accounted for the possibility of me being far deadlier than before and readied her forces to bring an excessive level of kill to bear against me. That Phelia had a growing reputation as a necromancer following her performance against Viras—and was thus considered fair game by much of the world—was another worry.

So was it a trap?

No, I decided. That wasn't Amira's style. And even if she killed Phelia and me now, that would still leave her with a lot of problems. Solitaire alone was one thing. Beam, now, might be even worse. In terms of sheer killing power, he was the deadliest thing in the entire region. That wasn't the sort of thing she'd antagonize if she could help it.

Which still left me unsure about what she had planned. Oh well, only one way to find out more. We headed through the mansion, coming shortly to the governor's office.

Or her office now. She certainly suited it more than her father had, not being a fucking moron for one thing.

"Hello, Shango." She beamed, as if seeing me made her happier than anything else in the world.

"Why did you not use the hundreds of mercenaries outside to help fight Viras?" I asked her, not bothering with the pleasantries. She didn't seem offended—she never seemed anything but bubbly and pleasant—and her eyes practically shone as she answered.

"Because they weren't here, silly. They only just arrived a few days ago in bulk. I called them in from out of the city."

"And you thought they'd arrive a few days earlier?"

She hesitated a second, caught between two answers, both of which would give me something. She chose the one that gave me less, but I still gained.

"No," she said at last. "I wasn't expecting them earlier." Had she claimed otherwise I'd have had grounds to push her on keeping their arrival to herself, but even still I'd caught her on something.

"So you knowingly brought in a stronger military force after Viras' defeat," I continued idly. "Why is that exactly, Amira? Are you feeling less friendly with my family all of a sudden?"

Phelia stiffened beside me, hand moving to the enchanted ring about her finger. Her control over that strange undead summon was still imperfect. Didn't matter. Imperfect control over a missile launcher resolved a remarkably large variety of situations.

Amira didn't shy away from my accusation like most would. She, of course, did not feel shame, and I was fairly sure she didn't really feel fear either. But she did have a sense for cause and effects, and certain consequences she'd rather avoid.

"Of course not," she replied evenly, carefully. "But you understand that, in all the chaos, I have to take certain precautions to maintain what is mine."

There it was, the meat of the matter.

"And what's that?" I prodded. The real negotiations started now.

"Elswick." She beamed. "My family's city. I am, of course, the governor's last child. It's mine by right."

Solitaire would've had a few colorful retorts for that concept, but now didn't seem like a good time to start smashing her face into the desk, so I decided to keep all the leaves of his book untouched and continue using mine.

"And you'd be willing to fight us over this," I tested her.

"Gosh, no!" Amira looked aghast. "But I won't have to, will I? These mercenaries are *very* professional, all quite good at fighting, and extremely loyal. I'm afraid paying them to turn traitor would be a waste of your time. So unless you think another bloodbath is worth my seat, it would seem ... ah, that I've got the better position?"

I ground my teeth and tried to find a hole in her reasoning, but there wasn't one. Sad fact was we'd exhausted the majority of our strength in all the fighting, and a week had been just long enough for Solitaire's orcs to head well out of the city. As things stood, Amira could do an awful lot of damage even if we beat her, and I didn't think she'd blink about doing so.

"You knew this would be the situation after Viras' defeat," I said at last. "Which was why you killed your family."

"Of course." She nodded happily. "Do we have a deal?"

I paused at that.

"Not yet. You've given me your offer. Now you need to hear my counter-proposal."

Amira frowned.

"Do you think you have the leverage to do that?"

"You've shown me I do, because all of this has been you skirting around what you clearly recognize as a bad group of enemies to have. You want us to remain friendly, right? So form a new Elswick Coalition with us."

Amira's eyes narrowed.

"You're suggesting you make yourself a new Viras."

Funny way of putting it. Ironic, in the nasty sort of way that induces self-reflection and moral discomfort.

"Yes," I replied, burying all of that. "Accept." It wasn't a request.

She accepted.

Phelia and I made our way out of the office without further ado, a victory in our hands. Of some small kind. Truth was, Amira had gotten more out of this than we had, relatively speaking. She really had made a good move. With any luck, her obvious fondness for me would keep the woman on our side.

"That's seen to," Phelia remarked, sounding oddly relieved. Had she been expecting it to go wrong? Fair enough. It nearly had.

"Now we can focus on—"

"*Necromancer!*"

The mace almost hit her, almost. I barged Phelia aside just before impact and felt it crunch into my own shoulder, sending me stumbling back. I thudded against a wall, bounced off, spun around, and threw a punch without thinking. Knuckles met steel, a helmet. Thicker than most. Not thick enough. The eye slit caved inward, and the attacker rattled backward.

I recognized him instantly, recognized his partner now coming at me with a great two-handed blade. Both in full plate, both preternaturally quick and strong. My arm throbbed from where I'd been struck, and my eyes were perceiving their inhuman motions as slower-than normal speed.

Witchfinders.

The sword whipped by my face as I lunged back. Its attacker closed in, stepping one foot forward and twisting his weapon back around. I hardened the air into a shield that bounced it overhead, then kicked him hard in the side. He flew into a wall, striking it and bouncing off amid a spray of broken rock. The other's mace caught me in the temple.

Everything was blaring noise and blurring light for a few seconds as I stumbled, wits knocked out of me. I righted myself, turned back, saw something move. Raised a hand with wind magic gathered and lead darts shooting out.

My projectiles powered through the Witchfinder's armor and body, eviscerating his torso and leaving pints of ichor to leak out from between mangled plates in a few seconds. But not before his sword came down hard on my wrist, neatly slid through the space where one bone was bound to another . . . and hacked the hand off.

I stared at the stump where it'd been, blinking, amazed. Heard Phelia scream, felt the rush of necromantic magic as her familiar burst forth. Then felt the other Witchfinder's dagger slide across my neck and open up the artery.

All my strength leaked away, and I dropped down onto my back. Eyes focused on the ceiling, mouth filled with my own blood. Heartbeat slowing. Slowing.

Slowing.

Ian B. Urns is the coauthor of the Author's Nightmare series, originally released on Royal Road. He writes dark fantasy stories with all the action, humor, and horror he can cram in. Having penned six novels thus far and developing his skills with each new book, he hopes to continue expanding into other genres. Urns lives in the United Kingdom, where he avoids natural light and eye contact with other living things.

A. C. Erinle is the coauthor of the Author's Nightmare series, originally released on Royal Road. A Nigerian novelist who favors character-driven fantasy and world-building, he has penned several books now, sharpening his writing skills with each one. He spends his free time frolicking in nature and otherwise enjoying life, before marching back into his Writing Hole. His stories are dark, but they never fail to be optimistic. Erinle currently resides in Lagos.